THE
SPARK
IGNITES

THE SPARK IGNITES

SAMANTHA CHRISTOPHER

Spark Productions

PROLOGUE

Evelynn
Oregon Health and Science University
Five Years Prior

"Professor Mayfield!"

I hold up a finger as I study the sample under my microscope. The elongated, circular organisms dive-bomb the brown tissue like ravage-hungry beasts. It's not quite what I was looking for, but it'll be enough to prove my theory.

"Evelynn!"

The voice grows closer, and I hold back a curse. I don't know when I started on a first-name basis with my students. It was endearing at the beginning—that they felt they could have that kind of relationship with me—but there is an obvious line they need to hold. I let the line blur for some of them. They need me, especially the Elementals who feel isolated on campus. They don't have it easy. Even the other professors treat them differently. It's despicable, but so is the culture of attending a Com school. They chose to be here, I remind them too often. But barging into my lab like this is stepping too far beyond that line.

I jot down my findings and ignore whoever is pestering me. If I don't get these numbers now, I'll be late picking up Cal from the sitter, and I don't want Maya trying to cook dinner again to surprise me. I adore my daughter, but cooking is not one of her strong suits. I doubt it's any thirteen-year-old's strong suit, though.

"Evie."

I stiffen at the nickname and drop my pencil. It bounces off my notebook and falls to the floor. Nobody calls me that here. A man's fingers wrap around the pencil. Slowly, he offers it to me. I grab it with the tips of my fingers, not wanting to touch his skin, and look into a pair of bright green eyes.

"What are you doing here?" I cast an uneasy glance around, but we're alone, thankfully.

This isn't the first time he's shown up unannounced—not like I ever gave him a way to warn me. Nonetheless, he's not supposed to be here. The first time I saw him in eight years was last year when he visited with another colleague working on a research project. I never told him about Henry's death. I was worried about what he might do...or ask. But he's been bugging me since, showing up with an annoyingly valid reason just to get under my skin. He has to know about Henry by now. I mean, it wouldn't be hard just to ask another professor. But even with Henry gone, he shouldn't be here, and definitely shouldn't call me Evie. Who did he even get that from?

"You need to go right now," he says.

His deep voice does weird things to my insides as he takes the words right out of my mouth. And those piercing green eyes and full lips… Is saliva actually accumulating in my mouth?

I lock those betraying feelings down immediately. I've been widowed for four years now, and I'll never feel that way about another man. *It's just a hormonal reaction, Evelynn. Nothing more. You can never, ever go there with him.*

"Something bad is coming, and you need to get your kids out of here." He presses something into my palm and wraps my fingers around a cool thin object.

My eyes narrow at him even as heat spreads from where he touches.

"You have to trust me. This is someplace safe. Go there tonight."

"Tonight? Are you crazy?" I get up. He's much too close for my liking, but he grabs my shoulders and forces me to look at him. His eyes are ablaze, fire flashing around his pupils.

"They. Are. Coming."

Understanding clicks into place. I thought it was just rumors. No. It's too soon. There weren't any signs. But weren't there? The segregation. The heightened hostility towards Elementals. The looks and whispers that have been becoming more rampant by the day.

My babies. I need to get to my babies. I swallow the rising panic and nod. His shoulders relax, but his jaw is still clenched, accentuating the lines on his face.

"Will you be there?" I hate the hope that breaks free from those locked away irrational feelings.

"No." He winces. "I don't know if you'll ever see me again, actually. There is something I need to do before chaos breaks out and—" He shakes his head. "But there will be more. More will come. Build a community, Evie. And survive. Promise me you will survive?"

"I promise."

He looks at me, and for one brief, terrifying moment, I think he might lean in and kiss me, but then he says, "And Maya—" He breaks off, swallows, and then nods. "Tell her—" He stops himself and restarts. "She'll be safe," he says almost to himself.

He pushes me towards the doors before I can respond, and I almost trip over my feet. I place my hand on the door to push it open, but before I do, I turn around to say goodbye. The room is empty. He's gone.

I blink away the hot tears gathering in the back of my eyes and rush down the hallway, holding tight to the key he gave me.

The highway is a mess. Roadblocks are everywhere, and construction crews line completely fine roads. Guilt and worry claw in my chest. I could only warn a few of my students and friends before leaving. I hope they get out in time. I hope I get out in time.

I lay on the horn as the Honda in front of me finally moves ahead, enough for me to squeeze through and take the exit ramp. I round the corner to our neighborhood, almost hitting the curb, and pray that Maya will be home from school. I know she stays late sometimes with Abby. Her pink bike is against the front side of the house, and I exhale sharply. Leaving the car running, I dash inside and yell for her.

She peers over the upstairs railing with a smile, her strawberry-blonde hair cascading down her frame. "Hey, Mom. You're home early."

My heart sinks. Her life is about to be altered forever. How will she handle going into hiding? Leaving her friends, school, and everything behind—her entire life. And this house. This is where she grew up, where we have so many wonderful memories of her father. That all will be ripped away. But she will be safe. That is all that matters now—her and Cal's safety. I will do whatever is best for them, even if they don't understand, even if they grow to hate me for it.

1

Remembering

Maya
Present Day

My hand throbs. The gash is long healed, but the remembrance of the pain and what it means pushes me forward through the trees.

"This has to be it," I grumble to myself.

The letters in my pocket burn a hole through my pants as I scan the face of the rocky wall. The fissures that run down its surface are oddly shaped, too uniform. I squeeze my fingers between the cracks and pull, but nothing happens. I continue to trail the fissure to the ground, giving a pull every couple of inches.

"Here, let me." Abby pushes me with her hip. Her short auburn bob bounces on her shoulders.

Sweat trickles down the nape of my neck. It's an unusually hot day as the summer heat bears down on us. I feel bad for dragging Abby out here again. But the cave system has to be here. I'm like eighty percent sure this is where James and I were when those two guys kidnapped me. I told Commander Wixx she shouldn't have closed the main entrance to the caves when we left two months ago after rebuilding the manor.

The rock groans under Abby's fingertips, creating more fissures and spreading until it gives way. I leap back as the slab of rock bangs onto the forest floor. My pulse quickens as I stare into the dark abyss ahead.

I grin. "I knew it!"

Actually, I didn't. I was searching purely based on the hope of a secret entrance in this area. Snapping my fingers, I create a single flame and enter the opening. My steps falter. My fire does nothing to light the way.

"I told you we should have brought William."

The words barely leave Abby's lips when an iridescent white orb floats into the space. I jump back as William steps forward with a sly smirk.

"As you wish," he says in his thick British accent.

The light dances off the walls of a long cave hallway stretching before us.

"Did you follow us?"

He only shrugs. I shake my head as we enter the cave. I can't be too mad. He had impeccable timing. The sounds of the clicking of our footsteps and the occasional drip of water bounce off the walls of the cave. My heart constricts. I know this is probably a fool's errand, but what else am I supposed to do? It's been ten weeks since I heard from him. If I'm going to find any information on this mission of his, it'll be down here.

William takes the lead, always protective. I study the walls, looking for anything I recognize. A door or a different texture of rock. Who am I kidding? Bare rock gives way to more bare rock. It's all the same.

We come to our first fork, and as my friends contemplate which way to go, I press a hand to the cave wall. It melts under my palm, searing a small hole into it. The fire from my hand dims while Abby raises her brow at me.

"It's easy to get lost down here." I shrug. Fire comes as naturally to me as water now, partially because of the help of my new Igna instructor—third, to be exact—but also because of the bond that I refuse to acknowledge since that awful first night down here when I realized Sebastian was still alive. James and I had gone to Don, the High Aura who performed the ceremony, the following day.

"There has to be a way, please!" I shout, tears streaming down my face, holding my hand away as if it's an infected piece of my body. Don looks at me with patient eyes, his eyebrows turned down in sympathy as he glances at James.

"I'm sorry, Maya, you are bound to him. There is no way to reverse it without the bonded pair present. And even then. It is a very painful process in which you may lose some of your abilities. It's very risky."

"I don't care." I choke, gripping James for support. "I don't want to be bonded with him. He forced this on me. Don't I have a say?"

Don shakes his head. "Unless he passes and the bond fissures or you bring him to me to perform the reversal ceremony, there is nothing I can do. The elements of this earth have bound you with him by blood."

As we reach the first signs of civilization, I swallow the memory. Dark doors line the hall in front of us. I pick up my pace, reaching for the first knob. William's arm shoots out as he eyes me. I nod toward it impatiently. The chance of somebody being down here is next to none, but I know William.

He pushes it open and jumps through with one swift movement. I'm right on his heels as light envelops the space. Shelving lines the walls, and we find ourselves in a cramped storage closet, William looking like he is about to throttle a broomstick.

Abby snickers from the doorway. "What did the poor broom do to you?"

William grunts and shoves the broom away, knocking down several containers. Abby laughs louder. I roll my eyes and head for the next door.

The other rooms are locked or deserted, precisely as we left them. We enter the Circle—a large room with circular tables and chairs on one side and a wide opening on the other that leads to the kitchen. The same kitchen with the refrigerator I was locked inside so long ago. I had a fear of the thing for a while, but with James's help, I overcame it and would come often to help with food preparation.

"James's old room was this way," I say monotonically as the others take in the eerie space. This room was always full of noise and laughter, the smells of our next meal wafting through the space. I swallow around the lump in my throat. This is probably a huge mistake.

I get to his door, only a few doors down from the flower room I called home for the month we lived there. Before I turn the knob, there is warmth on my shoulder. William's gray eyes scan my face—a line creases between his eyebrows underneath his overgrown, dirty-blond hair. It seems to be his usual facial expression these days, the constant smile from the past replaced by a mask of worry. He's still sunshine incarnate but more watchful, probably waiting for me to have another mental breakdown.

"I'm okay," I reassure him, and he lets me go. "Check the other rooms, just in case."

He scans me, looking like he wants to say something before turning on his heel.

I take a deep breath and shut the door behind me, pushing down the memories of this space before snapping my fingers. A small flame dances on my fingertips. It grows in my palm until the fire casts ominous shadows along the walls. I bite my lip and head for the table pushed into the corner. I do my best to ignore the bed. I'm not ready for that yet. I shuffle through the drawers with my free hand.

I slam the last drawer closed with an irritable sigh. How can there be nothing? Wixx won't tell me anything. Those first letters told me nothing. And this damn room.

"Nothing!"

I lean against the bed, my eyes growing hot. I fiercely grab hold of the numbness to shield me once more, but it won't take. The flame in my palm begins to dim, but before it does, I look at the bed I'm on. It's exactly how he left it, neatly made, with the black comforter and pillows. My heart skips when my eyes land on the one lone shirt still bundled against the pillows where I threw it. My flame snuffs out, and I fall back, grabbing the shirt and pressing it to my nose. His earthy sweet scent barely hangs on to the fibers. My eyes water and I curl into a ball, letting myself finally remember.

"What are you doing?" I ask as James grabs clothes from the chest at the end of his bed. He stuffs them into a duffle bag, a deep frown lining his face.

He's been spending more and more time in his old room, away from me. I haven't even had the chance to talk to him today since he kissed me goodbye this morning and has been who knows where, doing who knows what. Swallowing my pride, I came to talk to him. Seeing him packing was the last thing I expected.

"We have to go," he says without looking at me.

"Okay… You weren't going to talk to me about this? I mean, I guess I'm okay with leaving…"

He pauses for a moment before throwing another garment in, his eyebrows forming a deep V. "No. I have to go. Me and my team."

I shake my head, confusion and fear stabbing into my gut. "What are you talking about?"

"We got a call from higher up. I have another mission."

Hurt slashes my heart. After everything that has happened, he wouldn't dare leave me like this. There has to be more of an explanation. But I'm not in the mood to see reason as the hurt morphs into anger.

"And you were just going to leave me? Just like that?"

He winces and turns. His hazel eyes are unreadable. "Of course not. I was planning on talking to you. But I do have to go."

"And I can't come?" Emotion heats my throat, and he sighs, pressing his palm against my cheek. I lean into him.

"I thought anyone could join you guys?" The whole speech after the Coms attacked us about choosing to join them comes to mind. Was that all a lie?

"Yes, but it isn't that easy. Is this the life you want for Cal? What about Abby?"

"Yeah, what about Abby? And your mom? You're just going to leave them too?"

He stiffens and returns to packing.

I grab a T-shirt from the bag and throw it against his pillows. "James, stop!"

He sighs and turns back to me, rubbing the back of his neck. "My family will understand. This is my job, my duty. But you? You're bonded to Sebastian."

I step back, not expecting this conversation to go there. We haven't spoken about it since that morning two weeks ago.

"You heard Don. There is no way to reverse it without the bonded pair present, and even then, you may lose your abilities." His face softens as his voice lowers. "And I can see how it hurts you for me to touch you. It's better this way."

I wince as the fire building in my veins turns into ice. He's noticed that? He's been more distant since we realized Sebastian is still alive, but I never thought he was considering leaving.

"You're leaving because of me?" My voice wavers, and I swallow the rising whirlwind of emotion—first my mom, and now him. My pulse quickens, my heart begins to fissure.

His shoulders slump forward, but he finishes zipping the duffle and throws it over his back before facing me again. "Of course not."

I search his eyes, looking for the truth, but he's unreadable.

"But I am needed." He steps closer but doesn't touch me. "I think it'll be good for us until we figure out how to break the bond between you two. I can learn more about his whereabouts while I'm gone, and you're much safer here." He leans down and brushes a kiss on my lips. "I love you. You know that, right?"

I nod, and he kisses me harder, softening my breaking heart and waking my body up along with the ever-present growl that I push down. Not now. I pull him roughly against me as heat licks up my spine, molding my body to his. My hands find his thick hair, and I knot my fingers into it, not wanting to let him go. Will he ever return to me? I don't realize I'm crying until he pulls back and wipes my face with his thumb.

"You'll be back?" My throat is thick with emotion, but I force the words out anyway. I need to hear him say it.

"I'll send word." He kisses each tear-stained cheek.

A rock settles into my stomach. "But you'll be back, right?" I grab onto the collar of his jacket and lock eyes with him until he finally nods.

"I promise." His deep voice pierces through me and wraps around my heart.

I touch the two letters he sent in my pocket. Two months ago. It's been two whole months since I've heard anything from him. I don't know where he is or even if he's still alive. Wixx says she hasn't heard anything, but I honestly don't think she's telling me the truth, since she doesn't seem to know where the Coms took our commanders or my mom either. Out of everyone our last remaining able-bodied commander has sent, why is it that no one knows anything?

I thought I would find something down here. I swallow the tears threatening to escape and roll over to get up. A crackle sounds from beneath the blanket. I fight with the folds of the blanket until my hand comes across a sheet of thick paper. My heart leaps into my throat as I hold my flame in front of it. I don't recognize the handwriting, but it's addressed to James. If hope were a living thing, it would be bursting out of the cave it's been sleeping in, ready to devour its next victim.

Before I can process the words, the door bangs open. Abby scans me and the missive I'm holding. "Did you find something?"

I nod.

"We did too."

"What is it?"

"More like who." Abby's eyes flash.

2

A Little Reckless

I walk ahead of our now group of four on our way back to the community, not wanting to be anywhere near our new recruit, so I'm the first to find Wixx. She's just stepped from the grand staircase and is turning the corner toward the commons. By the way the place smells like sweet potatoes, I'm guessing lunch is about ready. The new front foyer fills with light from the windows that now line the main wall. I have to admit, it's even better than before Sebastian's fire burned down half the place. It still even has that fresh paint smell.

The Lympha commander's blue eyes light up when she spots me. She cocks her head, scanning me head to toe. The sunlight hits her dark skin just right to give her an unearthly glow. I get ready for her to accuse me of breaking into our previous living quarters. Even though she can't help me with the information I'm searching for, she seems to know about everything else happening within a half-mile radius around us.

"You don't look like the dead anymore," she says.

I scrunch my eyebrows and hold off on the explanation I was about to word vomit at her for breaking her rules. When have I looked like the dead?

She waves me off. "What do you need?"

I hold out James's missive to her, and I can't help but smile.

She does a double-take before looking at it. "I've missed that smile."

"I found this…in the caves," I add hesitantly.

Wixx has been more open and honest with us than my mother ever was with me. She filled everyone in on the many secrets our leaders kept from us, and she let us decide as a people to take the risk of staying here and rebuilding instead of relocating after James's group left. Some of them decided to go with him. Now, there are no more strict rules, and more importantly, no more matching. We've all been living as one, and it's been a beautiful system. And yet…she's still a commander, and there are some rules to keep us safe. Rules like not going in the abandoned caves we lived in for a month. But, if she hadn't done such a good job of burying the entrance, it would have been safer. I know it was because she didn't want another group finding it and holing up next to us—but still. She could have left a small opening for my relentless heart.

Her eyes narrow but she doesn't say anything as she scans the paper. "Texas?"

I nod enthusiastically. "We know where to go now. I was thinking we could gather a team and—"

Before I can finish, my friends walk through the brand-new oak doors of the manor. A homeless-looking man trails Abby and William.

The man was curiously absent when we lived in the caves, but I'd recognize that face anywhere—short blond hair and an overgrown beard. He could be attractive, but the permanent sneer on his face ruins it. His name is Josh, and he's one of the men who kidnapped me. He wasn't the kind one.

Wixx gives me a loaded look and waves us up to her office. Once there, she settles in her chair behind a desk and waits for us to explain ourselves. William launches into the story of finding him in the caves. Josh explains that he's been alone for a while and that James kicked him and Arnold out of the alliance. He avoids looking at me, and I know exactly why he was kicked out—because of how they treated me all those months ago. Knowing he got punished for it gives me a certain level of satisfaction, but it's followed by a tiny bit of remorse—very tiny, almost nonexistent.

He tells us that he and Arnold, the other man who assisted in my kidnapping, went their separate ways. He had nowhere to go, so he decided to return to the only other place he could think of.

I tap my foot, wanting to get this over with so we can continue our conversation about going after James. Even though I can't help but see the irony of the fact that a creepy man made the cave system his home, despite Wixx's attempts at keeping it locked down.

"You're a Commoner?" Wixx asks.

Josh nods slowly. "I wasn't planning on intruding." He throws a glare at William. "But they made me come."

"He hurt Maya," William says, like that's all the explanation we need.

"I did not, you liars." He turns to me. His sneer is so hateful, I know he blames me for everything.

William is in his face instantly. "You do not bloody speak to her," he growls. Then he turns to Wixx. "What would you like us to do with the bloke?" His voice returns to a normal, non-threatening tone. It's pretty impressive, the switch.

Wixx gestures to me. "Maya?"

All eyes are on me, including Josh's glaring ones.

"They did hurt me," I start.

Josh stands, his hands in fists. "I was doing my job."

Wixx puts a hand up before William decides to jump him. "We hold no ill will against Commoners, but this is a community to protect Elementals. We could make an exception for somebody in the alliance, but you were kicked out and we do not know you."

"I don't want to stay. Just leave me alone. I'm fine in the caves." His words say one thing, but his appearance says another. Not only with his overgrown facial hair, but with his protruding collarbones and thin arms. His skin even has a gray sheen to it. Who really wants to be alone down there? If he's already been alone for all this time—

"We sealed those caves for a reason." She catches all of our eyes before settling on Josh's. "You can stay as long as you don't pose a threat, you agree to work, *and* Maya is okay with it."

They look at me expectantly, except for Josh, who keeps his eyes on Wixx.

I sigh. "Like I was saying earlier—" before I was rudely interrupted, "—he hurt me, but I understand he was trying to do his job."

He doesn't react to my words, just keeps his face forward, unflinching.

"It was a long time ago, and no one deserves to live alone. He can stay." I move William aside so I can turn my threatening gaze onto Josh. "But if you come within ten yards of me, I will burn you to a crisp." I let the fire dance in my eyes, and to my delight, he flinches slightly.

"Okay," he says quietly after a few tense moments. It looks like he wants to stay, after all.

William nudges him out the door and mumbles, "Twenty yards."

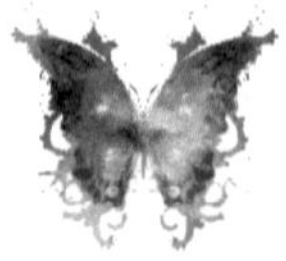

William lounges on my couch, one arm behind his head, as he stares at the ceiling, patiently listening to my tangent. With his other hand, he throws a ball of light at the ceiling, where it fizzles out on contact, before throwing another one.

"*No?* That's all I get? No reasoning? Just *sorry, Maya, the love of your life is missing, and you possibly know where he is, but no, you can't go get him?*" As I pace, I throw my hands in the air, trying to keep my fire at bay. My eyes are trained on the missive and the only two letters he sent me lying in the middle of my bed— my only two references that he was at least okay two months ago.

I talk out loud, piecing what I know together. "James and his team were sent to an alliance base in Texas, and by the details of the missive they should still be there, instructed to return after a small mission in Louisiana. But it doesn't make sense, because there isn't even a hint of him being in either of those places in the letters he sent me." I'd like to pretend I don't know the reason for James not telling me. *He didn't want me following him.* I put more energy into my next steps, timing them with my thoughts.

It doesn't matter.

Step.

I need to see him.

Step.

Talk to him.

Step.

Embrace him.

Step.

He promised me he would return.

Step.

He promised that he would never leave in the first place.

Stomp.

I put a hand on the wall and breathe through my frustration before turning around, pulling my fire into a tight ball in my chest. He hasn't broken either of those promises on purpose. "There has to be a reason for him not returning."

"Maya?"

I turn on William, studying his now grown-out golden waves that have been bleached by the sun this summer and reach his chin, and the line on his forehead that's made itself a permanent part of his face when he looks at me.

With a sigh, I sit next to him. He takes my hand and rubs his thumb over the back of it, a gesture he's been doing more and more since that first night he stayed with me. A trickle of calm flows from his touch.

When James left, I was a mess. It all became too much…between him, my mom, and Sebastian. I broke. I stopped eating. Sleeping was nonexistent, plagued by nightmares that I could never remember. I knew I was scaring Cal, but everything inside me was just dull. It's like James took with him the part of me that made me…me. I couldn't be there for my little brother. I couldn't be there for anyone. Abby's mom took him in, and William came in his place. When I *could* sleep, I'd wake screaming to William's soothing voice. The next night, he just stayed, making my couch his permanent home.

"I'm sorry," he says.

My head falls against the couch, guilt crashing into me. I'm the one that should be sorry. I've been so selfish these past months. This renewed hope and anger has opened my eyes. I didn't realize how much William watched me and did things to protect me. He's freaking sleeping in my room and casting colorful nightlights every time I have a nightmare. He's my best friend, but I don't know if he does these things because he feels the same way or still has lingering feelings from our courtship.

"William, why do you stay here with me?"

He stops the soothing circles on my hand and looks at me quizzically. "Because it helps you."

"But what about you? Sleeping on my couch can't be the most comfortable thing. I've been selfish."

He takes my other hand into his. "Maya, I'm doing it for the whole building's ears, mine included." He grins. There's the sunshine.

I giggle. "No, seriously."

He smiles. "It's been a while since I heard that."

I cast my eyes down. "That bad?" I mumble. Wixx saw it too. Numbness has been my constant companion until today. Today, I can't feel those emotions stirring. Today, I feel angry but also…hopeful…and a little reckless.

He lifts my chin to look at him, his eyes full of sympathy. "Nobody blames you, Maya. It's just lovely to see some hope in your eyes again." His smile grows mischievous. "And I *really* fancy this couch."

He's too good for me. I've known that since I had to break his heart all those months ago. I push him playfully. "You barely fit on it. Really, you can go back to your room. I've been doing better."

I get up and stalk towards the letters on my bed. Falling onto my stomach, I fan them in front of me as a crazy, probably foolish, idea forms. I may not know where my mom or Sebastian—or even my birth father—are, but I do know where James is. If Wixx won't send people, there is only one thing I can do.

My body tilts sideways as William sits on the edge of the bed. "Why did you let Josh stay?" he asks.

I side-eye him and bite my lip. Should I tell him the truth? He'll want to come. I want him to come. But I also don't want to wrap him up in this crazy idea.

I lean on my elbow to look at him fully. "What if I told you it's because I wasn't planning on staying?"

He lifts an eyebrow, his back stiffening. "Then I would ask you if you were planning on giving me a heads up or just escape in the middle of the night."

I shrug. "Depends on if you would stop me—you know, in this hypothetical situation."

He taps his chin before laughing. "Like I could stop you."

"Good, then there's no problem."

He raises an eyebrow. "You're not traveling across the country by yourself."

I lean back. "Wasn't planning on it."

A smile grows on his face. "When do we leave?"

3

Death Mission

*D*arkness wraps around me like a warm, familiar blanket as screams echo through the concrete walls.

My limbs ache as I stretch them out on the too-thin mattress, metal rings digging into my sore, bruise-ridden back. I close my eyes as flashes of images envelop my mind. I don't know what's real or imagined by this mind that doesn't feel like my own anymore. But vivid green eyes haunt most of the images. They bring me peace in this constant hell that has consumed me inside and out—a green-eyed angel.

The door flies open with little warning, then rough hands wrap around my arm and chains lock around my wrists. I've learned it's best not to fight it as they drag me from the darkness.

There is an explosion of pain in my right leg as the man growls behind me to move faster. The floor meets my face before I can react, and he laughs. I stifle a groan when he kicks me in the side, the pain in my face and ribs blossoming into one.

"Get up, freak, before I teach you what real pain feels like."

Anything he does to me will be better than what's prepared for me upstairs, so I take my time in rising. He must get angry with my lethargy, because I'm suddenly against the wall, and he's cutting off my airway. White spots blur my vision as a coffee-infused putrid scent is on my face. I hold onto those green eyes, not hearing the rancid man's speech. Maybe he'll knock me out again, and I'll have a nice respite from what awaits me.

Before I can get my wish, he releases me and pushes me forward.

Before long, I'm welcomed by the blinding light of my nightmares as people in white coats surround me, tying me to a table. There is a pinch in my arm, and the power that lies dormant deep inside of me sparks, its tendrils reaching for me before fizzling out completely.

"Patient 306 is ready for you, Dr. Harris."

Dread crawls through me. He's the worst of them. Medical jargon is passed above me as I try to prepare for what's to come. My whole body tenses as white-hot ice explodes into my veins. My back arches off the table when the sensation of burning alive and freezing to death, combined in one, rips through me.

Those green eyes appear again, this time attached to a lovely face. The memory of her resurfaces. The tug is so strong that it distracts me from the pain for half a second before slamming back into me with a force that opens my airways against my will. A scream rips from me, but my throat is so raw that only a rasp of one word forms on my lips. One name.

Maya.

I sit bolt-straight in bed, sweating and gasping for air. A shiver runs up my spine, remembering the too-real dream before the hazy edges of it expand and blur it completely. I reach for it, trying to remember the details before they're gone from my mind forever. I sigh, still feeling the horror of the dream but not knowing why, and look for William. He's usually at my side, sleepily comforting me or casting colors onto the ceiling. However, I see him on the couch, the sun's rays shining, making him look like he has a halo for hair. Fitting. A blanket lays haphazardly on his body, and a pique of regret pulls at me again. I need to convince him to sleep in a real bed.

There was no screaming, and I slept through the night this time. I reach under my pillow and pull out the black vest I keep hidden, my piece of James. I curse myself for not bringing the shirt I found of his. This doesn't even smell like him anymore, but it's still a comfort. I wrap myself around it and lay back down to catch my breath and calm my racing heart. Maybe I can tell Cal he can return to my room now that I'm no longer screaming through the night. He's better off with Abby's mom, though. He needs a parent, and with me planning to leave soon, it would just hurt him more.

A small thought occurs to me. I could bring him with me. His Lympha abilities manifested just last month, and he's already so good.

No, it would be too dangerous, obviously. Just me, William, and hopefully Abby and Juliet, if they want to join, but I would understand if they don't. Abby, my lifelong best friend, has Trevor now—her one and only match. They haven't made the bond yet, but they're pretty inseparable since the death of her other match, which left her depressed for that first month after the Coms attacked us. Just as she crawled out of her hole, I went in. And Juliet has her 11-year-old little sister, Ann, to take care of. Maybe it should be just William and I. Abby would surely kill me if I didn't say anything, though.

I tiptoe to the bathroom, careful not to wake the sleeping beauty. The water strengthens me as it washes over and absorbs into my skin in the shower, and I go over what I will say to my friends.

"You should try again," Abby says.

Abby braids Juliet's long white-blonde hair down her back as they sit on Abby's canopy bed while I lounge against the pillows, watching them. Ivy crawls up the four posts before creating a blanket of flowers above our heads. The beauty of it makes me almost wish I could control the earth like Terras. But no. Water and fire are plenty enough for me.

Both girls are still in their pajamas. Juliet is in a light-pink nightgown with lacy sleeves, while Abby wears her cheetah-print short set. As Abby's fingers twine around Juliet's hair, I wonder if she misses braiding her own hair, but she hasn't said anything about regretting her decision to chop off her curly locks. Or maybe she has. I haven't been a good friend in the last few months.

Abby and Juliet's friendship blossomed during my mental disappearance, reminding me of when I befriended Juliet because I couldn't talk to Abby. I'm glad I have both of them.

The hair does suit Abby, though. But she could be bald and still be beautiful. Abby is just one of those people with the facial features that can pull off anything.

They took my acquisition without surprise. Abby probably saw this coming after I found the missive, but Juliet? Abby must have told her. They didn't even pause the braiding session after my proposal to travel across the country.

"Abby," I say, folding my arms.

Juliet throws me a cautious look. "She's right. This could be really dangerous, Maya."

I didn't want to ask them to come with me, but I have to be realistic. William and I traversing the nation by ourselves? I need them. They're right, though. I feared they would try to talk sense into me. I should pull out all the stops to get permission before just running away. Running from my problems has never aided me before.

"I mean, I'm coming either way, but it will be easier with Wixx's support," Abby says.

My heart warms. Abby's water-wielding beau, Trevor, is taking over training duties as he's jumping through all the hoops to become a commander one day. He can't leave, so I thought there was a good chance Abby would tell me no. But she continues to surprise me and show me insurmountable support, more than I deserve.

"What about you, Juliet? I totally understand, with Ann—"

She holds up her hand and flashes me a small sideways smile.

"Don't move!" Abby yanks Juliet's head back into position. "Almost done."

She pulls the tie off her wrist and winds it at the bottom of the braid that almost reaches the bottom of Juliet's spine. If she continues to grow her hair out, Juliet won't just look and *act* like a Disney princess, she'll be one. She just needs a tower and a Prince Charming.

"I want to come. But, yes, there are things I would need to figure out first," she says, careful not to look at me again.

I smile and then sigh. They're right. I was very emotional the first time I talked to Wixx after finding the missive. I can try to persuade that rebellious side of her that let me run away from my bonding ceremony with Sebastian. And it would be nice to have her support.

"Fine," I relent.

I slide off the bed and head for the door.

Abby finishes and slaps her thighs. "There." Then she turns to me. "You want us to come?"

"Nah. I can't imagine it helping." And Wixx would then know exactly who to watch for if we try to sneak out.

"Good luck!" Juliet yells as I close the door behind me.

I turn and run right into a hard chest. "Oof!" I step back as two hands stabilize my shoulders. "Oh, hey, Trevor."

"Sorry, Maya. I was just—"

"Juliet is in there, but I'm sure she'll be happy to kick her out," I say with a small grin.

Heat crawls up his freckled neck, and I bite back my widening smile. It's so easy to get him to flush when talking about Abby. It's probably something that comes with red hair. He's always turning the color, like me. But mine is more of a strawberry-blonde, so hopefully I don't get *that* rosy.

He goes to move around me, but I say, "Wait. I've been wondering. When are you going to pop the big question?" I study his reaction so I have something to relate to Abby later.

He scratches the side of his head and shifts his feet uncomfortably. "Believe me, I want to. But I don't want to throw her into a bonding ceremony too quickly. My parents may be gone now, but they raised me with…you could say, more traditional values. I think they dated for like two years before getting bonded.

I mean, I won't wait *that* long, but still. I love her too much to push it."

My heart swells and then fissures when I think of James. I miss him. I miss him so much. But I am also so angry—angry at Sebastian for forcing the bond on me and taking away my choice.

Trevor seems to realize what he said, because his face burns even hotter, almost the same color as his hair this time. "I'm sorry. Jeez. I totally just put a foot in my mouth. I know that—"

I hold up a hand, really not wanting to get into this conversation with him, but I'm the one who brought it up. "No worries. I'm sorry about your parents, though." I remember Abby telling me that he lost his mother young, but I didn't know that both were gone.

He shoves his hands in his pockets and shrugs. "We've all lost people."

I nod, and when the silence extends a bit too long, I shift to step away.

Then he says quietly, "I barely remember my mom. My dad was harder. Losing a parent when you're older is a different experience. Like, you know the probability of outliving them. We will all lose our parents eventually. It's just life. But when it actually happens…" He shakes his head, his eyes locked on his feet.

I bite the inside of my cheek, thinking of my own parents and how it will affect me if my mom is truly gone, compared to losing my dad as a little girl. He's wrong though. It's not normal to lose them this soon.

I swallow, not wanting to think more about how this war is affecting the rising generation, normalizing our deaths.

"At least we have the choice."

I cock my head. I don't see us having many choices. "A choice about what?"

He looks up from staring at his feet. His blue eyes capture mine. "Life or death."

Gooseflesh rises on my arms. "How is that a choice?"

"We choose to kill or be killed."

I shake my head. "We don't *choose* to be killed."

He nods. "But we do. When we put ourselves in situations where we might die. That's a choice."

I have no idea how this conversation wound so off course, but I'm getting more uncomfortable by the minute. He seems to sense it, too, because he smiles.

"Sorry. Abby is always telling me that such grim topics are rude for normal conversation." He laughs.

I force a smile and say goodbye, but as I walk away, I can't get his words out of my head. *We choose to be killed.* What an odd thing to say. But then I remember what I had originally asked him and turn around before he goes into Abby's room.

"Abby loves you, Trevor. You have nothing to worry about."

He beams at me before walking in.

Abby's squeal of delight follows me down the stairs, and I smile. I'm happy for her, despite my screwed-up love life. At least one of us gets to live out the fairytale romance of our childhood dreams.

Once I'm in front of Wixx's door, the nerves return. I knock before walking in.

There is a large sitting area in front of her desk. I'm pretty sure this was Commander Lawrence's old office, but I can't be sure, since it was burned down. For all I know, she could have combined two or three offices. It's not like Commander Lawrence is in need of it. Kirt Lawrence, the Aura commander of the entire legion and family friend, got captured along with my mother and a few other commanders. Maybe that's why Wixx hasn't found them. She doesn't want to give up her extravagant office.

I shake my head, knowing that's not the truth. A door in one wall, I know, leads to her living quarters. I settle myself on the beige couch to wait for her to finish with whatever she's working on at her desk.

Unlike my mom's organized chaos, Wixx is very orderly. There is not a single paper or knickknack out of place. I look for a family picture, card, or anything to get to that soft side of hers. But there is nothing personal on her desk. The walls are blank and the few tables in the room hold only nonconsequential items. I know nothing about her.

Finally, she clasps her hands together and looks at me expectantly. Her hair, which is usually wild and free around her head, is braided in tiny strands down her scalp, making her look edgier. My reluctance to talk to her grows. I take a deep breath. I might as well jump right in, but before I can, she speaks first.

"I'm sorry, Maya, but your mom would never forgive me if I let you go on a death mission to save her."

I open and close my mouth like a gaping fish before crossing my arms trying to control my emotions. My Igna trainer is always getting on me about controlling them. In through the nose and out through the mouth. *Think happy, calm thoughts, Maya.* But she can't just deny me before I say anything. What happened to equality and all the other stuff they spewed at us all those months ago? If reason isn't going to work on her, maybe guilt will.

"But what about my choices being mine alone? I want to join the alliance. Are you going to imprison us like the other commanders did?"

She winces, and it doesn't make me feel good. I know she's nothing like the other commanders. She has given us so many freedoms.

"No. You are not a prisoner here, and you can join another group of people if you wish. But neither you nor your brother will be under my protection if you choose that."

I suck in a breath. She's got me. I'm not going to uproot my brother. He's grown attached to Abby's mom, Mrs. Stevens, since Mom's disappearance. I can't do that to him. And these are our people, even if they sometimes infuriate me.

She takes my silence for my response and continues. "Unless you fully break from us, you must abide by our rules. Maya, you are an eighteen-year-old girl. Traveling into enemy territory is very dangerous. And we can't send anybody right now. We've had scouts looking for our people, and we can't risk sending any to Texas at the moment. It's too far. Maybe in a couple of months."

A couple of months? Who knows where James will be by then. And what if he's in trouble? That could be why he hasn't returned.

A tendril of fear wraps around my heart as anger rises. I stand, not being able to hold still any longer. The scouts have accomplished nothing.

Throwing my hands in the air, my voice rises. "So where is my mom? They have been looking for months, and nothing has come from it! James's people can help." The fire swirls within, threatening to take over.

She gazes at me, unblinking. "I said no. Now, you need to control yourself. All you're doing is proving you are too naïve and inexperienced to go on a dangerous mission like this."

I swallow, trying to control the fire that is searching for an outlet. My control is almost as good as this third trainer of mine now, but even I'm not perfect.

I turn on my heel and storm outside the manor. My fire curls around me, traveling over my body and lapping at my ankles. I take off, pumping my arms, unleashing my control on the flames. They expand up and around me.

I ignore the stares from a group of Terras making their way into the gardens and pull up to the huge slabs of concrete that lean against a wall from the rubble of Legion Headquarters, the lake directly behind me. I form fireballs bigger than my fist, letting my anger lash out. I chuck them as hard as I can, repeatedly hitting the center of the bullseye sprayed onto the surface in red paint.

After a dozen fireballs, my energy dips as fast as it rose, just as my trainer has warned me would happen when I use emotion to guide the fire. After a high always comes the fall.

I collapse to my knees, sucking in air as the flames diminish around me until I'm left cold and alone.

I haven't talked to or hugged my mom in three months. She could be dead for all I know. And James. The man I love either decided I wasn't worth it, or something terrible happened to him too. Tears run down my face. I touch them, surprised that the numbness didn't stop them.

Oh yeah. The numbness is gone, since it got replaced by hope. Stupid hope. It makes one believe in the impossible. My heart is wide open again, vulnerable, ready to be carved out once more. How can I put Cal at risk? And my friends? Would we all be kicked out of the community, including our families, if we tried to go without Wixx's permission?

"Maya, are you okay?"

I turn to the sound of Cal's voice. He's holding a basket filled with oranges as he makes his way from the gardens, but he sets it down when he notices my tear-stained face and runs into my arms. His small, skinny frame wraps around me. He rubs my back tenderly as I cry into his hair. The scent of apples, dirt, and sweat wafts into my face.

After a minute of holding his big sister, Cal leans back to look at me with a timid smile. "You're back."

A wave of guilt crashes into me like a tsunami. It's all I can seem to feel lately. I'm a terrible sister. I've left him all alone these past few months as a husk of me has been walking around. I've been terribly ignorant to think it wouldn't affect him.

"Oh, Cal! I'm sorry!"

He shakes his head. "It's okay. I felt the same way. I still do." He breathes in deeply. "Does this mean you want me back in your room?" He blinks nervously.

I laugh and wipe my eyes. "You can stay with Mrs. Stevens."

He smiles, but then his face grows serious. "Maya, I've been wanting to ask you something, but with everything going on…"

I tilt my head. "What is it?"

He bites his lip before his almond-shaped blue eyes—Dad's eyes—land on mine.

I've always been grateful for Cal's constant reminder of Dad, his little mini-me. But it's become more of a comfort since learning he wasn't my biological father. It explained why I could never see Dad in me when I looked in the mirror. That doesn't mean he's not a part of me, though. I feel him in the way I wield water—the way he taught me.

"Can you train me?" he asks.

A surge of warmth, along with a tiny tendril of guilt, runs through me as I wrap my arms around him tighter. The perfect thing to redeem myself. "Of course."

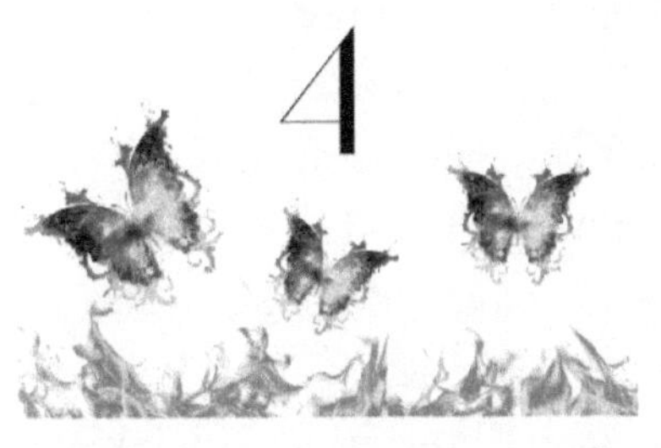

4

Brilliant Brother

For the next week, I rigorously teach Cal all that Dad and Seth taught me, ignoring the pain wrapped around my heart that grows heavier day after day as the numbness refuses to return.

We're throwing balls of water at each other on the pond's edge when he suddenly asks, "Do you think she's with Dad?"

The question shocks me. My eyes widen as his water hits me square in the chest, soaking my clothes. At least the sun is out, but there is a chill in the breeze, carrying a promise for fall.

He frowns. "Never mind."

I try unsuccessfully to recompose myself. "No."

His face falls.

"No, she's not with Dad, because she's still alive."

He peers up at me, biting his lip, his big blue eyes filling with hope. "You think so?"

"I know so."

"How?"

I walk over and place a hand on his bony shoulder. His head now reaches my chest, and he's getting taller every day. "This is Mom we're talking about. Super smart, never taking no for an answer Mother." As I say it, I know it's true. I'm not just trying to make him feel better. There is no way that she's dead. Nobody would want to hurt that brain of hers. They would want to use it.

He drops his hand but still looks like he's about to cry.

"Can you keep a secret?"

He perks up, a mischievous look twinkling in his eyes.

I smile. "I'm going to save her."

He blinks at me as his mouth slowly falls open.

"I just need to figure out how to let Wixx let me go. But I know where James is now, and he'll help me. He has people on the inside."

His mouth snaps shut, and his eyes light up as he looks around. "Just go."

My heart aches. I wish I could just go. "It's not that easy, bud. Wixx told me that, if I disobey orders, then I put you at risk."

He furrows his eyebrows. "Why?"

"She would kick both of us out."

"She said that?" He looks at me, unconvinced.

I think back to her exact words and shake my head slowly. "Well, no. Just that if I decided to join the alliance—"

"But you're not joining the alliance. And you really think she's going to kick a nine-year-old out by himself?" He puts a hand on his hip, reminding me of Mom.

I bite my lip but realize that he's right. She would not do that. And she wouldn't do it to Abby's or Juliet's family either. Wixx is not like the other commanders. Yeah, she'll be angry with me but wouldn't take it out on our innocent family members. And she was talking about whether we should decide to *join* an alliance, not just leave for a bit. Our disobeying of her orders would be on us, not them.

So what am I waiting for? Without realizing it, I've returned to my obedient, never-asking-questions self. If I want to go, I should just go.

"Cal, you're brilliant." I pull him into a hug, and he wiggles out of my grasp.

"Ugh! You're all wet."

"And whose fault is that?" I say, grabbing him tighter. I laugh and let him go.

He pushes off of me.

"Will you be okay without me?" Worry and guilt wrap around me once more.

He looks over the swaying grass and wildflowers that have replaced the crater-filled landscape thanks to the Terras, then back at me with a lift of his chin. "I've really liked the training sessions, but we can start up again when you get back. It's worth it for Mom." He smiles wide. "I'll be okay."

I sling an arm over his shoulders and we stride toward the manor. If I break a rule this big by going on a *death mission*, I have to warn my friends of the ramifications, at least.

"Of course, you'll be okay. Nobody will be here to tell you to slow down on the chocolate from Mrs. Stevens."

Road Trip

Abby walks through my bedroom door the next night, her face red and splotchy, eyes swollen. I quickly grab her hand as William hangs back, sifting through our gear and the supplies we've collected the past two days.

"Are you sure about this? You don't need to come, Abby."

She sniffles, wipes her face, and squares her shoulders. "Of course, I'm coming. Avery is my brother. And you need me. You'd probably starve or poison yourself without me."

Hearing her call James by his first name makes me pause. We really haven't talked about him much these last few months.

I squeeze her hand. "I do need you. But Trevor is your person. I'd understand—"

She cuts me off. "He can't come. It's fine." She walks past me to where William is carefully combing through our supplies and putting them into four black backpacks. "Need any help?"

I turn away from them to peer out my windows toward the fading sun. Pink and purple beams slash through the darkening blue sky like somebody spilled paint on the heavens. My gut swirls with remorse that Abby is choosing to help me over staying with Trevor, but there's also a surge of warmth that she decided to come. And she's right, James is her brother. Of course, she cares about his well-being.

"Where's Juliet?" Abby asks.

"She's going to sneak out once her family is asleep," I say.

"You two should get some sleep. It's going to be a long night," William says, standing.

I already feel the nervous jitters. There is no way I'll sleep, but I nod and lay on the bed, fully clothed, shoes and all. William laughs, shaking his head. I've already packed my bag. Nothing left to do but wait.

I stare at the ceiling, tracing the swirling patterns, thinking about seeing James soon. Well, in three *days* soon, if everything goes according to plan.

The next thing I know, I'm being shaken awake. Abby is curled next to me, still asleep.

I sit up, William's gray eyes scanning my face.

"It's time."

I check my watch. "Is Juliet—" I say groggily.

"Right here!" comes her musical voice from the depths of the room, way too chipper for two in the morning.

I nudge Abby. She yawns and blinks. Once she realizes what's happening, her eyes widen, and she nods. We sneak out my back door one by one. I'm the last to leave. I pause and glance at my darkened bedroom.

Running to my side table, I throw open the drawer and draw out James's knife.

"Just in case," I whisper, tucking it into my boot. It feels odd pressed against my ankle as I catch up with my friends, but having something other than my powers to protect myself is also incredibly comforting. It's not like I know how to use it. It can't be hard, though. Point and stab.

We move under the cover of darkness, which is sparser than the last time we snuck out at this hour, thanks to the bombing. Terras did their best to regrow trees around the manor, but a whole forest takes a while. When we're far enough away, William or Juliet casts a small orb traveling just at our feet so we can see. I've got to admit, traveling with Auras is quite handy.

My thoughts drift to Cal. I gave him clear instructions on what to say to Wixx to give us some wiggle room before they realize the four of us are gone. Abby said Trevor won't rat us out, but he also can't lie. It'll hurt his chances of becoming a commander. We just need enough time to get out of the area.

Even though I believe Wixx won't kick Cal and our families out, I don't feel comfortable taking that chance. Because of that small risk, we decided telling Mrs. Stevens the plan was best. I'm sure there was more to the discussion, but according to Abby, her mom wants us to find James, and she agreed that, even if they were kicked out, Cal would be safe with her. But it's not going to happen. Wixx is nothing like Commander Lawrence or even my mom.

I peer at Abby, but she's showing no dismay about leaving the manor and traveling further away from her beloved Trevor. Her eyes are focused, searching the space far ahead.

"What is it?" I whisper.

She eyes me before saying, "This is just making me think of another time is all."

My heart squeezes at her words. I look at her knowingly. The last time we were out here at this hour was with James, and it didn't end as planned—with him going after that Com, who ended up being one of his people. They probably had a good laugh between them, while Abby and I thought he was dead for a couple of days. I never did bring that up with him. When I see him, that'll be the first thing I ask after I embrace or slap him. I'm not sure how I'll feel when I see him. Angry? Relieved? Probably a mixture of both.

Our footsteps slow as we reach the wall. With a quick wave of Abby's hand, the vines crawl away. She's done this many times now, but here in the darkness, with her hair cut short, she looks exactly like James as she does it. My heart constricts again. Three days, I remind myself.

"How do you think Wixx will react?" Abby murmurs.

I shrug. "She'll know where we've gone, but our numbers are too low for her to send people after us. She already told me so. Heck, they're too low even to have proper guards. We were able to cross the border without a problem."

"Yeah, I doubt she'll be surprised. It is weird that there were no guards out tonight, makes you think she wanted us to go."

I shake my head. No way.

We walk for quite some time, enveloped in the sounds of crickets and rustling animals, before the trees separate, and we come into a large opening up against the mountainside. A field of moonlit yellow grass extends until it ends along the edge of rocks that cover the face of a large cliffside, with giant boulders on the bottom looking slightly out of place, too perfect. The tall grass encasing the field leads to another opening in the trees on the far side.

"This is it," William calls. "This is where they brought us chaps when I first arrived, where the scouts keep the Jeeps."

Abby walks ahead of him and points at the boulders. "And they're obviously hidden in there." She scoffs. "Not a very good hiding spot."

"Well, if you're a Com, I doubt you'd be able to tell the difference," Juliet says.

We all watch Abby as she strides to the boulders and sets a hand on one of them. "What would you have done without me?"

William fights a smirk as she closes her eyes in concentration. The rock shudders but doesn't budge. Her eyebrows rise, and her mouth pinches as she steps back. William smothers a laugh with his hand. She glares at him.

He raises his hands in defense. "It's supposed to require two of us. Not like you asked."

She gestures towards the wall irritability. "Go ahead, know it all."

He shakes his head, bringing his hands forward. "Ready?"

Abby rolls her eyes at him and places her hands back on the rock. The other boulders begin to shift as the giant middle one rises off the ground, revealing a massive pitch-black cave. Juliet casts an orb, and yellow spots flash at us from inside. As the orb enters the cave, black SUVs, camo-green Jeep Wranglers, and large trucks with more wheels than I think necessary line the space. William and Abby work together on the other large boulder as the cave fills with more light.

William whistles. "Blimey, we have our pick, girls!"

We walk down the row of smooth, shiny vehicles, the temperature dropping as we advance. I rub my arms, trying to bring heat into my maroon leather jacket—the material reminded me of James when I picked it from a pile of discarded clothes in the caves. I've missed being able to wear it.

"Wait, does anyone know how to drive?" Abby asks.

My heart drops at the realization. I certainly don't.

"I do!" Juliet chirps.

"So do I," William says.

Abby and I look at them.

Abby raises an eyebrow. "Good, you two can take turns." She reaches into a black and green Jeep with its windows down and rattles a pair of keys in front of them. "Who's first?"

After carefully steering the Jeep through the dark field and then through the opening I saw earlier, William weaves smoothly in and out of the trees with one hand on the wheel. I hold tightly to the handle on the door in the back seat, like my life depends on it. The side of my head aches from hitting it twice on the window. I'm surprised it hasn't cracked yet. Then, I'll bounce right through the glass and onto the road. No. It's not even a road.

Juliet's soft snores take up the front seat. I can't imagine how she's sleeping through this, but staying up all night waiting for her eleven-year-old little sister to fall asleep must not have been easy. Juliet is constantly complaining about Ann being a night owl. Her head rests against the window, bobbing up and down slightly. A sleeping princess, her lips puckered perfectly. Of course, she sleeps like that. My mouth would be wide open and drooling all over myself if I was her. I have a sneaking suspicion William didn't sleep either, but he's not complaining. He's as cool as a cucumber.

I force the panic down, even though I'm pretty sure we will hit something, and we'll all end up dead or injured before we have even left the forest. Instead, I focus on the sound of the engine and

Abby's moving hands. She's making grass grow back over our tire marks, but I worry as she becomes increasingly lethargic.

As her eyes droop for the third time, she places a hand on William's shoulder, panting slightly. "William, stop, please. I need a break."

He stops and looks back at us. "No problem, we should check the map anyway."

I release my vice-like grip on the handle and reach into the one bag we left in the car with us—the rest stuffed in the rear compartment—and pull out the large map and hand it to him.

"Aw, this isn't the one. I probably put it in the other pack. Hold on." The door swings open and he walks to the back, opening the door to the trunk, when I hear a loud, slightly high-pitched scream.

Abby and I jump out simultaneously as Juliet says groggily, "What? What's going on?"

William stares wide-eyed into the space, one hand raised before him, as if ready to blow somebody into the air and the other over his heart. Abby sucks in a sharp breath as I round the door of the trunk blocking my view and see what the two are staring at.

At first, all I see are the black backpacks we brought on one side and red gas cans on the other, but as I study the lumpy objects more, I notice two big brown eyes from one of the bags blinking at me.

I jump back, startled, but on closer inspection, it's not a bag at all. But the outline of a young girl.

"Is anyone going to tell me what's going on?" Juliet calls as she joins us and sees our dumbfounded expressions.

I hold back a smile and point at our little stowaway. Her eyebrows turn down, but she sits up straight as her sister finally spots her.

"Annabelle!" Juliet shrieks, loud enough to wake anyone in a mile radius.

6

Stowaway

Ann bites back a smile as she swings her legs over the edge of the rear compartment and hops down. The head-to-toe black, combined with her dark hair and eyes, makes her easy to miss. But not invisible. There was absolutely no sign of anyone following us out to the caves.

"What in the world? How did you get in there?" Juliet says, her mouth agape.

Ann's face twists guiltily before she vanishes before us.

A second later, Ann's voice comes from behind us. "I followed you guys. I knew something was up when I saw you packing."

We simultaneously jump and twist around. After all these months, I still haven't gotten used to her doing that.

Juliet's face turns a shade of pink as she sputters, "You were…? You promised not to use… How did I not hear…? I can't believe…"

Ann frowns and steps warily toward her sister. "How could you leave me?"

That makes Juliet snap her mouth closed.

Ann's chin quivers, and she wipes her face furiously. "Aunt Jodi would have blamed your disappearance on me, like she blames me for everything. And without you there, my life would have been awful. How could you?"

I share a glance with Abby and William, feeling like we shouldn't be here for this. But there's nowhere else to go, and I do share the blame.

Juliet's eyes glisten as she blinks repeatedly, seemingly rendered speechless.

"Ann?" I say.

She turns her tragic gaze onto me.

"It's my fault. I asked her to come with me to find James and my mom. We weren't going to be gone for long, two weeks tops."

"You're not leaving for good?" Ann turns back to her sister.

Juliet wraps Ann in her arms. "Did you not get my letter?"

Ann shakes her head.

"I put it at the bottom of your bed."

Ann shrugs.

"You have to know that I would never leave you like that. It's just too dangerous for you to come."

Ann leans back. "Please don't make me go back. I can help if trouble comes up." She disappears again. Juliet's arms hover oddly in front of her, like she's in the middle of a dance. The girl does have a point.

Juliet looks to me for a response, and I give her a look that means, *What else are we going to do?* We can't go back, and we can't send Ann back alone.

She rubs Ann's nonexistent back. "You can come."

A shriek pierces the air before she pops back into existence. "Thank you, thank you! This is going to be so much fun! You don't have to worry about a thing. I packed my own bag and everything." She disentangles herself from her sister and reaches in the trunk to grab a small green duffle bag between the black backpacks.

William mumbles something that sounds like *bloody hell* as we pile back into the Jeep.

Abby nudges Ann's shoulder. "I'm glad you're joining us. We didn't have enough girls."

William chokes out a laugh as Ann giggles.

"Sorry, William."

I settle in the passenger seat as William says, "No worries kiddo. You know I grew up with all sisters. This is my normal."

My eyes flick to him as he throws a knowing grin at Ann, and she beams.

William guns the engine as Juliet begins murmuring to her sister. Something about talking to her first and not believing she used her abilities like that. The headlights flash ahead of us, the beams bouncing off trees, brush, and the occasional yellow eyes. My pulse quickens. The front seat is so much worse than the backseat. One wrong move from William, and I'll be impaled by a tree limb. I wince at every swerve and bump before deciding to study William to get my mind off it.

He has dark circles under his eyes that are alert but relaxed. His face seems calm and worry-free, even though he's white-knuckling the steering wheel.

"When did you learn to drive?"

"My parents taught all of us at a young age. It's a little different being on this side of the car, though."

"Oh yeah! They drive on the right side in the UK." I risk a glance out the window and gasp as a wide tree trunk comes a hair away from the side mirror. "How have you not hit a tree?"

He flashes me his boyish smile. "Your guess is as good as mine."

I whack him on the arm and he laughs.

"You just have to keep your eyes far enough ahead, not on what's directly in front of you."

I try it. Looking where the beams flood the forest ahead instead of at the nearest trees we're dodging. It's still too much.

I look away with a shake of my head. "Maybe you can teach me. Well, when we're on an actual road, of course."

He glances at me, holding my gaze as something flickers in his eyes. "I'd love to."

There's meaning behind those words, and I try not to linger on his emphasis on a particular word. "Keep your eyes on the trees," I mutter. Does he look at me like that often? Have I been that out of it these past few months?

The exhaustion eventually sets in, and the bumps, jolts, and rocking become less terrifying. I finally put my trust in William and my eyes slide closed.

I wake to the sun beaming me in the eye. Abby is chatting happily with William. As I shift in my seat and stretch my cramped legs, I notice the car's movements are smoother. I sit up with a smile. The pine trees on either side of us shoot into the bright blue sky, the road winding before us.

"William, don't you need sleep?" The clock on the dash reads 9:32.

"Good morning," he replies.

"I've been keeping him awake, unlike *somebody*," Abby responds.

"Who? Me?"

"Yeah, if you get all that room to yourself up there, it's your job to keep the driver awake."

"Sorry, didn't know," I mutter as I look in the back seat. Abby is squished against the window. Ann's head is in her lap, and Juliet is asleep on the other window, her body taking over half the seat and her long dress taking over the rest. Why she chose a dress to wear for this beats me. I'd probably be more stunned to see her wearing pants, though.

I bite my lip as Abby narrows her dark eyes at me. At least she has a blanket.

William's lips twitch upward. "I'm doing alright. Once Juliet is awake, we'll switch," he says with a yawn.

"Where are we?"

He nods to the map in the cup holder. I grab and unravel it. A giant rectangle, with lines going every which way, opens up before me. It's Oregon. He points to a green spot in the middle. "We're on a back road around here. We should come upon Highway 26 soon."

"A highway? Isn't that dangerous?"

He shakes his head. "They only check cars entering the big cities. We're only going through smaller towns until we hit Idaho. And we have enough gas cans to make it halfway across the country. We'll be fine."

"And what about when we run out of gas?" I say, anxiety gnawing my gut.

"Don't worry, Maya, I planned our route so we don't go through any extremist communities."

A fuzzy conversation I had, from when I was first in the caves with James, dances on the edges of my mind—a story about extremists, alliance groups, and peacefuls.

"How do you know where they are?"

"We have a map back at headquarters…er…the manor. Extremists are in the bigger cities in most states along the East and West Coasts."

"And what about places like ours?" The Elemental extremists. Even though that name doesn't suit us anymore. Our group in the mountains is somewhere in between with Commander Lawrence and my mom gone.

A heavy feeling settles in my gut as I remember her last words to me, before she told me my birth father's name. *They can't know about you. Don't let them find you.* She would not want me crossing the country like this. But I have to find her. And I can't find her without James.

Abby chimes in. "Texas, Montana, Iowa, Arizona." She ticks off her fingers as I glare at her.

"How do you know?"

"Trevor tells me everything."

Lucky her to have a partner who tells her the truth. Neither of mine did.

"Then there are peaceful communities, right? That have Elementals and Coms?" I try to show that I know *something*.

William nods, and another thought occurs to me. William gave me a peek into his mind about his choosing to come to our community, knowing that we were a group of extremists, but I never asked why.

"William, why did you choose to come to our community? Instead of joining a group of peacefuls?" I don't think I would have chosen the same if my mom had given me the choice.

"I always knew I wanted to help. I know some call us Mentals, and after everything that's happened, maybe we are mental."

"Wait, back up. Mentals?" Abby says, a little too loudly for the small space.

Ann groans and shifts in her sleep. Abby smooths down her hair.

"You haven't heard that? That's what others call us. The 'Elemental extremists.'" William raises two fingers in air quotes. "In reality, we're just trying to do what's best for our kind, but others see us as war-obsessed zealots."

I shrug. "Makes sense."

William eyes me and sighs. "Yeah. Knowing what I do now, I honestly don't know if I would have chosen the same path." He purses his lips. "I understand what the alliances are trying to do. Even though they might be a little impertinent in their ways. But sometimes they're not much better than the peacefuls, who just stand back and do bloody nothing while our world burns."

I grunt. "You're starting to sound like my mom."

He smiles. "The commanders got obsessed with upping our numbers instead of focusing on trying to win the war right here, right now. Not twenty years from now. Keeping you guys in the dark about the world and forcing everyone to their ways wasn't right. Everyone should have a choice."

He looks at me with a sad smile. "I'm sorry I didn't tell you. If I had known how much you were in the dark back then, maybe none of this would have happened."

I place my hand on his arm. "You can't think like that. What's done is done. It's what we do now, moving forward, that counts."

"After getting to know James's people, I think James made the best choice in joining an alliance."

We're all quiet as we think that over. Knowing what I do now, an alliance does seem to be the way to go. I wonder what my mom would choose now.

"The highway is just ahead," William says before I spiral into thoughts of my mom.

He slows the car as we come to a stop sign. One car is coming from the left, fast. My heart hammers in my chest. What if it's a group of Com extremists?

I clutch at William's arm, and he wraps a hand around mine, rubbing the back with his thumb. My breathing regulates, but I bite my lip as the car passes without a glance in our direction.

"You're going to have to get used to cars passing us. We've got a long road ahead."

I nod, but I can't speak as he enters the highway. After a minute, I withdraw my hand, feeling embarrassed by my reaction. At this rate, I'm going to run back home with my tail between my legs before we even come to a town.

"Wrong side, William!" Abby suddenly screams.

The car swerves into the right lane, and my elbow knocks into the door hard.

His eyes are enormous. "So sorry. I guess I am pretty knackered, and I'm not used to driving on this side of the road."

"Well, I'm awake now. I'll drive before you kill us," Juliet mutters.

I look at her. I think it's the first negative thing I've ever heard her say.

She raises her eyebrows as she pulls her hair into a high ponytail. "What? I'm not a morning person."

I giggle, William laughs, and Abby starts snickering from behind. Juliet glares at the three of us, and we all laugh harder, waking up Ann and breaking the heaviness in the air from our earlier conversation.

"What's so funny?" Ann groans, stretching out her arms.

"Just that Juliet isn't the perfect princess we all thought," Abby retorts with a sigh as she repositions now that Ann is off her.

Ann snorts. "I don't know who ever told you that. You should see her when she's hungry."

We all start laughing again, and this time, Juliet joins in.

7

First Stop

After graciously letting William have the front seat, I'm now squished in the back with Abby and Ann, wishing I knew how to drive, just for the extra legroom. William is snoozing away as the sun rises high in the sky. Houses begin to blur past. My heart speeds up as the car slows, preparing to enter the first town. William said nobody would bat an eye at us passing through, but also said Oregon was one of the states full of extremists.

I catch Abby's eye as she looks away from the window, her face sketched in apprehension. Her mouth stretches into a thin line before returning to study our surroundings.

"How's our gas, Juliet?" I say, swallowing my unease.

"We should be good until we hit Idaho."

I lean back, fiddling with the necklace at my throat that William gave to me during our courtship. More cars than I've seen thus far crowd the street ahead of us as we pass a *Welcome to Madras* sign. A few people line the sidewalks in front of restaurants and shops, and my stomach unexpectedly rumbles. Hunger breaks through my nerves. I would kill for a cheeseburger.

We come to a stoplight, pulling up next to a hatchback. Young kids are in the back, and one looks my way. I dip my head down, worried they'll see me through the window and somehow know I'm an Elemental.

Juliet's hands grip the wheel tightly. The car is dead quiet except for William's soft snores. I stare at the light; this has got to be the longest red light ever. I peer back out the window to the little boy smiling at me. He waves, and I jump back, bumping into Ann. I look at her to see her smiling and waving back.

"Don't do that," I hiss, yanking her wrist down.

"What? It's just a boy," she says, hurt lacing her tone.

"He's a Com."

She seems to realize the tension in the car as she looks at Abby and then her sister, who is shooting daggers at her.

"Oh," is all she says as she settles back into her seat, her lips turning down. Thankfully, the light turns green, and we're off again.

I wish I still had Ann's innocence. She's lucky not to remember the chaos from the start of the war, having grown up in communities like ours. She was in the bunker when the Coms attacked the manor. She doesn't even know what they're capable of.

Bodies strewn across the field flash in my mind, and I wince. My innocence led to my ignorance and inevitably making the wrong choices. Ann should know what the world is like. Heck, I still don't fully understand what the world is like.

Even though I was told that places were rebuilt and relatively normal in certain parts, a part of me was still expecting bombed and destroyed buildings and rubble, communities with barbed wire around them, and Coms walking around with those big guns of theirs. But everything is…normal. People are going about their day like we don't live in a war-torn world.

An ache builds in my chest, thinking of all the lies and fear-mongering that the commanders and my own mother fed us to keep us locked inside the manor. There were so many lies. But I can't get angry with my mom for her past mistakes. She apologized for keeping me in the dark, and I forgave her, even though I never told her that. I just need to find her and hope she's still…herself.

The sun drops below the horizon when we stop and stretch our legs at a deserted rest place. We fight over who gets to use the bathroom first—which I immediately regret, as the trees would have been a better place to relieve ourselves than that nastiness. Then, after we fill up our water bottles, William and I walk around an overgrown pond while eating dried fruit and protein bars. It's only been a day, and I'm already tired of this food. Abby is in charge of our rations and insists that the nasty stuff will last us a week, but with Ann, that will probably shave off a few days now. Maybe I'll get my burger sooner than I thought.

"Whatcha thinking about?" William says, breaking the silence between us.

I smile, and he does a double-take as if he hasn't seen one on my face in months. He probably hasn't.

"Cheeseburgers."

He chuckles. "Of course you are. Those fast-food restaurants are tempting, huh?"

I nod and kick a rock into the swampy water. My intense need to be in or around water all the time has tampered down the more I harness my Igna abilities. Usually, I'd be itching to dive in, even though there's no telling what kind of bacteria is in it.

"I know it's too dangerous," I say.

"Eh. We probably could if you really wanted."

I stop and turn to him. "Really? Wait, don't we need money?"

He nods, swallowing a handful of nuts. "We have plenty."

"We do?"

"Mm-hmm," he says, looking away and popping some dried cherries into his mouth.

"Do I want to know?"

"Nuh-uh."

I smile, but it quickly turns into a frown.

He looks back at me with one eyebrow raised, probably surprised I'm not trying to get him to tell me where he got the money. But something else is still making my insides twist and ache.

"What?"

I start walking again. "As we're driving through those towns, everything seems so normal. It's one thing to hear about it, but to see it with my own eyes, knowing that I was isolated for so long from…normalcy."

"If it helps, it's still pretty bad in the cities. The best place for you probably was in that manor."

"What?" I turn on him.

He runs a hand through his sun-bleached hair. "Hear me out. Your mum had one motive—protect her children. And that's what she did. Right?"

"No, that was not her only motive."

"I'm saying that was probably what her motive was in the beginning and then it changed and morphed into something else. But at the root, I still think she was trying to protect you."

I sigh, because it's very close to what she told me when she apologized for everything. "You're probably right. And I did forgive her for it. It just still hurts sometimes."

"All feelings are valid here, love," he says casually, throwing an arm around my shoulders as some cows meander over a hilltop in the fields that line the rest stop. His comfort makes me want to be more open to him.

I turn into him, but his face is only a breath away, and my eyes lock with his. For a brief moment, he doesn't hide anything, and feelings that I thought—hoped—went away a while ago flash vulnerably on his face. Then he blinks and plasters on a big smile. His sunshine returns so quickly that I think maybe I imagined that look on his face.

There is a cough from behind us, and we look over our shoulders as Juliet awkwardly hangs back, her eyes lingering on where our bodies are touching. Seeing the two of us, I can imagine what she must be thinking, so I slowly detangle myself from William. He's such a good friend to me. But a small feeling in my gut warns me to be careful with him—with his heart.

"I, uh, put more gas in the car. We're ready to go," Juliet says.

I watch him join Juliet. He knows I'm in love with James, that we're just friends. There's nothing to worry about.

My eyes peel open as Abby shakes me awake. "We're here."

"Already?" I answer groggily. I look around. Everyone is already out of the car. I rub the sleep from my eyes. A street-lamp shines brightly behind Abby, bathing her in yellow light.

We're in the parking lot of what looks like a small motel. There are four other cars in the lot, but no other people. It must be pretty late. The last thing I remember is a whole lot of nothing around us as I watched the stars in the night sky from the car window. Juliet is holding some of our bags, and Ann is leaning against her with her eyes half closed, clutching her bag tightly to her chest.

"Where's William?"

"He's getting our room," Juliet says, nodding towards the building.

I blink through the darkness and catch silhouettes through the window. I nod uneasily, and Abby grabs my hand.

She smiles. "We're okay. This is Burley, a small town in Idaho, surrounded by peacefuls. We can't get any safer."

Juliet hands me my bag, and I swing it onto my shoulder. She smiles softly before turning her head to the building and biting her lip.

The chime of a door rings, and William strides over to us, a hand in his pocket, wearing a tired smile. He holds up a key card.

"Room 16 is this way."

He takes the rest of Juliet's bags, and we follow him to a line of brown, beat-up doors, a dim light blinking to the side. I can't help but study our surroundings, waiting for somebody to jump out with a gun. We're too vulnerable. My spark flickers as I rub my fingers together, ready.

William opens the door, and we practically run him over trying to get inside. I slam the door behind us and chain up the top as William laughs half-heartedly.

He gestures to the room. "We're safe, ladies. Chill. Not a five-star inn, but there are two beds and a pull-out sofa."

I eye the grubby gray couch shoved into the corner as he falls onto it and leans his head back. None of us move as we take in our home for the night. The smell of mothballs and cigarettes hangs in the air like it's permanently attached to every surface. Two full-sized beds with a tiny side table squeezed between them take over most of the space, with a TV hung on a wall across from them. A door in a small alcove—which the couch is a hair from blocking— must lead to the bathroom.

Ann is the first to jump onto a bed and crawl into the worn, floral sheets, immediately closing her eyes. Juliet scrunches her nose slightly before following her. Abby and I take the bed closest to the door. I peep out the blinds, scanning the lot again. It's black besides the few streetlamps and there's still nobody to be seen.

I slide off my shoes and settle onto the rock-hard mattress, peeking at William. He hasn't even bothered with the pull-out and lays haphazardly on the couch, his long legs hanging off one side. He should have a more comfortable place to sleep since he does most of the driving. I could offer him my spot, but I doubt Abby or the other girls would take to sleeping with William. I wouldn't mind it. I've woken up enough times with him passed out next to me after comforting me from another nightmare, it wouldn't be much different.

I turn to Abby, about to ask her to sleep on the couch, but she's already out like a light, her auburn hair splayed across her pillow. I sigh and try to get comfortable. Despite my worries, I nod off quickly into a rare dreamless sleep.

8

Will the Hunk

I didn't wake early enough to get first dibs on the shower. The water is freezing when it's my turn. As the ice-cold water slides down my body, I grab onto my spark, pulling my flames up to heat my skin. It helps a little. The water energizes me as it soaks into my pores. It's bizarre that I can feel so grubby from just sitting in a car all day, but I also slept in that bed. A shiver runs down my body that has nothing to do with the water. I swear something crawled on me in the middle of the night.

Once I'm out and dressed, I throw William a ruthful expression, knowing he doesn't have Igna abilities to warm the water. There's an assortment of food on our little table under the TV, which is playing old cartoons, pulling me back to a simpler time when all I had to worry about was losing a favorite toy, instead of losing the boy I love. Ann sits across from it, her eyes locked on the screen in some sort of daze.

I smile and look back at the tiny cereal boxes I haven't seen in years, bagels that look less than appetizing, and over-ripe fruit.

Abby grabs a banana, and it slowly brightens from brown to a brilliant yellow before she peels it. Juliet hands her a bruised apple, flashing her puppy dog eyes. Abby purses her lips before sliding a finger around the rim of the apple. It reddens and brightens before our eyes.

"Save the seeds. I can use those," she says.

I munch on a packet of Fruity-O's. "Ugh, I used to like these?"

Abby peers at the box in disgust. "You've been on an all-organic diet the last five years. Of course that junk will taste disgusting. Oh, and you're not four anymore."

"At least this has a taste—" I cut off when Juliet's eyes widen at something behind me.

My heart leaps, and I whip around, grabbing hold of my flame. If somebody has broken in, they are about to regret that decision.

Instead, William is standing before us, wrapped in only a towel from the waist down. His bare chest shows off his six-pack abs, still glistening wet from his shower. My eyes zone in on a single water droplet making its way from a patch of fair chest hair, down his muscled abdomen, and disappearing into the top of the towel. Then my eyes roll up his frame to his broad shoulders and down large biceps laced in veins that coil with the movement of his arms.

He doesn't notice us gawking at him until he grabs his bag off the couch and turns toward the bathroom. His eyes find mine first and one brow lifts. I swallow hard and quickly look away, but his bare chest is burned into my mind.

Abby's eyebrows are raised high into her hairline, and Juliet has yet to close her mouth. She's gazing at him like he's a mix of a Greek god and a prince who just stepped out of her favorite fairytale.

"Uh, just forgot my clothes," he grunts before the bathroom door closes.

Abby busts out laughing. "Need me to pick your chin up off the floor, Juliet?"

Her face turns beet red, and she whips around to stare at the food. She grabs a bagel, even though there is a half-eaten apple in her other hand and continues to stare at that. I join Abby in her laughter but don't blame her reaction. I've never seen William quite like *that* before.

"Stop it, guys, he's going to hear you," she mutters.

Abby laughs harder. "Oh, come on, Juliet, it's just William." She then elbows her in the side and drops her voice. "I mean *Will the hunk*. Who would've thought?" She snickers again, and the pink in Juliet's cheeks travels down her neck.

I would've thought. I remember feeling those muscles during the few times we touched during our courtship, but I haven't thought about William in that way since. I especially haven't imagined him looking like that without a shirt on. Sure, he's good-looking. I've always known that. But he's always been so…cutely boyish. But that body. That is the body of a man, nothing boyish about it.

Don't even think about it, comes a deep voice, almost a whisper, something carried by the wind.

I startle and look back to the bathroom, thinking William is out, but the door is still closed. Abby and Juliet didn't say anything, as they're still in front of me, and neither of them have that deep of a voice. Where did it come from?

"What's wrong?" Juliet says, as Abby is still poking fun at her.

I stand, shaking off the nagging feeling at the back of my mind, feeling like I'm ignoring the obvious. "Nothing, just thought I heard something." I drop the extra food into one of our bags and hand a cereal box to Juliet. "Come on, we've got to get on the road. But you should get Ann to eat something. I think she's lost all sense of reality."

Juliet nods, but still eyes me, the color of her face finally returning to her milky white pallor.

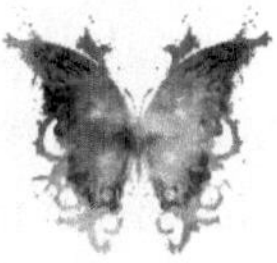

After a couple of hours of driving and nobody being able to look at William seriously, he finally snaps. "Okay, what is going on with you lot this morning?"

William raises his eyebrows at me as crickets come from the back seat. I peer behind me to find Abby with a hand over her mouth, trying to cover the huge grin on her face as she looks out the window, and Juliet is looking out the other window intently. Ann just shrugs.

Great, I'm the lucky one in the front seat and can't ignore him. I peer at him, but abs and chest hair flash in my vision as I take in his form. He's wearing a plain white T-shirt and jeans, his normal daily wear, but today, I swear his shirt is tighter than usual.

His gray eyes hold mine before he has to look back at the road. "Hmm?"

"I don't know what you're talking about." Yes, I'm a coward.

"Come on, you can tell me. Are you guys just worried? I promise we're going to be fine," he says.

I don't respond, but I feel his silent probing in my mind. It's been a while since he's used his Aura air link to talk to me. He must be really curious.

I bite the inside of my cheek and send him a silent *no*, not allowing him in.

Please, let me in. His silent plea caresses my mind, and I hold back a shiver.

I suck in a breath, breathing through the strong desire to give in. I widen my eyes, and he gives me a guilty smirk. The air link only works if I accept it, but I didn't know of his ability to sway me into accepting. I try to scowl at him, but his face distracts me.

His newly washed hair has dried in waves that travel over his ears; one plays on the top of his upper lip, and he blows it away. I forcefully remove myself from staring at his lips. What has gotten into me?

Well, you guys are leaving me out. Not fair.

I shout a hard *no* at him in my mind, and the tendrils of his presence leave as he slumps against his seat with a silent *humph*.

I sigh, feeling guilty. What am I supposed to tell him? Sorry, we're being weird because we all realized how smoking hot you are and now can't look at you the same.

This is stupid. It's just William for crying out loud. I will myself to wipe away the image of his naked torso and turn back to him.

"Have you decided if we're going to go through Salt Lake?" I ask, pulling the map from the cup holder.

He gives me a side-eye and a beat of silence before answering. "We could go around, but it adds an extra five hours. Salt Lake City should be one of the few cities that is safe for us. What do you ladies think?"

"Should be?" I swallow.

He presses his lips into a thin line and nods. "Yeah, they have more peacefuls than not. But, you never know with a city. Abby, Juliet?"

"I vote let's go through. I'm done being back here," Abby says.

"I don't know," Juliet says. "I don't think we should take the risk."

"I vote yes!" Ann smiles.

Juliet nudges her. "Sorry, you have to be an adult to vote."

She folds her arms. "Not fair."

William glances at me. James's hazel eyes flash in my mind as I take in the flat landscape stretching for miles around us, mountains rising in the distance. I could see him in five fewer hours. We've gone through two states and haven't seen any extremists. This trip is turning out much smoother than I imagined. Something swirls in my gut, but I push it down. The world is calmer than I thought. How bad could a city be?

"Let's do it."

9

Utah

An hour later, we are amongst more cars than I have seen on this whole trip. Growing up near Portland, I know this is normal for a city, but the feeling in my gut only worsens. I had gotten used to peering at strangers in cars who seemed to not care less who was in the car next to them, but I'm back to keeping my eyes cast down.

We stopped to fill the Jeep with gas so there would be no reason to stop within the city's borders, and I graciously gave the front seat to Abby so I wouldn't have to listen to her irritating sighing anymore. Ann is drawing between me and Juliet, who has her eyes trained on William and a mystified expression on her face. I hold back a smile. She must be imagining him with his clothes off.

Juliet notices me staring at her and blinks away from him. *What?* she mouths, as color crawls up her neck.

My eyes move to William, then back to her. She shrugs like she has no idea what I'm talking about and faces away from me.

I'm not sure why she's so embarrassed. Is she looking at him like that because of this morning, or could something more be there?

I have to admit, I haven't given Juliet's love life any thought since she was matched with James, but I know she stopped dating her other match, the Igna, and I haven't seen her with anyone else. Knowing that I've been in my own world these past couple of months, grappling with grief, it's totally plausible I missed something between Juliet and William.

I study her as she tries hard to avoid my gaze. Finally, she looks back at me, and I raise my eyebrows in silent question, nodding towards William. She shakes her head. What is that supposed to mean?

I open my mouth to whisper across Ann, when the girl notices the shift in our body language and peers up at us.

"What are you doing?" she asks.

My finger taps on the paper in her lap. She has a colored pencil poised between her fingers. "What are you drawing?" She's the smartest of us to bring things to do on this road trip. I study the picture of a block house surrounded by cacti.

"It's my home. Juliet said we might get to see it," she says with a grin.

"Annabelle, I said we may *drive* through the town, but we won't be able to go through any neighborhoods," Juliet interrupts.

Ann shrugs her shoulders and keeps drawing.

"New Mexico, right?" I ask.

Juliet's face grows somber. "We moved around a lot, but Ann was born in New Mexico. That house there is the only thing Annabelle remembers from before the war."

"Yeah! This is where my mom and dad lived before…" The pencil in her hand stills. She outlines the house with her finger. "I was happy there."

The mood shift in the car pulls unwanted memories from my childhood up, but I push them away as I put my hand over hers. "Maybe we'll get to see it."

Ann whips her head around, eyes big. "Really? Thank you, thank you!" She bounces up and down, and Juliet smiles at me knowingly.

As Ann continues to chat about what she remembers about her home, Abby says from up front, "What does that mean?"

I look up as she points at the dashboard.

"The tire pressure is low, but it's fine. I'll check it out the next time we stop," William responds.

Swirling colors above Ann take my attention away from their conversation. Ann is immersed in happy chatter with us, but still has a hand on her drawing. The colors from the picture peel off the page and dance in the air.

I suck in a sharp breath as my eyes widen at the strangeness of it.

Ann stops momentarily, following my stare. "Whoa!" She uses her hand to twist the red, yellow, and brown strands in the air, shaping them into the image on her paper.

I look over to Juliet. Her eyes are as big as mine.

"Ann…Annabelle, how are you doing that?" she stutters.

She smiles up at her sister. "I don't know. This is so cool!"

Abby turns around to see what all the commotion is about, and her mouth pops open. "Juliet, are you doing that?"

She shakes her head. "No, that's all Annabelle."

Ann shapes the colors into a dog, a cat, and then a tree.

"Isn't that an Aura ability?" Abby asks.

William shifts the rearview mirror until I see his eyes zoom in on the dancing colors. "Huh. Not quite. But very similar to what we do with light."

Ann glides the colors back onto the page.

"Wait a minute. Your dad was an Aura, and your mom a Terra?" I ask slowly.

She looks up at me and nods, her dark eyebrows turning down.

"Oh my! I can't believe I didn't make the connection earlier," Juliet says, her face awestruck. "Besides you, there never has been anyone else. I assumed—"

Ann looks from me to her sister and back. "What are you talking about?"

"Annabelle, you're poly—"

Juliet's sentence is left unfinished because a loud pop sounds at that moment, and I'm thrown against Ann and Juliet as the car shakes and squeals loudly—the smell of burning rubber stings my nose.

William curses as he tries to get control of the vehicle. Other cars swerve around us as he switches lanes. He barely misses the median as the Jeep slows and we enter the exit ramp. Ann, Juliet, and I hold onto each other as the car grinds harshly against the ground. I wince as my head knocks into Juliet's.

Finally, he stops as we get off the ramp, and pulls into a grassy area next to a stop light. A gas station and burger joint are on the other side of the road. Tall buildings are just across the highway to our left. My heart thumps wildly in my chest. We're directly in the middle of the city, every route blocked by cars and people out and about. This is the worst possible place to stop.

"William!"

"I think we have a flat tire, girls. I'm going to check it out. Don't worry." He closes the door behind him.

I want to slink into my seat, but sigh, instead, kicking my door open, joining William in the hot afternoon sun. I shield my eyes and peer at other vehicles passing us. Some look our way, but most ignore us, thankfully. If there has ever been a time I just want people to mind their own business and not think of others, it's now. Maybe I should glare at them.

William pulls tools out of the trunk, which I didn't even know we had, and unscrews the spare tire off the back door. His eyes are focused, but he doesn't seem panicked or worried.

I shift on my feet, studying every person and car nearby. "Uh. Need any help?"

He grimaces. "I bloody wish I could use my abilities right now."

I walk around the back to assess the damage. The tire is indeed flat to the ground. "How did that happen?"

"Beats me." He grunts as he lifts the tire to the ground.

I unhelpfully watch as he expertly jacks up the Jeep and switches the tires. At this point, the others have piled out of the car and we're all watching. The sleeves of his white shirt are rolled over his broad shoulders, and sweat glistens on his neck, reminding me of that single water droplet I watched run down his chest this morning. A sweaty guy should be gross, but for some reason, the sight of William working on the car like this…

What is with my thoughts lately? I shake my head and turn to Juliet, who can't keep her eyes off him either. Abby and I share a private giggle. Ann flits around the tire, asking a million questions. William even lets her screw in the last of the bolts. He high-fives her as he stands. He lifts the bottom of his shirt to wipe a sheen of sweat off his face, and Juliet practically swoons at the sight of his abdomen.

"Bob's your uncle!" William says, clearly happy with himself.

Juliet twists a wisp of her blonde hair around her finger. "I'll drive if you're tired," she says sweetly, batting her eyelashes.

I swallow my laugh as William responds, "Sure. I should probably take a turn in the back. Maybe this one can show me some more of her cool powers." He ruffles Ann's dark-brown hair. She giggles while Juliet deflates, probably cursing herself for being able to drive and not being able to snuggle up with him in the back.

I move to open the passenger door when another car pulling off the highway captures my attention. It's a white and black police cruiser. My heart picks up its rhythm as I meet William's eyes. A line forms between his brow as he follows my stare. The cruiser slows, coming right for us.

"Everyone, get in the car now. Lock the doors. I'll handle this. If anything happens, stay off the highway. Take the back roads," William says, voice laced with command.

"William," I hiss and grab his hand.

He shakes me off, desperation in his eyes. He lifts a hand to my cheek. "I won't let anything happen to you." Static moves through me at his touch, and his face inches closer.

For a moment, I think he's about to kiss me, and a feral growl rumbles in my mind. I freeze at the sound, but instead of closing in, he opens the door and pushes me inside.

I watch him in the side mirror as he shoves his hands in his pockets and casually strolls to the back of the car. He waves at the officer who has parked behind us.

"Juliet! Turn on the car!" Abby yells from the backseat.

Juliet sits in a shocked state, staring into the mirror like I am, but at Abby's voice, she shoves the key in the ignition, and the Jeep rumbles to life. "What are we going to do?" Her voice trembles.

I shake my head as the officer walks towards William, my pulse pounding in my ears. After all he's done for me, I can't let anything happen to him. It's not like I can use my abilities, though. That would be a death sentence for all of us.

"Stop freaking out. I'm sure he's just seeing if we need anything. It'll be fine."

"It's a Com officer, Abby!" I whisper-yell at her.

"Are we doing anything wrong?" she asks calmly.

Abby's right. He will assume we're just regular Coms having some car trouble. Nothing suspicious.

Suddenly, I realize Ann isn't in the car with us. "Where's Ann?" I shriek.

"I'm here," comes a small invisible voice.

Juliet and I both let out a breath.

"Good, stay like that," I say.

I watch as William talks to the officer, gesturing towards the tire. The officer is wearing a blue and black uniform with dark sunglasses, his hair slicked back. He nods, also gesturing with his hands. I risk opening my window a crack to listen.

"Glad you made it off the highway okay. That could have been a very dangerous situation. If you need a new tire, there's a guy in West Jordan you can visit. He'll take care of you." His voice is deep and scratchy.

I sigh in relief as the officer shakes William's hand.

"There's just one more thing. I see you're from out of town." He gestures toward our Oregon plates then reaches into his jacket pocket and pulls out an orange block-shaped device.

"Sir, we're really late to visit my little sister in the hospital." William's voice comes out strained.

"This will just take a minute. Protocol to check noncitizens. There seems to me more and more of those damn Elementals popping up all over the place these days."

No! No! No!

"Oh no," Juliet whispers. Her hands quiver on the steering wheel.

"We can't leave him." I go to pull on the door handle, but it's locked.

"Do you want us all to die?" Abby hisses. She's leaning over Juliet with her finger on the lock controls.

"We can't leave him," I whimper.

"He's a legionary. We need to trust that he can take of himself. He's trained for this."

William can't object to the testing, that'll be too suspicious. William gestures towards the road. "Normally, I would love to comply…but my sister. Please, sir. How about you follow us to the hospital, and I'll take it there?"

The officer scratches his chin and looks towards us. I stiffen, holding my breath as my heart seems to stop beating and sweat gathers on my neck. Maybe he'll let him off. We can try to lose him as soon as William is safely back in the car. He just needs to get back in the car.

The officer drops his hand with a shake of his head and holds out the device to William. My heart plummets.

I watch William bend over and spit into the device, his shoulders stiff. He shifts his weight so he can glance in our direction. While the officer's head is down, he mouths *go,* then quickly looks away.

No way we're leaving you! I scream at him in my mind, wishing to open up an air link.

He scans the downward slope of the hill we're on as the device makes a clicking sound. There's nowhere for him to go. No forest to run into and disappear, just streets, stoplights, and convenience stores. He could just jump back in the car, and we could make a run for it. But could we get away? We might all be doomed unless we take out the officer.

My fingers twitch as a plan formulates in my mind, but before I can do anything, a loud beep sounds out, and William takes off as fast as a bullet down the slope.

"Go! Now!" Abby yells.

I gasp as the car lurches forward. The officer looks from us to William and then down at his scanner. He pulls out a black and yellow gun from his belt and points it right at William's back.

"No!" I cry and pound on the window. I desperately look to Juliet, who has tears running down her cheeks, but obediently drives away just like William asked us to. She runs the red light as cars honk.

I twist back to where I last saw William. He's still running but suddenly his back arches abnormally, and he falls to the ground.

A sob bursts from my chest as the car rounds the corner and he is lost from sight.

10

Death Wish

"Stop the car!"

"We can't," Juliet whimpers. "He told us to go."

Fire courses through my veins, pressing against my fingertips, whipping through my body like a wild animal wanting to break free. I give her a look of pure rage, letting my fire take control and burn in my pupils. She better listen if she doesn't want us all burned to a crisp. She looks at me and slams on the brakes with a gasp.

The car lurches forward, and I break free of its imprisonment before it stops, barely hearing Abby yell after me as I run back to my best friend. My rock. My sunshine. My William. He may already be gone.

I push the thought from my mind. I won't lose another person.

I round the corner of the gas station and spot the flashing lights of the police cruiser. I slow to a fast walk, reeling in my flames, and glance around at the growing crowd. They stand on the edge of the parking lot, blocking my view. With no plan, I march through them, pretending to be another concerned citizen. Nobody pays a small, skinny girl any attention. Sirens wail in the distance. I can take out one officer, but more? I elongate my stride.

When I get to the front of the crowd, I see him. The officer has William's arms pinned behind his back as he stands him upright and leads him to the cruiser. His face is pained, his white shirt covered in grass stains and dirt, and his jeans torn. But no blood from a bullet hole.

Relief floods me. He's alive. How is he alive? I saw him go down. And if he's alive, why isn't he trying to escape?

I take a step to cross the road when William's head snaps in my direction. His eyes widen, and he shakes his head. I feel his words slam into my mind. *Get out of here!*

No, I respond, letting him in. *Why aren't you fighting back?*

He's got a gun on me. Get out of here. I'll find a way to escape and find you. I promise.

Tears prick my vision. I'm not letting them take away another person I love.

I step into the road. That guy may have a gun, but I have a whole lot more firepower.

Whisk that bad boy away. I'm coming if you like it or not.

No! He growls back. *I won't risk you or our friends. I'm giving you a chance to escape. They'll be after you next. Go!* His voice is deafening in my ears as he urges me to leave.

I cross the road, ignoring his shouting in my mind. By the time I reach the grass, the cop notices me. He has just opened the cruiser door and is about to lower William inside.

"Stop there, young lady. Unless you want to get arrested for obstruction."

I spot the black gun that he's jamming into William's side. "What did he do?"

"He's an Elemental." He grunts like that explains everything. "Now get back."

Hesitantly and studying his reaction, I take another step, choosing my following words very carefully. "But why is he being arrested?"

"Are you new to the city or somethin'? Their kind isn't allowed here. You an Elemental lover? Want to go with him?"

I smile and take another step forward, not having the faintest of idea where my confidence is coming from. William looks at me, horror-struck, but is radio silent.

"Maybe."

I move closer, and the cop slowly points his gun at me instead. My smile grows, adrenaline coaxing my fire hotter and hotter as it presses up against my insides, seeking release. Maybe I do have a death wish.

Before I get the chance to set myself aflame and really show the cop I mean business, William uses the wind to throw him across the road and to push me back a few steps as he barrels my way. "Damn it, Maya!"

He's still fast, even with his hand in cuffs behind his back. The officer is untangling himself from the crumpled heap on the ground.

"How are you okay? I saw you get shot!" I ask as he reaches me, and we race across the road.

"It was a taser," he grunts. "It still bloody hell hurt."

As we reach the other side, gunshots ring through the air. Chaos breaks out as the crowd decides things have gotten too violent for them and starts dispersing, helping our cover. I risk a backward glance, and a massive earth wall forms between us and the officer.

I look around for Abby and notice our Jeep at the end of the road, past the gas station, one wheel precariously on the curb. I wince, hoping William's new tire holds.

Abby climbs out, and Juliet looks frantically between us and the host of police cruisers who have just rounded the corner. We're not going to make it to her in time.

"Go!" I shout, waving my hand for her to take off before the police see her.

An air link between us opens. *I'm sorry. I'll stay close, but I don't want to involve Ann. Keep me updated on where you are. Good luck.* I can feel her conflicting emotions with those words. She wants to stay and help but also protect Ann.

She gives us one last crestfallen look before rounding the corner. Looks like we're on foot now.

A dozen officers pour out of their vehicles. I look between Abby, who is running for us, and William. We're really doing this.

Before they get a chance to start for us, a giant crack forms along the road, traveling straight for them. Most leap out of the way, but some of the bigger ones, who look like they had one too many donuts this morning, fall into the fissure.

As Abby reaches us, I finally unleash my fire. It's like a rubber band wound tight. The relief is immediate as flames engulf my arms. For one heartbeat of a moment, I marvel at their silent ferocity. Unlike a fire made with wood or coals, it doesn't crack or make a sound. It's just there, ready and waiting to devour.

"What's the plan?" Abby asks as she sucks in huge gulps of air. We've both been training more, but neither of us are true legionaries. We don't have the same stamina they do, built up from their rigorous training schedules.

"Uh," I respond, biting my lip.

"Of course, she doesn't have a plan!" William growls.

I roll my eyes and grab his cuffs. My fire melts away the metal until he's able to break free of them. He rubs his wrists where my flames got too close.

I wince. "Sorry."

"I'll heal myself later."

The cops who jumped out of the way now have their guns pointed at us. I shoot up a wall of flames as Abby motions toward the earth blockade that crumples toward the officers, and a new one forms right outside my flames. My hair flies upward as a thin twister touches down from the sky, swirling around our massive walls of earth and flame. The twister isn't big enough to do much damage by itself, but it's quite intimidating combined with Abby's and my powers.

"That should hold them! Come on!" William shouts.

The three of us sprint towards a large stone wall that the gas station is pressed against, separating us from uniform gray rooftops—a neighborhood, probably. Before I can even think of how to get around the wall, William grabs my hand, and I'm flying into the air.

A scream escapes me as all three of us shoot over the wall. There is a moment of weightlessness before we hit the ground on the other side. My legs buckle, but William holds me steady.

"That was kinda fun!" I laugh uneasily.

We're in the middle of a cul-de-sac. Three teenage boys stare at us, their faces slack, one with a basketball in his hands.

"Juliet's close," William calls as he runs ahead.

Abby and I look at each other before racing after him.

We weave through the suburban streets, staying on William's heels, until I spot the forest-green Jeep up ahead. We're only a block away when a police car turns onto the road we're on. Without its siren or lights on, we almost miss it. William dives behind the shrubs in front of a brick home.

I hit the ground hard on my elbows and Abby lands beside me. Pain radiates up my arms as I press my body into William's. We're too big to be entirely covered by the shrubs.

Abby waves her hands in front of us, and the vines from the bushes wrap around our bodies, encasing us, but leaving a gap so we can watch where the cruiser goes. I focus on my breathing, which is much too loud.

The cruiser slowly passes a black Jeep. Wait, *our* black Jeep—not green. It stops momentarily, and I suck in a sharp breath. *Please keep going. Please keep going.*

I notice something different about the plates too, they start to blur if I look too closely.

The seconds stretch impossibly long. Finally, the cruiser drives forward. When it passes and the Jeep comes back into view, I can't see Juliet nor Ann inside. The police car continues down the road and disappears from view.

I launch myself from the bush, the muscles in my legs screaming at me as I watch for more cruisers. I clear the road as the door to the Jeep swings open. Abby and William pile in behind me. The Jeep speeds off without a driver in the seat, somehow steering itself. We're a tangle of legs and arms in the backseat as we all try to reach for the steering wheel.

Juliet and Ann appear in the front, and I gasp. Ann removes her hand from Juliet's arm and beams at us, as if what we did was as exciting as winning a close race, not running for our lives.

"That was close," she giggles, enthralled by the whole incident.

I gawk at her and shake my head, as I try to detangle myself from William's and Abby's bodies.

"Guys!" Abby gushes. "I can't believe we just did that!"

"We're not in the clear yet." William grunts, moving towards the steering wheel. "Here, I'll drive."

Juliet jerks from under his touch, looks at him wide-eyed, and then back at the road. "I've got it."

"You know where you're going?"

She stiffly nods. "I studied the map of these streets while you three tried to kill yourselves."

William slumps back, knocking his shoulder into mine. I shift so he can have more room in the middle. Juliet white-knuckles the wheel while she takes us through the streets, weaving through side roads, parking lots, and neighborhoods. I strain my ears, listening for sirens, but the further we get from the city, the more the sounds go with it.

We keep off the highway until the sun starts to lower, and we have no choice but to get back on so we can get to the mountains and out of Utah. We pass signs of the war that transpired here—houses and buildings in ruin, hate speech sprayed on old signs, and cars melted to driveways. It's how I imagined the whole world would be.

"It wasn't like this outside of Boise," I recollect.

"We were on the main roads. There are places like this all over the country but mostly outside the cities."

"Like Portland," I mutter.

Images of our chaotic exit the night Mom took us out of Portland and to the manor absorb my mind. She had come home from work, announcing that we were leaving our home. I remember being frozen in my bedroom, not knowing what to take or leave. Then she was back with Cal, and I just threw whatever was in my closet at the time into a bag, and we left forever. We thought we were okay and had left early enough…until we came to the wall of fire. It was my first time using so much of my Lympha abilities. And if I had failed, we would have died.

William gives me a sympathetic arm nudge, breaking me from the horrible memory.

"How do you know all this stuff?" Abby asks from his other side.

"My parents made me do a ton of research before I transferred here, and the commanders keep us updated on everything going on around the country," he says.

"Must be nice," I grumble.

William rolls his eyes at me. "Hey, I didn't know you knew how to cast allusions," he tells Juliet. "I have yet to master that."

"I'm still working on it. I can only hold it for a short while. I wanted to change the car completely, but the most I could do was the color and a little of the plates."

William nods. "Good job."

Juliet's cheeks pinken. "It was a team effort. I don't think it would have worked if Ann didn't make us invisible."

William shakes his head. "Ann continues to surprise us."

Ann sits up a little taller, and he offers her his fist. She touches her knuckles to his happily.

After an hour of dark, and nobody following us, I finally let my eyelids slide shut.

"Thank you," William whispers.

"For…for what?" I stutter, opening one of my eyes at him.

His gray eyes hold mine. "For saving me. I haven't thanked you yet. You were brilliant out there. I was more afraid than you were."

"Oh, well, you would have done the same for me." I shrug.

He puts an arm around my shoulders, and I can't help but nuzzle into his warmth. Despite the sweat and dirt caked onto him, he still somehow smells like honey and warm tea, like home.

Before long, I feel myself drift off, but not before I hear the words, *I love you, too,* trickle into my mind.

11

Santa Rosa

Please, please, please!" Ann whines, pulling on William's shirt sleeve.

William is driving. We made it out of Utah and halfway through Colorado, William and Juliet taking turns driving through the night, only stopping once to refill the tank. And even then, in the middle of nowhere, everyone was on edge. Today has been harder, as we are all itching to get out of the car. Now that we're three-quarters of the way through New Mexico, taking the long way around Albuquerque to avoid the city, Ann may very well get her wish.

"After Salt Lake, I don't think we should risk stopping in any towns," William says for the third time.

"I can make us all invisible!"

"Can you?" Abby asks, astonished.

"Well, I haven't tried. But Juliet was easy enough. I'm sure I can!"

I still can't get over Ann being polymental, with Terra and Aura abilities. It's a relief that I'm not the only one, and means there's a higher chance there are more of us. Although, most are probably too young to come into their elements, since we've only done the matching in the last five years. It makes me wonder if my mom had a hand in Ann's parents coming together—another one of her science experiments, leaving ruined families in her wake.

I shake the thought away. I can ask her myself soon enough. And who knows, maybe it can happen naturally, without medical interference amongst couples from different groups. If we hadn't been so prejudiced among our own people, we could already have stronger Elementals with multiple abilities.

"No," William repeats.

"Let's vote!" she says, looking between me, Abby, and Juliet. Juliet shakes her head.

Ann pierces me with her big brown, puppy dog eyes. "You said—"

"Yeah, yeah, I know. I'm fine with it," I concede.

Her face lights up as she looks at Abby in the passenger seat.

"I'm sorry, kiddo, but it's too dangerous."

She whips her head to Juliet, who bites her lip and looks from her to the window before her shoulders slump. "Ugh. Fine."

"Yes, yes, yes! Three to two," Ann says triumphantly, looking like she's trying to hold in sticking her tongue out at the front-seat passengers.

William grumbles to himself but doesn't argue. We all need to get out of this car before we start ripping each other's heads off anyway. I can practically feel the grumpiness radiating from the group from being confined to the small space.

Before long, he pulls off the exit for Santa Rosa.

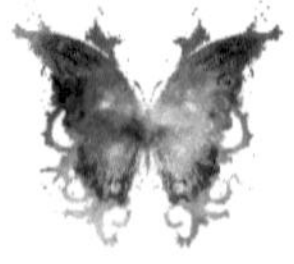

"There it is!" Ann squeals, jumping up and down in her seat.

William makes a U-turn at the stop sign and pulls across the street from the house. Ann smashes her face against the window on top of Juliet, while we all nervously take in our surroundings.

A small bluish-gray concrete house with two windows and a triangle roof faces us. Flat rocks line the yard of dead grass and a huge evergreen tree in the middle.

Juliet wiggles out from under her sister's weight, moving to the middle next to me.

"It looks the same!"

"It does," Juliet says, surprise laced in her tone. Despite the dead grass, the house seems to be in good shape, with no broken windows. There is even a welcome mat in front of the door.

"Like maybe they never left," Ann whispers.

"Oh, Annabelle." Juliet moves to wrap her arms around the little girl, but she's gone, the car door flung open. "Annabelle!" Juliet shouts as she's about to jump out of the car after her.

I grab her wrist. "Wait, she can't be seen, but *you* can."

"We can't just leave her!"

I hesitate and let her go. Her long blonde hair comes undone from her top knot as she races across the road, her navy-blue skirt whipping around her legs.

"Here we go again," Abby mutters, climbing out.

William and I join her on the side of the car, scanning the deserted road. There are other houses, but they all seem vacant like this one.

Juliet climbs concrete stairs and peers through the windows of the house. She waves us forward.

"Where did she go? It's not like she can walk through walls," Abby says, then looks at Juliet. "Can she?"

Juliet doesn't respond, so Abby looks at me. I shrug. I wouldn't put it past her. I don't even know the full scope of *my* polymental abilities.

"Mom? Dad?" comes a small voice from inside the house.

"She must have gone around back!" Juliet tries to open the front door, but it doesn't budge. With a flick of her wrist, I hear a click, the knob twists, and the door flies open.

The calling has now turned into sobs as we locate her at the bottom of the stairs in the living room with her face in her hands. Juliet folds her into her lap. The living room has a brown lumpy couch, but based on the musty smell permeating the house, it hasn't been touched in years.

"I know it was stupid to think they would be here, but part of me hoped that nothing happened to them. That they've just been here all along, waiting for us to return," Ann says between sniffles, muffled in Juliet's shirt.

From what I can remember from the story Juliet first told me, she and Ann share a dad. Her dad left Juliet's mom for Ann's. Juliet would come to visit. This must be that house.

I'm surprised Ann remembers it, with how small she must have been when the war started. I know Cal doesn't—thank goodness, with our traumatic exit.

William steps into the living room from the kitchen. He must have been checking if the coast is clear. He nods, and I join Ann and Juliet on the stairs.

"It's not stupid. Nobody can take away your hope." Juliet nudges Ann's chin until she looks up at her with a red, tear-stained face. "Hope is the only thing that can get us through the hard stuff. You are hope, Annabelle. Dad and your mom would be proud of you. These amazing abilities of yours are just the beginning of the hope they had for you. You are going to accomplish so much, and the world is a better place with you in it. I bet they're watching you right now."

Ann wipes her eyes and gives her a little smile. "Really?"

Juliet nods. "I can feel Dad sometimes. Mostly when I use my ability. Feels like he's my Sage—grounding and strengthening me." Juliet turns her palms upward as they start to shine, colors forming and shooting into the air. The colors swirl to create an image of a white-haired man resembling Juliet. Ann must take after her mom with her darker features.

Ann gasps and then tries it for herself. She rubs her palms together. More colors join, swirling around the image of their dad until it explodes into a world of color.

She lays her head against her sister's shoulder. "You're right. I can feel him." Ann places her palm on the ground. Vines slither from the door and up the wall, colorful flowers blooming and traveling all over the house. "And there's Mom."

Tears prick my vision, and my throat burns as I think of my dad. I look at Abby, who is leaning against the wall near the front door, silent tears sliding down her cheeks. We've all lost people. It's not fair for Ann to be going through this so young. It's not fair for any of us.

William grabs my hand and rubs the back of it with his thumb, sending soothing tendrils through my body.

There is movement behind him in the kitchen. Before I can react, there is a clinking sound, and a metal ball slowly rolls toward our feet, as if time has yet to catch up.

The last thing I feel is William's hand tightening on mine before an explosion of smoke envelops us, and everything goes dark.

12

Strangers

I wake with a start as a groan escapes my lips. When I open my eyes, there is only endless darkness. Something is wrapped around my head, obscuring my vision. I go to remove it, but my wrists are tied behind me. I shift on the hard-backed chair and bump into a warm body.

I startle. "What's going on?"

"Maya?" comes a high-pitched voice from behind me.

"Juliet, is that you?"

"Yeah, I can't see anything. Can you?"

"No, what happened? Where is everyone?"

"I don't know," she whimpers.

My ankles are tied to the chair, too, but I'm able to knock my knee into the body next to me again. I hear a soft groan.

"What the…?"

"Abby! Thank goodness." I wiggle my wrists and feet, trying to get free of the binds, but they're too tight. My knife! I wiggle my foot, still feeling it pressed against my ankle. Only if I could get to it.

"Ugh. What in the world?" Abby murmurs.

"Annabelle! Are you here?" Juliet calls.

No answer.

"Annabelle?" she sobs.

"William?" I call hesitantly. I grab my flame and direct it toward the bindings, hoping it's a rope or something that can burn easily. Fire licks my pointer finger.

"Oh, no yer don't," comes a rough voice with a strong Southern drawl as water hits me.

"Oh!" The ice-cold liquid drips off my clothes, instantly putting my fire out. Well, little do they know.

I grab hold of the water droplets, then stop. I should get information first, then unleash a surprise attack. For all we know, we could be in a metal box.

"Who are you?" I call.

"We have a few questions for you ladies before we take off the blindfolds," comes a different voice.

More than one, and William isn't amongst us. I store that tidbit away. There's a musty smell in the air, so there is a good chance we're still in the house.

"You have questions for us? We're the ones tied up. You all could be murdering Coms for all we know," I say.

A feminine voice barks a laugh, and I hear a quiet *shoosh*.

"As I was sayin'," says the rough male voice. "We need ya'lls names, abilities, and where yer came from."

"We're not telling you psychos anything! Where are our friends?" Abby yells.

"If you want those blindfolds there off, answer our quest'ns," he says again.

I sigh. Well, they already know about my fire.

I open my mouth to speak when Juliet says, "Where's my little sister? Is she safe?"

There's a beat of silence and then muffled whispers. "Answer our questions."

"I'm—" Juliet starts, but I interrupt her.

"I'm Amanda and this is Rachel and Nikki. We're Ignas just passing through. We don't belong anywhere. Our community just got wiped out up north. Now let us go."

"Now, was that hard?" he asks as the blindfold slips off my head.

I blink as my vision clears. A man in a cowboy hat with a handlebar mustache that falls past his chin sits in the middle of the couch pushed against the wall, one foot balancing on his knee as he studies me. I was right. We haven't been taken from the house.

I crane my neck, counting two more: a redhead leaning against the couch with a bucket full of water at his feet and another standing in the shadows in the corner of the room. The sky outside is darkening, with the fading sun lowering over the mountains and casting long shadows into the living room.

"They're not Rogues," whispers a feminine voice behind me. So, at least four.

The man in the cowboy hat grunts in agreement. "What brought yer to this'n house?"

"I'm not answering any more questions until we know our friends are okay," I say.

He looks at me for a moment before pointing behind him. "The man is in the back there. Reckon, he's still out, had to give 'em an extra dose." He looks behind me. "And the little girl is upstairs, asleep. She's just dandy."

I hear Juliet sigh with relief. They haven't hurt us. There are no weapons on them—that I can see. So that must mean only one thing.

"Are you guys Elementals?" I ask.

He shares a look with the redhead before nodding.

Relief sweeps through me. "Why did you tie us up?"

"Make sure yer not Rogues," he grunts, like it's obvious.

"Well, can you untie us?"

"Nope. And don't think about using yer fire abilities again. We need to check the male fella first."

There's a thump upstairs and then a bang as a skinny young man with blond hair rushes down the stairs, his eyes blown wide. "The girl is gone! She just disappeared!"

"What do you mean she disappeared?" Cowboy Hat and Redhead say at once.

As they bicker, the binds around my wrists loosen. Ann! I easily wriggle out of them as Juliet opens an air link with me.

I'm free. What's the plan?

Wait until a couple more of them leave to go find Ann, and then let's show them what we got. Abby and I will hold them off. You and Ann wake William and meet us at the car.

Say what? Abby says, apprehension filling her thoughts around the part of the plan where we take them down by ourselves. And she's probably right. We'll need all of our abilities to take them down. We don't even know what types of Elementals they are.

Okay. How about Ann goes to wake up William, and the three of us combine our abilities? Abby, you tie them up with your vines. I'll soak them. And Juliet, you freeze them into human popsicles.

A unanimous agreement reverberates from their thoughts. We don't have to wait long. As two of them break off and rush upstairs, I prepare to jump up, grabbing hold of the closest water source in the kitchen.

A loud crash sounds from another part of the house, and William comes barreling around the back of the stairs, his face bloodied and eyes wild. They turn lethal as he catches sight of us tied to the three kitchen chairs in the middle of the room.

William unleashes a roaring tornado inside the house. The few still standing in the room smash against the ceiling, as Abby, Juliet, and I race around it toward the front door. Vines capture my foot, and I fall hard on my knees, pain radiating from my left side. I shoot fire behind me and jump back up.

Juliet stands at the door, pushing an invisible force outside. Good, she must have run into Ann. As Abby races out behind Juliet, I twirl around to find William outnumbered five to one.

The ones he threw against the ceiling are regaining their footing, and the other two have just slid back into the room, holding onto the banister for support. I gather a ball of fire in my palms and launch it toward the whirlwind in the middle of the living room, turning it into a flaming tornado. It scorches the ceiling, and flames lick up the side of the walls.

A spark lands on the couch and catches, causing the upholstery to melt and burn. Smoke thickens around us, and William dives for me. We rush out of the house.

We get to the car where Annabelle and the others await us. We pile in and William starts the engine. I hesitate on closing the door, though. Something wraps around my heart, tugging me back to the house. The flames have now reached the second story, where smoke billows from the windows. Those people are still stuck inside.

We can't let them die. Without giving it another thought, I jump back out and run to the house.

"Maya!" William shouts.

I ignore him, tripping over the entrance to the living room. The redheaded man has a fire bubble around him and the others. He must be an Igna. But screams are coming from upstairs. The man with the deep southern drawl has his cowboy hat pinned to his chest, looking frantically from the fire to the stairs. He spots me, and his eyes turn pleading.

He shouts something, but I can't hear over the crackling, spitting, angry flames. It's not hard to know what he needs.

I take the stairs two at a time and find a woman with short gray hair pinned at the end of the hall with a wall of fire in front of her. I throw my hands out, dividing it enough so she can squeeze through. She runs past me, down the stairs, and out the door.

The group is almost at the back door when I return. The raging fire has devoured the living room and half of the kitchen. Words from my instructor spring to mind: *There comes a point when you can't control the fire any longer. It will continue to burn and devour until everything in its path is gone. The only tool in your arsenal will be directing it, and you better hope there is something to which it can be directed.*

I grasp the flames and do my best to give them more room to get out, but it's like fighting an out-of-control beast ten times your size. The stairs give way, crumbling at my feet, but I hold it. Just a few more feet, and then they'll be out.

The house screams, and I know I need to get out, but as I step back toward the front opening, part of the wall crumbles. I try to jump out of the way, but I'm not fast enough. My hands fly up to protect my head, but it never hits me.

William stands in the doorway, using his Aura abilities to hold the crumbling house together. I crawl underneath the floating, fiery wall that almost killed me. When I touch the porch, he pulls me into his arms, and we fall down the steps and onto the grass.

As I cough the smoke out of my lungs, I see the group rounding the back of the house, Juliet using the wind to keep the flames from reaching the neighboring houses, and Abby erecting a wall of rock on either side. William helps me to my feet as I grasp the body of water nearby with my mind. Before I can do anything with it, the skinny, blond-haired boy in their group douses the flames. Juliet and Abby lower their hands, panting.

"Thank you," comes a voice behind me.

I turn around to see the redhead. For the first time, I notice he has bright green eyes like mine. I didn't really get to study his features in the shadowed house. But there is also something else about him I can't place.

"We tied you up and you saved us." He shakes his head in disbelief.

I shrug. "You didn't try to hurt us."

"Speak for yourself," says William, rubbing his jaw where a nasty bruise is rising. There is also dried blood under his nose.

"Sorry. You didn't immediately knock out at first, and you seemed a little roguish."

"Rogues? You guys used that word earlier," I say.

The man with the handlebar mustache comes up behind the redhead. But he doesn't stop. I tense as he's suddenly upon me...but not trying to hurt me. He's *hugging* me.

"Thank you for saving my Marla. I owe you my life." He releases me and bends down to kiss the back of my hand.

When he looks up, his brown eyes are shining with tears. I look behind him at the rest of their group, who are hanging back. The woman with the short gray hair looks unscathed.

"Thank you." He straightens and fixes his cowboy hat, which now has scorched black tips. He looks much older than I thought, now that I can see him properly, his face lined with wrinkles and gray hair sticking out from underneath his hat.

"You never heard of Rogues? What, yer come from an isolated group of Mentals or somethin'?" He jumps right in like he didn't just hug and kiss me.

But then his words register, and I stiffen, looking to William, who raises his eyebrows.

"Well, I'll be damned," the man says, turning to the redhead and nudging him with his elbow.

Abby comes up next to us, dusting off her palms. "Well, thanks for the wonderful hospitality and all, but we should be getting out of here." She does a double-take of the redhead and squints. "Wait a minute, do I know you?"

"Butter my butt and call me a biscuit!" the old man shouts, slapping the redhead on the shoulder.

"Where did you guys say you were from again?" the redhead says slowly, as William murmurs, "Butter your what?"

I look at William, but he's scratching his chin and staring at the other man. "Up north," I say, not wanting to give him our exact location.

"You don't mean Oregon, do you?"

William finally realizes what we're talking about and eyes the redhead. I shrug, keeping a cold mask on my features.

"He's only askin' 'cause he escaped one of those crazy communities. How long ago was that?"

"Four years," he murmurs. His face pales as he studies me.

Now that Abby says it, he does look familiar—the red hair, green eyes, oval face shape, and tan skin. The only other person I knew with the color was the young man that…no…

"Do you have a daughter by chance?" Abby asks.

My eyes don't leave his as he stiffens at the question. Could she be thinking what I'm thinking?

He carefully looks over the three of us, eyes widening. "No, you can't be from LindonGale Manor."

William gives me a questioning look.

"That's what we called it when we first arrived," I murmur.

He *is* exactly who we think he is. The man who was matched to Claire. The same man who was a part of the story that was told for so long to scare matches into obedience. If he really is that guy, then he supposedly murdered Claire's original match when he found out that her child was his. He bonded to Claire, who then ran away from him. He took off with their child shortly after, never to be heard from again—until now.

The man pushes a hand through his hair. "This can't be happening. Claire won't believe it. It's been years since we left. Can't believe the place is still standing."

"Wait, Claire is here?" I ask as Abby gapes at him.

"Yeah. Why wouldn't she? We left together with our daughter."

"But, I thought…wow…" Abby says, blinking at him.

The old man lifts his hat to scratch his balding head. "This is quite the coinkydink. But ya'll can discuss it later. We can't stay here. The smoke will bring others snoopin'. Ya'll follow us to our camp. We're in the orange truck around the corner."

I take one last look at the redhead, who's still watching me. He cocks his head as something sparks in his eyes. I'm sure he's as shocked to see us as we are to find him, but I have a gut feeling that that's not it—that the intense curiosity in his eyes has nothing to do with where we came from and everything to do with me.

13

Stories

I can't peel my eyes away from Claire and her two green-eyed children as we sit around a fire, having just finished the most delicious chili I've ever tasted, filled with bacon, beans, brown sugar, and who knows what else that danced on my tongue. A beautiful little girl with long orange hair sits next to her, and a baby boy with dark hair is on Claire's lap, happily chewing on a jerky stick. Thomas, the redhead, holds her hand as he takes in the flames. They look like a happy little family, not the murdering, crazy, lunatics we thought. Occasionally, he sweeps his eyes toward me but looks away before I meet his gaze.

Sal, the older gentleman with the cowboy hat, explains why they tied us all up. "You see. Rogues are lower than a snake's belly in a wagon rut."

I stifle my laugh at another one of his weird sayings.

"They can be like any other Elemental, but their eyes are dead." His eyes glaze over as he gives us his best impression of Rogues. "Like nothin' is inside of 'em—just shells of the person they once were. The extremists change their minds—twist and turn 'em into weapons that hunt their own kind."

A shiver runs down my spine.

William blows out a breath. "I've heard of them but didn't believe it could be true. Just thought it was some dodgy propaganda from the Coms to try to turn us against each other."

"It's something out of a horror movie," comments Juliet, having just returned from helping Ann find a place to lay down. She sits next to William in our little circle—the fire crackling in the middle, like in the house that burned down earlier. Ann was so distraught, she only took a few bites of her dinner before asking to go lie down. I feel awful for burning down her childhood home. I've apologized profusely, but she keeps saying I did nothing wrong and that she's not mad at me. It hurts, though, seeing her heartbroken over something I caused.

After following their group to the next town, which they share with peacefuls, we learn they're an alliance group like James's but not nearly as big. They told us they just recently started gathering a group from others in the area in the past year. Sal and Marla had come from a small town in Texas. I assumed the two were together from his reaction to me saving her, but I think it's more of an unrequited love situation as I get to know them. His eyes follow her and hang on her every word, but she doesn't even give him the time of day.

Abby, who's on the other side of me, continues to stare at Claire and Thomas's family like I am, probably still not believing that the rumors we grew up hearing were just that…rumors.

"So that's what happens to us if we get captured?" I ask warily.

"Yes and no," murmurs Thomas, setting his eyes on me. He looks like he wants to tell me something else but looks away.

"Only a lucky few are chosen for that path," Sal finishes. "The rest get drugged so they can't use their abilities and are forced to work for the Coms or are experimented on, depending on their usefulness."

"And they call *us* Mentals?" Abby scoffs.

Claire looks at her apologetically. "I know it's not the best nickname, but it stuck. Took us a while to get used to it too."

"And what's Thomas's real story then, about why you left? There are plenty of rumors back home. But I'm guessing they're not true. Since you don't seem crazy and you're still with him," Abby says to Claire without reservation.

I balk but Claire meets Abby's stare. To her credit, she doesn't even blink in surprise.

"I can only imagine what they said about us. But we had to do what was best for our family and get our daughter out of there."

Abby seems to digest that information and then eyes Thomas before asking, "Did you...?" She makes a gesture of slitting her throat. "The other guy?"

"Abby!" I hiss.

She ignores me and stares down Thomas, who sighs.

"No, I did not hurt Simon."

"Horrid people to spread such lies," Claire chokes out, tucking the now-sleeping toddler against her.

I want to push Abby off her tree stump, but she's too far away, so I settle on throwing a pebble at her, which she bats away.

"Simon was sick long before I gave birth to Loreline." Claire looks down at her daughter, who notices her mother's attention and smiles. "I didn't think he would make it before I gave birth. Simon made Thomas promise to watch out for us after his passing. So when Simon found out she was Thomas's, he was happy." A tear slides down her cheek. Thomas leans in to wipe it away. She looks up at him and smiles, eyes full of love. "I did truly love both of them," she finishes, leaning against her mate.

Her declaration of love for another man doesn't seem to bother Thomas as he holds his little family.

"I never wanted to take Simon's place, but when he came to me to tell me his dying wish, I couldn't say no. I wasn't planning on bonding with Claire, but I promised to take care of them. As Lori grew, I knew I needed to do more than just be there for her, so when Claire was ready, we sealed the bond and left, knowing nobody would truly understand. At that point, we were questioning the commanders anyway. We decided to figure out things for ourselves. We lived with the peacefuls for a while, but when we had Freddy." Thomas strokes the baby's chubby foot poking out of the blanket he's wrapped in. "We knew we wanted to make a better world for our children. I didn't want them living in fear. So we sought out an alliance group."

I absorb his words. How isolated they must have felt and how brave they were to decide to leave our community. Their children are lucky to have such parents. I only hope that, one day, this world will be better for them.

There was a time, before the matching, that I was counting on the next generation being the ones to make it better. How selfish that way of thinking was. We need to make it better for them now. Today.

A resolution rises within me as hot as my flames. I will make a better world for my children. One day, when I have a child, they will live with freedoms that I have gone without. They won't be afraid of their neighbor or worry the next day will be their last. They'll just live.

After begging us to stay at least one night, Claire sets us up in their house, where Ann is already passed out. Since they have young children, they get the biggest home in their community of refurbished houses. They offered to split us up, but we refused. So, as we finish laying out blankets and pillows in what must be Freddy's nursery, I pad to the kitchen to find a glass of water.

As I close the refrigerator door, I jump, catching Thomas watching me from the living room couch that shares the same space.

"Oh, sorry. I thought you guys went to bed. I was just getting some water."

"No need to apologize. Like I said, you all are welcome to anything you need. I remember what it was like to be on the road."

His eyes don't leave my face. I grow more uncomfortable at his blatant staring, looking away, but I still feel his eyes on me.

Finishing the glass of water, I set it in the sink. When I turn, he's still watching me. Now it's creepy. Do I have something on my face? A hole in my pants?

"Is there something else?" I ask hesitantly.

"I'm sorry. I've just never met somebody outside my family with the color," he says.

I look at him oddly.

"Your eyes."

"Oh!" That's why he must have been staring all evening. But what does he mean it's only in his family? "Really? I mean, neither have I, but it's just a rare color, not nonexistent."

He shakes his head, his eyebrows turning down. "No, it's only in my bloodline."

I scoff, not believing him for a second. "Yeah, okay."

"I'm serious."

My next step wavers and I tilt my head at him. "So, what are you trying to say? We're related?"

I'm still waiting for him to laugh or say he's joking, but his face remains serious. He stands and moves toward a shelf that holds binders with music notes on the spines, a couple children's books, a ukulele, and one old leather book that he pulls out. Turning to me, he sucks in his lips as he taps the top of the book.

"That is exactly what I'm saying."

I shake my head. "I'm sorry, but I barely know you. And saying we're related because we have the same eye color? Thank you for letting us stay in your home, but I need to go to bed. I have a long day tomorrow."

He places the book on the arm of the couch and raises his hand. "No. I'm sorry. You're right. Goodnight, Maya." He sits down and pulls the book into his lap.

Before I slip down the hall, I catch the title. *Divina Origin: A History*. Pictures of the four elements are painted around the words.

I waver, my curiosity piqued. Was he going to show that to me? Does it explain why he thinks we're related?

I sigh. "Is there another reason you think we're related?"

He turns his head with a slight smile on his lips. "Would you like to hear a story?"

When I don't answer, he turns fully toward me, his smile widening. "It's a good one, I promise."

I look back toward my room down the hall and then at him. It will be impossible to sleep now, knowing there's something he wants to tell me. And it's not like I'm driving tomorrow.

"Fine." I sit on the couch next to him and he places the book so it balances on both our legs. On closer inspection, I notice that the drawings on the front must be hand painted, even the letters. They don't have the same uniform shape as printed books. Whatever is in this book must be pretty special.

"What is this?"

"A story."

"You already said that."

He shrugs and opens to the first page. Inside, there are aged yellow pages bound between the covers. An image of a person with bright green eyes and dark hair is on one side. The other has words written in a cursive that is almost unreadable.

My eyes snag on the eyes that look like mine and Thomas's. A slight shiver snakes down my spine.

"Once upon a time—" he chuckles under his breath before continuing, "—there were a people called Divina. They could wield all the elements of nature. This manifested through their emerald eyes, a sign of their power. They ruled over those who had no abilities for centuries. They were seen as gods by people who didn't have those powers—Nomagi."

My stomach does a tiny flip as he turns the page. This page depicts people locked in an intense battle. Swords clashing, elements swirling, and crimson paint smeared throughout.

"The Divina didn't know, but tension and unrest was rising amongst the Nomagi toward them, as they became increasingly desirous of the Divina's unique abilities. The first war broke out.

The Nomagi fought back, and most of the Divina, unprepared for such violence from a usually peaceful people, got slaughtered. Before they knew it, they were bowing before the Nomagi."

He flips through the next couple pages too quickly.

"Hey wait. I want to see those."

He cocks an eyebrow at me. "Don't worry. I'm just passing the boring parts. The Divina and Nomagi were locked in a power battle for centuries. Sometimes the Divina ruled and other times the Nomagi did. But this is where it gets good." He lands on a page with six green-eyed people. "There came a point where Divina were on the verge of being wiped out. They began mating with Nomagi to continue their race, but it dimmed their powers, making it so their people could only wield one element, not all four."

I stiffen but he continues.

"Three couples chose not to interbreed and found an isolated part of the world, far from Nomagi, to continue their pure genes. That's where they live today." He goes to turn the page, but I stop him, placing my hand on his.

"What is this book?" I whisper, unease spreading through my veins.

"I think you know what it is." He scans my face.

I shake my head, releasing him and standing up. "This can't be our history. It would be common knowledge if it was."

He stands up, pushing the book into my arms, passion burning in his bright green eyes. "There is a reason this isn't common knowledge. Look at the last page."

A stone drops into my stomach as my wonder grows. I take the book and turn to the end. An outlined family tree covers both pages, little orange blossoms holding the names. At the top are six names—the six Divina that left.

With a trembling finger, I trail the dark, hand-painted branches through each generation. I reach a branch that goes lower than the others, following the blossoms until I reach a name that I recognize at the very bottom. Michael Ali.

The book hits the floor with a thump.

"Where did you get that?"

His eyes light up in fascination. "You recognize a name on there, don't you?"

"Where did you get that book?"

He shakes his head, his lips quirking up as he bends down to grab the book. He opens it back to the page with the family tree and points to a name.

I take a deep breath before looking down. He's pointing to the name Izalia on the bottom row, before it branches off by itself to the bottom.

"This is my great-grandmother. She gave me the book."

"She's a Divina? But…how?" My mind races, not being able to grasp onto a single logical thought.

"My great-grandmother fell in love with an outsider and was banished from her home. They had one child." He moves his finger to the next name underneath hers. Teddy. "My grandpa married an Igna and had my father." His finger lands on the last blossom with the final name, Michael Ali, and he studies my face.

I shake my head, stepping away. "Say this is all true—"

"It is."

I ignore him. "Does this mean you can control all four elements like the Divina?"

He closes the book, and finally, that bottom name stops blinking at me like a flashing neon sign of the truth that I'm working hard to overlook.

"After the second generation, the abilities filtered out, and my dad only has fire abilities to my knowledge. My parents never bonded, and I was their only child. The green eye trait, I guess, takes longer to filter out. I'm surprised my children got the trait too." He looks at me intently. "So where are you from, Maya?"

My heart falls into my stomach, and I forget how to breathe. He doesn't know that I don't know who my biological father is. He doesn't even know that I have two abilities. Is that why I'm able to do what I do? Because I have Divina blood? No. Ann is also polymental, and she doesn't have the green eyes.

"Is your father here?" I whisper, not knowing if I'm ready to meet this man who is probably my father. I still don't even know if I believe this far-fetched story—a history of Elementals that nobody else knows except this stranger I just met. My knowledge of our history is bare, to say the least. Nobody truly knows where we came from. But this is crazy.

He shakes his head, standing up and placing the book carefully back onto the shelf. "I haven't seen my father since I was a young child. The bastard left us."

The hope that arose so suddenly withers and dies before it can blossom.

"I…don't know my biological father. You really think we could be related?" I swallow. I study his features, looking for anything similar between us, but besides the eyes, we couldn't be more different.

He shrugs, looking back at me with those all-too-familiar green eyes. "Did your mother ever tell you your biological father's name?"

14

Divina Eyes

I ponder Thomas's words all night and into the morning. When I do sleep, I dream of green-eyed beauties.

I don't tell anyone about my chat with Thomas, and by the end of breakfast, William nudges me under the table. I look at him. Without said or unsaid words, he asks what's wrong. I shake my head a fraction of an inch and try to eat a couple more bites of the heavenly scrambled eggs and sausage. I catch bits and pieces of the conversation.

It starts with a question about where they get their food and somehow turns into discussing the corrupt government that is full of Com extremists. Before the war, the government had Coms and Elemental members, and the people had a say, each state making its laws. Now, with the Elementals pushed out, the extremists have taken control, forcing states to abide by the same corrupt rules that alienate Elementals. Still, they can only really be enforced in areas with a significant number of extremists, and some states have managed to hold back. Peacefuls are mostly left alone in those states, but nobody thinks it will last much longer, as more are forced to choose a side. All this leads back to their relationship with the peacefuls in town. They keep a farm, often trading food and supplies with them.

Before long, we're hugging our new friends goodbye, and promising we'll visit again. Having somewhere we can go if our plan falls apart is nice. The longer we're here, the more I can imagine living this life. They are free to make their own choices. They don't have the same level of protection but make do with living in the middle of nowhere. But the reality is that it won't last forever. We have to fight back.

Thomas leans in for a side hug and whispers in my ear. "It's good to have a sibling."

I lean back, looking him in his eyes, my eyes. My brother. Emotion threatens to rise, and I push it down. I've had all night to come to terms with the fact I have a brother, but I can't seem to make the connection stick. When I told him my birth father's name, he didn't seem the least bit surprised. It's still hard to believe. I need more time to process before I tell anyone else.

When I give his children high fives, it clicks that I'm their aunt, and my eyes well up. Did my mother know about Thomas? He was a part of our community; she would have had his samples. I can do nothing with these thoughts except let her secrets and lies hurt me, so I banish them for now.

As we load up, they trade our license plates. Our run-in with the Coms in Salt Lake was all over the radio channel they use to communicate with other communities.

"Why don't you guys just use phones?" Abby asks.

Sal looks at her. "Don't let your brain rattle around like a BB in a boxcar."

"What he's trying to say," Thomas says with an annoyed glance at Sal, who shrugs, "is that phones are trackable and hackable."

"Well, yeah. But, at breakfast, you were saying the peaceful groups are left alone. Why would they care?"

"They may be left alone, but that doesn't mean they're not watched. Any talk of fighting back and they're goners."

Sal pulls out a map for William, directing him to the largest alliance group he knows of in Texas and telling him which roads to stay clear of.

Once they pack our car full of food and supplies, we thank them and wave goodbye. Thomas's and Claire's eyes linger on me as they stand on their porch. He must have told her of the revelation, but thankfully she didn't say anything to me. It's just all too much right now. Maybe one day I'll be able to return and act like the family I truly am to them—the family they deserve to have.

"I wish we could stay," Ann huffs as she sits between Juliet and Abby in the back seat.

"I know, kiddo. It was nice not being in a car for a bit. But we have a mission, remember?" Juliet says.

"Yeah, but still. They were so nice."

"What have you been teaching this kid, Juliet?" William chuckles. "They did knock us out and tie us up."

"They didn't tie *me* up," Ann mumbles, pulling more laughter from William.

After an hour of driving, William reaches out to me with his mind.

You don't have to tell me, but is this about this Thomas guy? I couldn't help but notice him staring at you all evening yesterday. And the way he hugged you...

I sigh, feeling the jealous edge to his thoughts and contemplating whether I should tell him. This will open up old wounds I don't want to get into. But I can't help myself. *Do you know the Elemental history?*

There is confusion in his thoughts. *Yeah, what about it?*

What exactly do you know?

What does this have to do with Thomas?

Ugh, never mind. I go to nudge him out of my mind when he launches into a history lesson.

It's all the same stuff that I knew, how we're not sure how we got the Elemental gene that gives us our abilities. There are theories ranging from it being a gene mutation to involving magic in our blood that some being blessed our ancestors with. He mentions the same war Thomas did but nothing about a people with all of the powers of nature or Divinas.

I stop him.

Now that we got that history lesson out of the way. Are you going to tell me?

No, I respond and push him out of my mind, snipping the mental link.

He turns on me and balks, but I say nothing. I twist my body away and look out the window to watch the most flat and dull landscape I've ever laid eyes on. I miss Oregon, the lush green, rolling hills, and mountain peaks. William will be upset with me, but there's no way I can tell him something like this over a mind link. I still don't know if I believe it. I do think I'm Thomas's sister. Could there be more than one Michael Ali who is an Igna with green eyes? Maybe. But I strongly doubt it.

This story about Divinas, though? I'm keeping it to myself until I hear it straight from the horse's mouth. Great, Sal is rubbing off on me.

I'll tell him and all my friends about Thomas eventually…as soon as I get the guts. It's too fresh and overwhelming right now. I don't even know if I can say it out loud—which is what I tell myself while William shoots daggers at the back of my head for the next several hours.

The late afternoon sun shines in my eyes as we near our destination. Juliet is driving, and I'm in the backseat with a moping William, who's talking to everyone but me. Juliet is over the moon about the attention and is chatting away. Abby sends curious glances between us in the rearview mirror but says nothing. And Ann is none the wiser. I'm just glad she's doing better since yesterday. She's back to drawing pictures but not of her home she was so desperate to see and which is now a pile of ash. Ann draws pictures of us, our different powers swirling around our bodies. She's even added Sebastian and James in the background. Dirt is in a halo around James, but Sebastian is powerless. I hold my question on why she chose not to include his fire and look away. I'm unsure what she knows about everything that's happened, and I don't feel like explaining it if she has questions.

The nerves kick in once we pass into Texas. What if James isn't even here? What if he's changed? What if he doesn't love me anymore? I bite my lip, trying to push the thoughts down. Abby seems to have the same anxiety, as she won't stop arguing with William over the plan.

"And we're all just going to stride up to the front door?"

"Why not? They're an alliance group, not extremists," William says with a pointed look.

Abby's eyes widen. "Because they have guns."

"Abby. They are not all Coms. They aren't going to hurt us."

"Then why aren't we letting Ann stay visible?" She raises an eyebrow.

William sighs, pushing his hair out of his face. The ends have curled against the nape of his neck. "It's better to be safe."

She smacks the seat. "Exactly!"

"Then what do you suggest?"

She chews on her lip and shrugs.

"You can't argue against the plan unless you have another idea," he says.

She sits back in a huff. I know she's only arguing because she's worried about James. I would voice this, but talking without the urge to puke hasn't been easy. Why do nerves make me want to launch bodily fluids out of my body?

I scan our desolate surroundings, waiting for a giant building or something to appear as I ponder Juliet's sweet conversation with Ann yesterday before all hell broke loose. She had talked about their parents being part of their Sage. Is my father a part of my Sage? Is that why I had those dreams about him healing me and seeing my biological father? Was he trying to tell me something? Was it why I saw him under the waterfall when I almost died escaping James's people? Could he really be with me in a way? Or am I just a little crazy because I come from a bloodline who married their cousins?

With a sigh, I knock my forehead against the warm glass window as my green Divina eyes stare back.

15

Texas

"That can't be good," Juliet says as sirens ring through the air.

We barely stepped beyond the chain-link fence surrounding the white square-shaped buildings when we heard them.

"Should we turn around?" Juliet looks at us frantically. Her ponytail, with a purple ribbon entangling with the white-blonde strands, whips across her face.

I shake my head. "They already know we're here."

"Ann, stay invisible, okay? If anything happens to us, get to the car and radio the base. There's one in the glove box. It should already be tuned to the right channel," William says, looking at the spot next to Juliet, where there is a barely there fuzzy outline of Ann, with a hard expression.

A small "got it" comes from the spot.

It's hot. Not just a hot summer day hot, but being transported to the surface of the sun hot. Sweat sticks to me everywhere, like

I've been dumped inside a sauna. The water in the air is heavy, even though there isn't a cloud in the sky. Suitable for my Lympha abilities, I guess, but literally nothing else. Why would anyone choose to live here? And it's so loud. A high-pitched buzzing sound follows us wherever we go. The bugs here must be huge to make sounds like that. The thought makes my skin crawl.

"Now we wait for them to come to us," William says. His voice isn't worried—it's even a little cheerful—but his shoulders are stiff, betraying his unease.

Lights blink from within the buildings, announcing our arrival. There is no doubt that this is the facility Sal told us about. It's right where he told us. There is nothing else around to mistake for it. Barren land stretches in each direction on the mountain-less horizon, adding to the ever-growing list of cons about living here.

I share a look with Abby, who's trying to keep her face expressionless and failing. Her mouth turns down, but her eyes are alight with hope—the same hope that fills my heart. I've tried telling myself that James might not be here, but it doesn't matter. My heart longs for him, even though I know I can't do anything about it because of this bond holding me back. Knowing that he's okay and well will have to be enough for now, until we figure out how to break the bond with Sebastian. It's only temporary.

That's what I tell myself as the doors at the front of the building open and people pour out, some wielding weapons and others with their hands raised, ready. Those must be the Elementals. And at the head of the group of about a dozen is a man with curly chestnut hair dressed in all black.

My legs are about to buckle underneath me as the other faces fade away, and I take in my James. Well. Whole. Just like the last time I saw him.

I want to run and jump into his arms, but something holds me in my place. I would never hope for him to be anything else, but seeing him okay punctures a hole into my chest. Why did he stay away, then?

I wait for him to recognize me as his eyes travel over our small group.

As their group closes in, James raises a gloved hand and those with weapons lower them. His eyebrows lift as his mouth falls open, stopping a few yards away from us. He still hasn't looked at me. Why hasn't he looked at me?

His eyes are on Abby as he snaps his jaw closed, studying her. Once he's done with his assessment, his eyes finally slide to mine. He stares at me stone-faced for a split second, his eyes traveling down my person like a warm caress, but they're gone too soon. There is a flicker of emotion before he moves on to William.

James strides up to him, his face expressionless. "You need to leave immediately," he growls.

"Avery! It's us," Abby says, smiling, like he wouldn't recognize his own sister.

He ignores her, as he stares down William. "Now," is all he says before twisting back around and heading to the building.

I peel my eyes away from the back of his head and glance at William, who looks like he's trying to do statistics in his head— the same confused expression we all share.

My stomach bottoms out as a loud ringing in my ears blurs my vision. No, this can't be happening. We didn't come all this way just for James to act like he doesn't know us and tell us to leave. The James I know and care for would never look at me like I'm nothing but a stranger. But it *is* him, with the same dark brown curls, hazel eyes, and hypnotizing voice.

"James!" I cry out.

His footsteps waver, but he keeps his pace toward the buildings—his group marching as one.

My emotions swirl faster and faster. Flames gather, building and growing as his back gets farther away, and my heart breaks in two.

I take a step toward them. "You have to help us find my mom, James. Please!" My whole body shakes, and I clench my fists. "Please don't leave me!" I scream. "You promised," I say quieter.

His back stiffens, and he halts in the grass. For a beat, everyone is still—my friends next to me, the group of people in front of James, their hands half on their weapons still casting glances our way and confused expressions towards James.

I hold my breath. *Please turn around. It's ME!* I want to yell just like Abby did.

He turns and makes his way back to us, his face sketched in anger. I exhale, relief flooding through my body.

He stops a few feet from us and, without meeting any of our eyes, says, "I do not know you. You can come in. We can see what we can do to help but I am not Avery or James here. Got it?"

His head rises as he looks into each of our eyes, and my friends nod silently. Abby cringes as she does so. When he reaches me, his eyes flash, but the lines of his mouth harden.

I nod. He isn't James, not anymore.

16

A New Name

"Stevens, you didn't tell me you would have friends visiting," the woman introduced as Talia says with a twinkle in her eye as she studies us. "Please, tell me your names."

Talia is a tall woman with straight white hair, cut bluntly at her shoulders. Her face is all sharp edges, and even her silver eyes look like they could cut somebody with one look. She wears a long black coat paired with red heels, making her features look even more deadly.

I look to Juliet, who is closest to her in the circular lobby we stand in, expecting her to start the introductions, but another voice speaks.

"Juliet, Abby, William, and Grace," James says.

I swallow the shock of him calling me something else, because the woman is studying us too intently. There has to be something going on here that explains why James is acting like this. And giving me a new name? He must not want her to know my true name. But why? They are an alliance group, not extremists.

My mother's words come back to me again. *They can't know about you. Don't let them find you.* Was she talking about these people, too? Don't they already know about me, though?

Whatever it is, James knows something we don't. So, I keep my mouth shut and act like a Grace.

She smiles at us—not a warm smile. "We don't usually get visitors, but you are welcome, nonetheless. I'm guessing you come from the base in Oregon? Stevens was a bit naughty up there, making so many friends."

I keep my eyes on the concrete wall behind her, not wanting to give anything away. After we came through the front and I experienced my first pat-down—which they did a poor job of, because my knife is still safely tucked in my boot—James brought us to this little receiving party with Talia, his intense commander. And I thought Kirt was bad.

"Yes, we do. We came for some help. You see, Coms attacked our community, and we lost many of our commanders," William says.

Talia frowns. "I know. That was not meant to happen." She cuts a look in James's direction before continuing. "But I'm sorry to tell you that there isn't much we can do."

"You don't have to do anything. Just some information would suffice."

She nods. "I see. You want some intel on the extremist communities?"

"Yes, exactly." William smiles, putting on his most agreeable front—his specialty.

It doesn't seem to work on her, because her frown only deepens. "Well, you are strangers to me. Do you think telling people you just met such information is very smart?"

William shifts on his feet as his smile wavers.

"Perhaps if you tell me about your relationship with Stevens, your abilities, and your background, then maybe I could get to know you," she says with a slight smile in my direction.

I swallow.

"They—" James starts but is silenced with her finger.

"From them, Stevens." She points to Juliet.

"Oh, um. I'm Juliet." She looks to James, who gives her a small nod. "I'm an Aura. Me and James were friends. Actually, we were matched, but that obviously didn't work out."

"Why is it obvious, Juliet?" Talia asks. She studies her like she's a specimen under a microscope.

"Well…" she starts but stutters and blinks, "he wasn't my type." Then she makes a show of shyly looking at William and biting her lip.

"I see," Talia says, glancing at William. Then her eyes move to Abby.

Abby exhales. She opens her mouth to speak, but her eyes fill with tears. "Abby. Terra. I knew him through Juliet. But my mom, one of the commanders, got taken…" She sniffles, and an actual tear falls from her eyes. "So that's why I'm here. I drug the rest of them along," she says, shrugging and wiping her eyes.

"I'm sorry. That must be so hard," Talia says dully before laying her eyes on William.

William goes along with Juliet's story about wanting to protect us.

Then she turns her frightening gaze onto me. My insides squirm. We're not just specimens under a microscope. We're worms under a magnifying glass on a bright, sunny day, and she wants us to burn.

"And you?"

Lie. The word comes from William, but if I could open an air link with James, I have a feeling that's exactly what he'd be telling me with that intense gaze of his. I allow William inside my head, but he doesn't give me any more information.

I take a steadying breath. "Yeah. I'm Grace, a Lympha. Juliet and Abby are my best friends, so, of course, I had to join them. I also knew James through Juliet. Still a little bummed it didn't work out for them." I give Juliet a sympathetic smile, laying it on thick.

She scrutinizes us for a long moment before waving an irritated hand at James. "Stevens will tell you what we know. You can stay one night, then you need to go. We have more important things to deal with." Then she turns on her red, dagger-pointed heel and strides down the hall without a backward glance. I hold back my sigh of relief. We've passed some sort of test.

Now that the witch of a woman is out of the room, I risk a glance at James. He's smiling at us, and I instantly regret it. All I want to do is throw my arms around him and never let go. I take a step forward, but William grabs my hand. I look up at him as he brings me back to reality.

She can't know who you are, Maya.

Why?

James didn't tell me that much.

So, he did talk with William, probably feeding him, Juliet, and even Abby, all that stuff they said.

What did he tell you? I almost growl.

Nothing.

That's what I get from his silence. I cut the link with my mental scissors, so he doesn't feel my heart tearing apart.

I hesitantly look back at James. His smile is gone, and his eyes are zoned in on mine and William's interlocked fingers. I'm about to let go but realize that maybe it's a good thing if I show William some affection. That is what James wants, isn't it? For me to be *Grace*. Maybe Grace is in love with William. In the worst-case scenario, he shows that he still cares for me by getting jealous.

I tighten our grasp and even lean into him a bit. William shoots me a look, but I'm too busy studying how James reacts.

He stiffens and looks away, mumbling something to the others in the room, which I now realize consists of one familiar face. Laura, from the underground bunker. I smile at her when she meets my gaze. Her lips move up faintly—a small acknowledgment.

But that's all I need to know that my relationship with James wasn't all in my head. What we had was real. Only a few months ago, James was professing his love for me in those caves after my capture, and Laura was trying to explain the outside world, the truth, to me. She was among the few people who were honest with me from the beginning. Whatever is going on with James now, I need to hold on to those memories. Every kiss, every touch, every feeling we shared was not a lie. It couldn't have been.

James leads us to a room similar to the bunker underneath the manor, with bunk beds lining the walls. This room has sunlit windows, at least.

"You can choose any of the bunks that don't have crap on them. Get settled. I can't imagine your journey across the country was easy. Dinner is in an hour, and then we'll talk." He tilts his head toward a camera blinking at us in the corner of the room, and leaves without a glance in my direction.

I fall onto one of the empty bunks, trying not to look disappointed. I need to remember that I'm supposed to be happy right now. We'll be getting information on my mom soon. Well, *Abby's* mom. I look at her as she sits beside me and leans in for a hug.

"At least he's okay," she murmurs before pulling away. Her eyes are downcast. It can't be easy, having to ignore the fact that her brother is right here, having to pretend that she barely knows him.

I nod before looking at William and Juliet.

"Now what?" Juliet asks.

William stretches out on a bed, looking like he could nod off in no time. "We wait."

And you girls pretend you're crazy in love with me.

Juliet's face reddens, signaling that he sent the message to both of us.

William turns his head to wink at me. *It'll throw them off your tracks for good.*

And I wonder why we need to do that, I want to respond. Instead, I roll my eyes and stare at the bars of the bunk above me. I can't admit that I was thinking the exact same thing earlier but for much more selfish reasons.

As we walk to meet with James, my stomach makes a strange noise, trying to digest the almost inedible food I forced down at dinner. I didn't think I would ever miss the cooking of Terras. Com food is so much worse, like I'm eating something that sat in a closet for ten years first. Don't they have a couple Terras here to help? There's James. I try to imagine him in the kitchen and smile before the thought turns sour. Things must be run differently here than the manor, and it's not like I saw a farm on the grounds on our way in.

I try not to look at James when we walk into a room with a large round table and chairs, but my whole body buzzes with the knowledge that he's close. William reaches for my hand, and I let him take it. We sit next to each other, while Abby and Juliet take the seats to our left.

A chair scrapes from across the table and I finally lift my eyes to James's. His stare is hot on my skin, his expression tense, as if he's trying to communicate something he can't say aloud. Now would be an excellent time to be an Aura.

His gaze flicks to William and then back to me, questions in his eyes. I peel my eyes away. Let him question it.

A large binder lands on the table and I jump. James puts his gloved hand on it, and I allow my eyes to travel the length of his muscular arm corded in veins. Have his arms gotten bigger? I swallow the sudden desire to wrap myself in them.

"This has information on all the extremist strongholds. I don't know which one your mother is in, but my best guess is San Francisco." There is an edge to his voice as he keeps his eyes on Abby.

William squeezes my hand as hope flourishes in my chest.

"It's the highest security clearance facility on the West Coast."

And my hope dies.

Abby speaks my mind. "So how do we get in?"

"You don't."

I can't control the influx of emotions that cross my face. James keeps his eyes trained on Abby's, but his controlled mask slips a little as his eyes soften.

"But I could."

"You're coming with us?" Abby says, rising in her seat.

He leans back into his chair and pushes his overgrown dark locks out of his eyes. "I want to. But we can't spare my squad." A war is fighting in his eyes, and it takes all my strength to remain seated and not jump over the table and shake him.

I take a deep breath and lean forward in my seat. "So what exactly are you saying?"

It seems to take great effort for him to look me in the eye, but once he does, I almost forget my anger. His hazel eyes pierce me, and memories flood into my mind. His lips on mine, his fingers in my hair and on my skin, blue flames that are only triggered by him.

"I need air," I announce suddenly.

I stand and leave the room before anybody can stop me.

I turn down the white, tiled hallway, passing people and ignoring their stares until I find an unlocked door and throw myself inside. Flipping a switch, I find myself in a small room with one bed. My head falls against the door, and I try to calm my racing heart. He's not going to help us, and this whole trip was for nothing—us going against Wixx and risking our families, the Coms almost taking William, burning down Ann's childhood home, risking our lives to travel across the entire country, all of it, for nothing.

I can't do this. I can't be here and pretend any longer. I'm going to scream or, more likely, set the place on fire.

The doorknob turns, and I jump deeper into the closet-sized room, preparing a poor excuse about getting lost. The door opens and closes, but nobody is there. I take another step back as Ann appears in front of me.

"Oh!"

She throws her arms around me, and I stroke her dark hair. "I've been waiting forever for one of you to go somewhere."

"I'm sorry, Ann." Honestly, I had forgotten about her. Juliet must have been freaking out. I pat her back, feeling horribly guilty about being caught up in my own selfish desires.

"What's the plan?" she asks, looking up at me eagerly. But her face is lined in exhaustion as she blinks slowly.

"We're staying the night. Have you eaten?"

"Juliet got me something."

"Oh, that's where she went at dinner," I say, remembering her sneaking off and then feeling wretched for not thinking of it.

"Juliet told me to stay in the bunkroom, but—" she yawns, "—I'm really tired, and I feel weird." She wobbles, and I catch her before she crashes to the floor. I gently lay her on the bed. This is not good. She shakes her head weakly. "I can't hold it anymore."

I look around, trying to figure out whose room this could be, but the walls are blank. There are no personal items besides a few books on one low shelf. Whoever's room this is could walk in any moment. I shout out with my mind, wishing I could open my own air link, but I'm met with silence. Crap. *Think, Maya.*

"Are you capable of air links?"

She shakes her head weakly. "Never…tried. I dunno."

"We need to hide you. Is under the bed, okay?"

Her eyes flutter closed.

"Oh boy," I mutter to myself.

I pull her into my arms and gently place her on the floor. Thankfully, there's nothing under the bed. Could I be so lucky that nobody stays in here?

Her eyes remain closed as I push her body far under the bed, cradling her head. I tuck in her loose clothes and stand when she's entirely underneath and hidden. I reposition the blanket on the bed over the side so it covers her.

"Stay here," I murmur, but she doesn't respond.

I wipe my sweaty palms on my jeans and turn towards the door. Inching into the hallway, I look around and try to casually walk as fast as I can back to the meeting room.

Nobody meets my gaze as I settle back into a chair. Maps are strewn across the table, and they're discussing something with James that I probably should know, but I can't pay attention, only getting a few words here and there.

Finally, I kick William under the table after a few minutes of casting obvious looks at him and Juliet and practically bouncing up and down in my seat.

Are you okay? he asks in my mind.

No! Ann is in somebody's bedroom, passed out under their bed. We need to get her out.

Impressively, William's expression doesn't change as he responds, *Okay, let's wrap this up.*

"Thank you for the information. But we're leaving in the morning with or without you," William says to James as he stands. "Let us know what you decide." He walks around the table towards the door with me and the girls on his heels.

I resist the urge to look back at James as the door shuts. They follow me, as I assume William fills them in on what's happening with Ann.

We turn down the hall and slow when a group of four approaches us. A taller man with short, jet-black hair, probably around James's age, breaks off from the group and heads straight for the room Ann is hiding in.

"That's the room," I murmur frantically as I pick up pace. My heart falls into my stomach as the man grabs his doorknob.

Abby jumps ahead. "Hey!"

He pauses from fully opening the door when she almost runs into him.

"Hi! I was just wondering where the bunkroom they have us in is? We've gotten all turned around." She makes a big show of throwing her hands up and looking like a lost puppy.

My breathing stalls as he cocks his head at her.

His hand loosens on the doorknob. "Oh. Sure."

Abby turns to us, placing a hand on her hip. "See, we just needed to ask for help." She giggles and turns back toward him.

He points over his shoulder. "Down this hall, take a left, then a right, and it's the first door."

Before we can stop him, he opens the door and steps into his room.

All four of us move toward him.

Abby waves a hand at us to stop as she places the other around his bicep.

He looks back, confusion on his face.

"You see. My friends were on their way to a meeting, but I left something on my bunk. Would it be too much trouble for you to show me the way? I would hate to get lost all by myself," she says, fluttering her eyelashes.

The confusion turns into a slight smile as he finally steps away from his door and closes it. Abby hooks her arm around the poor guy and looks up at him expectantly. He seems a little taken aback but obliges as they walk down the hall.

Once they're around the corner and everybody else in the hall is gone, Juliet and I squeeze into the room and leave William to keep watch.

We throw ourselves onto the floor. Ann is still asleep under the bed, her dark hair splaying around her head. Juliet grabs her arm and gives it a slight shake. She stirs but doesn't wake. Based on how far away the bunk room is and the lengths Abby will probably go to keep the guy's attention diverted, we have anywhere from two to ten minutes.

"What are we going to do?" Juliet asks me, her blue-gray eyes wide.

"I have no idea."

17

Broken Promises

I take quick stock of our surroundings. Not even a window to work with. We don't have another choice but to get his help.

"I need you to reach out to James," I tell Juliet.

She looks back and forth between me and Ann, her eyebrows turning up in worry. "But what if he tells them?"

"He won't." I won't tell her how I'm not entirely sure he won't, but he's trying to help, isn't he? My mind goes back to our meeting and how unhelpful he was.

She makes a face. "I don't know if I can reach that far."

I sigh. "I can get William. Come on, we're losing time." I start to get up.

"No!"

I turn back.

"No. I've got this," she says, her eyebrows pinching in concentration. She closes her eyes for an achingly long twenty seconds before— "I got him! What should I tell him?"

"The truth."

Her face pinches again. "He's coming." She opens her eyes and looks at the door nervously, then reaches under the bed. "Annabelle, this would be a great time to wake up." Juliet shakes her again.

The doorknob rattles and I jump back. Juliet angles herself in front of the bed.

William and James fall into the room. William has James by the arm, and James is cursing him to let go.

"It's okay!" I say, stepping forward to break them up.

William shoots me a look before letting go and closing the door behind them. Everyone's body heat and tension radiates in the air, warming up the too-small space.

James eyes each of us before shaking his head. He pushes one hand through his hair, but it's so long, it just falls back into his eyes. "Where is she?"

Juliet and I both glance at the bed.

James raises an eyebrow. "Are you kidding me?" He snorts. "Connor would get a kick out of this," he says, kneeling on the ground.

I watch his arms and back flex as he pulls her carefully out from under the bed and lays her on the mattress. He does it so swiftly and gently that I almost miss it, distracted by his body. He *has* gotten bigger. His muscles are more filled out and they strain against his tight shirt.

I look away towards Ann, her head falling to one side as her chest rises evenly.

"Who's Connor?" William asks.

"The guy whose room we're commandeering," James says, gently pushing Ann's hair out of her face, a tender gesture I don't miss.

My heart leaps, and I hold myself back from moving closer to him.

"I'm guessing you had her using her camouflage abilities this whole time."

Juliet nods sheepishly.

"We all have our limits," James mutters. "But I would have done the same thing. It's hard enough keeping *you* under the radar." He briefly looks at me, and I can't read what's there before he turns back to Ann.

"Pull some clothes out of there." James nods towards the chest in the corner. "There's a shift change at six o'clock, but just in case somebody's watching, they shouldn't look twice if she's wearing our uniform. Then I'll take her to my room. She can rest there."

Juliet and I slip the too-big, dark clothes over her body. Juliet's hair falls around her shoulders as she pulls the ribbon from her ponytail. Of course, she uses ribbons instead of hair bands. She ties it around Ann's waist to hold the pants up.

"When I realized what room you were in on the way here, I sent somebody to give Connor a task, so we should be good for a while. But you guys need to join Abby before somebody starts asking questions," James says.

"No. I'm staying. You two go," I say. This might be my only chance to talk to him. I can't waste it.

William gives me a pointed look. Even though he doesn't say anything out loud or in my head, I can read him loud and clear. He's worried.

Juliet pulls her eyes away from her sister and nods at me. "I trust you."

"Absolutely not. It's better if it's just me taking Ann to my room." James's voice is rough.

My heart cracks a little, but I hold firm. "I'll catch up. Tell them I'm in the bathroom or something."

Juliet and William ignore James's protests and leave with one last glance at Ann.

James stares hard at her. We're alone, and he still refuses to look at me. Two more minutes pass before I can't take it anymore.

"James."

He turns his head, his face an uncaring mask. It hurts. It hurts more than ever. I mean to ask him what's been eating away at him, but I only want to hurt him back. Make him feel the same pain that's plagued me for months.

"It's a good thing I'm not bonded to you."

He flinches and his mask dissolves. Different emotions cross his features—shock, hurt, anger. I immediately want to take it back. But I don't because at least he's feeling something, showing me emotions besides indifference.

"So, you're happy to be bonded with a psychopath?" he asks, dark eyes piercing mine.

I shake my head. "He's not psycho."

He laughs. "He hurts people and forced you to bond with him."

I flinch. Yes, Sebastian made mistakes—*huge* mistakes that will affect me forever, and I will never excuse his actions. But Sebastian isn't standing in front of me right now. Sebastian isn't the one who is breaking my heart at this very moment.

James promised he would never leave me, then he did.

James promised he would return, then he didn't.

"*You* hurt people." I can't control the rising emotion that breaks through in those words. My fire is a chaotic living thing as it rages under the surface of my skin. I'm able to push it down, but the hurt is too much. Heat gathers at the back of my eyes.

His face falls. "Maya, you have—"

"What's going on?" comes Ann's voice.

The emotion in his eyes disappears as he turns to Ann. "You're weak from overusing your abilities. We're going to get you somewhere safe."

She looks at me, and I nod, swallowing the swell of emotions breaking free and blinking back the tears threatening to fall. I won't let him see me cry or worry Ann.

We both help her up.

James checks his watch. "We have a couple minutes until shift change." He turns to her with a smile. "So, you're still just as sneaky."

She shrugs her small shoulders. "Comes in handy." Then panic crosses her features as her brown eyes blow wide. She looks down at herself and the too-big clothes. "Wait, did I mess everything up?"

James cocks an eyebrow and I hastily shake my head. "Everything is going to be fine," I tell her. *Hopefully.*

After we shuffle through the hallway full of people going to their new positions on the base, we make it to James's room without anyone glancing our way. The room is exactly the same as the other one with matching blank walls.

"Does nobody decorate in this place?" I ask.

He looks around. "This isn't home."

"And where is home?"

He opens his mouth to answer but looks away. "I haven't had a home in a long time."

I flinch. Those words cut deep. I thought *I* could be his home.

Ann is already curled up on his bed, exhausted from the walk over. She's not paying us attention, facing the wall, but that doesn't mean I can say what I truly want with her listening. Do what I truly want.

"What happened to you?" I ask finally, not being able to keep my emotions at bay.

He rubs his chin as his dark eyes look everywhere but at me. "Have you found him?"

"This is why you've stayed away then? Because I'm bonded to Sebastian?"

He doesn't immediately respond, and anger and grief well up inside of me. First of all, one of *his* reasons for leaving was to try to find Sebastian. Looks like that was just another lie. And second of all, he told me to stay put. How could I have found him?

It all hurts too much to contain anymore. Too many lies and broken promises. My breathing becomes more rapid, and I peer at Ann, who's overcome by sleep, her chest rising rhythmically, before unleashing myself on him.

"I didn't want him, James! I never wanted him. I wanted you!" I grab his shirt in my hands, balling it into my fists, forcing him to look at me—to see how he's breaking me. "I wanted *you.*" My voice cracks.

That does it. His eyes soften, and the next thing I know, I'm enveloped in his arms, in his familiar earthy male scent that opens up a hundred memories and desires. The past few months without him crash into me, and a sob breaks free, the grief overpowering the anger. His body feels like home. He may not think he has a home, but he does. It's with me and his family, not in this building with these people.

He rubs my back and nuzzles into my hair. "I've missed you." His rough voice rumbles against me.

I look up at him with what I'm sure are tear-stained cheeks, cursing my eyes for letting them fall. He palms my cheek, his fingers intertwining with my hair. He looks at me like I've imagined him looking at me for all these months. It's him—my James. He still loves me.

I lean into him as he dips his head down, our lips mere inches apart. My heart thrums as fast as a butterfly's wings with expectation.

A deafening growl erupts in my ears, and I stumble back, hitting the wall.

James's face lines in confusion and hurt as the heat in his eyes dims, the growl just a distant echo. "I'm sorry," he says.

I shake my head. "No." I reach for his hand. He takes it but is more hesitant when wrapping his fingers around mine. Once I feel his skin, I relax. "I've missed you too."

His eyebrows turn down. "I broke my promise."

"I don't care, just come back with us." I say, leaning into him once more.

But again, the growl sounds through me. This time, there are words. *No.*

I gasp, cringing away from the man I love. But he didn't say those words.

"Did you hear that?"

He shakes his head in confusion, but then his face slackens. "You're not mine, Maya."

My heart bottoms out and I'm unable to fight the tears. He can't be about to—

"You know I love you, but it's better this way—the distance," he says, emotion swirling in his hazel depths.

I shake my head, not wanting to hear any more. How can he do this after everything we've gone through? Just give up on us.

"I...I need to go." I trip to the door, not feeling entirely sane. "Keep her safe."

I stumble through the hallway, looking for an exit. There has to be one somewhere in this godforsaken place. There's no way Sebastian could be talking to me. It has to be in my head. I've never heard of bonded mates being able to communicate in such a way. And he's an Igna, with no ability to use an air link like William and Juliet can. I'm just cracking, breaking. I've kept my emotions bottled up for so long that I'm now leaving pieces of me everywhere I go, absurdity filling in the gaps.

Sebastian *can't* be talking to me.

Somehow, I find my way back to the bunkroom…or somebody led me here. William is at my side in an instant.

"Is everything okay?" Juliet says frantically.

I look at her and nod. William slides an arm around me and takes me to a bunk. After trying and failing to get anything out of me, he leaves me alone to be swallowed by my self-pity.

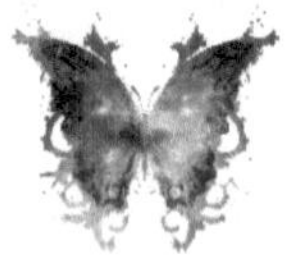

I'm quiet and restless for the rest of the night, but I don't shed another tear. I welcome back the familiar numbness like an old friend. Juliet keeps up constant communication through an air link with James about Ann. By morning, despite their failed attempts at getting my input, they have a plan to leave early and head to San Francisco with or without James's help.

Talia and some of her men, including James, stand in the foyer as we descend the steps. We stop at the open front door, where we received our pat-downs. I should return James's knife, but when I try to move to grab it out of my boot, my body doesn't listen. My fingers only twitch.

"Safe travels, William, Juliet, Abby, and *Maya*," Talia says with a wink at me. She turns on her black and red heel, which looks like it's been dipped in somebody's blood.

James stiffens, keeping his place near the door as she leaves. Well, whatever he didn't want her to know, she figured out. It's not like he'll touch me anyway with what happened last night.

James goes down the line, giving Abby and Juliet a hug, a handshake for William, and then it's my turn.

I tense, expecting another hallucination, but nothing happens as he loosely pulls me in.

"Don't stop fighting," he whispers before pulling away.

Fighting for what? For him? No. He's already stopped fighting for us. He doesn't get to tell me to be strong while he's given up. I want to yell at him for giving up, but all fight is lost from me. He doesn't get to tell me what to do. If there was still something between us, he would have shown me that he loved me by explaining what's going on or coming with us. Heck, he could have even tried to make another broken promise of returning soon. But no. This is a true goodbye.

I swallow the emotion as James hands William an extra pack I didn't see earlier. William nods and slings it across his shoulder without a word.

"Good luck." James's eyes land on mine, something building in his expression. He opens his mouth, but I turn away, keep my head down, and walk for the Jeep.

The tether that usually pulls me to him is no longer there. I didn't realize that it was severed when he left two months ago, and I've been trying to tediously tie it back together this past week. But I can't tie what is not there. There is a pull in another direction, toward San Francisco, to the person who will truly always love me…my family, my mom.

18

San Francisco

The next few days are a blur of towns, roads, fields, cars, and sleepless nights in the Jeep. I know she'll be there. I can feel it. The closer we get, the stronger the feeling that we are going in the right direction. It's the only thing holding me together at the moment.

Nobody talks to me. William doesn't even bother getting in my head. I'm sitting in the same spot with my head against the window like I have been for two days when Abby curses loudly. I blink as the edges of my vision clear. Abby is turned around in her seat staring daggers at me.

"You need to snap out of it. I don't want the return of emotionless Maya."

I glare at her but don't have it in me to fight back and return to looking out the window.

"Stop the car, William," Abby says.

"What?"

"Now!" she roars.

The Jeep comes to a sudden halt on the side of the barren highway, and Abby leaps out.

I gasp as Abby throws my door open, and I almost fall on my backside onto the gravel.

"Abby, what the hell?"

"Oh good, there's something," she says with a scowl-like grin, her hands on her hips. The top half of her hair is pulled into a bun on her head, a few pieces escaping to frame the dirty look on her face.

"Ugh. Leave me alone."

"No. You are done moping."

"You are not allowed to tell me when I'm done moping." I can't believe I just said that.

Grabbing the car, I prepare to swing myself back to my seat, but Abby pushes me off balance. This time, I do fall. My flame leaps as I jump up and push her back.

"Okay, so my brother broke your heart. He's a dirtbag, okay?"

She stuns me for a moment. As fast as the fire came, it dwindles. I shake my head. "No. It's me. I've changed."

"Yeah, you're not the same helpless girl he met. His loss if he can't see how badass you are now."

I shake my head. "No! That's not it. Well, he was acting like a dirtbag, but I didn't…want him. He tried to kiss me, and I freaked out."

Everyone is quiet inside the car, I realize a moment too late. Yeah, that was definitely too much information. I peer over at William, Juliet, and Ann, who are at least pretending not to listen, looking the other way. William starts to whistle loudly.

I suck in my bottom lip and turn back to Abby. She's studying me.

"Maya. That could have been a number of things. A lot has happened since you last saw him." She grabs my hands. "You are amazing. My brother is dumb. He should have fought harder. This is on him, not you. Now I want you to forget about him. I need my badass fire- and water-wielding best friend back, because we're about to go kick some Com butt and get your mom back."

I grimace. I really don't want to let the numbness go. I'm not ready to feel…or move on from James. Just thinking about it makes my insides twist. But she's right. I shouldn't put all the blame on myself. James was definitely acting strange, and something is going on there. I shouldn't let him affect me like this. I've already let him affect me too much, two entire months too much. I can't do that now, not when my mom needs me—needs that person Abby is talking about. I can at least try to be her. What's the saying? Fake it till you make it?

"Okay," I say.

"What was that?"

"*Okay*," I say louder, but it still sounds wimpy, even to my ears.

She pushes the sides of my mouth up until I slap her hand away and smile for real.

"One more time."

"Okay!"

She throws her arm around my shoulders and leads me back to the Jeep. Before we get to the door, still wide open, I trip her, jump over her flailing body, and land in the passenger seat. She gawks at me from the dirty rocks, her hair having come loose from the bun. The pathetic knot dangles in her face like a dingleberry.

I lose it in a fit of giggles. "You deserve that," I hiccup between laughter.

As soon as we're back on the road, I jump into the conversations I've missed. The heartache is still there, but I push it down as best I can. My mom needs me. I can do this for her. I learn that James gave us detailed instructions in the pack on how to get in and out of the city undetected and even a contact who works at the facility who can help us. There are Com uniforms and even weapons in the pack that I'm sure Talia didn't know about. The thoughtfulness he put into this pack pricks the back of my throat, but I refuse to give in to it. I refuse to let my feelings over that man control me any longer.

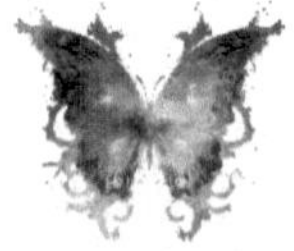

The sun is setting when we pull up to a townhouse about two miles from downtown San Francisco. The usually vibrant colors in the sky during my favorite time of day are dull and lifeless behind the city landscape. Day becomes night, and there is no magic in between. It's as if the Coms here even suck the joy from the sky. We triple-check the address before stepping out.

"Stay here," William says, stepping out of the car.

"I'm the one that can go invisible. Shouldn't I check things out?" Ann whines.

William closes the door on her, and she falls back into her seat with a huff, crossing her arms.

Juliet pats her leg. "You did so good in Texas, we just want to be more careful about you using your abilities after what happened."

Ann rolls her eyes in my periphery. I watch William walk casually along the sidewalk, like he's been here a hundred times. I hold my breath when he reaches the door and knocks.

After ten seconds—I counted—the door cracks open. William says something through the door before it closes in his face.

"What are we going to do now?" Abby whispers.

"We're not going back," I say, more to myself than her. I can't go back to Oregon without Mom, and I'm certainly not going back to Texas to have another encounter with James that will roll me back into depression.

Suddenly, a yellow light falls onto William, and a giant hand pulls him inside. We all gasp collectively.

But then his head pops back out, and he gives us a thumbs up. His face is replaced by a burly man, twice William's size, with a buzz cut. His smile contradicts his body as he walks toward us. Is the ground shaking with his steps, or am I imagining that?

He knocks on the car window. Abby throws a panicked look at me before rolling it down an inch—like a thin layer of glass would stop this dude.

"You're welcome to come in. Make sure to pull the E-break. Cars are known to roll away on this hill." His voice isn't as deep as I expected. It's more soothing.

Once we shuffle out of the car, the man seems impossibly bigger. I have to lift my chin and step back to look at his face.

"I'm Sawyer," he says, offering a hand.

I feel like a child as his hand envelops mine. He smiles a toothy grin and grabs my bag. He does the same with Juliet, Abby, and Ann. He easily holds all our bags in one hand as we follow him to the house.

Each skinny home is a replica of the one next door. Red brick surrounds a narrow black door with a number in yellow, chipped paint. Sawyer elbows number thirty-six open. There's a sliver of grass between the house and the sidewalk. My eyes follow it down, down, down. It's the steepest drop I've ever seen on a road. If you even trip, you'd turn into a ball of arms and legs and roll right to the bottom.

I suppress a shiver and enter the small hallway that leads from the front door into the living room, where William is sitting on the edge of a gray couch, talking to a guy with short dark hair and glasses.

I briefly take in the small living room that leads to an even smaller kitchen, where a bar with two chairs divides it from us. The only light comes from one pendant light in the middle of the popcorn ceiling that looks like it's missing a couple of lightbulbs, casting dark shadows on the brown walls.

William and the guy stand when we enter.

"Welcome! Glad to meet some friends of James. Didn't think he had any," the guy with glasses says, chuckling. When we don't laugh, he clears his throat and directs us to the couch. "I'm Marcus. I work in the labs at USF."

"Do you know anything about Evelynn Mayfield? Strawberry-blonde? Kind of looks like me," I say, not wanting to waste any time when we're this close. The pull is incredibly strong right now, like I can practically feel her in the vicinity.

"I haven't heard that name, but I also don't have the highest clearance level. But I assure you, we'll find her if she's here. Not sure about getting her out. But I can probably get you in to talk to her," he says.

I step toward him, shaking my head. Somebody puts a hand on my arm, probably Abby, but I shake her off. "No. We have to get her out."

He fixes his glasses and licks his bottom lip. "We'll see what we can do. Let me show you to your rooms."

"We can't go now?"

He shakes his head. "It's the end of the workday. I'm scheduled for tomorrow morning. I'll get you in then."

I sigh, but don't push it. If this guy is willing to help us, I have to do it on his terms.

"Thank you, Marcus. I just really want to see her."

His blue eyes soften. "I understand. Nobody could stand in my way if I had the chance to see my mom again." He turns to head up the stairs behind a half wall.

I swallow the emotion from his words as we follow. My mom is still alive. I can feel it.

19

Mice in a Snake's Den

William, Marcus, and I drive up to the front gate dressed in Com military green. It's too risky to take any more of us. Abby is probably still sulking in that tiny bedroom we stayed in. Ann took it pretty well, though. She followed the giant around all morning. Sawyer may look big and scary, but he's a teddy bear in disguise and adores Ann. They were playing a game of flower guessing when we left. Juliet is just happy that Ann wasn't complaining, but she did give us both a too-long, borderline awkward hug and flashed me a worried look at the door.

I sit between Marcus and William in the front seat of Marcus's pickup truck as we slow down at the check-in window. Staring straight ahead, my heart pounds in my ears as my palms sweat. I resist the urge to wipe them off on my itchy pants. William rubs circles on the back of my hand. He's been doing that so much lately that I'll probably have permanent indents.

A couple of words are exchanged before the gate rolls to the side, letting us through.

"That was easy," I breathe out. For some reason, I thought getting into a high-security Com facility would be hard.

"Only because they're used to me bringing military personnel through. Don't forget. You are mice in a snake's den."

I swallow as that fact settles into my stomach and twists my insides.

"Now comes the hard part. Usually, we're not wanting to see the people in their jail system," he says.

I give him a sharp look.

He pushes the glasses up his nose and fidgets with the steering wheel. "It'll be okay. James wrote a very believable story for you guys. Brought tears to my eyes." He gives me a slight smile.

I look at William, and he shrugs. James really thought this whole thing out. I push down the feelings that want to rise with that knowledge.

"You two are brother and sister, who want to visit a woman who is the best friend of your deceased parents," Marcus says as we pull into a parking garage.

"They allow visitors?"

"Sometimes. If the convict is on good behavior."

"My mother is not a convict."

Marcus winces. "I know. I'm sorry. Some of them are."

"And the rest?" I ask.

He gives me a heavy look that silences my questions. Most of them are good people. Their only fault is being born with Elemental abilities like us. Marcus though, is not. He's a Com in the alliance, who is stationed here. Part of me doesn't want to trust him, but James does and that's all that matters.

"And how do we get her out once we find her?"

Marcus doesn't answer my question, but his grip on the steering wheel tightens.

"Marcus?"

"Not a word once we're inside, got it? Follow my every step. Heads down. Don't look at anyone."

William and I nod. I swallow the rock in my throat as we climb out of the truck. I peer from under my cap at our surroundings once sunlight bathes us. In front of us rise four white pillars with gray, pointed tops reaching toward the sky. It reminds me of an old cathedral in Portland I used to pass on my morning ride to school. To our right, a high chain-link fence with barbed wire at the top surrounds an overgrown grassy landscape between the castle-like structure and another building made of all glass. I have to stifle my gasp. It looks just like our old Legion Headquarters.

As we approach the brown front doors, I notice words carved in gold lettering at the top: Lone Mountain. My eyes want to migrate up, following the panels of glass and pillars, but I cast my eyes to my feet as we enter, as Marcus instructed.

Our boots click on the golden tile as we weave around people and through another set of doors. I focus on the scent of paper and freshly pressed clothes to ground me, like we could be walking through any office building—not an extremist Com facility. William's hand brushes mine occasionally, reminding me he's right there.

Soon, we're outside again, and my curiosity flares, but I keep my eyes glued to the concrete. We enter another building, and I wonder if it's the glass one. These floors are smooth marble. We start down a set of stairs when we're stopped.

"Marcus Bullsby. What are you doing out of your lab?"

I slow down my heart rate, willing myself to relax and breathe. *I'm a mindless, simple soldier. I'm a mindless, simple soldier.*

"Hello, sir. I still have another half hour before my shift, and these soldiers are acquaintances of mine. They are here just for the day to visit somebody in the jail. I told them I would show them the way."

The man grunts, and I watch him tap his black boot. "If you're late, it's coming out of your pay." Then his footsteps fade behind us.

Marcus lets out a breath before continuing down the steps. We descend one, two, three, and then four sets of stairs before stopping. The suffocation of being far underground presses in on me, and the musty smell makes me want to gag.

The walls and floors are all concrete and metal. Walking down a dimly lit hall, I realize we're far from the elements, too— no weather to control, no access to the earth or water, and no flames in sight. Luckily, I can create my own fire.

I count the glow of yellow lights on the concrete floors to resist the urge to look around, or worse—run in the opposite direction.

I get to light twenty-three when Marcus's footsteps slow, and a gate creaks in front of us. A pull, intensifying by the minute, emanates from in front of us. It feels as if a physical rope is wrapped around my heart, pulling me toward my mom. I know she's here.

"May I help you?" comes a feminine voice. Here is the moment we see if James's story gets us in.

Marcus recounts the same story he told us but with a few added details.

"What is her name and age?"

"Evelynn Mayfield, forty-five," I say, raising my head, unable to ignore the pull any longer. I need to get in there.

Marcus eyes me behind the rim of his glasses before smiling back at the woman. A woman with short black hair and a pierced nose looks at me momentarily before her eyes sweep back to her computer.

"No. No Evelynn Mayfield here."

"She has to be," I bite out.

William nudges me, and I bite my tongue, willing myself to stop talking.

"Could she be under a different name?" she asks.

Marcus looks at me and nods towards her.

Oh, *now* I can talk. "It's possible."

She moves her long, manicured fingers over the keys. "When would she have arrived?"

"April."

"We have two women that came in that month, but only one matches her age. Her name is Sandra Yulloc."

I search my mind for anyone or any instance where Mom might have used that name, but there is nothing. No way that's her. My heart falls. I can't believe we got this far, and she's not even here.

She looks at me expectantly, and I don't know what to say.

"We'll see her," William responds. He smiles faintly at me. He's right. We have to try, at least. And there is that undeniable pull.

He grabs my hand as the woman pushes a button, and the concrete door slides open. "What are your names?"

"Grace and Gabriel Miller," says Marcus.

I'm glad he knows our fake names because I had already forgotten.

"A guard will meet you inside. You may talk to her through the window of the door, and you only have five minutes."

We both nod as Marcus steps back.

"You're not coming with us?"

"I'll wait right here," he says with an encouraging smile.

I hold tightly to William's hand and enter willingly into the jail, deeper in the belly of the snake, where, if they knew our *true* selves, we would never see daylight again.

The first thing that hits me is the strong smell of urine and chemicals. I have to bite back the bile that rises. Then, a weird sense of déjà vu has my steps faltering. William squeezes my hand, as if feeling my reluctance. Moans and shouts come from our left and right as we meet up with a heavily armed guard, one massive gun in his hands and two on his belt. Those are the visible ones, at least.

We nod to him, and he falls in step with us without saying a word. We make our way deeper into the cellar, unworldly moans and cries rising from its depths. I intertwine my fingers with William's and squeeze tightly. I'm honestly hoping she's not here now. Heat gathers in my throat just thinking about her being stuck in this hole for the past three months. These poor people, *our* people.

My flame pulses. Nope, you have to stay nice and small right now.

The guard stops and lifts a hand toward a door. I swallow and step to the window. I stand on my tippy toes to look between the dirty iron bars, catching the faintest of glimpses inside the cell.

At first, I see nothing, but as my eyes adjust, I notice a lump on the bed in the corner, which kind of looks human.

"Hello?"

The lump moves, shifting until it's sitting up. I hold my breath as their heavily matted hair falls down their back—dark hair. Even in the terrible lighting, I know it's not her.

The person looks my way. I can't see her eyes clearly, but she rises from the bed and jerks toward the door. I step away, shaking my head.

William wraps his arms around me and peeks in. He wrenches away as a shrill scream rings through the walls.

"My boy! Please come closer. It's been so long since I've seen such a handsome face. *Ha ha ha!* Come! Come!"

The guard pulls us away from the door, looking bored, and directs us back.

"I'm sorry," William mumbles.

I barely hear him over the woman, who's now shrieking obscene remarks. It causes a stir in the jail, and people begin speaking as we pass, asking us to visit them or peek in, saying they have surprises for us.

My eyes burn, and I swallow the tears. What are we going to do now? This was our only chance. If she's not here, then where?

I cling to William as we rush for the door at the end of the grubby hall, but a familiar voice stops us in our tracks.

"William? William!"

I practically hear William's heart take off in his chest as we turn toward the voice of liquid silk. My own heart stops beating altogether.

Behind the bars of the concrete door is a dark, handsome face with bright-blue ocean eyes. His eyes slide to mine, and something flickers in them.

"Do I know you?" comes the unmistakable voice of my nightmares.

20

The Prisoner

Sebastian." William's voice comes out so soft I almost miss it. His state of shock equals mine as we stare at the man in front of us.

"It is you." Sebastian's voice breaks, and something inside me tightens, pulling me to him as I step forward.

"Sebastian," William says, rougher—colder—as he grabs my arm, keeping me from stepping closer. His voice is too cold for a man seeing his best friend for the first time in months.

We haven't spoken much of Sebastian over the last few months. He knows that he forced the bond on me and that I saw him get shot in the chest. He knows that I believed he was alive somewhere still.

My body drifts away, watching the scene unfold from afar, not knowing what to feel or think.

Sebastian's eyebrows rise in disbelief. "You're not here for me." He says it as a statement, but I can tell he's confused by the words.

A strange noise comes from William's throat before he spits, "No. You bloody deserve this."

The hostility surprises me, pulling me back to my body like a rubber band snapping into place. I take a step back, gasping for air. He's never once told me he was angry with Sebastian.

Sebastian blinks back in shock. I wait for the fire to fill his eyes, but he just looks sad and beaten down, like this place has sucked all the life from him.

I'm unable to pull air into my lungs as they squeeze tighter. I need to get out of here. I peel my eyes away from Sebastian to tug William to the exit, but he's staring at him with all the vile and disgust one could muster. I've never seen him wear such a face. It makes me stiffen, even though my lungs scream at me to breathe.

"I'm glad you found somebody," Sebastian says, barely a whisper.

My eyes return to his as he stares at mine and William's entwined hands, before trailing up to my face.

"Be good to him," Sebastian says to me. "He deserves to be happy." With a faint smile, he disappears from the window.

I don't have time to be confused as the edges of my vision blur. William steps toward Sebastian's, but I pull again—this time, he notices. I suck in short gasps of air. No matter what I do, I can't get the air to my lungs.

"I need to get out of here. Can't. Breathe."

His face is a mask as he nods, leading me to the exit without a backward glance. We bust through the door, and Marcus jumps up from his slouched position on the wall. His face falls as he sees my state.

"She's having a panic attack. We need to get back now."

Marcus nods quickly, and we rush down the hallway and up the stairs. I only take a few steps before vertigo hits me, and I fall into the wall. *I can't breathe. I can't breathe.*

"I can't breathe!" The air goes down my throat, but it's not giving me any oxygen.

William places his hands on either side of my face, forcing me to look at him. "Breathe with me."

I focus on the lines of his cheekbones, his dark eyelashes that contrast with his blond eyebrows, and the shape of his lips as he breathes. I suck in a slow breath with him and blow it out. We do it again and again. I follow his movements exactly, letting his calm flow into me like I'm learning how to breathe for the first time.

"Can you walk?"

I try to nod, but he's still holding my face. He lets me go and takes my hand.

As soon as we're outside, I collapse onto the nearest bench, breathing in the cool, fresh morning air. I don't know how anyone lives down there.

William paces in front of me, pushing the hair out of his eyes repeatedly and balling and unballing his fists. Marcus patiently waits to the side with his arms crossed, watching us. We're in a courtyard with trees and an open sky above our heads, surrounded by the buildings we must have walked through. The beautiful spires of the first building we entered towers above them all. We're the only ones out here for now.

"I have to go now. You can take my car back to the townhouse. I'll get a ride home," Marcus says.

William stops and looks at him. "We can't just leave with him down there. Alive. I can't believe he's alive." He shakes his head and starts pacing again.

Sebastian is alive.

I look down at the palm of my hand, the white, slightly puckered scar still visible. I knew he was still alive. But to actually *see* him.

I close my eyes and lean back, counting my breaths.

"I take it Evelynn wasn't down there?" Marcus asks.

"No shit."

"William," I hiss, shooting him a look. He never curses at people, especially those who just risked their lives to help us.

He grimaces. "Sorry, mate. I'm just rattled."

"Whoever you saw down there is never getting out. You can return to the—"

William silences him with a glare. I stand slowly and put a hand on William, so he stops pacing. He's making my anxiety skyrocket.

"This is a good thing," I say.

William's eyes look like they are about to tumble out of his head.

"We know where he is now. Not knowing was the worst part."

"Are you kidding me? I thought being bonded to a lunatic who forced himself on you and tries to off people if he gets a little miffed was the worst part," he snaps.

I've never seen him so— *What did he say? Rattled?*

"Shh!" Marcus says, looking around and nervously fixing his glasses. "Come on."

He pulls us through the courtyard and into another building. We keep our heads down, and William enters my mind.

I'm sorry for snapping. What are you thinking?

I don't know what to think. I almost don't let him in, but after one look at him and his puppy dog eyes, I do.

I forgive you. Was it just me, or did he seem to not know who I am?

That was definitely an act.

His thoughts are swirling with emotion. Usually, he's good at only sending me words, but wisps of his true thoughts attack me. Mostly anger and hurt, but surprisingly, also a little hesitation, like part of him doesn't believe it was an act.

But what about the last part he said?

He replays Sebastian's words—when he implied that William and I were together, instead of being bonded to *him*—in our minds. I'm grateful he doesn't add the visual. But I still cringe.

I don't know, he admits. *That was weird. But he's probably just trying to get in our heads.*

Despite what he said, though, Sebastian barely looked at me or acknowledged me—just William.

I hardly notice that we enter another building as we keep to Marcus's heels, and our footsteps change, echoing off the walls, as we walk across a tiled floor in a seemingly empty room.

I still think this is a good thing.

He scoffs in my mind, but I continue.

Now that we know where he is, maybe we can get him to reverse the bond.

That would require getting him out of here. There's silence for a beat before he's shouting in my mind. *No. No way! That's mad. We are not breaking him out of here after what he did.*

Do you really believe he belongs here? I didn't know you were so angry at him.

Angry is an understatement. I hate what he did to you, Maya. I hate him.

I wince, feeling the heaviness and truth of his words in my mind as we round a corner.

He's done some bloody terrible things. Things you don't know about. But I'm not an Igna. I don't have to struggle with intense emotions like that, and he was like a brother to me. He had a good heart. I believed he could get control of his anger issues, and he did. But I should have seen the signs during our courtship. And after he attacked me, I should have done more to protect you afterward. I didn't think he would ever force the bond onto you. Good men do not do that. I'm so sorry I didn't stop him.

He's silent as I absorb his words. How long has he been holding all of this anger in? If I had known that this guilt of not saving me from Sebastian had been eating away at him, I would have nipped that in the bud real quick. None of that is on him. I was so naive and clueless back then, in the middle of falling head over heels for James and distracted by how my body reacted to Sebastian's heat. I missed all the signs with Sebastian too. But what happened isn't on me, William, or even my mom. It's on Sebastian. It was his choice to take my agency away.

We turn another corner, and a faint antiseptic smell permeates the air.

Why didn't you tell me any of this before? I ask.

William looks at me, and suddenly, he doesn't need to answer. I was in a dark place back then. The last thing I needed was to hear his thoughts on the matter. And despite it all, I am still bonded to Sebastian. Now, there's a chance we can break the bond and fix this whole mess.

Okay, I understand. But still, you're not the one bonded to a lunatic who forced himself on you and tries to off people if he gets a little 'miffed,' I say with a terrible attempt at a British accent while staring him down.

He looks away from me. Oh, *now* he has nothing to say. But then I realize why.

We're standing in front of glass doors that lead to a laboratory, very similar to the one my mom worked at when I was a kid. It hits me like a punch to the gut when I remember why we came here in the first place.

My mom isn't here.

The crushing weight of grief threatens to crash onto me. My steps falter, and William eyes me, but I keep my face down, trying to push away the emotion and stay in the moment.

"In here," Marcus whispers.

We turn through a doorway on our right and enter a bathroom. Marcus hurries down the rows, looking under each stall, then comes back and bolts the door.

"We can talk freely here." He looks at his watch and sighs.

"The loo? You know, I kind of need to go," William comments, but the joke falls flat as his voice is missing its regular cheery cadence.

I shake my head at him. "You can leave if you need to," I tell Marcus, who is fidgeting with his lab coat.

He shakes his head. "It's fine. This is more important."

William takes my hand, his face twisting in sad acceptance. "Okay, let's bust your lunatic fiancé out of here."

"Mate," I correct him and immediately regret it. A bad taste fills my mouth at the word.

"*What?*" Marcus yells, startling the both of us.

I look at him, and the shock on his face is almost comical, with his glasses making his widening eyes even bigger.

"I'm sorry. Did you just say mate? As in a bonded mate? Your bonded mate is down there?"

I bite my lip and nod. "And we need your help to get him out."

21

Breakout

I wake screaming his name.

William has me in his arms before my eyes fully open. "Shhh. It's okay. He's not here. He can't hurt you."

I barely hear his words as the dream fades into the recesses of the part of the mind that harbors all the nightmares plaguing me. Before it does, I have a strong impression that I'm not screaming Sebastian's name because I'm afraid of him but because I'm afraid *for* him.

"I can't remember it," I pant.

William pushes my sweaty hair out of my face. "I know. Just breathe."

I nod and lean my head against his shoulder. "Thank you."

"I'll always be here for you, Maya."

My heart warms because I know he will. William is my best friend. I don't know what I'd do without him.

"Did I wake anyone?" I try to look around him, but it's too dark to make out faces.

His chin rubs against the top of my head as he shakes it. "They're asleep like the dead."

"Sorry I woke you. You should get back to sleep. We have a big day today," I say.

He pulls back. "You don't need to come. I can do this on my own, you know."

"No way. It was my plan. I'm coming."

"Stubborn," he murmurs.

I lie back down and watch him do the same on the cot beside mine. We face each other in the dark, only the outline of his face visible. "You are too," I whisper.

His teeth flash. "The proof's in the pudding."

I laugh and he smiles. Only William could pull a laugh out of me after another awful nightmare.

Eventually, his breathing evens out, and I'm left staring at the ceiling.

Shortly after returning to the townhouse a week ago, I realized that Sebastian was holding the other end of the tether that I thought was pulling me toward my mom. Even though I haven't necessarily heard about something like that, I'm not surprised. It's more prominent now that I know what it is, and I'm growing more restless by the day. I'm nervous about him being physically close to me and how I may respond. Our blood is intertwined. A bonded pair is always supposed to be together. We amplify each other's abilities. Feeling a pull toward my mate makes more sense than feeling pulled toward my mom. She's still out there somewhere. I'm not giving up. But I don't want to spend the rest of my life bonded to Sebastian and doomed to be alone. Breaking him out and fissuring the bond is my only chance to be truly free to make my own choices.

It took a whole day to convince everyone that we could bust Sebastian out. Once Marcus told us that he could swipe some injections for us to keep his powers at bay, everyone was begrudgingly on board. I won't admit it, but our plan will probably get all three of us locked up or killed. I don't want anyone else coming, no matter how much Abby begged that she should be inside with me. She has a part that I have to keep reminding her is equally important. Her distance this week tells me she doesn't believe me, though.

Today will be Marcus's first day working with the prisoners, and we hope Sebastian will be among them. It took time for Marcus to transfer to the experimental lab and then gain access to the prisoners.

By the time the sun rises, I'm already up and ready in my military uniform, filled with nervous jitters. The door creaks as I open it, and William's head pops up, his hair sticking out in every direction. The others are still fast asleep around him. Ann is curled up against Juliet's back, and I can barely see Abby, who's entirely under her blanket.

William blinks sleepily before rubbing his eyes and narrowing them. "You didn't go back to sleep, did you?"

I grimace and leave the room before he can say anything stupid like, *you have to stay because you didn't get enough bloody sleep.*

After breakfast, we make our way back to USF. As the castle-size building looms ahead of us, my nerves weirdly lessen. The tether strengthens, practically vibrating, knowing I'll be reunited with him soon. I try to push it away, like I've done all week, trying not to let it affect me and ignoring the fact that it's affecting me much more than I'd like.

"I won't let him hurt you," William murmurs as we walk down the hall to our imaginary post, where we will stay until Marcus gives us word. William will be in his head the whole time, and we'll be ready if anything goes awry.

"I'm not scared of him," I say, trying to believe it, as flashes of him losing his temper fill my mind.

I wish I could tell him that that's not what I'm worried about, but he won't look at me the same if I do. Even though I know, *I know*, that I should be nervous about seeing him again. My body wants so badly to reunite with Sebastian. That thought terrifies me even more.

"The moment you two are separated from the bond, he'll get what he deserves."

I haven't thought much about what will happen once we're separated. I've had a hard time hoping that would ever happen. Now, it's a real possibility. Will James take me back?

I kick myself for thinking it. He broke up with me—or whatever *that* was. The point is that he has no desire to stick it out or even attempt to find Sebastian to break the bond to be with me. He gave up.

That familiar ache rises, and I return to thoughts of Sebastian. What will we do with him? Even with what he did, I don't want him dead or even in a prison like this. Unlike William, I don't think he deserves to live the rest of his life like that. Far away from me? Definitely. Inside a Com prison, where he's probably being tortured? No. On a deserted island with an anger management program where he can't harm anyone? Maybe.

I shake away the thoughts—one thing at a time.

"Do you really think this will work?" I ask.

He peers at me. "I'm certain it will."

I raise my eyebrows in question. He winks and bows his head, closing his eyes. It's go time. And I'm sure he's planning something I don't know about.

I try to look like a guard, swiveling my head up and down the hallway. We came to an almost deserted part of the building, close to the labs, to wait. Sounds bounce off the white cement walls and linoleum easily, so we'll be alerted if anyone decides to come this way. I feel silly, like I'm playing dress up, especially with this fake gun strapped to me.

Ten minutes pass before the impatience creeps in. William's eyes have remained closed the entire time. I should let him concentrate, but come on, no updates?

"What's happening?" I whisper.

He shakes his head, his blonde hair swaying back and forth. "Nothing yet. Marcus is still waiting for the prisoners to come up. He's just getting his station ready."

"How do you know all that?"

"He's sharing everything. Letting me have a front-row seat. It's brilliant."

I slump back. I'm glad he's entertained. I go back to fiddling with my fake gun. Well, it's not fake. But it has no bullets. I didn't want them. Even holding the thing brings me back to when I had to point one at Sebastian's chest after he nearly killed James. A shiver curls up my spine. I feel more comfort from the knife in my boot. I still haven't used the thing. Maybe I'll finally get the chance.

Another five minutes pass before he straightens. I grab his arm.

"They're filing in."

I wait with bated breath. Is Sebastian going to be among them? Please let him be there. Please *don't* let him be there. My brain and my heart fight back and forth. I want this to work, but part of me hopes it doesn't. I breathe in and out and harness my Sage. I need to calm down. How am I supposed to get through this if I'm already freaking out?

I'm tapping the wall behind my back, trying to ground myself, when William curses. I freeze.

"Ouch," William says, peering at me.

I release my grasp on his arm and find moon-shaped indents on his uniform. "Sorry."

He holds my gaze. "He's there, Maya."

The tether pulls roughly, slamming into me with such force, it almost takes my breath away. I take a step, but William reaches out and grabs my arm.

"You can go if you need to. I can handle this by myself."

He thinks I'm trying to run away. What would he think of me if he knew I have an overwhelming desire to go to Sebastian?

I step back and shake my head, resisting the pull.

He studies me for another moment before closing his eyes again. He frowns. It kills me not to know, but I keep my hands at my sides, breathing the stale air in and out. If it's important, he'll say.

William shakes his head. "What they do to them is despicable, Maya."

"What are they doing to him?" Panic rises in my gut, and I want to run to him right now. I grab the wall, holding myself back from doing something stupid. I need to wait.

"They're injecting him and the others."

Well, that's not that bad. Didn't Marcus say that's how they keep them from using their powers?

"And—" he winces, "—they're cutting into him. His body is covered in bruises and unhealed cuts."

"He can't heal himself," I gasp. Emotion builds in my chest.

"Oi. Now they're—"

"Stop!"

William blinks at me as my eyes burn with unshed tears.

"I can't take it. Please stop."

He furrows his brows. "Sorry."

The next ten minutes pass with me watching William cringe and frown occasionally.

"How can Marcus do these things?"

"We asked him to, Maya."

The thought makes bile rise in my throat. "Aren't we close?"

"There! Marcus slipped. He's rushing Sebastian to a different room."

"What do you mean he slipped?"

He grimaces. "You don't want to know."

Footsteps sound on the tile, and we both jerk our heads down the hall.

"Time to go."

We slip around the corner and head straight for the double doors that lead to the supply platforms where Juliet and Abby are waiting for us with our camouflaged Jeep. Juliet took her job very seriously. She sat with the Jeep all week in the townhouse's garage, working on changing its color and even the body of it.

As William opens a double door, we crash into somebody. The woman stifles a gasp before regaining her composure and smoothing her uniform. "What are you two doing here?"

"We were sent to gather some supplies, madam."

Her eyes bounce between us. "Soldiers are never sent down here. Whose orders?"

At William's hesitation, she grabs a pager from her belt and lifts it to her pink lips. William swipes it from her hand.

"Excuse me?" Her eyes widen in anger.

"I'm really sorry about this." William twists his hand, and she goes flying across the room, landing in an unconscious, crumpled heap. I help William take her into a supply closet and close the door.

"We need to hurry. They're on their way," he says as the door closes.

We throw the door to an outside loading dock open and panic surges when I don't see our Jeep, but then I remember that Juliet is making it look like all the other military vehicles.

A commotion sounds from the opposite door to the room. "Oh no."

A gurney is shoved through the doors, Marcus pushing it from behind, his eyes wild. The body on the gurney is too still. My heart plummets.

"Is he dead?" No. I still feel the bond, and the tether is stronger than ever.

There is no time to answer that question, because lab techs barrel through the doors behind Marcus. I throw my hands out, and fire erupts past him, creating a wall between us and the white coats. Marcus's eyes impossibly double in size, but he keeps his pace until he stops before the door. William dashes in front of me.

"I'll hold them off. Help Marcus!" William yells.

I launch myself at Marcus, only to come to a halt when I see Sebastian. His eyes are half-lidded, and he's staring back. His face is dirty, an untamed beard taking over most of it, and his dark ringlets are overgrown and matted to his head.

Marcus grabs and hauls him up, placing his arm over his shoulder. Sebastian's face turns away as Marcus leads him down the ramp. Abby jumps out of the car and runs to Sebastian's other side to help put him in the back seat.

I'm frozen in the doorway, just staring at the scene unfolding.

I faintly hear shouting behind me, but I can't peel my eyes away from the back of Sebastian's head until he's inside the Jeep. It's him, my bonded mate. Alive.

"Maya!" William shouts.

I jerk, turning around in a daze. Soldiers surround William, raising their weapons and pointing them directly at his head and heart. He slowly raises his hands as they circle him. He's mouthing at me to run.

"No!" I cry, jolting forward. They can't have him.

Lighter fluid ignites in my veins as heat laces my body.

Some of the soldiers break off and start for me. My flames erupt. I throw all I have at them, but I'm not fast enough. They shoot. Pain envelops my shoulder and then my side as I fall. A bright, dazzling bolt of lightning strikes from the sky as the fire reignites in my veins, growing to an impossibly high level, and I detonate.

Everything is red as I smack into the ground, and the pain spreads across my chest and into my head. I open my eyes as the red fades, angry gray clouds open, and mammoth-sized water droplets splash my face. The last tendrils of my fire snake back into my limbs, my vision blurs, and darkness threatens to overtake me.

A white-haired angel rises in front of me, and I fly upward. Is this death? Has it finally come to claim me? The black abyss opens its wide jaws and swallows me whole.

22

Trauma Reincarnate

When I open my eyes, the faded polka-dot wallpaper of the room we've been staying in stares back. Soreness in my right shoulder and side makes me wince when I sit up. I push the blankets off me and lift my shirt nervously. A faint scar is settled right below my rib cage. Huh. I lower the neckline on my shirt—which I realize is *not* my shirt—to view the other sore spot and find a matching scar right next to my collarbone.

My cheeks heat as I pull down the shirt, noticing I'm in one of William's white ones. I look around the room at the blankets and pillows strewn about and hear faint voices outside the door. I stand and stretch my muscles. Ouch. My body aches in strange places. What on earth happened and where is everyone?

I open the door slowly and peer out. The voices emanate from down the stairs. I glance down, feeling the air on my bare legs. Right. I should probably put on pants.

Once I've covered up, I leave the room. As I step down the stairs, I try to think of the last thing that happened, but all I remember are flashes. I know we were at Marcus's labs. I don't remember what we were doing. There are flashes of white coats, lightning hitting the building, and an angel? I shake my head. That can't be right.

The smell of eggs and bacon drifts up the stairs, and my stomach rumbles as moisture gathers on my tongue. Marcus has been feeding us so well. It's going to be hard to leave.

When I get to the bottom of the stairs, Sawyer's big frame blocks most of the kitchen as he hands plates to Ann, who's loading the dishwasher. She giggles as he flicks soap bubbles at her. Marcus sits across from Abby at the table, chatting with somebody diagonal from her. Juliet is at the end of the table, also looking at the person I can only assume is William, blocked by Marcus. Abby nods and bites a piece of bacon.

"Was anybody going to wake me up? I'm starving," I say, bypassing the table and walking straight to the food on the stove behind Sawyer. Scrambled eggs with melted cheese oozing gloriously on top wait for me in a pan.

Somebody grabs my wrist, and I twist to see William gawking at me from a stool on the other side of the counter.

"You're awake." He jumps up, rounds the corner to the kitchen, and pulls me into a hug.

"No thanks to any of you," I joke, but his lips don't so much as twitch to smile.

"Do you not remember?"

"Oh. Um. Bits and pieces." I try to shake him off to grab a plate, but he doesn't let me go.

"You were shot. You've been out for two days."

I cock my head at him. What? I got shot? Well, that explains the scars, at least. "Dang. No wonder I'm so hungry. Tell me what happened while I eat," I say, trying to give him a hint of how hungry I am. My stomach growls again.

William blocks me from getting to the eggs.

"Hey!"

William shakes his head. His eyes are careful. "We just need to talk to you first."

"We?" I look around then, realizing everyone has quieted down.

Sawyer stares down at me from beside William, his large, round face sketched in worry. Abby rises from the table. Then I remember that William was at that table. *No.* He was at the bar. If he was there, then who is sitting over there? I step around William, the obvious answer sitting right at the edge of my mind, just out of reach.

A chair screeches against the linoleum, breaking the silence.

Sebastian stands behind Marcus. His bright-blue eyes are a door to my memories and everything slams into me at once. Coms shot me while trying to break Sebastian out. *We got Sebastian out.*

I gasp, and before anyone can stop him, he moves past the table, reaching a smooth, dark hand toward me.

My body gravitates toward him, wanting him to touch me, to feel his warmth on my skin again. I almost close the distance, but William yanks me away and shoves Sebastian's chest so hard that he falls onto the table full of dishes. The legs of the table buckle, and everyone leaps away to avoid getting squished. Glass shards fly but freeze in midair, before they can do any damage, then scatter on the ground.

Fear clutches my chest as Sebastian's eyes redden. Sawyer is on him in an instant, but he doesn't fight back. He lets the hulking man lift him and push his arms behind his back, which have a few bleeding gashes on them. But Sebastian doesn't take his eyes off of me, doesn't even flinch in pain. The flames are gone, and only a calm, blue ocean surrounds his pupils.

William is in his face in an instant, forcing Sebastian to tear his eyes away from mine. "You don't touch her, you don't come near her, you don't bloody look at her," William yells, inches away from him.

To my surprise, Sebastian hangs his head and nods. Sawyer leads him from the room. William's entire body stills as he works to control his breathing.

When Sebastian is gone, I exhale and look around. My senses return to me. Abby and Juliet stand frozen in the corner. Marcus is where Sawyer was next to the sink, with Ann halfway behind his back.

William turns and steps toward me carefully like I'm a frightened animal. "Are you okay?"

"What in the world did I miss?"

William shoves a hand through his hair and exhales as Abby glides my way.

"Sebastian lost his memory of everything," she says nonchalantly.

My mouth unhinges as William elbows Abby.

"What? She should know."

"Is that true?" I ask.

"It seems to be," he says irritably, looking in the direction Sebastian went.

"You don't believe him," I say.

"I don't know. It seems oddly convenient that he doesn't remember blowing up the manor, trying to kill me, and forcing himself on you."

Marcus steps forward. "It's a side effect of the treatment he's been undergoing."

"Treatment." William scoffs. "You mean those people treating Elementals as lab rats?"

"It's why I don't work in that department," he says, eyeing William like he's the loose cannon instead of Sebastian. I don't blame him, though. He just threw Sebastian—*Sebastian!*—across the room like he was football.

"What does he last remember?" I ask.

"He says he doesn't remember you at all…but what he just did there. Bollocks. He knows who you are."

I don't want to tell them about the tether. If I feel it, Sebastian must feel it too—this overwhelming desire to be near each other.

I shake my head, trying to understand this turn of events. "What does this mean?"

Abby and William's eyes are full of pity.

"What do we do?"

Abby answers. "We were waiting for you to wake up to discuss it. We didn't want to make any decisions without you. But I don't see why we shouldn't go ahead with the original plan. If anything, this makes things easier."

"Easier? How am I supposed to hate him if he doesn't even remember me?" My voice takes on a whiny pitch. I don't know why I'm reacting like this. I should be jumping for joy that he doesn't remember. What's holding him back from unbonding himself to me? I'm a stranger to him now. But it's all so…unfair that he gets to just forget, while I hold all the traumatic memories. The man doesn't *remember* me!

My fire builds inside me, pushing on my insides. I want to scream.

Abby grabs my shaking hands. "It's still Sebastian. Him not remembering doesn't erase what he did. This does not give him a pass, Maya."

"I need some air," I gasp and throw myself toward the back door.

Nobody follows me when I go outside to pace the small sitting area in the backyard. The fresh air on my face helps calm my racing emotions. I'm still too riled up to go back in, though. Instead, I use my five senses to harness my Sage and ground myself. You wouldn't think the smell of industrial emissions and wet asphalt would do the trick, but it does. I sigh, missing the trees.

"I want to talk to him," I say when I finally return.

William and Abby share a look before William nods and leads me into a room behind the stairs.

Sawyer is leaning against a wall of a tiny bedroom that I'm pretty sure is supposed to be a storage room. Sebastian lies on the too-small bed in the corner with one arm behind his head, staring at the ceiling.

When I walk in, he sits up, and that tether pulls tight again. This time, I'm ready for its onslaught. I breathe through the intense desire to run to him and remember the last thing I said when I talked to him—that I hated him. I felt terrible, knowing they were my final words back when I thought he died, but now? He deserves what I said to him. I should be mad.

I use all my willpower to block the desire to jump into his arms and hold onto my feeling of anger towards the man that forced me to bond with him, tried to kill his best friend and James—twice—went off like a freaking bomb, and burned down the manor because of his anger. All in the name of "love." I glare at him, wanting to slap that starstruck expression off his face.

"I want to talk to him alone."

"No," comes William's voice behind me.

I turn. "I don't need protecting. And anyways, he can't use his powers, right?"

A muscle in his jaw pulses. "He's twice your size. He doesn't need powers to—"

My expression makes him shut his mouth, and he nods toward Sawyer. "We'll be right outside the door." He reaches for my hand and squeezes it, relaxing me the tiniest bit. He means well. My safety has always been his number one concern. And it's not like I ever minded before.

He shoots Sebastian a lethal glare. "Don't forget what I said earlier. Touch her and you'll, indeed, regret it," William hisses.

Sebastian looks at him momentarily, as if he still doesn't believe he's the same William he once knew. Finally, he nods.

William leaves the door open a crack, and I roll my eyes. He'll probably have his ear to it the whole time. It's at least better than having him breathing down my back while I try to talk to my…mate.

The room is small, with only the bed in one corner, which they probably drug in here just for Sebastian. There's a stool where Sawyer was leaning. I grab it and pull it towards me, not wanting to be closer than necessary. There's no need to make that tether stronger.

It's silent between us as Sebastian looks at his hands. He's wearing a short-sleeved navy shirt and sweatpants. His condition is a step up from when I last saw him. A blue-gray bruise is healing on the side of his face. His hair is longer now that it's clean, almost touching his grown-out beard that makes him look a bit like a homeless person. Scars, old and new, run down his biceps, and little bandages from the earlier incident are on his forearms. His shoulders sag. I can't help but compare this image to the one of when I first met Sebastian. I thought he was a model with his confident stride, sharp cheekbones, breathtaking smile, and eyes full of light. He's so far from that dauntless gentleman that courted me months ago.

I take a deep breath. "Do you know who I am?"

"Maya. The woman I'm not to talk to, touch, or look at. Even though every fiber of my being wants to." He glances up at me. Sorrow fills his eyes. "Sorry. The pull is hard to resist."

My eyes widen, and there is a slight flutter in my stomach. I curse myself for reacting to his words.

A familiar light fills his eyes. "You feel it too, then."

"Yes. We are a bonded pair." I may not know exactly why it's so strong, but I certainly have my theories…involving the fact that we haven't been intimate yet, sealing the bond like a normal couple. But I'm certainly not going to bring that up. Instead, I say, "In any other relationship, this pull to each other would be useful, instead of a hindrance."

"You don't want to be bonded with me." He furrows his eyebrows. There is no way the confusion in his eyes could be fake, after all he did to me.

I take a deep breath. I don't want to get into my past trauma, but I need to know. "What do you remember?"

He shakes his head, a deep line curving between his brows. "It's like trying to remember a dream. There are images. I recognize you, but I don't know how. That's why I assumed you were with William when I first saw you." He cocks his head. "You two do have something there, though. Am I wrong?"

"He's my best friend."

He fights a smile. "You're wearing his shirt."

"No, I—" I look down, remembering that I *am* in his shirt, though I'm still not sure why. I shake my head. "Doesn't matter."

"Do you love him?"

"Of course."

The smile he's been fighting breaks through a little before vanishing. "But not *in* love."

"Why are we talking about this? My relationship with William is none of your business," I snap.

"It's just odd. William is my best friend. I don't remember ever hurting him. But the way he acts around me. He can't stand to even look at me. And the way he acts when you're around…" He exhales, his eyebrows scrunching together, like he's trying to solve something. "He's in love with you and, even though he hates me, my feelings haven't changed for him. I want what's best for him."

I shake my head. "You're misinterpreting. Didn't they tell you what you did? He's protective."

He looks back at his hands. "Yeah. They gave me a pretty clear picture." He winces.

"Wait. Did they *show* you?"

"Yeah. The girl. Juliet. And William took turns throwing into my mind all the horrible things I did."

It's as if he's talking about somebody else.

He looks up at me, eyes pleading. "That wasn't me, though. I would *never* do anything to harm you or anyone."

I stand, having enough. "That *was* you!" My hands shake. I clench them into fists and breathe through the sudden flare of anger. "*You* did those things. You may not remember now. But a part of you is that person. Nothing you do will ever take away you bonding yourself to me without my permission or threatening my friends or trying to kill James—" I choke on the stupid tears escaping, remembering the sound of his fists against James's body, thinking he was dead.

He stands, and I step away, my back hitting the door, making it click shut. "I'm so sorry. I swear to you I will spend the rest of my days trying to make up for those vile acts." He bends down on one knee, clasping his hands in a silent prayer. "You don't have to forgive me now or ever. I will do whatever you wish to make amends and prove I'm not that man. I will do anything. Just tell me what I can do."

"Don't come near me, and when it's time, break our bond."

His eyes widen. "But the ramifications—"

"No!" I yell. I see red and I know there are flames burning in my eyes. "You *forced* the bond onto me, and you *will* break it if any part of you actually believes those words."

His shoulders slump but he nods.

And without another word, I turn my back on him. I walk past William, who looks like he was about to knock the door down, Sawyer in the hallway, and the rest hovering in the living room. I avoid all their watchful glances, taking the stairs two at a time.

I slam the door behind me, then collapse onto my bed, my chest heaving, but no tears escape. I just faced my trauma reincarnate and came out unscathed. Maybe I can do this after all.

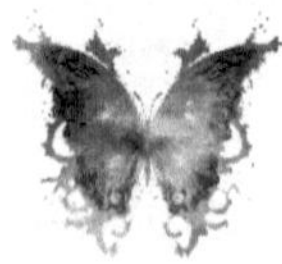

Abby and Juliet fill me in on what I missed the past few days when they bring me breakfast. I had almost forgotten how hungry I still was. I eat like I haven't seen food in a week.

"It's ten hours back to the manor if we drive straight up. You can be free of him by tomorrow," Abby says excitedly.

I smile at her enthusiasm, but there's a pang in my gut. I bite my lip and shake my head. "I haven't done what we came out here to do."

Abby's face falls.

"I'm sorry we didn't find your mom," Juliet says, placing a hand on mine.

"I hate to say it—" Abby starts.

"So don't."

"Abby's right, Maya. I don't think we should risk trying this again," Juliet says for her.

"I won't ask that of you guys. You should go home, Juliet. Take Ann and go back to the manor where it's safe. I've already put all of you in enough danger. Abby, you too. I know you're missing Trevor. Go home to him. But I'm not giving up on her."

"Maya," Abby says, her face pained.

I grab my plate with only a few crumbs rolling around on it and start to head out. "I've got William. I'll be fine."

I'm almost to the door when Abby says, "And Sebastian? You trust him? What? You already forgave him?"

I whip around. "Of course not. Ugh!" I sit back down, my plate rattling on my knees. She has a point, though. He can't go with them.

"You're not thinking this through. We have to all stay together," Abby says.

I can't take Sebastian along on a mission. And if it's just William and me having to take shifts watching him, we won't get anything done.

"All of you should go back, then. I'll check out one more facility on my own. The next one on the list James gave us is in

Portland, right? It makes more sense she would be there. I'll meet you back at the manor in two days."

Abby looks at me like I'm crazy. I probably am. "*Or* we can talk to Wixx about all this and maybe get some help."

I shake my head. "Are you kidding me? After what we did? I'm sure we're in heaps of trouble. And anyway, if she were going to save my mom or the other commanders, she would have done something by now."

There's a knock on the door. William strides in with Ann on his heels. He takes one look at us and his next step wavers. "Am I interrupting something?"

Abby stands. "Just Maya acting like a martyr," she scoffs and storms out.

William raises an eyebrow at me. I grab my pillow, shove it on my face, and fall back on my bed. Somebody grabs the plate from off my lap before it falls to the ground. I hold myself back from screaming out my frustration. Instead, a gurgled moan comes out.

I hear William's muffled speech before the pillow is plucked off my face.

He sits down on the bed. "It'd be really great if you don't try to get yourself killed or captured, or did what we saw in that prison give you the warm fuzzies?"

I glare at Juliet, who must have shared everything with him through an air link. She shrugs. She's so goo-goo eyed over him, she'll tell him just about anything.

"I have a plan, if you want to hear it," he says, playing with a stray string from the blanket.

Motioning with my hand for him to go ahead, I sit back, folding my arms. Ann smiles wide, moving closer until she's practically in my lap so she can be involved.

"Abby?" he calls.

She steps back in and leans against the wall like she never left. She eyes William. "It better be good."

He looks at the four of us and flashes a crooked smile before plucking the string off the blanket and twirling it in his fingers. "Oh. It's bloody good."

23

Dark Desires

"You've got to be kidding me."

I stare at myself in the mirror of the motel right outside Portland. I've got a new head of short black hair and face full of eccentric makeup. I don't dare look at the too-tight dress.

"You turned me into a woman of the night!"

"That's the idea," Abby sings.

"Easy for you to say."

Her long bleach-blonde wig makes her look even hotter, highlighting her ivory skin. A red snakeskin dress covers her figure…just barely. I turn on William, who pokes his head through the door that connects our adjoining rooms to check our progress. His eyes lock on my dress, dragging them down my frame.

I squirm. "There's got to be a better way."

His face reddens, and he clears his throat as he looks away. "Come on. You ladies look…nothing like yourselves *at all*."

"He's right. Nobody will be expecting this," Juliet says, who has a short, wavy, light-brunette wig on, making her milky-white skin tone shine. She's wearing a short, poofy, cream-colored dress with a sweetheart neckline and white stilettos with pink bows attached to the toes. She looks amazing.

I glance at her, then back at William, wearing his usual white V-neck and jeans. "And you get to be you. It's unfair."

He cocks a boyish smile, opening the door wider. "I will be invisible, so it doesn't matter what I look like."

I roll my eyes and stomp out of the bathroom, carrying my awful black heels. The motel room is small, with two full-sized beds. William hangs out the door to the room next door, where he and Sebastian are staying.

I catch sight of Sebastian on the couch, handcuffed to a side table that's drilled into the floor. He gawks at me before tearing his eyes away and studying the ground. He's a little more dressed up, with a black, collared shirt, but still nothing like our ridiculous outfits. He's been good at not coming near me, talking to me, or looking at me. On the way up, he had the back compartment to himself, after we tied all our bags to the roof rack, and didn't even complain once.

I avert my eyes and peer at Ann, who is relaxing in bed, saving her energy for our mission. William's plan's success is on her tiny shoulders this evening.

After William told us of his plan, it took a while to get Juliet on board because of Ann's involvement. Ann has been thrilled to play such a key piece in getting William in and out that she's been on her best behavior, even overdoing it on the "resting" before tonight.

We eat a quick meal of vending machine food and pile in the Jeep to make our way into downtown Portland. I watch the lights of the cityscape, nostalgia washing over me. Driving in and out of the city was a weekly occurrence growing up. An ache for my childhood home forms in my belly as I imagine taking an exit and going to that house. This is how Ann must have felt in New Mexico and look where that got us. Those worry-free lives are gone now.

We find a parking garage a few blocks from the club next to the facility where we believe my mom is being held, based on James's list. This facility isn't anything like the last two. The Com Extremists here are using the "hidden in plain sight" angle. Lucky for us, the facility shares a wall with an infamous nightclub—our way in.

There's a soft drizzle coming down, and the smell of wet cement and garbage permeates the air. The water absorbs into my exposed skin—which is way too much—strengthening me and making me feel more brave. I pull my arms around my chest, glad that Abby let me keep my maroon leather jacket on over this so-called dress.

The sounds of cars driving through puddles, the honking of impatient drivers, and the chatting of groups of people intensify as the city lights bear down on us. As we round the corner to where the club is, the steady beat of a bass makes my heart begin to pound. I touch the itchy wig on my head to ensure it's still in place and step in line behind a group of Coms wearing tight pants and short dresses with brightly colored hairstyles. A girl with neon pink hair bumps into me and turns around.

"Sorry," she giggles. "Ooo. Love your dress, girl."

I look down at the leather fabric that hugs my curves. It covers about as much as a napkin would, and I have to keep pulling it down to cover my butt. I smile my thanks a bit too late, and she shrugs, turning back to her friends with not a care in the world. It's not like Elementals are being experimented on and tortured right next door. I envy her ignorance. Or maybe she's not ignorant and just hates our kind.

I lean away from her and bump into somebody else. An electric shock goes through me, and warmth travels through my body, making my blood roar. I whip around and tilt my head up at Sebastian.

I quickly step back, not realizing we were so close. His eyes flick to my lips, and my traitorous heart actually flutters.

"Excuse you," Abby says, wiggling her way between us.

I shoot her a silent thank you.

A tall guy in dark clothes and biceps that could put William's to shame stands over us with a clipboard. He shines a flashlight into my face. "ID."

I share a look with my friends. ID? Like to check if we're Elementals? I was worried they might do the scanner thing, but an identification to prove we're Coms? Abby shrugs and Juliet frowns looking off to the side. William steps forward, digging something out of his back pocket.

My spine straightens. He's not supposed to be visible. William hands a small ID to the man. Sebastian is right behind him following suit. He studies both of them briefly before unlatching the rope to let them pass.

At the very moment he pulls the rope towards him, a scream rips through the air.

We all whip our heads towards the sound, even the man. Juliet points towards a dark alley, screaming so loud that I go to cover my ears. But before I can, somebody grabs my hand and pulls me past the rope. When I look to see who did it, nobody is there. Then I realize my arm is gone. I follow the ghostly limb and look down to find my whole body missing.

"Come on!" comes a small familiar voice.

I instantly relax and let Ann guide me through a throng of people looking towards Juliet, who is *still* screaming. It's a pretty good diversion, but how is she going to get inside? This was not supposed to happen.

Once the music is loud enough to pulse through my body and the dancing bodies envelop us, my body comes back into view, along with Abby's. We stare at each other with the same wide eyes. She must be thinking the same thing—how completely odd but thrilling it was to be invisible. No wonder Ann does it all the time.

Lips are on my ear, and I almost jump back before the familiar British accent comes.

"Change of plans. Juliet is going for the car to wait for us. Her distraction was the only way to get you and Abby in. Sebastian and I had fake IDs issued to us when we joined the legion. I honestly don't know how Sebastian still had his. I should have known they'd ask, but something so…mundane didn't occur to me. I apologize for that. I need to get through to the facility while Ann is still capable. Don't let Sebastian near you. I'll be back in twenty minutes tops."

When I turn, he's gone—or he was never there, hidden under Ann's invisibility.

I briefly take in the club around me. Under different circumstances, I might have fun at a place like this—being carefree with friends. I don't even know what that's like. Colorful lights blink around me, lighting up part of a bar on one end with stools and an opening to the left where restaurant-style booths peek out. That must lead to where William and Ann are heading. *Mom, please be here.*

Sweaty bodies knock into me. I take a deep breath and make my way over to the bar. *Stick to the plan.* I sit on an available stool and breathe through the fact there has already been a hiccup. It's still going to be fine. Abby will use her Terra abilities to get William and Ann through the wall where the map of the place showed a door that may or may not be there, and Juliet will be ready to go as soon as they come out with Mom, no biggie. If anything, this is probably a better plan.

I thrum my fingers on the stained wooden counter as somebody says, "What are you having?"

I look up at a woman with bleach-blonde hair wearing a purple crop top and low-rise dark jeans looking at me from behind the counter. She smacks her lips and raises her drawn-on eyebrows at me. Oh right, this is where people order drinks. I try to think of a suitable drink, but my mind is blank. Would she laugh if I asked for water?

"Um."

"Two Cokes please," a smooth, deep voice says from behind me.

I don't look at Sebastian as he takes the stool to my right, ignoring the tingling sensation along my skin at his proximity. I shift towards the dance floor instead. Bodies move in rhythm to the chaotic music, sliding against each other in a way that makes me blush. I scan the space for Abby. How long does opening a door take? Juliet was supposed to stay with Sebastian, but now I'm his babysitter, even though William warned me to stay away from him. My stomach twists, hoping Abby hurries.

"Here you go," says the woman, placing two glasses of dark liquid before me.

Sebastian's hand shoots out to take one, making me flinch at the close contact. I grab the other and sip on it. Carbonation stings my throat. Wow. I forgot what soda tasted like. I don't remember being too fond of it when I was little. But this is pretty good. I take a big gulp and wince.

"It's good, isn't it?"

"Yeah. It really is," I say without thinking, then kick myself. I wonder if I could get a burger here. I push the thought away. I should not be thinking about food right now, or Sebastian, or Sebastian with a giant cheeseburger in his hand as he looks at me from underneath his eyelashes. My stomach flips.

I glance at Sebastian, who has a faint smile hovering on his lips like he can read my thoughts. No. He can't do that, not as an Igna anyway. I've heard of bonded Auras being able to, though. They don't even need a link.

The disco lights bounce off his face. I haven't let myself get a good look at him today. But he does look really nice. His sleeves are rolled up to his forearms. If I were to reach out, I know I'd be able to feel his veins there. He'd probably even flex a little under my touch.

I bite my lip, keeping myself from reaching out and trailing my fire along the length of his arm. His long hair, styled in tight braids, has Ann written all over it. I'm surprised he hasn't cut it yet, but his beard is trimmed short. It was a bit easier not to get caught up in his perfectly sculpted looks when he reminded me of a vagrant.

A high-pitched laugh in my ear jostles me, and I realize that I've been unabashedly staring at him, and he's staring right back, heat pulling in his gaze. He drinks the rest of his drink before setting it down, never taking his eyes off mine.

I meant only to glance at him quickly, but words tumble out. "Your hair is different."

"Well, unfortunately, they don't give you scissors in prison." He smirks.

I shake my head. "You haven't cut it yet?"

"It grew on me." His smile widens at his joke, and I bite my cheek to keep from smiling back.

What is wrong with me? I should turn around and continue ignoring him, but I ask him another question. "Was it terrible?"

He lifts his shoulders. "It could have been worse."

I scoff, not believing it. "How much memory did you lose?"

"Only the important stuff, it seems." He scans my face before raking his eyes over me. It feels as if his fingers are skimming my skin. Heat flares where his eyes touch.

I cross my legs and pull my dress down, but it doesn't move lower than my thighs.

"I really wish I could remember you. I know almost nothing."

"I honestly don't know you either. The time we spent together was a lie." The reminder sobers me, and I start to turn away, stopping when he speaks again.

"Despite what I did. I know that my feelings for you weren't—" he stops, correcting himself, "—*aren't* a lie."

I shake my head. "It's just the bond."

"I'm sure that plays a huge part. But there is something else there too. You must have left a mark on my soul, Maya. Please give me a chance to at least get to know you."

My heart beats erratically when he says my name. His hand moves to hover over mine when somebody taps me on the shoulder.

I jump and swivel on the stool, almost toppling off. The person grabs my elbow, holding me steady. I notice the dark curls that skim his chin and almost throw myself into the man's arms before my brain can catch up. I don't recognize the face at all. This man has a thin face and a goatee.

"I'm sorry, didn't mean to scare ya. I was wondering if I could buy you a drink?" He smiles a boyish smile that reminds me more of William than James. I need to stop making comparisons. There are thousands more men than my three guys.

"Actually, I'd rather dance." I need to get away from Sebastian, and for the moment, this guy could be a great distraction.

He smiles and nods, placing his hand on the small of my back to lead me into the hoard of swaying sweaty bodies. Maybe this wasn't the best idea.

Before we get too far and claustrophobia sets in, I say, "This is good. I don't want to get lost in there." I laugh, hoping I sound sane. I do need to keep an eye on Sebastian too.

I sway to the music and the man places his hands on my hips. I risk a glance at Sebastian and regret it. His eyes are laser-focused on the man I'm dancing with, seeming to calculate his every move and probably planning a hundred ways to kill him.

The thought has me closing my eyes and throwing my hands in the air, wanting to lose myself to the music. The best thing for me right now is to get out of my head. I try to imagine the hands on me are somebody else's. James's. I wonder what he's doing right now and if he's worried about me.

Ugh. This is not working. I open my eyes and am startled by how close the man is. He pushes his hips up against me, and his hands travel to my backside. I try to step out of his arms, but the bodies around us have closed in. I'm stuck.

I look around looking for an escape, but I'm smashed between so many bodies I can hardly move. My breathing hitches as panic claws at me.

"Get off!" I yell but my voice is lost in the music.

"You feel good under my hands. Wanna get out of here?" the guy whispers in my ear, his breath tinged in alcohol as it swirls around my face.

I shove him off me, and his eyebrows pull together, hopefully realizing my resistance. "I need some air. Please let me go!"

Another set of arms wraps around my waist, and I'm pulled free. I look up into Sebastian's worry-filled eyes.

"Are you okay?"

I nod but am distracted by the heat running through my veins at his touch. He seems to feel it, too, as his eyes spark.

"Want me to hit him?"

Despite myself, I smile. "No, I don't think he meant to trap me in there."

"I still want to hit him."

"Aren't you supposed to be controlling those violent urges of yours?"

His blue eyes bare into mine. "You're right. I'm not that man. But maybe I can see a little how I could become that man. I feel… protective over you."

His hands don't move from my waist, and I hesitantly put my hands on his shoulders. His eyes light up. This is a terrible idea, but I can't help myself. He's so close, and I want to touch him *so badly*.

"I promise I will never hurt anyone unless you tell me to." His voice resonates deep within my bones.

I want to believe him. Everything in me wants to believe him. It could just be the bond, but it could also be something else. I let myself lean into him, and we sway to the music. His heat consumes me, burning away my doubts. Could this be the Sebastian I fell in love with? Maybe his losing his memory will make it so we can truly start over. He's not that jealous, raging monster that hurt me anymore.

I let him nuzzle my hair and breathe in his new smell. It's a mixture of his old smoky scent, but there is something unknown there, too. A hint of sweetness? Flashes of us kissing and laughing surge, and I tilt my head, welcoming him in. My hands glide over his arms' smooth, hard muscles, up to the nape of his neck. The time in jail did nothing to his physique. I look at his lips, wanting to feel them on mine again. His head dips down, closing the distance.

Sebastian barely brushes my eyebrow with his mouth before my body gets yanked to the side.

"Maya! There you are. Come on!"

I startle as Abby glares behind us at Sebastian. She then gives me a—'Are you having a psychotic break?'—look. Maybe I am. The tether that was so tightly wound around us slackens as I gain some distance from him.

My eyes widen, and the hand that Abby doesn't have a death grip on covers my mouth.

"You're welcome," she mouths, rolling her eyes.

My cheeks fill with heat. I can't believe I was about to kiss Sebastian. I definitely underestimated the bond. All normal reasoning seems to go out the window with a single touch from the man.

A shiver runs down my spine as I think of why that is. My theory is getting more probable by the minute. Then I realize Abby is talking to me.

"We should have heard from William by now."

"What?"

"Good gracious, Maya. Snap out of it." She pulls me into the opening I caught sight of earlier. There are booths with people chatting and eating. The red, peeling walls are covered with old records. As soon as we turn the corner, the noise level decreases, but a slight ringing in my ears remains.

"I was saying that it's been about ten minutes since William and Ann went through. I spent the last five looking for you," she says irritably. "William said he would keep me updated, but I haven't heard a peep."

"What about Juliet?" I ask, finally catching up.

She shakes her head and bites on her newly manicured nail, which we did back at the motel. It was the first seemingly normal moment of this whole trip when us girls sat down to do each other's nails to prepare for this outing. William was making silly comments in the background about feeling left out and telling us about a time when his sisters painted his toenails hot pink.

"Well then, I wouldn't worry. Maybe there's just too many people in here for them to find us," I say.

"I was thinking about that, but—"

"What's going on?" Sebastian asks, pulling up next to me.

A jolt goes through me as his arm brushes mine. Abby notices and yanks me away from him. I can't even look him in the eye. I keep my eyes straight ahead as Abby gives him a vicious glare.

She turns to me. "But they have linked with us so often. The crowd shouldn't be a concern," she finishes.

"Hello? Maybe I can help?" Sebastian says.

"Nuh-uh. All you want to do is get your grubby hands on my best friend. Go back to the bar and keep lookout or something."

She's forgetting we're supposed to be watching *him*, but it's not like he's going anywhere. He's had several chances to bail on us this evening and hasn't.

"He could help." I look at Abby and she narrows her eyes at me. I tilt my head and her eyes widen. I tilt my head more and they finally soften, giving in.

She nods, and I turn to Sebastian. The sight of him brings the heat but not as intense as before.

"Would William be able to create a link with us in a crowd this big?"

"Yeah. It's a part of his training. It's important to keep up the links in combat."

I can't help but watch the way his lips move.

Abby groans and falls into a booth. I should be worried about my best friend, not staring at Sebastian's lips. I put my fingers on my temples and try to message thoughts of Sebastian out of my brain as I sit across from Abby.

"I still think it's a good thing that we haven't heard from Juliet. Maybe it's something else preventing them from communicating and not that they're in danger," I say.

"Could be," Sebastian says casually, scooting beside me in the booth.

I eye him to make sure nothing of his touches me.

Abby gives him a look and he shrugs. "They were testing a device on Auras to block them from communicating with people back in the labs. I don't know if it worked. Didn't have access to that information, but maybe they have something like that here."

"It's only been fifteen minutes. How was getting the door open?" I ask.

She glances toward the serving area where I'm guessing the door is and sits up. "William was right. They had walled it off. But I got through it just fine."

I nod and sit back in the booth, scooting as far away as I can get from Sebastian, and pick up the menu. "Then we wait."

After half an hour and two rounds of mozzarella sticks, the three of us stand outside the door located past the serving area, a hallway that leads to a dead end with the wooden door. Surprisingly, nobody pays us any attention except for some rolled eyes.

"Probably makes a good hook-up spot," Abby comments.

I look at Sebastian's gorgeous face and the two of us girls with him and almost gag. Gross.

In disgust, I peer around at the cement walls and faded linoleum, avoiding Sebastian, who hung back near the hallway's opening to warn us if needed.

"Are you ready?" I ask, peering at Abby who's shifting her weight.

"No. Juliet's going to kill us."

"That's the least of our problems if they actually got caught."

"I don't see how though. They're freaking invisible!"

A knot formed in my stomach back when we hit the twenty-minute mark and they still weren't back. Now it's the size of a bowling ball. I won't admit it to Abby, but I'm terrified for William and Ann. And now we're about to just stroll into the high-security Com compound that may or may not be a trap and somehow get them *and* my mother out. Sebastian can't even help us since he has zero use of his powers.

"I just wish we had a better plan," I murmur.

"Well, that's what happens when we follow William's plan. I wanted to go back to the manor and get reinforcements." Her voice rises in pitch.

"Now's not the time, Abby."

"Actually, it's the perfect time. We still could, you know. The manor is, what, a couple-hour drive?"

"We're not leaving them!"

She pulls at her hair. "We're a couple of teenagers. What do we know? Did you really think we'd be able to break your mom out of a high-security prison? Now we're about to be doomed just like them. I won't do well in prison, Maya!" Abby wails, going from borderline hysterics to a full dive into crazy town. Her breathing quickens and her eyes widen in fear. She clutches her chest.

"Abby. It's okay. You don't have to go in there. Stay here with Sebastian, okay? If I don't come back, then go get help."

Abby's eyes are still panicked as she stares at me.

"Sebastian?" I call.

He's at my side in an instant.

"Stay here with Abby. If I'm not back soon, go back to the manor and get help."

"No. Absolutely not. You're not going in there by yourself," he says, fear lacing his tone.

I turn on him. "Yes, I am. You said you were going to try to make it up to me. I need you to do this. I need you to protect Abby. It's the least you can do."

He looks at me for another beat, conflict raging in his eyes, before he nods and steps toward Abby. Surprisingly, she goes to him and slumps against his side. She must really be freaked out.

I turn toward the door and take a deep breath. I reach for the knob, but Abby grabs my hand, her eyes filled with worry, despair, and maybe guilt?

I pat her hand. "It's okay. This is on me. I shouldn't have asked you to go in there. If anything were to happen to you, I would never forgive myself. I'll be right back." I give her a weak smile.

Sebastian's face is pinched in the same expression Abby gave me, but I ignore the spark igniting in my chest and open the door.

24

Break-In

I step into a dimly lit hall and immediately take note of the stench of death.

The mozzarella sticks threaten to reappear as I breathe through my mouth and take a few more hesitant steps. Allowing my eyes to adjust to the dark, I reach out to feel the walls. My hand grazes rough concrete, and I let it guide me forward. Faint voices come from somewhere in the building. The wall dips underneath my hand as I touch a different, smoother texture.

Hoping it's a door, I wait, listening, but nobody seems to be inside. I feel for a knob and twist. An even darker space opens before me. That foul smell hits me in the face, and my eyes water as I feel for a switch, covering my mouth and nose with my other hand. Finally, something sticking out of the wall slides under my palm.

A bright light blinds me momentarily. I scan the space as my vision clears. Rows of tables line the room with bulky objects covered in white sheets. Next to those tables are smaller ones with various sharp, silver tools organized. A nagging sense of unease spreads over me. I shouldn't have come in here.

I retreat until my back hits the wall. I turn to find I bumped into a set of cabinets. They creak open, and a pale face stares back.

A scream bubbles inside me, but the face doesn't move or even blink.

No. No. No. No. I launch myself out the door and run down the hall. I need to get back to Abby and Sebastian. I can't do this.

My shins hit something hard, and I fall, my elbows smacking into the ground as I collapse onto more hard edges. My arms flail out as I find the wall and then a railing. Nope, this is definitely not the door that I came from.

I'm about to turn around when voices drift from the top of what must be a staircase. Far above me is a door with light filtering through the crack at the bottom. I rub my sore elbows, tiptoe up the steps, and put my ear to the door.

"Patient 391 needs you," says a feminine voice.

"Oh good. I did *not* want to go down there." Another woman.

"Well, you still need to. The patient can wait a minute."

"Can you? I can't stand the smell."

The woman scoffs. "No. Dr. Ally sent *you* to check the door, not me."

"Ugh. I still don't know what the point is. That door has been sealed for a decade."

My heart drops. She's coming down here. They're talking about *this* door. William and Ann must have been caught if this doctor wondered if the door was still sealed.

I tiptoe back down the stairs. When I reach the bottom step, the door opens, shining yellow light all the way down the hall. I throw myself into the shadows and hold my breath. Shoes click on the steps.

As soon as I see a head of blonde hair, I throw myself on her. Twisting her arms behind her back, I shove the woman forward like Seth taught me back when he showed me some self-defense moves. She falls onto the ground with a squeal. I jump on her squirming body and cover her mouth. I glance up the stairs, but there is no movement.

"Be quiet!" I hiss, blinking flames into my eyes.

She stills when she sees them, her eyes as big as saucers.

"Now listen. And you won't get hurt."

She nods.

"I'm going to release your mouth but don't scream. If you do, I'll burn you."

She nods again and I slowly pull my hand free.

"Are you going to kill me?" she cries. Tears slip down her cheeks, and I feel a pain of regret.

"Come on," I say, helping her up, while keeping a good grip on her arm, just in case she tries to run. "I'm not going to kill you. But I could really hurt you." Snapping my fingers, a flame dances on my hand.

She gasps and I nudge her forward.

"Is there a different room down here besides that one?" I ask grimacing towards what must be their morgue.

"There's a closet down there," she whispers, her voice shaking.

I follow her lead and open the door to a cleaning closet. "I'm going to tie you up."

"No! Don't leave me down here," she sobs.

"Shhh!" I shove her into the closet.

"I'm sorry," she sniffles. "I don't like it down here."

I think briefly about pushing her through the door for Abby and Sebastian to watch, feeling guilty. The smell down here is rancid. But now is not the time for empathy for these people. They have my friends, and maybe my mom, doing who knows what awful things to them. If those bodies were any indication, I don't want to know what they do to the living.

"You're going to tell me everything you know about this place and Dr. Ally while we change outfits. Then I'll leave you in the safety of this closet, unless you prefer one of the gurneys in the other room?"

She whimpers and shakes her head.

"I didn't think so."

After a few minutes, I have the necessary information and a new outfit. I leave the silently crying nurse tied up with vacuum cords and a dust rag shoved in her mouth before heading back up the stairs.

Before gently opening the door, I smooth down my scrubs. I take the name tag, shove it in my pocket, and pull my hair up and out of my face into a loose ponytail. The wig would have been too obvious in this environment. Hopefully, I look the part.

I step into the brightly lit, chemical-smelling hallway with my head held high and pretend I belong here. It's just a few flights upstairs to the offices to find Dr. Ally, the head of the hospital division. He must know where my friends are if he's asking questions about the door.

White coats walk my way, so I veer into the closest room. A sleeping man lies on a cot with tubes sticking out of him. I grab a clipboard off the bottom of his bed and face away from the door.

I wait for the footsteps to continue down the hall when one word jumps out on the document attached to the clipboard. I suck in a breath and look at him again, noticing the chains on his ankles and wrists.

"Terra."

The monitor beeps rhythmically. He's still alive at least. What terrible, awful, dreadful people. I was feeling bad about the nurse I tied up, but now…maybe I won't tell anyone where she's at, let her rot.

But would that make me any better than them?

I shake off the thought and drift closer to him. He's older, maybe in his fifties. *How long have you been here?* I go to touch his arm. Perhaps I could get him out of here too.

He jerks and his eyelids open. He stares at me for a moment with dead, unblinking eyes before he begins to thrash. He yells non-intelligent things and arches his back, flinging his head side to side.

Horror-struck, I take a few steps back and slip out the door. I look around to make sure the white-coated men are gone and bolt down the hall. What on earth are they doing to these people?

My blood boils, anger threatening to make me react in a way that will surely get me tied to one of those tables. I take a few deep breaths, trying to wrangle my emotions, or I'll burn this doctor to a crisp before I can get any information out of him.

I reach the upper floor and scan the office numbers. 205. 207. 209. 211. I glance at the other side. Room 212. There it is. The office she said he would be in.

I reach for the knob but freeze. She could have told me anything. I could enter this room and find out it's the security office. There is no window to check who's on the inside.

I look around one last time before slowly turning the knob and sliding into the room. It's a risk I have to take if I want to save William and Ann.

A man, probably in his mid-forties with dark, styled hair and a nice beard, stares down at a document in his hands.

"Just a moment. I'll be right with you." He doesn't even look up.

I don't know what to say…or do. I honestly didn't believe I would get this far. Shoot up in flames? Threaten him? Or continue to play the nurse angle and find out more information? As I'm contemplating my next move, he looks up.

"What is it, Nurse…wait, are you new? I don't believe we've met." He stands and walks around the desk. "You must be one of the new girls from the recent…" His words fade as I stare into his eyes. His *emerald* eyes.

Eyes that look just like mine.

He smiles warmly, stepping closer, and shoves a hand out. I don't move, and his eyebrows furrow.

"Miss, are you okay? Do you need to sit down?"

I let him guide me to his sitting area, but I don't sit.

He cocks his head. "You know, maybe we have met. Your eyes—" His words freeze on his lips. "What did you say your name was?"

"I haven't," I gasp.

"What is your name?" His voice grows serious.

I back away from him. "I'm sorry. I didn't mean to come in here. I'll just be leaving."

He moves to block my path to the door. Without thinking, I grab my spark and unleash it, letting the fire consume my hands.

"I'll be leaving *now*."

He smiles. "Remarkable." He steps toward me and reaches out a hand as if to touch me. Is he crazy?

"I wouldn't do that if I were you," I say, forming a fireball in my palm.

He takes another step and I throw it at him.

He smiles wider and catches it, passing the flaming ball between his palms before extinguishing it. I suck in a breath. It really *is* him.

Not Dr. Ally.

Dr. Ali.

Dr. Michael Ali.

"It's so good to finally meet you, Maya. It's nice to see that you developed my Igna abilities."

25

The Doctor

"Where are my friends?" I ask, skipping the family reunion.

"Ah. It makes sense now. They're with you. You have very good friends. They wouldn't tell me a thing. And the scrubs." He nods as if approving my breaking and entering before his eyebrows turn down. "You didn't hurt Nurse Clarissa, did you?"

"*Where* are my friends?" I say louder.

He puts his hands up. "They're okay, Maya."

"Stop calling me that," I snap.

"Do you go by a different name now? It's been so long since I've seen you."

I shake my head, my stomach tightening. "You can't be him."

"Maya Mayfield, daughter of Evelynn and Henry. I am your birth father, Michael Ali."

I suck in a breath as my fire extinguishes. "No, it can't be. You're here. Helping *them*. No." I shake my head, backing away from him. This can't be possible. He can't be here. This is not how I meet him.

A line forms between his eyebrows. "I'll explain everything. How about we get your friends and maybe you can tell me where you put poor Clarissa?" He rubs his chin. "She was a good nurse. I'll hate having to get rid of her."

My heart surges for the girl. "No! Don't hurt her! I made her tell me."

His face falls. "You think I'm a monster?"

"I don't *know* you."

He sighs and taps his finger on his desk. I look toward the door, analyzing my chances of getting around him. He doesn't know I wield water. I'll have to use that to my advantage.

A strange scraping sound fills the room as the bookcase behind his desk shudders. It swings open like a door, revealing a large library.

William and Ann stand from a couch in its center.

"Maya!" William yells, jumping over the back of the couch, and then sliding over the desk like he's in an action movie before pulling me into a tight hug. He wraps one hand around my waist, and the other threads through my hair.

"You guys are okay." His shoulder smothers my voice.

"Yeah, we're fine," he says, leaning back and looking me up and down. "What are you wearing?"

"I had to come save your butts." I shrug. "I improvised."

Michael clears his throat, and William twists around, moving his hand from my hair to my hand, tugging me half behind him.

My biological father studies us and nods. "Clearer by the minute."

"I told you he's trying to help us," Ann says, stepping out of the secret room.

"Ann," William and I say at the same time.

She rolls her eyes but hurries to us, and I pull her against my side.

"I think I'm getting the picture now, but I still need to know why y'all are here in the first place. Your *friends* told me nothing."

William squeezes my hand, but I pull away a bit to face the man. "Is my mom here?"

If my mom is here, my father's got to be one of the most despicable human beings in existence. But if she's not…my heart falls into my stomach. He doesn't seem despicable, even though he's standing here as the head of the hospital wing that tortures Elementals.

Without any valid reason, I suddenly know she's not here.

He frowns. "No. Of course not. Why would she be? What happened?" His voice goes up an octave, like he cares about the answer.

I catch William's side-eye as I shake my head. "I told you why we're here. Now let us go."

He nods and folds his hands. "Three more questions, and then you're free to go."

Before I can respond, he asks, "Are there any more of you I should be worried about?"

William and I share a look.

His eyes turn thoughtful after a beat of silence. "Okay. We'll figure that out. Two. Where's Clarissa?"

"She's in the closet in the basement, and no, I didn't hurt her."

He visibly relaxes. "And three. Would you and your friends like to join me for a meal at my home? I don't live too far from here. It's safe. I promise."

"Bloke, are you loony? Why in the world would we come to your house?" William finally speaks up.

"William," I caution.

"What?" he says, looking between the two of us, possibly seeing the resemblance for the first time. His eyes widen incrementally.

"I'm Maya's birth father, and I would love to get to know her and her friends and answer any questions you may have." He looks at me. "I'm hoping to be somebody you can trust. Even though this place may not be what you think it is, it's still not safe to talk here." He moves to his desk, pulls a piece of paper from a drawer, and scribbles something on it.

"This is my address. Maya, you have to believe me. I've been wanting to be in your life since I learned about your existence."

He offers me the paper, but I don't move to take it. There is no reason to trust the man. I can't help but think about that dream—or rather, memory—I had about when he arrived at our home when I was five years old. He did want to know me then. Could he be telling the truth?

"Please. Just one meal."

His face is so full of hope that I take the piece of paper and shove it in my pocket. It doesn't mean we'll actually go, but at least I'll have the choice.

He smiles warmly. "Come as soon as you've all rested. I'm working the night shift." He lets out a deep, airy laugh. "Lucky for you lot. Soren would not have been as accommodating. But I will be home this afternoon, and even if I'm not, Sarah will let you in."

I open my mouth to speak, but nothing comes out. He seems to sense my reluctance.

"I hope you greatly consider it. Now, it's probably best for you all to return the way you came in. The door from the club next door, I'm assuming?" He shuffles us through the door when I turn back around. He has one hand on the door when he looks at me with those hopeful, bright-emerald eyes.

"Would you be able to help me find my mom?"

He smiles a sad smile, but something sparks in his eyes. "I can certainly try."

That's enough for me. I nod. "We'll be there."

William gawks at me, but I pull him and Ann along, leaving my father in the doorway.

I look back, remembering the dream again. The last time I saw my father, he stood in a doorway, trying to get to know me.

Thirteen years later, he'll finally get his chance.

26

One and Only

"I told you so!" Ann sings as we drive toward the address Michael gave us.

She claims to have gotten good vibes from Michael and kept telling William to trust him when they got caught. How in the world she would know that, I don't know, but she was somewhat correct. We still don't know if we can trust him. But if he can help me find my mom, then we have to take the risk.

I replay our conversation on the way back to the motel early this morning after William, Ann, and I returned to a hysterical Abby. Sebastian did well on his part in keeping her safe and refusing to let her follow me, which she tried once I left. My stupid spark sang at the knowledge. Juliet was in even worse shape by the time we made it to the car, since she'd been unable to communicate with us. We guessed that Sebastian was right about the facility having a device that blocks Auras from creating air links. Juliet even tried to get into the club a couple more times and almost got arrested when they called the police on her.

"We would have been fine if we hadn't run right into the guy," William said.

"You walked into him? While you were invisible?" Juliet shrieked, still not all the way calmed down.

"Should have seen his face." William laughed and then stopped at the sight of Juliet's open mouth. *"Sorry. I take full responsibility for Ann and our short kidnapping. It was a terrible mistake on my part."*

As we wind around lush, green trees, the sun high in the sky, I still don't think Juliet has forgiven him. She hasn't ogled him once today.

"Told. You. So," Ann says again.

"Yes, Ann. We all got it. You were right, and I was wrong," William announces.

"Thank you," she chirps. "I hope he's got pancakes."

As Ann rambles about food, the Jeep turns onto a street with a large open gate. Huge, beautiful white houses with perfectly kept yards you would only see in a magazine stretch before us.

"Whoa, your dad is rolling in cash," Abby says.

We still haven't talked about last night, but I'm sure we will soon. She has nothing to feel guilty about. She was scared, and I shouldn't have put her in that situation.

William parks the Jeep into the driveway of a white two-story house with black trim and window panels to match. We pile out, all of us a little giddy.

"You think he's expecting all of us?" William smirks.

"He said he wanted to get to know *all* my friends."

"Oh, does that mean I'm your friend now?" Sebastian asks as he climbs out of the trunk and stretches his limbs. He twists his torso, and I can't help but stare at the strip of dark skin that shows when his shirt lifts. I wonder if his muscled abs and chest still feel the same. I can almost feel the way his arms would wrap around me as flames lick my skin.

"No," Abby says for me and gently shoves me toward the house by my shoulders. I give her a look and shake her off, but she avoids my gaze. I'm grateful she's serving as my buffer, but she's starting to get on my nerves.

As we walk up the white staircase, colorful flowers in pots flanking us, the front door opens wide, revealing an elderly lady in a bright orange floral gown. Her face is frail, lined with wrinkles, and her dark gray hair falls in ringlets around her face that lights up at the sight of us. Her all-knowing emerald eyes focus on me.

"Come here, my child. Let me see you!" she says, taking a shaky step outside.

I jolt forward, fearing she's going to topple down the stairs. Another person comes from behind her, gently grasping her shoulders.

"Mrs. Izalia. You should not be answering the door!"

"Oh hush, Sarah, this is my granddaughter!" she exclaims joyfully, trying to take another step.

I hurry forward. She obviously should be sitting down. Her warm hands encase mine. She grips tightly for such an old lady.

My *grandmother,* I realize with a jolt. I've never met a grandparent. Both sets of grandparents from my parents have long passed.

"You are a beauty. It's true. You have the Divina eyes. But that seems to be the only thing you got from your father." She threads her hand through my hair and pushes it behind my ear like she's done it a hundred times, such a tender, motherly gesture.

"You must take after your mother." She smiles, showing a row of too-perfect white teeth. "But your father told me what happened. You definitely have my tenacity," she says with a wink.

She takes in my friends behind me. "Come in, come in! Sarah was just preparing lunch. Michael will be up soon."

I help her walk back in, and Sarah leads her toward a high-backed chair in the corner of an extravagant sitting room. I take in the high ceilings, elegant portraits of gardens and landscapes on the wall, and plush carpet. A white-bricked fireplace that I imagine a whole family gathered around during the holidays takes front and center.

"Should we take off our shoes?" I worry, feeling like I'm getting dirt everywhere.

She still has my hand in hers as she shakes her head. "Nonsense, this place needs some roughing up." She finally releases me when she sits but points to the white couch beside her.

Sarah, a curvy woman with short dark hair, wearing scrubs—who I can only assume is her caretaker—looks at her warily before disappearing around the corner.

Izalia pats my knee. "I've been waiting so long to meet you."

"How long have you known about me?"

She tilts her head, looking at a spot far off. Her skin, in this light, has a much darker complexion. It's not as dark as Sebastian's, but I had no idea I had ethnic blood in me. "Michael told me about you…was it five years ago?"

"Seven," responds a deep voice.

I look over to Michael, who's now standing behind Abby's chair. All my friends are sitting around a small glass coffee table that has dried flowers pressed under the surface. William and Sebastian are next to me on the loveseat. Abby is in one of two matching oversized red chairs. Juliet and Ann are squished in the other.

"Yes. But you waited much too long to tell me I had a granddaughter." She casts him a scolding look before her eyes come back to mine. "You're my first."

"Grandchild?" I ask, remembering Thomas uneasily, hoping I'm not harboring some huge family secret. Luckily, I haven't told my friends either. I bite the inside of my cheek. It's one thing to keep it from them, but Thomas is her grandchild, with whom Michael supposedly had a falling out.

"No, no, no. Grand*daughter*. You come from a line of only sons. My son Teddy had only Michael, and he had—"

"Noni," Michael hisses.

I relax a little, but not before catching a look shared between my friends. They heard the obvious meaning—I have a sibling, and Michael doesn't want me to know.

Izalia's cheeks redden. "Right. I apologize. I'm getting ahead of myself. You and your father have much to discuss. I'll keep your friends company. Go ahead!" she says, shooing us out.

Ann takes my place next to William, beating Juliet to it as she sits back down and casts her eyes about, looking a bit sullen. It seems like she has forgiven him after all.

I try to hide my smile as I follow Michael through the kitchen. Something delicious wafts through the air, making my stomach growl. But, unfortunately, we don't stop. We pass Sarah, who's too busy to notice us, stirring a pot with one hand and taking biscuits out of the oven with the other.

"I hope my office is okay?" Michael looks back at me with a smile.

I nod and rush to catch up with his long stride. We round another corner and come to a set of double doors. He opens one and offers me to step inside first.

The office is quite bland compared to what I've seen of the house. Books cover the wall on one side, and the other has a huge window that overlooks a small garden. My heart compresses. It reminds me of the manor in a way. There are no bobbles or pictures to indicate he has a family. He rests against a massive oak desk and offers me the seat behind it.

I sit in his big, comfy office chair, bouncing it a little before facing him.

"I am so glad you came, Maya." He looks at me meaningfully.

"Why did you do it?" I blurt, finally voicing the words eating away at me since I talked to Thomas. The story he told me about Divina is still sharp in my mind. If everything he said was true about the rarity of our bloodline, why would Michael give a stranger part of his valuable DNA?

"Excuse me?"

I take a deep breath. "I know about Thomas."

"How…how is that possible?" he stutters.

I shrug. "Chance, really. He used to live in the same place I did after the war started, and then we ran into him in New Mexico. He told me there was a possibility that I was his sister and told me some of the history about your—*my*—ancestors. Is that all true?"

He looks past me out the window. A soft smile forms on his lips as he mutters something under his breath that sounds like, "He went after all."

"Michael?"

He looks at me and blinks. "I'm sorry, what?"

"He told me I was his sister and shared some history about our ancestors. Is it true?"

"Yes. I'm sure everything he told you is the truth."

"So why did you do it? Give my mom your..." I hesitate, suddenly feeling awkward, being on the topic of his manhood.

He smiles. "She was quite convincing. Honestly, she could have asked for my left leg, and I would have given it to her. I've never met a woman so, so—"

"Demanding?" I scoff.

He shakes his head and looks me in the eye. "Inspiring."

If I didn't know better, the look in his eyes is one of adoration.

"Did you know her well?" Suspicion taints my tone. From what I got from my mom, supposedly, this man is her perfect match. She chose him in the hope that I would have multiple abilities. Was there more going on than just a sperm sample? Would she have done that to Dad?

"No, not at all, actually. But she is a brilliant woman, and the few interactions I did have with her..." He seems at a loss for words as he clears his throat. "Her research on genetics and heredity was before her time. It was a sight to behold."

"Did you know *I* was her experiment? That she used you too?" The feelings of betrayal I had when I first found out swirl like a tornado, looking for a place to touch down. *I forgave her*, I remind myself.

He sighs and pushes himself off his desk. "Yes, I knew." Before that swirling tornado of betrayal can land and my anger flares toward this man I barely know, he adds, "But *you* were never an experiment. You were created with love, just like any other person. Your parents love you very much, and I would like to include myself in that statement. I've loved you since I first got the notice of your birth." He pulls something from his back pocket, a black leather wallet, and opens it up. He hands me a picture. I hesitantly take it into my palms. It's an image of me around eight years old, outside next to the stream in the backyard of my old house.

I fall against the back of the chair, rocking it back and forth. "Your father sent me updates on you."

My heart leaps. He did? This picture must have been taken right before he died. Heat gathers behind my eyes.

"I know it was hard for him to do, but he knew I wanted to know you and obliged me in this. I couldn't see you, but I knew you."

I shake my head, a tear slipping down my face. "I don't think Mom knew he was doing that… He…he died." I add the last part because I want him to know why the pictures stopped—that he didn't just stop on his own accord.

His warm hand finds my shoulder as he kneels in front of me. "I know. I am so sorry."

I nod, unable to look him in the eyes with all the emotion this conversation is pulling to the surface.

"He was a good guy, and he raised a wonderful, talented daughter despite her not having his abilities."

I look at him then. "He died before they manifested." His smile turns sad. For a moment, I almost don't share that I have two abilities, but I can't think of a reason not to tell him. "And I don't just have Igna powers."

His eyes bounce between mine as they slowly widen in realization. He falls back on his butt, one hand on the side of his desk in support. "You're also a Lympha?"

I smile as he shakes his head. "Astonishing...I really wish we could have been in your life, Maya. I'm sure that was so hard to figure out on your own."

I do hold back that I recently discovered my Igna abilities, not wanting to tell him *how* I did.

"They were both adamant I have no contact. It's what I agreed to." Sorrow fills his eyes…or maybe regret.

"But you did come," I say hesitantly, still not 100 percent sure that my dream was a memory.

He leans forward on his knees. "Yeah, I did. They were pretty mad about that. I had to see you just once, though. That's when your father started sending me pictures. I think he was worried I'd come back." He chuckles. "But I did catch a glimpse of you peeking around the corner." He smiles at the memory. "I could never forget that. But I am surprised you remember."

I nod. "You had my eyes."

His smile widens. "Glad the trait passed down to you too. Pa would be happy."

I ruffle my eyebrows. Would be?

"Your Grandpa Teddy. He and Mom died a few years ago."

I cross and uncross my legs. "I'm sorry."

He puts a hand up. "Your Great-Grandma Izalia, though. She still has quite a bit of life in her."

That's right. She's my great-grandma.

My eyes widen. "Wait, so the one that got banished?" I say, trying to remember the story Thomas told me and kicking myself for not putting together the pieces earlier.

"The one and only," he says, rising to his feet. I sit back in a daze as Michael rubs his palms together. "Smells like lunch is almost ready. We'll have plenty of time to talk more. I want to know more about you and this boy of yours." He eyes me, pushing away from his desk.

I shake my head, embarrassment reddening my cheeks. Great, I've had a father for a total of twelve hours, and he's already asking me about boys. He has no idea.

I go to give him back the picture of me as a little girl, but I freeze. "Wait. What about my mom? The Coms took her when they attacked. You said you might be able to help?"

He nods. "I've already started to look into it. I have some access to their records, but not all. It'll take time to shuffle through everything."

I sigh. It's something at least.

We join the others around a huge table that could fit a dozen more people in a fabulously decorated dining room draped in colorful tapestries showcasing different animals from the African plains to the tropics. A china cabinet in the corner holds elegant white dishes that I'm sure they've never used. Somehow, I end up sitting between Sebastian and William.

I'm so highly aware of Sebastian's every movement that I can hardly eat the delicious soup before me. I ignore his sideways glances and how his hand hovers dangerously close to mine as we eat. It's so nice to eat real food, though. Everything tastes almost as good as the Terra-made food back home. The sweet liquid full of spices warms my throat, continuing all the way down to my toes.

We find out Sarah, who sets some more rolls on the table and bustles back into the kitchen, is a Com. Izalia tells us she's a trusted nurse friend who helped her for the past three years as her health declined—or so other people say. I agree with her. She's full of vigor and energy for a ninety-something-year-old. I especially feel it when she practically throws herself on me after lunch, enveloping me in a tender, grandmotherly hug. The backs of my eyes sting. I have a grandparent.

"It's my turn," she says once she releases me. Sarah comes to assist her, and she swats her away. "I'm alright. My granddaughter will help me, won't you, dear?"

I nod and take her arm as she leads me through the house. I think we're going back to the sitting room, but she steers us left, down another hallway to the first room on the right.

When she opens the door, I'm struck speechless by her decor.

Canvas paintings cover every square inch of her walls— paintings of white sandy beaches, of sunsets and palm trees, of people dressed in floral dresses and palm leaf skirts. One captures my attention of a young girl with sweeping dark hair and a monkey on her shoulder. I don't realize that I've walked towards it until my fingers hover over the beautiful woman.

"Is this you?" I ask, twisting to face her.

She sits on her vibrant, colorful bedspread, watching me. "Yes, my dear."

"You had a pet monkey?"

She looks at the picture fondly and nods. "Beau."

"That's amazing." Next to it is a painting of her with flowers in her hair and a man who looks a little like Michael, but blonde. A gorgeous sunset in the background outlines their faces, which hold so much love for one another. It's beautiful that the artist was able to capture it. "Did you paint these?"

"Oh no. I'm not an artist. That boy's mother painted all of those."

"So, my great-great-grandmother?" I guess.

"Yes," she says, answering my underlying question about the boy in the painting being her partner.

"You must have quite the stories."

"Oh, someday I'll tell you them, but first, let's talk about you," she says, patting her bed.

I join her, and she rubs my knee affectionately.

"You're bonded to that boy aren't you?" She just dives right in. It would almost make me smile if it weren't for the ball of knotted yarn that is my love life. "Sebastian is his name?"

"How do you know that?"

"The way you two move around each other. I can practically see the gravitational force of the bond. It's been a while since I've sensed one so strong."

"It's complicated," I say hesitantly and study my hands. The ocean-blue nail polish—that now reminds me of Sebastian's eyes—from Juliet's manicure at the motel yesterday is already starting to chip off.

She waits patiently for me to continue. Her silence makes me look up, which is a mistake. Her deep emerald eyes pierce mine, making me want to spill all my secrets. Is this how it feels when others look at me?

I swallow. "It was a mistake. My mother made the match, so that's why I'm guessing it's so strong." I put my head in my hands.

"Right. Your mother is a geneticist?"

I nod. "She's really good at it."

"Why do you say it's a mistake? You don't want to be bonded with him?"

I look at her, debating how much to say. "He did some things that I don't want to get into, and we plan on breaking the bond. But I don't know…it's just…"

She nods in understanding. "Ah. I see. You love another. Is it that other boy? William?"

"No! Ugh. Why do people keep saying that? We're just friends." I shift uncomfortably, tucking my feet underneath me and looking back at the pretty paintings.

She giggles. "Love doesn't begin and end the way you think. It can be unpredictable and hard to understand. But the bond only amplifies what you already feel."

"But I don't—" I begin to say.

"Just because you feel something for him, even if it's deep down, doesn't mean you have forgiven him for what he did. Love is an unruly thing. Other feelings can overshadow it, but it never truly goes away."

I'm getting more uncomfortable by the minute. Then I remember the story Thomas told me and look back at her. "Can you really wield all four elements?" I ask, changing the subject.

She eyes me for a moment but caves. "Oh yes. I was once a spritely young thing, walking on water and all that, but now…" She looks down at her aged, wrinkled hands. "I'm lucky if I can wield one on a good day," she says sadly. But then she looks back up with a smile. "Those days are behind me. But *you* have a long life ahead. Tell me about your friends."

I'm relieved to hear a knock at the door. Michael peeks in.

"You're just in time. Maya was just talking about her friends."

He smiles and sits on the wooden rocking chair in the corner. "Go on."

Dang. I take a deep breath and tell them about my friends, family, and upbringing. It's a bit therapeutic talking about everything. By the time I'm done, I feel a slight weight lifted.

I don't realize how much time has passed while talking to them until I yawn. "Oh, man. What time is it? We should go," I say, standing.

My father stands with me. "No need. Your friends have all found rooms, and I have one for you prepped as well."

"Oh." I shift on my feet. Having a meal is one thing, but staying the night in the house of a man I just met is another.

His face falls. "Well. You certainly don't have to. But all your friends were pretty enthused by the invite." He smiles.

Yeah. To not have to sleep at the motel for another night, they probably would have wholeheartedly agreed to sleep in the same room as him, let alone this extravagant house. I'm pretty sure I heard rats in the walls the first night at the motel.

I shrug. "Okay. But I'd rather stay with one of the girls."

He probably would have had a heart attack if I told him I wanted to sleep in William's room, and I imagine Izalia would have given me a knowing smile, along with another speech about love. I've just grown accustomed to sleeping in the same room as him. His light snores and heavy breathing lull me to sleep instantly, and he's always there if I have another of those awful nightmares I can never remember. Although, I haven't had any this past week.

After I say goodnight to my grandma Izalia, he leads me up the stairs and down a narrow hallway lined with doors. We walk into one of the rooms and find Abby, Juliet, and Ann sitting cross-legged on a bed in the middle of the room.

"This is a guestroom?"

I can't take in everything fast enough as my head whips every which way—the dark-purple, moody walls and matching crown molding, Victorian paintings that hover between wistful and creepy, a floor-length gold mirror in one corner, a black dresser with gold knobs, and a matching king-sized bed with a curved gold and black headboard that reaches halfway up the wall. I feel like I'm in a Gothic-Victorian home of the sixteenth century.

Abby jumps up when she hears me.

"The previous owners had quite the eclectic taste. Every room is different." Michael shrugs.

"Thank you again, Mr. Ali, for letting us stay," Abby says, looping her arm in mine and drawing me to the bed.

"I'll see you girls in the morning. Sarah makes fantastic pancakes." He smiles and shuts the door with a soft click.

"Yes!" Ann squeals.

"This is so much better than I imagined," Abby says, hopping on the bed.

"Are you all really okay with this?" I ask as I sit on the bed and practically moan. I lie fully down. "What is this thing made of? Clouds?"

Juliet giggles. "What was that again?"

"Are you kidding me? Real food. A heavenly bed. Come feel the pillows." Abby falls into them and throws her hands in the air. "Air conditioning!" She giggles.

I look at Ann, who looks like she's holding back, saying, "I told you so" again. "It just seems too good to be true. You know?"

"Oh. Stop being so pessimistic. You found a parent!" She taps me with her foot.

"Not the one I was looking for," I grumble, but she has a point. I have found more family on this trip than I could have ever imagined—a brother, niece and nephew, father, and grandmother.

"Come on. He's amazing! He's so kind and generous. And that sweet old lady. What'd you learn about them?"

I get ready to launch into everything, but I close my mouth. Huh. I didn't learn much. "Nothing, really. *I* talked mostly. They had *so* many questions."

"Understandable," Juliet says with a smile. She gets up with Ann and heads for the door. "Tomorrow, it'll be your turn to ask the questions."

I nod as she leaves, but something turns over in my stomach. I really don't know anything about them. Thomas had said his dad *left* him. Michael doesn't seem like the type of father who would do that, though. Could he be hiding something? Why does he have this huge house anyway? And what's up with his job? He *is* working for the Com Extremists.

Another yawn escapes me, and I scramble to the pillows and nudge Abby over until I have enough space to pull the covers over my shoulders. Juliet is right. It'll be my turn to ask the questions tomorrow. More questions pile up as I let the feather pillows pull me under.

27

First Breath

James!" I yell, sitting straight up in my bed, sweat sticking my clothes to my skin.

I kick the covers off and try to slide out of bed without disturbing Abby. The room is pitch-black. Only a sliver of light peeks through the drapes from a streetlight outside. I tiptoe to the door, grab an extra shirt from my backpack, and peek out. The house is silent. I find the bathroom down the hall. Blinking against the harsh bright light, I peel my top and shorts off. I splash water on my face and breathe with both hands on the side of the porcelain sink.

It was just a dream, I tell my reflection. But I remember this one. My family and friends' bodies laid disfigured on the manor's grounds. James and Sebastian stood in the woods, beckoning to me. I was drawn to Sebastian's arms despite fighting to get to James. When I made that first touch, I was overcome by the bond, and James had to watch as Sebastian took me away. No matter how many times I told my body to stop, that I was making the wrong choice, I had to watch the light go out of James's eyes.

"My family and friends are not dead. James doesn't want you anymore. Stop dreaming about him." I worry about how this bond is affecting my mental state, though.

Grabbing a towel, I dry myself, throw the clean shirt on, and wad my sweaty clothes into a ball. I step into the hall and am halfway to my room when a floorboard creaks behind me. I freeze, feeling exposed in only a T-shirt and underwear.

I look back, but it's too dark to see anything. I take another step and hear another creak, closer this time.

My heart rate accelerates, and I break into a run. I hit a solid fleshy wall of muscle and fall onto the floor.

"I'm so sorry!" comes a deep voice. "Are you okay?"

"Yeah," I respond, trying to get up and pull my shirt down at the same time. Relief floods me when I realize it's too dark for him to see what little I'm wearing.

"Angel?" he says. His hand wraps around my bicep, pulling me to my feet.

Fire shoots down my arm, making me shudder.

"Um. No. Maya," I snap and shake him off. Who is Angel? I don't have to see to know it's Sebastian, by the way my skin electrifies in his presence and the pull intensifies.

"Were you running?" I can feel him smiling.

My cheeks redden. "I thought I heard something."

He chuckles. "I don't like the dark either. Why didn't you turn on a light?"

"I didn't want to wake the whole house."

"I meant your Igna abilities."

Right. I'm so dumb. I could snap a flame on right now, but then he'd see me in only a T-shirt, which would not help the tether.

And *he* obviously can't provide light, because his powers are still suppressed. I watched William inject him with the stuff once, and that was enough. I couldn't watch without thinking about what he endured the last couple of months, and I'm trying not to feel sympathy for him—anything to keep my emotions hardened and the pull from intensifying.

"Right. Well, I'm almost to my room. Don't want to set off any fire alarms." I go to step around him and run right into him again. Ugh.

His arms come out, steadying me. Heat blasts into me from the contact, traveling to my stomach and continuing right down to my toes. They curl, and I can't hold back the gasp that escapes me.

He pulls me closer and threads a hand in my hair. "I'm so sorry, but I can't not touch you when you make a sound like that..."

His whisper caresses the shell of my ear. His hot breath curls around my neck as a growl rumbles in his chest. Sparks ignite and race through my body like shooting stars. I bite my tongue, swallowing a terribly undignified sound.

My hands move on their own accord, feeling the ridges of muscles on his chest. The growl grows louder as my hands make their way to his collarbone and over his broad shoulders. He shudders beneath my touch.

How is it possible that he feels more sculpted than the last time I traced him like this? My eager touch explores the plains of his body, and he holds impossibly still. His breath comes in short gusts on my neck, his lips just mere inches from my skin.

"That feels as good as I imagined, my angel."

"Why do you keep saying that?" My voice comes out breathless.

"Angel?"

I nod into him, my whole body thrumming with energy, the tether winding around us so tightly I can hardly breathe.

"In the darkness of that hell, I would see your eyes. I forgot everything else about you, but those stuck with me. I started to call you my green-eyed angel. You stayed with me during the worst of it."

My heart speeds up as flashes of forgotten nightmares briefly fill my mind. I bury my face into him and breathe in his scent, letting the spice and subtle sweetness ground me, bind me, electrify me. He strokes my hair.

"I think I saw you too," I say, looking up at him, even though he's only a silhouette in this all-consuming darkness.

I'm on the verge of something when his thumb brushes my lower lip. All thoughts are banished from my mind. He tilts my chin up to him and I oblige, thinking of no reason not to. His other hand snakes down my arm, making a fiery journey to my waist as he pulls me flush against his body. I welcome it like a moth to a flame.

This man is going to ruin me, and I don't care.

His lips crash into mine. And it's like I have not truly taken a breath until this moment. He is the air in my lungs and the blood in my veins. The fire within me combusts, consuming our bodies, tearing down the wall, and burning every wrongful deed between us away until I am him, and he is me. There is no Maya without Sebastian. The tether interlocks our hearts, our minds, our very souls.

He pulls me into his arms, and I jump, wrapping my legs around his torso, greedily deepening the kiss, never wanting to let go. The growl returns as his hands find the bare skin on my legs. Desire floods my system. He tastes like the hottest fire and the sweetest dessert, as flames dance between our joined lips. I thread my fingers through his long hair as he presses me against the wall. I can't get close enough. My heart leaps, knowing there is one way we could get closer, and I wouldn't say no. I don't think I *can* say no.

He seems to read my mind as he fumbles for the doorknob behind me. I feel the corners of his lips lift against mine. Oh. How I wish I could see that smile. He manages to get the door open, and we fall through the opening. I giggle as he trips over his feet and we crash to the floor. He turns so he doesn't crush me, and I land on top of him, all without breaking the kiss. Moonlight streams through the window of the room, and I pull back to see him better. His eyes are as blue as the brightest sky and full of heated desire.

"You are the most beautiful creature," he says, caressing my cheek.

I smile back and touch his lips.

"What? You're not done with me?" The deep timber of his voice vibrates under my fingertips.

I shake my head, my heart beating irregularly as I pull on the bottom of his shirt. His smirk lifts as he pulls it over his head in one swoop. His hand roams down my leg, tightening on the inside of my knee. He pulls it up and hooks it on his hip, my shirt lifting slightly with the motion.

I gasp but there is no embarrassment or shyness between us. Why not take this to the next level? We are one now, bonded for life.

My hands slide over the smooth planes of his chest as he pulls me back to his lips. This kiss is soft and slow, a promise for more to come. He rolls us over until he's hovering over my body, one hand splayed on my thigh.

The light brightens overhead. I whimper as Sebastian's heat disappears and cold air slams into me. An invisible force pulls me up, and I land in another's arms.

To my horror, and greatest embarrassment, I look into William's hardened face. He's looking menacingly at Sebastian.

"How dare you." His voice is dangerously calm, an intense contrast with his rigid posture and pure rage twisting his features.

Without a glance at me, he shoves me behind him and slams Sebastian into the far wall with a hard gust of air. A crack crawls up the wall behind him at the force.

"You broke every bloody rule. You know what would happen," William says, stalking toward a surprised Sebastian pressed against the wall.

William's fist slams into his jaw, and Sebastian's head snaps back. He spits blood on the floor but does nothing to fight back. William wraps his hands around his throat. When Sebastian's face starts to turn purple, and choking sounds reach me, I finally break from my shocked state.

"William! No!"

I throw myself on William's back, grabbing and scratching his arms and wrists, trying to pry them off Sebastian, but he pays me no attention. His lethal stare is only on Sebastian as his eyes roll to the back of his head.

"You're going to kill him! Stop!"

I move to stand in front of him, but his eyes don't see me. So I slap him across his face as hard as I can.

He blinks back in surprise, his eyes finally moving to mine. I twist back to Sebastian, who, released from William's grip, falls to the ground into an unconscious heap.

I throw myself on him. "Wake up, wake up. It's okay." I press my ear to his chest. His heart is beating strong, thank goodness. I push the hair off his face and stroke his jaw.

"What's wrong with you?" I snap at William.

He's looking between us, one hand on his cheek. His eyebrows pull down in puzzlement. That's when I remember that I still have no pants on. I tug my shirt down slightly to cover myself. He closes his eyes, and a blanket lifts from the bed of the otherwise empty room and drifts towards me. I grab it and drape it over my legs.

"You can open your eyes now. Not like you haven't seen my legs before," I say irritably. He's seen me in a bathing suit, for crying out loud, but still, embarrassment reddens my cheeks for how he saw me and Sebastian twined together moments earlier.

"I don't understand." The puzzlement turns into hurt as he opens his eyes.

"What's not to understand? He's my mate, William," I snap a little too harshly. Of course, he doesn't understand. I don't even understand. But I do feel more…whole, like the rubber band tethering us has finally snapped into place. I was fighting against nothing this whole time. I place my hand on Sebastian's chest to make sure he's still breathing.

"He'll be fine," William whispers.

I look back at him but he's already walking away. His shoulders are slumped as he rounds the corner out into the hallway.

I look down at Sebastian, who looks like he's sleeping peacefully. His color has returned to normal. I stand and chase after William. "Wait!"

He stops but doesn't turn around.

"I don't know how to explain it, but you're right, you don't understand. The bond isn't something he or I can control. It was coming for the both of us, no matter how I once felt about it."

He turns, his eyes boring into mine. "So, you forgive him then? For all the awful things he did?" He steps toward me. "Or did you forget? Do you need reminding, Maya, that he's the one who *forced* this bond onto you?" He takes another step, thrusting a finger behind me. "Or that he tried to kill us!"

I flinch. "Stop."

He steps again until he's only inches from my face. His voice drops, the rage taking on a painful note. "I've been there for you, helping you get through the trauma he caused. He did this! Sex won't solve anything."

I flinch again. "We didn't—" I stop myself. I don't have to explain myself to him. He just doesn't understand. It's not something I can control.

He shakes his head in disgust and walks away. I watch him go until he closes his bedroom door behind him, not sure what to think or how to feel. The hatred I once felt about Sebastian…I just don't feel that way anymore. That trauma he's talking about. I know it's still in me, but it's like it's been shut away and locked up, when those doors were wide open before.

I return to Sebastian, who is starting to sit up. "Are you okay?"

He nods. "It would be nice to have my abilities right now. Especially when somebody is trying to kill me."

"He wouldn't have." I shake my head.

"Oh yes, he would have. But it's okay, I deserve it. And it helps me keep my promise." I raise my eyebrow and his lips quirk up. "I didn't hurt him, did I?"

Despite myself, my lips pull up. "You didn't." I help him up, and he eyes the blanket covering my bare legs.

"That's definitely for the better. It's hard enough to control myself around you."

He walks me back to my room and is careful not to touch me.

Before I go in, I turn to him. "You don't have to try so hard anymore."

He tilts his head.

"You know…to not touch me." I rise onto my toes and kiss his cheek with a feather-light touch. Then I curl my hands into the blanket to resist doing anything more.

I shut the door on him with a smile, letting the blanket drop.

When I look up, Abby sits in bed, her curly bob askew.

"Where are your pants?"

I bite my lip, trying not to smile.

"William?" She gawks.

"What? No. Of course not."

Confusion washes over her face before her eyebrows shoot into her hairline. "No. No. No. Tell me you didn't."

"I didn't!"

Would I have if William hadn't caught us? A shiver runs through me, not quite sure if I'm okay with the fact that I wouldn't have thought twice about taking that next step with Sebastian. This bond is insanely powerful. It's like it wants us to jump each other and make us one in every way possible. If that didn't prove my theory about the tether, I don't know what will. I have a terrible feeling that I will continue to feel like this until we finally seal the bond.

I swallow hard as guilt creeps in. I feel bad for fighting with William, but he was definitely in the wrong. At the end of the day,

Sebastian is my mate, and whatever happens between us is for us to decide, not him.

"Well, what was that fight about then? I'm pretty sure you woke up the whole household. But I only caught the last half. And why are you in your underwear?"

"Give me some pants first," I tell her irritably.

So nosy.

28

Original Monster

I sit at the breakfast table, avoiding everyone's heavy glances in my direction. Well, everyone except for William. He won't even look at me. Nobody has said a word. And I can't decide if it would be better just to say something or continue to ignore the fact that everyone heard Sebastian, William, and I last night.

Abby initially was mad at me when I told her I kissed Sebastian, but when I described the tether, she seemed to understand or pretended to. As we dressed, she asked me if I was still planning on severing the bond. I didn't have an answer for her then and still don't as I glance at Sebastian across the table. His face is down as he focuses on his food, but he's only taking small bites of the pancakes and sausage on his plate.

Ann sits next to him, devouring her plate and talking to Izalia. She's either clueless or couldn't care less. My eyes move to Izalia and my father. They obviously heard something last night from the looks they gave me when I walked in. William came into the dining room last, gave Sebastian a hostile look, and ignored the rest of us. I feel more guilty this morning…but not for kissing Sebastian, only that William saw. Not sure what that says about me. William's words are still pulling on me. I want to talk to him, but he was pretty clear last night about what he thought, and I don't want to open that can of worms again.

"Did you really have a pet monkey?" Ann asks.

I might have divulged a few details about the pictures in Izalia's room this morning as I shared the bathroom with Ann, hoping for this exact moment to happen. I still haven't told them about Thomas and how I know Izalia's story about coming from an isolated part of the world full of people who can control all the elements. From the pictures on her wall, I'm guessing she came from an island. I want to know more. And who better to bring it up than Ann—an innocent child who is certainly not trying to determine if this family can be trusted.

My grandmother smiles. "His name was Beau; he was my greatest companion."

"Do you miss him?"

"Very much so."

"How did you even have a monkey? Did you live in the jungle or something?"

My ears perk up, and even William comes out of his moping to give Izalia his full attention.

"I grew up on an island."

Yes! I was right.

Ann smiles wide. "Like Hawaii?"

She taps the table and glances at Michael. "Something like that."

"Do you miss it?"

She nods. "I do at times."

"Then why did you leave?"

She looks over the five of us, puts her fork down, and sits back in her chair.

"Ann, maybe she doesn't want to talk about it," Juliet tells her sister. Glancing at Izalia, she mouths, *Sorry.*

Ann wrinkles her brows at Juliet.

"Oh, she's fine. Only curious. I'm sure you all are as well."

Izalia shares another fleeting look with Michael. I wonder if she'll tell the same story Thomas shared with me. There has to be a reason nobody knows anything about her people.

"Where I grew up," Izalia continues, "they didn't welcome outsiders. And if you left, you couldn't return. I chose to leave because…it was the right thing to do." She sighs and grabs Michael's hand. "I chose to follow my heart in the end and have never regretted it."

I bite the inside of my cheek, keeping myself from looking at Sebastian. Am I following my heart if I remain bonded to him?

"Never? So, you've never tried to go back?"

"Ann," Juliet hisses.

"Once I tried. After I had Michael's father. I was quite young and missing my family. But I didn't make it far." She grows quiet and sips on her tea, looking above our heads, probably reliving the memory.

"What happened?" Ann asks, ignoring Izalia's inclination not to explain what I'm sure are traumatic memories at the breakfast table.

Juliet looks like she's about to have an aneurysm, but Izalia just laughs and shakes her head. At that moment, Sarah walks in to gather dishes, saving Juliet from shoving her napkin in Ann's mouth.

"These pancakes were divine," William tells her, and everyone else offers the same sentiments.

Ann slumps in her seat to eat the last pancake after what appears to be a silent chiding from Juliet.

Sarah's cheeks redden with a smile as she shuffles back into the kitchen with our plates. I stand with my dish and follow her. It looks like what Thomas told me about our family was the truth. And Izalia won't be revealing much more information about her background.

Now for my father. If I want the truth about him, maybe I could get it from Sarah.

"Oh! You don't have to do that," she says, swiping my plate and turning the sink on.

"I insist. It's the least I can do." I hover before my eyes lock on a dishwasher. I open it up. "I'll load."

She sighs and hands me the wet plate.

After loading a few I say. "So, you like working here?"

"Yeah, the Ali's are wonderful people."

"And what Michael does for work doesn't bother you?"

She stops washing the plate in her hand for a second but then resumes. "I don't know why it would."

"Or the fact that his son isn't in his life?"

She turns to me with a pointed look. "What are you getting at?"

I shrug and put another plate in the dishwasher. "I just want to know more about him."

"Then ask him, silly girl," she says with a laugh.

"I've barely met him. I don't know if I can even trust what he says."

"The Ali's have been good to me when nobody else was. I would never say a bad thing about them."

I slump against the counter and continue to load the dishwasher.

Once I finish, I return to the dining room, where my father is waiting for me. "Hey."

He pulls a wad of clothes from behind his back. "Is this yours? Sarah gave them to me this morning. She found it in the middle of the hall."

Heat floods my face. I could say no, but he'll know I'm lying. I bite my lip and hold out my hand.

"I know I've only been your father for a day, but you can talk to me," he says, putting the clothes in my hand. "Noni told me you're bonded to that boy, Sebastian. I've never been bonded myself, but I have heard…things are amplified. I'm not sure how much your mother has explained to you about men, but I know quite a bit if you have questions." His expression takes on a playful edge, and I want to crawl in a hole and die.

"Oh. No. I'm okay. You know I'm eighteen, not twelve? I've had 'the talk' and all that." I fidget with the clothes, wanting to turn and run straight out the door. At least the dining room is deserted now.

He nods awkwardly. "That's good. Sorry. I've never had a daughter before. Not sure what I'm supposed to be—"

"What about Thomas?" I interrupt him. "He's your son, and he's bonded, with children. Have you met them?" I didn't mean to just throw that out there, but I might as well take the window while I have it.

He blanches, obviously not ready for a question like that. Good, maybe he'll tell me the truth.

He shakes his head slowly. "I did not know that."

I shift on my feet. "Thomas said you abandoned him."

"That's what he said?" He looks genuinely shocked as he slides a hand over his mouth and down his neck. "I didn't abandon him. His mother left me. Took my son and *left*." His voice rises with emotion, but he swallows. When he speaks again, it's softer. "But it makes sense she told him a different story, so I'd be the bad guy." He sits on a chair, folding in on himself slightly. "I was always the bad guy to her." He looks at me, his eyes full of regret that's clearly been slowly tearing him apart. "Tell me. Do I look like a bad guy?"

I study his expertly styled dark hair with a thin line of gray running through it and trimmed mustache, the rose coloring in his cheeks, and his bright-green eyes. He's so familiar, yet not somebody I genuinely know or understand.

"I don't know you."

"Fair." He leans forward and pulls a chair out. "Sit. I said I would tell you about my work."

I go to sit but stop. "Can I get my friends?" They need to be here for this.

He throws his palms in the air and smiles. "The more the merrier."

We all settle into the living room. Even Ann—with everything she did and saw, while still believing Michael to be a good guy—deserves to know the truth.

Michael wraps his hands around a mug in his lap as he begins. "First of all. I help Elementals. I do this job. The good and the ugly of it, for our kind." He looks at me. "Like your mother, I am also a scientist. That's, in part, how she first found me. I was in Portland for a dissertation." He rubs the rim of the mug in his hands. "I'm not proud of the work I was doing back then. But it ultimately got me to where I am today."

"And what were you doing then?" I ask warily, not sure if I want to know the details.

He sighs. "I was a part of a team trying to bring our abilities to those who didn't have them. We did tests on Coms, who volunteered. But most of them ended badly." He blanches before taking a steadying breath. "But one." He looks me in the eyes and something settles into my gut. "It worked! We were all thrilled. We transformed a Com into one of us. But we realized his abilities were not of our kind. They were a twisted version of ours. I see now, that was an inward representation for what this man was on the outside. At first he was somebody everyone liked, charismatic and charming. Easy to talk to. He fooled me." He leans back, taking a sip from his mug, as if biding time before saying the next part.

"This man became power-hungry. He managed to wiggle himself up into a position of control and revealed his true plans. Elementals are what gave him his abilities, but he insisted these powers needed to be abolished—that they were too dangerous. But what he really wanted was to be the only one of his kind. He got friends to turn on me and the other Elemental scientists. By the time I finally got out, I had already lost my companion and child to that job. She thought I was horrible for being in on those experiments, so she took my three-year-old boy and left."

Everyone in the room looks at me with widening eyes at the mention of my brother, probably wondering why I don't ask about him. I suck in my lips and keep my eyes trained on Michael. He doesn't notice the shift in the room as he continues his story.

"That's when I went to Portland, and your mother asked me to help give her and your father a child. I couldn't say no. That was the darkest time of my life. And after what I did, bringing a monster into this world, I thought it could be my redemption. I stupidly agreed to everything she wanted and signed away all my rights…another mistake." He looks at me meaningfully.

"Well, skip forward to when the war began. I didn't know how it started, but I knew. I *knew* it had to be that power-hungry bastard who wanted to wipe out our kind. And I was correct. He's the one commanding all Com extremists. I learned he continued experimenting on himself, strengthening his abilities, and obliterating any empathetic cell in his mind. He wanted to create more of himself now, build an army, to wipe out all of us. But he must have had difficulty replicating what was done to him, because he moved on to testing on Elementals, changing them into…monsters."

Out of my periphery, I catch William sharing a look with Abby. It's like what Sal was telling us about Rogues. They must be thinking the same thing. It's true. A shiver runs down my spine, and I look back at Michael.

"An old friend from that original team came to me shortly after and begged me to help him. So, I did. And I've been in San Francisco ever since. Yes, technically I am working for the Com extremists. They even gave me this house to butter me up. But I only rehabilitate those affected by the experiments, Coms and Elementals alike."

My mind goes to that man whose room I entered when trying to find William and Ann. His thrashing and dead eyes…was he a Rogue that Michael was trying to rehabilitate?

"You help them," Ann says softly.

His lips lift slightly. "I try."

"After you let them get tortured," Sebastian says, his voice hard as stone.

I look at him and want to reach out and grab his hand. He has gone through all these horrible things. I can only imagine how this sounds to him. But at least he's not one of those…things.

Michael's eyes fill with sympathy. "I won't pretend to understand what you went through. It's an abomination. But it will continue to happen with or without me. If I weren't here, those people would die…or worse."

"What could possibly be worse than death?" Abby asks.

He looks at her, his face forming into a mask of hardened pain, probably formed from years of experience in this field. "There are many things worse than death."

I again remember the patient I walked in on that day and cringe inwardly. But there are also flashes of somebody else getting tortured, over and over again. Screaming in agony. I blink and the images are gone.

"The only thing that keeps me going back day after day is knowing what could happen to those people if I'm not there."

"Why don't you do anything to stop it then?" Sebastian growls.

Michael blinks at him. "I wish I could. I feel at fault for all of this. If I hadn't helped create that monster, none of this would have happened." He looks at me, hopelessness shining in his eyes. "Now do you understand why your brother wants nothing to do with me? And I…I'll understand if you don't either."

The room is silent. Everyone waits for my response. My heart beats irregularly. I've wanted my father back for so long, and it happened in a way. Do I hold the past against Michael like I held it against myself for so long? Blaming myself for my dad's death. Like I held the past against Sebastian?

I take in a deep breath. "We all make mistakes. The past doesn't matter." I glance at Sebastian whose eyes widen. "It's what we do moving forward." I look back to my father. "And you're in a position to help end this war."

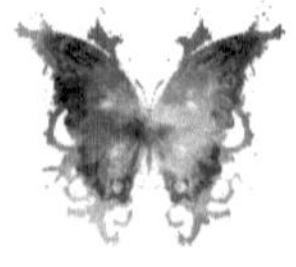

Izalia envelops me in her warm embrace. She has a sweet, floral scent. "Thank you," she murmurs.

I look up at her.

Her thin eyebrows turn down. "He needed this. He needed you."

"I'm glad to have met him and you. I can't wait to hear more of your stories."

She smiles, kisses my cheek, and squeezes my arm one last time before nudging me toward Michael.

"Do you think there is a chance my mom is…?" I start but can't say it out loud—that she's gone.

"No." He shakes his head furiously. "No. I will find her. And when I do, it'll be time to make up for the mistakes of the past." He pulls me in for a brief hug, and I realize this will be the last time I can tell him about Thomas.

Before I pull back, I whisper, "Thomas and his family are in Santa Rosa, New Mexico. I think he'd want to hear your side of the story."

His face is full of apprehension, but I give him an encouraging smile before stepping down the stairs.

My friends saved the front seat of the car for me. I settle in and watch Michael and Izalia—my family—waving as we drive away.

"Home?" William asks, briefly looking at me.

I nod, feeling the tension between us but trying not to let it get to me as I hold on to my dad's promise to find my mom. "Let's go home."

29

Home

I swallow hard when I spot Wixx waiting for us on the front porch of the manor, her arms folded, body posture as stiff as a pole, her face a blank mask.

We're halfway through the vineyard. I grapple with focusing on my Sage to calm the anxiety that's made me pick off the rest of my motel nail polish. I fixate on the green trees, breathing the fresh air straight from the source. Oh, how I missed them. The rising peaks around us add to my declining nerves. They're like a great wall, keeping out all the terrible things of the world.

During the couple-hour drive back from Portland, I told my friends to put the blame on me—tell Wixx that I forced them to go—but they refused. I can still try, but they'll outnumber me if they stick together. I just hate to pull them down with me. I've already put them through enough.

My worries lighten when a brown, moppy-haired boy pushes around Wixx and launches himself off the porch. Wixx steps to grab him but misses. Just as I make it beyond the garden, he slams into me. I pull him into my arms. A peculiar black-and-white striped butterfly lands on top of his head briefly before he flings his head back and it flies away into the rows of trees behind us.

"Did you get taller?" I say with a chuckle, looking back at the butterfly. That was weird.

His eyes light up. "Did I? I've been practicing everything you taught me, wanna see?" A silhouette of a ball of water forms above his hands as he tosses it between them, a wide smile forming on his lips. He then splits the ball of water in two, delight radiating from his being.

I smile. "So good! I want to see more, but first I need to talk to Wixx." I eye her nervously as she continues to stare at us from the porch.

He drops the water and it splashes both our feet. He looks back at her and rolls his eyes. "She's just pretending to be mad. She's glad you're back. Did you find Mom?"

A rock settles into my throat, and when his gaze drops, I know he can see it on my face. "I have somebody I trust looking for her, and I have reason to believe that he'll find her. It's just a matter of time."

Abby ruffles his hair. "Did you hold down the fort for us?"

He doesn't respond. His gaze travels to Ann, walking beside Juliet. His blue eyes widen and then narrow. *"No fair."*

Ann sticks her tongue at him, and he pales.

Juliet nudges her. "She snuck out."

"Without me?" He glares at her, and Ann has enough brains to look at least a little guilty as she stares at her feet.

"Come on." I grab his hand and make him face forward as I march to my doom. No matter how Wixx feels about us returning, I still left after she said no, and there's no way we're getting out of this unscathed. But knowing that Cal is still here at least gives me some hope. She didn't banish him and our families.

She starts for us. My steps slow, but hers don't. I hold my breath as she stops directly in front of me. She grabs my shoulders and pulls me in for a hug.

I stiffen. I don't think she's ever hugged me. Her warmth seeps into me. The scent of lavender stings my nose. She must use handfuls of it in her shampoo.

When Wixx pulls back, she looks me up and down, and then studies the rest of us. Her face is still unreadable. I don't know if she's about to cry with happiness or push us to the ground in anger.

"You all okay?"

We nod in unison.

She steps back. "You're all adults and you can make your own decisions. I'm not one for holding anyone hostage. But if you ever pull that kind of crap again. You will not be welcomed back. If you want to be here, you *will* follow my orders. If not, you are welcome to leave." She stares hard at each of us and waits until we all verbally tell her we understand.

She flings an arm around my waist. "Okay, well, let's hear what you guys found."

I finally release the breath I've been holding for the three weeks we were gone.

We're home.

I don't even know where to start with all the different people we found. Sebastian is beyond the border, waiting for us to get him, once we explain his presence. If only to prevent somebody from killing him on sight. I don't think anyone has forgiven him for burning down the manor and being the cause of so many deaths when the Coms found us and war broke out.

Once settled in her office, we start at the beginning and tell her everything about James and his people, about finding Thomas and Claire—leaving out the long-lost brother tidbit—and discovering my father. I skip over finding Sebastian, too, leaving that for the end. She has many questions about my father's role, and I can only answer some of them—the whole while kicking myself for not asking him more. In the end, she agrees that he will be a great asset.

"And we found somebody else," I say a bit hesitantly. Wixx has taken everything else with such grace. Will this finally push her over the edge and make her throw us all out of here?

She blinks. "Oh?"

"Before we went to Portland, we stopped in San Francisco and found—"

My words are left dangling in the air as a group of legionaries storms into the room, holding a bloodied man in their arms.

"Sorry to interrupt but look who we found just outside the barrier."

Wixx gasps before I can understand who they're holding. But then he manages to lift his head, his blue eyes finding mine. That's when I start to scream.

30

Forgive and Forget

Chaos erupts as I throw myself at the three legionaries, unleashing my fire.

The legionaries yelp in unison and drop Sebastian as flames envelop him. I grab his shoulders to steady him, but his weight is too much for me, and he falls. Something hits me in the side, and pain radiates down my hip. I cry out, reawakening Sebastian, whose eyes had shut.

He forms my name on his split lips as he reaches out to me. I palm his swollen and bloodied face with one hand, and fling the other towards the person who hurt me. Water surrounds them, and they collapse onto the floor, their face disfigured as they choke.

A surge of light comes from my left, and I throw my body over Sebastian's, releasing the water from my hold. Air rushes past us, and I peer up at William standing over me, protecting us from the legion members, all on their feet, stalking my way.

Juliet and Abby position themselves at my side. Three of them against four and a half of us. It looks like we have the better odds. I grind my teeth together, pulling my flame up.

That's when I remember Cal and Ann are in the room. I look for them, but they're not visible. Instead, I spot Wixx, who has thrown her hands out toward both groups, her black hair wild around her face, which is sketched with pure rage.

"Stop it!" she yells as she positions herself in the middle. "Stand down, legionaries."

The legion men lower their hands at the order, but we stay ready.

"This is not how we do things. You should be ashamed of yourselves."

The men gawk.

"Do you not know who that is?" a man with cropped brown hair says. His voice comes out rough, and he clears his throat, which doesn't do much. I'm pretty sure he's the one I tried to drown. "He's the reason our friends and family are dead or taken hostage," he hisses.

The two next to him breathe hard, nodding in agreement.

"This is not the way. He will answer for his crimes. You don't take it upon yourselves to deal out punishments." She shakes her head in disappointment.

The other two hang their heads, but the brunette glares at Sebastian, who has passed out again. I hold him tighter against me.

"Out. Now," Wixx orders.

The men file out.

The one who spoke lingers and catches my eye. "You're pathetic."

I see red and lift my hand to douse him in flames, but somebody beats me to it. A thick wall of water hits the legionary in the chest, and he sprawls out into the hallway.

"I said out," Wixx growls and slams the door closed. She turns to us, looking down at Sebastian. "Is he alive?" She doesn't say it with much emotion, making me realize that what she just did was for me and not for the man lying bloodied and unconscious in my lap.

My hand is on his chest as his heartbeat reverberates through my body, ensuring it doesn't stop. I nod.

She cocks her head. "You were indeed busy these last few weeks."

I open my mouth to speak, but Wixx waves her hand. "I'm sure you have quite the explanation, but let's get him down to the medic wing for now, and then you can tell me all about it."

William takes most of Sebastian's weight, and we head down the two flights of stairs and lay him on a bed. Sebastian doesn't even twitch at the movement. My stomach tightens as I pull a chair next to him and grab his hand. I feel for the pull between us, and it's still there, thankfully, woven tight as ever.

Dr. Rye works quickly, cutting Sebastian's clothes off his bloodied body. My rage flares when I see the whole of him, gashes and discolorations covering every square inch of him. They beat him so viciously. I wince when the doctor resets his arm, which was positioned awkwardly, and offer my fire to help heal the places he instructs. I'm a little surprised when it works, never having used it to heal before. His face slowly becomes more recognizable as my flames recede, leaving purplish-black bruises. The doctor works on his ribs. Pure, hot flames inside me search for something to devour at every sound of bone popping back into place.

Once the doctor finishes putting him back together, he leaves us and tells me to get some rest. Thankfully, Sebastian is still out of it. My friends have long since left, needing to tell their families of their return.

It's just me and my mate, his hand warm under my touch when a chair scrapes next to mine.

"You still love him," Wixx says, sitting beside me. It's not a question.

"He's my mate," I murmur, not taking my eyes off him, the rising of his smooth, marbled chest.

"Yes. The bond is strong between you two."

"It's not just that," I say, irritation rising in my tone. I quickly dampen it. She doesn't know that that's what everyone keeps accusing me of. *It's just the bond. You don't actually feel anything for him.*

"Would you like to finish what you started in my office now?"

I finally look at her. Her face is open, not angry. She's not looking at him hostilely like everyone else, just patiently waiting for me to explain.

I nod and launch into the story of finding Sebastian, grasping onto the task like a lifeline, anything to take my mind off Sebastian and the horrible sounds that came from his body moments prior. It was all too familiar, as if I'd somehow witnessed it before. But that can't be possible. I've never seen him endure such torture.

"If I remember right, you threatened me quite a bit," Sebastian croaks.

I had just told Wixx about learning about Sebastian's memory loss and my fighting against the bond. I stop and turn toward him. He flashes me one of his perfect smiles and my heart soars. I jump up and put a hand to his face. His smile widens as he grabs it and kisses it tenderly, striking my fire.

"How do you feel?"

"Like I got jumped by three full-grown men who thought I stole their girlfriends." He smirks, but I don't smile.

"What?" His eyebrows come together, wiping away the smile.

"You did a lot worse than that to them."

He frowns, remembering. "Right."

"He really doesn't remember," Wixx says, tapping her chin.

Sebastian looks at her and then back at me. "Who's this?"

Before I can tell him, Wixx stands. "I'm Commander Wixx. The one who decides your future."

His eyes widen slightly, but he nods in understanding.

Sebastian helps me tell the rest of his story, telling her about the prison he was in and the things they did to him. He glosses over the torture and testing bit. In any case, I'm left with an increasingly sickening feeling.

"I will let you know my decision," she says. Then she walks off, glancing back and gesturing for me to join her.

I squeeze Sebastian's hand. "I'll be right back."

Wixx closes the door behind me when I enter the hallway. "Nobody is going to be happy he's back. What those legionaries did to him is just the beginning. I don't think him being here is very wise."

I straighten. "If he leaves, I leave."

"I thought you might say that, and I don't want you to have to leave your home because of who your mate is."

She pulls a hand down her face and leans against the wall, looking more worn than I've ever seen her. She has bags under her eyes, and her hair is pulled into a tight bun, deepening the lines on her dark face.

"He'll always need to be watched. He has to earn back the people's trust, if that's even possible." She sighs. "And I'll have to work him *hard*."

I throw my arms around her. "Thank you, Wixx!"

She shakes her head and pushes me gently back. "There used to be a holding in the Legion Headquarters, which I'm sure you remember."

I wince. James was briefly held there as I was forced to go through with the bonding ceremony with Sebastian.

"Now that that's gone, we'll have to put him in the basement. He'll be watched around the clock."

I shift on my feet. Put him back in a prison? He won't like that, but he has no choice if he wants to stay. "For how long?"

"Until I can get everyone on board about this."

"So…forever?"

She shrugs. "He'll sleep in the basement with a guard at night, and during the day he has to work."

"Okay." I roll my shoulders, readying myself to give him the good and bad news. "Whatever he has to do, I'm sure he'll do it."

She looks at me again. "You sure about him?"

I ignore that slight flutter in my stomach that isn't sure and nod.

She places a hand on my shoulder, her blue eyes scanning mine. "Give the word, and he'll be gone."

"He's not that man anymore."

And with that, I return to my mate and tell him the news, ignoring the little nudge in my heart, telling me that that man could still be in there.

The following week passes quickly, only being able to see Sebastian at our allotted times after each meal. He tells me everything is going fine, but one day, I notice a limp in his walk, and the next day, he's rubbing a spot on his side. His black eye is the last straw, though.

"This is not okay," I say, placing an icepack on his eye despite his arguing.

We sit next to the lake, enjoying one of the last sunny days before fall officially sets in with its constant rain. Then Sebastian won't want anything to do with spending our days outside.

He pulls at my waist until I'm sitting in his lap. "It's worth it because I can do this." He brushes my hair to the side, pressing his lips to my neck.

My spark reacts, and I instantly have to control my breathing. My body's reaction to him is getting harder and harder to control. I thought it would be easier now, but nope, the tether that binds us makes me never feel close enough to him.

"No...they shouldn't... I..."

He hums against my neck, placing another kiss lower on my collarbone. I bite my lip, instantly forgetting what I was about to say. With a thump, the ice pack falls to the ground.

"I love your skin," he murmurs.

His kisses make their way up my chin as he threads a hand through my hair and turns me to face him. My legs come around him when he finds my lips. The fire in my veins ignites, and I pull him closer to deepen the kiss. His tongue teases my lower lip, and my spine tingles at the touch. I part my lips, returning the gesture. He pulls back, flames dancing in his eyes.

"You can't do that," he pants. "Not while we're in public. People may not like what they see if I lose control with you." His grip tightens around my waist, and my heart flips upside down.

I know he's not talking about losing control of his fire, since he still doesn't have his powers fully back, but losing control of something else.

Warmth crawls up my neck at what he's suggesting. I climb off of him, pick up the ice pack, and place it back on his face. He winces.

"You distracted me," I say with a glare.

He smiles wickedly. "I'm fine."

"You need to tell Wixx who's doing this."

He shrugs again. "I can handle it." He looks past the water and says softer. "I deserve it."

I grab his chin and force him to look at me. "No, you don't. You have to forgive yourself. The guilt will eat at you until…" I take a deep breath. "Remember when I told you about my dad?" Usually when we're not kissing, I've been trying to fill the holes in his memory. Telling him about me, which means me having to be vulnerable with him all over again. "What I didn't tell you is that I believed for a long time it was my fault. That I killed him." I swallow. "But I didn't. I know that now."

He looks at me sadly, caressing his fingertips down my cheek. "I'm sorry."

"I don't want this to hold you down for the rest of your life. You have to forgive yourself."

"I'll try. For you, I'll try." He leans in and plants a kiss on my cheek. "Time to go."

"Ugh. Already?"

He hops to his feet and pulls me up into his arms. "I'll do whatever I have to do to stay here with you."

I wrap my arms around his warm body, breathing in his spicy aroma. "That doesn't mean letting those ogres walk all over you."

He kisses me one final time before walking away, hands in his pockets, head held high.

I'm grateful he can't remember what he did. He's having a hard enough time forgiving himself for something he doesn't remember. If he did remember, I can't imagine the pain of those memories.

I shudder and turn back to the manor but spot something moving on a nearby rock—a black and white butterfly. Its wings flap lazily as it sits there.

I step toward it carefully and kneel. When I reach for it, it flies onto my finger. I smile as it tickles me. "I've seen you many times this week. Are you following me?"

"Maya!"

William jogs up to me, and the butterfly flies away. We still have yet to talk about that night, neither of us wanting to apologize first. With William being the sun he is, I knew he'd break soon.

"Hey," I start.

He shoves his hands in his pockets and rocks back on his heels. "I've been meaning to talk to you."

We both talk at the same time. He says, "Can I come get my stuff from your room?" as I say, "I'm not mad anymore."

"What?" I respond as he says, "You're mad at me? Are you kidding me?"

"I thought you came to apologize," I say quickly.

"I'm not sorry for protecting you, Maya."

"But you *weren't* protecting me. I kissed him, and then you tried to kill him for it!"

His lips pinch. "Can I come get my stuff or what?"

"No."

"What?"

"No." I almost want to stomp my foot like a child. Instead, I say, "No. Not until you apologize," which isn't much better.

He throws his hands in the air and turns around. "I'm not apologizing! Fine. Keep my bloody clothes."

"Hey!" I grab his shoulder. "You don't feel bad for trying to kill my mate?"

"Nope."

My mouth falls open. He shrugs and turns back around. My rage flares for a moment, then sputters out. I don't want this between us anymore.

"William, please talk to me."

He stops walking. I guess I will have to apologize first.

"I'm sorry you saw us like that, and I don't blame you for your reaction."

He turns slowly and looks at me with a frown pulling on his lips. "I just don't understand it, Maya."

I put my hand up before he starts spouting out all the awful things Sebastian did. "I know. And you may never understand. But it's my choice. I don't want to lose you. You're my best friend," I choke.

His eyes soften as he studies me. "He hasn't hurt you?"

I give him a look. "I wouldn't be with him if he was still like that."

"He fooled you once."

I step back, hurt. That was a strike to my character. But I breathe through the flash of anger. He's right.

"He promised me that he would never hurt anyone again. And he's kept it. You know those guys that jumped him? He didn't lay a hand on them. Didn't defend himself at all, just to keep his promise to me."

His eyes widen, looking impressed. "Okay."

He holds his hand out toward me. I grab it, missing his warmth. He rubs his thumb over the back of my hand, and I smile.

He pulls me in for a hug and murmurs against my hair. "I'm not happy with it. But looks like I have to deal with it."

I pull back. "I hope one day you can do more than just deal with it. It would be nice to see you two friends again."

He smirks. "You forget. I'm not the one bonded with the bloke. And that would be really weird if I was."

I giggle, glad to have my William back.

His face turns serious. "Don't get mad at me. But I believe the bond helped you forgive him so quickly. That doesn't mean I can do the same. I don't know if I can return to what we had before."

"But—"

"Hey. If you're allowed to feel how you feel, I'm allowed to feel how I feel."

"I'm not happy with it, but I have to deal with it?" I ask with a wry smile.

"Yup." He leads me into the manor with one arm draped over my shoulders. "Now I would really like my stuff back. I haven't brushed my teeth in a week."

I push him off of me. "Ew."

He chuckles and dangles his tongue out, coming closer like he's going to lick my face. I dodge him and run ahead as he chases me up the stairs. He catches me right when I reach my hall, grabbing my waist and pulling me into a bear hug.

"Breathe it in, Maya," he says, his mouth open wide, heavily breathing over my face.

"Gross! Stop!" I shriek, wriggling out from his arms, but stop short at the sight of Sebastian leaning against the wall beside my door. His eyes are on William, a cold mask on his face. I hold my smile, but William drops his, straightening.

"I'll see you later, Maya," he says stiffly.

"William, you need to get your stuff, remember?"

He hesitates. "Right."

I approach Sebastian, trying to ignore the tension radiating off the two men. "I thought you had work?"

He takes his eyes off William, and his face softens the tiniest. "I do. But I got some good news and wanted to tell you."

I grab his hand. "And?"

He glances at William and then back at me. "I don't have to sleep in the dungeon anymore."

"That's amazing!" I say, throwing my arms around his neck.

He hugs me back and quickly releases me, his eyes on William before peering down at me with a smile. Such different emotions raging war on his face. "I'll see you tonight, then?"

"Uh. Yeah, sure."

He gives me a quick peck on the lips and steps around William, not even acknowledging him.

I look at William. His face is similar to Sebastian's—a battle of anger and rage, and coolness and calm fighting to take hold. I shake my head and open my door. "Come on."

"Yes, I would love to come into your room, Maya, and get my things from the times I slept with you—" his voice grows louder and louder until he's not talking to me but yelling down the hall to Sebastian, "helping to calm you from the *constant nightmares she had after you destroyed her*!"

"On the couch! He slept on the couch," I yell over his shoulder as he moves into my room and closes the door behind me with a smirk.

"Seriously?"

"What?" he says innocently.

I hit his shoulder.

"He should know. He's your *mate* and all."

"Yeah, whatever. Get your things."

"Come on, you can't be mad at me," he chirps, flashing one of his adorable boyish smiles.

I roll my eyes and sit on the couch, waving my hand to the room as if to say. *Get your stuff and get out.*

It doesn't diminish my hope, though. They can be friends again, even if it's far, far in the future.

Blissful Nothingness

I wake up screaming.

My dreams are again full of James. No matter what I do, I can't get him out of my head. How can I still have this same dream? It doesn't make sense. Things are good with Sebastian, okay with William, and James…I'll never fix things there. He'll forever be the guy that got away. It's not like he was mine for very long. It shouldn't matter. Ugh. Sebastian is my mate, and I'm happy.

I am happy.

I keep telling myself that as I pull myself out of bed and head for the lake. It's the only thing that can clear my mind without William sleeping in my room. I would be crazy to ask that of him now, but it's still a tempting thought.

It's become my nightly occurrence, a middle-of-the-night swim. I dive into the water, letting the brisk water consume me and wash away the confusing emotions rattling through me. I swim and swim and swim until I'm out of breath. Then I pull myself onto shore and flip onto my back to stare at the stars, letting the cool night air dry me off. Now that my thoughts are clear, I think about my conversation with Sebastian before bed.

He came to my room. I know he wanted me to invite him to stay, but I couldn't build up the nerve to ask yet, so I let him go. I don't even know where he's sleeping. I should have told him he could stay. It would make things that much more real—to sleep with him. Even if we just *sleep*, I can't imagine how things won't get heated in the same bed, though.

But even then, it would be like we really *are* mated partners, waking up with one another. And if something were to happen…to consummate the bond… I don't know the technicalities of breaking the bond, but I doubt having it sealed will help.

No. I cannot sleep with him without being 100 percent sure I don't want to break the bond anymore.

The dream has brought up all these emotions I thought I moved on from, but no—James is still there, holding on to a piece of my heart.

I watch the stars blink at me, the full moon shining down, tiny bats flying through its rays. For once, I let myself think of him. How I could be swallowed whole in those dark hazel eyes, how the forest brought out a different side of him—a more tender side, how he touched me and made me feel a thousand different things, and how I always felt so safe and secure in his arms.

Oh, James. I still love him. That's why I can't give myself entirely to Sebastian. I slap my hands over my face.

"He doesn't care!" I shout into the night.

I grab my chest like I can force my heart to stop pounding for him. I sit up, wrap my arms around my knees, and watch the lake, like it can give me the answers I seek. The moon's reflection in the water steadies me, slowing my racing pulse. I focus on my

Sage and empty my thoughts, listening to the wind through the branches and the tiny sounds of night creatures.

That's when I feel a pull on the bond. It's getting closer. I turn around as a silhouette steps out of the shadows. I know it's him before I can fully make out his features.

Sebastian strolls up to me like it's midday, and he just happened to find me out here.

"I was wondering where you came every night." His voice is smooth, seeping into my very pores.

I cock my head at him.

"I can feel you. I could feel you pulling from a different direction, and this is the first night I could follow it."

"Did it wake you?"

He shrugs. "Can't sleep anyway."

I stand as he moves closer. His eyes are dark and fathomless in the moonlight, reflecting the rippling waters. He's looking at me differently.

"Sorry, I'm all wet." Nerves scatter my thoughts as his eyes drag over my body.

"I don't mind." His voice is almost hoarse as he draws me in.

His hands travel around my bare waist, and I stifle a gasp. Fire lurches into my very core. With only my thin bikini between us, everything feels...different. *More.* More heat. More desire. More him. Maybe if we did bind ourselves that way, I would finally stop caring. Let that love for James finally slip away.

His thumb rubs over a tender spot beneath my ribcage, and his voice comes out rough with emotion. "You were shot back when you saved me from the prison. Is this from that?"

I nod—or I think I do—his warm hands on my stomach muddle my brain and do weird things to my insides. Then he does something that will surely unravel me. He bends down and places a tender kiss on the scar.

Electricity courses through me at the touch and I'm done for. I'm gone. My feet are no longer on this earth. I have no idea how I get the next words out.

"And here." I tap a spot on my shoulder where the other bullet pierced me.

His eyes are full of heat as he kisses that spot too.

"Can you walk me to my room?" I ask, in an almost tortured gasp, before he fully pulls back. I need his lips back on me, and it can't be here, outside for all to see.

His eyes glow brighter as he studies me, then nods. I slide the thin T-shirt dress I had set on a rock over my head before taking his hand. It does little to dampen the invisible flames leaping between us.

We walk slowly, each footstep measured as I try to remember to breathe. He doesn't rush me as he keeps our pace. The wind blows over the long grass, raising goosebumps on my arms. I push the water droplets off my body as I harness my flame, warming my skin and shirt where the water soaked through.

We climb my back steps, and I open my door. He stops just before the threshold, my hand still in his. I turn. The tether is almost tangible now as it twines around us, nearly too unbearable to resist, but still he waits.

"Are you sure?" he asks.

I smile and tug him toward me. He trails his fingers up my arms, orange and red flames alight on my skin. We smile as he continues the fiery journey along my visible skin, until I'm entirely on fire. The flames ripple toward him, aching for his touch. They grasp for the edges of his smooth jaw, the slope of his nose, his high cheekbones, and dance around his eyelashes. He wraps a hand around my jaw, his fingers skimming my hair, and pulls me close to him.

He kisses me tenderly as my flames wrap around him and try to consume him whole. He sighs in my mouth, and I pull him closer.

"It's been so long," he murmurs against my lips.

I pull back with a tilt of my head.

"Since I've been on fire," he explains.

I giggle, and he silences it with another kiss. He strokes my hair and my back as I fumble for his shirt. He soon realizes what I'm doing and pulls back to look at me. He briefly studies my face before removing his shirt with one fluid motion. My heart stutters, stops, and restarts as I study his flaming chest. I trace the smooth panels and dim my fire until it's only in my palms. His eyes shutter closed as I trace fiery designs on his chest, feeling every muscle. I lean into him, planting a kiss on his collarbone. His eyes fling open, his own fire burning in his pupils. I smile and slowly back up until my legs hit the bed.

I draw him closer with a sensual curve of my finger.

"I don't want to do anything you don't want to do," he whispers, placing his palms on either side of my face, searching my eyes—nothing like the man who forced this bond on me against my will.

I nod and scoot into the middle of the bed. He smiles wide, and he's so absolutely breathtaking I want to cry. My eyes move over his smooth, dark, marbled chest, his pants so low on his hips that I avert my eyes.

The bed dips down as he crawls toward me. I bite my cheek as flutters take over my insides, turning me into a human birdcage. He reaches me, tracing his hands so achingly slow down the sides of my neck, my shoulders, over my biceps, caressing my forearms, and finely lacing them with my hands. He kisses each knuckle.

"The bond makes these emotions so much more powerful. It takes everything in me to not ravish you right here and now and worship your body for the rest of the night."

I swallow as the spark ignites in me once more. I release my hands and travel up his arms like he did to mine until I reach his face, holding it between my palms. "You are not that angry man with no control anymore. I know that now. I trust you. I…I love you, Sebastian." As I say it, I know the words are true, despite the bond amplifying everything. I do love him. What I feel for him has grown from love and nothing else.

His eyes widen, the red of his fire outlining his irises. A fire that isn't coming from anger but desire. "You don't want to break the bond anymore?"

I smile and shake my head. His lips smash into mine, the force making me fall into my pillows. He scoops me into his arms so we're lying chest to chest on our sides.

"I have loved you since before I met you, my angel," he murmurs against my lips, caressing his hand through my hair. "You were in my every dream in that prison. The thought of this mysterious woman in my heart was the only thing keeping me going. It didn't matter how dark it got, my mind always returned to you, waiting and ready." He feathers kisses down my throat, reaching my collarbone. He pulls back. "My beautiful green-eyed angel." He strokes my hair. "Better than the dreams. In some, I would sense you with other men and get so mad." He chuckles. "A woman I didn't even know. But I *did* know." He taps his heart. "You have bewitched me, body and soul."

My mouth hangs open. "Mr. Darcy."

He smiles. "I noticed the book on your shelf and have been reading it in the basement. It's quite good. That Mr. Darcy character has a way with words."

My smile widens as I bring him back to my mouth, but I pull back in a dawning realization. "You said you would get mad at those men in your dreams. Did you by chance, growl at them?"

His eyes widen, and his cheeks pinken in the cutest way.

"I heard you!"

A bemused look crosses his face, and he tilts his head. He closes his eyes and opens them again. "Did you?"

I nod, and he smirks. "Hmm, we'll have to figure out *that* little trick." His words come out almost growl-like, doing extraordinary things to the inside of my body, the tether pulling so tightly now I think I may split in two.

I giggle and he quiets me with another kiss. This kiss lights me on fire, and when he moves his mouth to my hairline I gasp, "Say it again."

As he kisses my jawline, he whispers, "You…have bewitched…me." His voice and kisses travel down my throat and over my chest as his hand bunches my shirt. "Body and…"

My heart takes off faster than a bullet. But I do trust him. He has proved to me time and time again that he's nothing like the man I once knew. This Sebastian and I belong together.

A faint memory pulls my mind in a different direction, wanting to take me away from him and into somebody else's arms, but I force it down. I turn my mind off and stop thinking, only feel, focusing on the intertwining of our bodies, his skin, his scent, and the heat pulsating between us.

"Soul," he growls at last.

And I let every desire and craving I've had for Sebastian the previous couple of weeks take over into a blissful nothingness as the tether finally pulls us together, sealing our bodies as one—sealing the bond.

32

The Letter

Fingers sweep along my back, drawing tingling designs.

I keep my eyes shut as I dwell on the rare, pleasant dreams from last night—*really* pleasant dreams about James. Is he the one caressing my back?

Smiling, I roll over, the hand sliding off. Sebastian is on his elbow staring down at me, a lazy smile on his face. The blanket is loose around his torso, and his dark, sculpted chest is almost too perfect to bear. A shock goes through me, and the memories of the night prior come flooding back, as do all the touches and tender kisses. Heat fills my cheeks, and he brushes the back of his knuckles on them.

"Good morning," he coos.

I pull the blanket up and around me to make sure I'm covered. "Um, I need a moment."

I roll off the bed, taking the sheet with me that is covered in dark scorch marks. My eyes widen. I'll have to burn this. No way am I ever letting anyone see *that*.

He chuckles as I shuffle to the bathroom. I look back and almost face-plant into the ground. To cover myself, I took the blanket off him—*all* of him. I gulp and avert my eyes, closing the bathroom door behind me.

After using the toilet, I wash my hands and face. The cold water soothes the fire swirling inside of me. I feel weird. Like last night was somehow a mistake, even though, in the moment, I was so sure it wasn't. Sebastian is my mate, and we are bonded forever. This is what mates do. And I do love him. It wasn't bad. It was actually the most incredible sensation I have ever felt, but still, I can't deny this sense of wrongness in my gut. It *was* my first time. That's probably it.

And it didn't help that I had that dream about James. We were back in the underground tunnels, in the flower bedroom, and we didn't stop at just kissing.

I shake off the dream and stare at myself in the mirror. I'm with Sebastian now. I chose Sebastian. My hair is in a knotted strawberry-blonde halo around my head. I pull a brush through it, trying to untangle the curls when I notice reddish bruises on my neck. I drop the brush in the sink, inspecting the marks closer. My eyes widen. Did Sebastian give me hickeys?

I explore the rest of my body and find six similar markings. Heat crawls up my neck, making the hickeys stand out even more. Crap. It's not even cold enough to wear a scarf. I'll have to get hold of Abby's makeup.

I brush my teeth and look around. Luckily, my pajamas from two nights ago lay in a bundle in the corner. I've never been so thankful for my messiness. I throw the shorts and shirt on and head back out. Sebastian is buttoning his pants, and I let out a breath, studying that smooth, marble chest. Again, heat swirls in my gut, remembering exactly how close we were.

"I have to get to get back before somebody notices. I'm on pretty strict guidelines—" he kisses me quickly on the lips, "—that I plan on adhering to so I can earn my place here once again." He taps my nose. "So, I can be the man as you see me." He pulls on his shirt and steps away but turns back, wrapping his arms around my waist. He kisses me long and hard, until we're both gasping for air. "I love you. Oh! I'll never tire of telling you that." His smile stuns me for a moment as I watch him go, pulling on his shoes as he races into the hallway.

I fall onto my bed and look at my ceiling until my breathing slows. The unsettledness from earlier has faded now. How could just one kiss make my whole body tingle after what we did?

After getting dressed in clean clothes, I head towards Abby's room. I knock hesitantly before opening the door. With Trevor always over, I never know what I will walk into.

"Abby?" I say, flipping the light switch.

No answer. She must have gone off to handle morning breakfast already. Everyone but me has easily returned to their everyday routines from before we left.

I open the first drawer in her bathroom, rummaging through different shades of lipstick, eyeliner, and eyeshadow before opening the one underneath. This one only has makeup brushes. I pull the next one out, but I'm wrong again. I move to the last drawer. A white envelope lies on top. I pick it up to look underneath and see the foundation. Score! Now, to figure out which one is my shade. Abby is much darker than me.

I return the envelope, but notice my name scrawled on the opposite side. I right myself and turn it over. Thumbing the contents, I pull out a piece of paper. I'm about to open it when I stop myself. Should I be looking at this? It does have my name on it.

I look at the envelope again, my name scrawled in a neat cursive. This isn't Abby's handwriting, though. But I do recognize it. Wait a minute. My heart stops and then takes off again. I would know this handwriting anywhere. It's the same handwriting of the letters in my drawer that I have read repeatedly for months.

My fingers shake as I unfold the paper.

Maya,

I'm so sorry for the way I acted while you were here. And I'm even more sorry that I broke my promise about returning. I wanted to explain everything, but I just couldn't put you in jeopardy. That's why I decided to put this letter in your pack. Hopefully, you'll read it when you're far from this place.

For your safety, I had to break my promises. I had to keep my distance from you to protect you. My supervisor wants to recruit you, and I couldn't let her get her hands on you. People have been making choices for you for too long, and I'm not about to let her take that freedom away from you. I've seen the signs of her corruption, and I'm trying to leave. I should be able to soon, but I have to make sure it doesn't put my squad in danger. Give me a couple weeks, and I'll meet you back in Oregon. I have a plan.

I hope, in the meantime, you're able to find your mom. Everything in this pack will help, but it is still very dangerous. I know you don't need me to tell you this, but please be careful. I don't know what I will do if anything happens to you. Kick some Com ass! See you soon. Promise. No. I swear it.

I love you,
James

My hands shake hard, my fire pushing against its tightly controlled cell within me, threatening to escape. I place the letter on the counter before I accidently turn it to ash.

No. This can't be happening. Why wouldn't Abby have given this to me?

I step back, balling my hands into fists as the fire envelops them. I lurch out of the bathroom and into the hallway, heading for the commons.

I throw the doors to the kitchen open and try to control the anger that is increasing by the second. "Is Abby in here?"

Carlos shakes his head. "Nah, she's on lunch duty. Check the gardens. I thought I saw her heading that way." His hands freeze above the fruit bowl mixture he's working on. "Are you okay, Maya?"

"Peachy," I hiss and turn around.

I run out the front doors and through the orchard. "Abby!" I turn a corner and head up another row. "Abby!" Flames crawl up to my elbows.

"Hey! Get out of here. You're going to burn the place down," somebody yells at me.

"You can regrow it," I snap but head out of the trees.

I turn around in place twice before I catch auburn hair rounding the corner of the manor. I break into a sprint, my fire cascading over my shoulders and down my back like a cape. Around the corner, I spot her and William heading for the lake.

"Abby!"

They both turn around with confused expressions.

"Whoa. Is everything okay?" Abby looks around nervously, clearly without the faintest clue why I'm in such a state.

I pause a yard away. "Is there something you want to tell me?" I ask through clenched teeth.

Her eyebrows pull down, and William steps forward and reaches towards me.

"Don't touch me! I don't want to burn you."

"You need to calm down, Maya," he says, his gray eyes widening with alarm.

"Don't tell me to calm down!" My fire twists with my wrath. In the back of my head, I know he's right. I need to calm down. But I can't seem to get in control of my breathing, let alone this fire. "Why is there a letter from James in your bedroom addressed to me?"

Her face doesn't change at my declaration. Her brows just furrow even more, which finally causes my flames to lessen. That's not the reaction I was expecting. Remorse maybe? Or, better yet, embarrassment for being caught? I know she can act, but she couldn't hold onto such a facade for me.

"What letter?"

My flames die even more, until there is just a faint flicker in my palms. "The one where James tells me he still loves me and he'll be coming back," I choke out. My anger turns into sorrow like a flip of a switch.

"Um, Maya?" William says, rubbing the back of his neck.

"What?" I look at him, and his face looks how I expected Abby to look. My anger pulses once more.

"I know about the letter."

My eyebrows shoot up as he confirms my rising suspicions.

"What letter?" Abby asks loudly, looking between the two of us.

William turns to her with one eye on me. "The one I gave you and told you to give to Maya."

"Wait. That was from James? I thought it was some love letter from you where you finally admitted your feelings." Then she looks at me. "Which I didn't want to give you because things seemed to be going well with you and Sebastian."

She turns back on William and smacks him in the arm. "What did you do?"

He bites his lip as my flames double. I step toward him, and he lifts his hands in surrender. "Let me explain."

"You have one minute before I burn you to a crisp."

He smiles boyishly, but fear flashes in his eyes. "You wouldn't do that."

I fold my arms. "Does it look like I'm joking?" I bite out, barely able to contain myself.

"Okay, okay. It was in the backpack James gave us. And I decided not to give it to you at first because you were so sad, and I didn't want you to get your hopes up. You were heartbroken the last time he gave you a letter. Then you seemed to be starting to get over him, and I didn't want you to spiral again and get all depressed like last time. I was just trying to help. I did give it to Abby once we got here, though, so she could give it to you. I mean, if you're set on picking between the two blokes, James is definitely the better choice. Even though, honestly, I don't think either of them are good enough for you. And I should stop talking."

Abby pushes William away from me. "You should run," she says.

His lips quirk up, trying to laugh it off, but steps back as I move closer to him. His smile disappears. Everything inside me is consumed by fire, burning away every ounce of any pleasant emotion toward him. I can't think or feel coherently. Rage courses through my veins as I stare at my best friend…but he's *not* my best friend. I don't even see his face. All I see is a jealous, fair-haired British boy, who has decided to stick his nose where it didn't belong.

"How could you?" The ice on my tongue has a strange effect on the fire.

William turns and runs.

"How could you!" I scream again as I chase after him.

"Maya, stop! You'll regret this later! Come on. You don't want to turn your best friend into ash!" Abby yells from behind me as she tries to keep up.

"Please don't turn me into ash!" William screams in a high-pitched voice that would be hilarious if rage wasn't flowing through every facet of my being.

Surprisingly, I'm gaining ground on him. I have never been faster than him. He's smart, though, heading straight towards the lake. I throw a fireball right past his head and he shrieks.

Without looking, he throws a force of air over his shoulder. It blasts my hair back, diminishing my fire slightly but not slowing me down.

"Maya!" yells Abby, sounding further away. She should work on her endurance.

A crack forms in front of me and widens, blocking me from William. I leap over it without a second thought. Blasting fire beneath my feet to keep me in the air for longer. I had never tried a move like that before, but it works.

I slam into the ground on the other side and almost fall. William is nearing the lake. I throw another fireball his way but barely miss as he dives into the water. His head bobs from under the surface.

"Bollocks, Maya! I'm sorry! I didn't know she didn't give it to you."

I stop myself on the bank, water lapping at my feet. "This is not on Abby! You had no right to keep that letter from me. This has nothing to do with you!"

"Who has kept you from completely falling apart, Maya!" He shouts back. "For months, I was there for you, and what did I get for it in return? To come upon you hooking up with the man that *forced* you into all this. Him and *not* me." He chokes on the last sentence.

"Oh, I get it. You wanted me to bang you for helping me those months instead of Sebastian, *my mate*. Is that it? Just petty jealousy because I wasn't giving you all my attention anymore?"

He looks as if I struck him and he swims for shore.

"You probably shouldn't do that," I snap. Some semblance of sanity is slowly returning to me, but I'm still much too angry.

"Oh, give it up. You won't hurt me." He stands, water dripping off of him, hair plastered to his face, his wet shirt outlining his muscled chest, and walks towards me, too confident in my ability to hold back. "No, I do not want you to *bang* me." He stops a foot away. "I'm in love with you, Maya. How can you not see that?"

I shake my head. "You're not in love with me."

He laughs darkly and throws his hands in the air. "You refuse to see it!"

"William. I told you I don't love you like that."

"Yes, you have made that bloody clear," he growls. Raw hurt takes hold of his features.

I can't stand it. I take his cold, wet hand, warming it with my fire. "I do love you. You're my best friend."

"It's just how you see me." He takes my other hand. "If you open your eyes, you'll see that you're in love with me too."

I shake my head adamantly.

He rubs the back of my hands. "Why does me doing this help you?"

"I…I don't know. It calms me."

"My touch calms you," he says, raising his eyebrows.

I nod hesitantly.

He slowly pulls me into a hug, and I let him. "And how does this feel?"

His cool, wet skin makes a sizzling sound against my heated skin. But more than that, my anger and anxieties melt away in his embrace. "That I'm safe," I whisper.

He pulls back, his hands still on my waist. "My hug makes you feel safe."

I nod again.

His hand slides to my throat, fingering the necklace he gave me that I never take off. "Why do you wear this?"

"Because I…love it." That sounds lame even in my ears.

He smirks. "Do you miss me when I'm not around?"

I sigh but nod again, and his smile widens.

"But—" I start.

He places a finger on my lips, and the words freeze in my mouth. He moves his finger to stroke my bottom lip.

"And this?"

A shiver runs through me that has nothing to do with his wet body. He moves his hand to the back of my neck and leans in. No. No. No. And then a terrible thought that scares me even more runs through my head. I *want* him to kiss me. Despite the other men in my life, what I tell myself *and* him on repeat, and how absolutely crazy this is, all I can think is how his lips would feel against mine.

I close the distance.

33

Beacon of Betrayal

The moment our lips brush, a deafening roar sounds, and I jump back, startled.

Hurt flashes across William's face, and I turn, knowing who's approaching us.

"Get away from my mate," Sebastian says calmly, so at odds with the roaring in my mind. He doesn't even know he's doing it.

William's face hardens as he intertwines our fingers. Rage flashes across Sebastian's face. William must have a death wish. Fire swirls in his palms. Wait, how does he have his abilities?

I step toward him. "Sebastian."

He pulls his eyes to me, and his features soften. He stops just a few yards from us.

"Would you like me to hurt him?" he asks, his eyes begging me to say yes.

I shake my head, and his bottom lip juts out.

"Okay. I won't. I'm keeping my promise." His voice is rough but he rolls back his shoulders and walks forward, tugging on my waist until I release William.

"I shouldn't let my jealousy get the better of me," Sebastian says into my neck. His shoulder and back are taut like a bowstring. Keeping his word is physically affecting him, but he's doing it. He's doing it for me. "But I didn't realize how much harder it would be to see another man touch you after what we shared…multiple times last night."

I gasp and pull back. He's staring past my shoulder at William. He moves aside my hair to reveal the hickeys on my neck like they're his little trophies. I push him hard, and he stumbles back with a smile.

I twist to face William and open my mouth to explain, but nothing can improve this situation. He looks between us, horror-struck and a little pale, then turns on his boot and walks away without a word.

"That was not nice!" I throw a fireball at Sebastian's face just because I can, then chase after William.

I pass Abby, whose eyes are dancing with mischief. She mouths, *Really?*

I wince and run past her as a smile begins tugging on her lips. Ugh, did he have to say that so loud? I should've known he'd play dirty if he couldn't get back at William physically.

I grab William's shoulder, and he shakes me off. "William!"

"Please tell me that's all you did," he says pointing to my neck.

I cover it with my hair as heat fills my cheeks. "He's my mate."

"Ugh. As you keep reminding me." He pulls a hand down his face. "I think I'm going to be sick."

"Oh, come on! William. Don't be a baby."

His eyes bug out, and he shakes his head, heading towards the gardens. I follow him, waiting for him to slow down or talk to me. Yell at me about how I just had sex with a monster or something. He's always trying to throw Sebastian's past mistakes into my face.

William finds a bench and sits, leaning onto his knees. I sit next to him and watch him studying his feet before he moves again. This time, angling his face toward the sun.

"I'm not going to say anything. What you do with Sebastian is between you and him. You're right. He is your mate. I guess I've just been in denial about it for so long. I thought that it was temporary. You would sever the bond and then realize that you loved me." He chuckles. "I know. I'm pretty daft."

"No, you're not. I *do* love you."

"But as a friend."

I grab his hand, not believing I'm about to do this. "No."

His spine stiffens.

I exhale. "You're right. I do love you like that."

He looks at me like he can't understand the words coming out of my mouth, and it physically pains me to say them because I know they don't change anything. But he needs to hear the truth.

"I miss you when you're gone. You make me feel safe, warm, and whole. And believe it or not, I did want to kiss you back there. I will be forever grateful for you being there for me after everything that happened. I don't know what I would have done without you holding me together. But it wasn't fair for me to ask that of you as a bonded woman. I'm sorry. It's my fault that we have these feelings."

He takes my chin, so I have to look at him. "No, I've had these feelings for you for a long time, Maya. And you have no idea how nice it is to hear that I wasn't crazy for thinking you had them too." Then his face slackens. "Even if you still choose him. It gives me closure, at least."

I throw my hands in the air and stand. "Does it? Because I feel like all this does is make everything so much harder. It's not that I *still* choose him. I already chose him, I can't un-choose."

He smiles at my logic and stands, pulling me into a hug. "It's going to be okay."

"Ugh. Why do you always have to be such a damn sun all the time."

He chuckles. "What?"

I sigh. "It's my nickname for you. Since I first met you. You've always had this happy, positive demeanor, and then you would make light for me whenever I had those nightmares. You're my sunshine."

He tightens his hold and starts to sway. "I like that," he murmurs into my hair.

He doesn't immediately let me go, and I worry I said too much. But then I remember. This is where we danced for the first time. Under this tree, next to this bench. I knew then that I could see a life with him—not the life I once thought, but one of a great friendship.

And so, I dance with him and let my love for him be the music. I will always love William, and I hope one day he can move on from me and love me as a friend. It'll be Abby's and my mission to find him a girl who deserves his all-consuming love, and who will love him back with the same passion.

Opening my eyes, I spot Juliet descending the manor's stairs. That girl might be closer than I thought. I lean back as he plants a kiss on my forehead.

"Love you," I say, wishing it was enough. He deserves so much more from me.

"Love you more," he says, his face full of emotion he's trying to hide. He's never been good at hiding his feelings. I've always been able to read him clear as day.

"I'm sorry I tried to burn you alive."

He chuckles, but then his face grows serious. "I'm really sorry about the letter, Maya. It was daft of me. I should have never kept it from you."

I nod. "What's done is done." A pit forms in my stomach, thinking James could be here any day, just to discover that I moved on.

But *have* I moved on?

I walk away from William, smiling, knowing Juliet is heading his way. I hope he'll see it soon—that she has feelings for him. And if not, I'll make him see it. They would be adorable together.

Sebastian throws fiery stones into the lake as Abby watches from the grass.

She stands when she sees me. "How is he?"

"He'll be okay." I look back at William and Juliet underneath the tree. "I hope he'll realize it soon."

"What?" She looks back and nods knowingly. "Ohh. That Juliet is crazy about him? Yeah, he will. He just needs to get over you first."

"I'm going to talk to Sebastian."

"Wait!"

I stop and look at her.

"Did you two really...you know?" She wiggles her eyebrows and pinches her fingers together like they're kissing.

I nod, and she squeals silently.

"Oh my gosh. I need to know everything. Was it wonderful? Did you guys burn down your room?" She giggles.

"No." Then I think back, remembering the scorch marks on the sheets. "Well, maybe a little."

"Whoa. Okay, okay. And what about James? What did the note say?"

"Well, it's still in your room if you want to read it. But he said he'll be up here soon. Could be any day, now, I guess."

"And he still loves you?"

I bite my lip and nod.

"But you're not going to sever the bond?"

"Ugh. Abby. Cool it with the questions."

She sighs loudly when I walk away from her. I honestly don't know what I'm going to do now. Knowing James didn't want me anymore helped me move forward with Sebastian, but now? Can I still live with this choice, knowing there's a chance between James and me?

"How long have your abilities been back?" I ask, as I stop behind Sebastian.

He turns to look at me as he lets another fiery rock go. It skips across the lake's surface before disappearing. "Not long. Wixx started lowering my dose two days ago. I haven't felt this good in a long time. Not being able to wield fire in four months...Dr. Rye was worried it would be too much too fast, so Wixx is tapering me off the injections to be safe and to keep an eye on me."

"I'm happy for you." And I mean it. Even though I'm a bit ticked at him for announcing our intimacy to the world, I'm glad he's starting to feel whole again.

He winds his arms around my torso. "I'm sorry, Maya. That was childish of me to say to William. What we do behind closed doors stays behind closed doors." He leans down to kiss my cheek, but he lingers and begins traveling down my neck. Heat threatens to take over once again.

I pat his chest. "Closed doors."

He chuckles and pulls back up, his blue eyes twinkling. "You're hard to resist."

That's when I realize I don't quite feel the same way anymore. I can resist him, unlike before when it felt as if somebody was spearing me with a red-hot poker when I tried not to touch him. The bond is still there. I feel the tether. But it's loosened, like I can finally breathe again.

"I need to talk with Abby. I'll see you later, okay?"

"Don't make me wait too long." Heat fills his eyes, and a shiver runs down my body. He gives me one final kiss before letting me go.

Abby is almost back at the manor, so I have to jog to catch up. "Abby!"

She turns and smirks at me. "I didn't think you'd be able to pull yourself off of him."

I shove her shoulder.

"So, was it as great as we thought?"

I bite my lip. "It was pretty remarkable, but—"

She stops and turns to me. "What?"

I look around. Sebastian is walking in the opposite direction, probably too far away to hear us. "Let's get to your room," I say, pulling her along.

When we get there, I snatch the letter from where I left it in her bathroom. After handing it to her, I flip onto the couch and observe her as she reads.

"That bastard."

"James or William?"

"Both," she says irritably. "I probably would have torched him too. And James! Like he couldn't have told you this earlier? Letters are not the way to go. Too risky and way too formal." She shakes her head and sits next to me. "Well, obviously, he lost his chance."

I don't say anything, and she looks at me.

"Right? You've forgiven Sebastian. You've done the deed. Sealed the deal. Finalized the bond. Wrote your name in blood and all that. Maya. Right?" She looks at me frantically like I'm losing my mind. And I'm pretty sure I am.

"One would think so," I say sheepishly.

"What do you mean 'one would think so'? You know so, right?" Her voice rises in pitch, and I bite my lip.

She grabs my shoulders and gives me a shake. "Ugh. Girl! This is like spring all over again. *I love Sebastian. No, I love James.* You can't be yanking their hearts around like that."

I swallow and rub my hands down my face. She's right. What's wrong with me? My heart has been sawed in half, stitched back together, put through a grinder, and is now ripping in two again. I can't imagine what I'm doing to theirs.

"I'm not. You're right. I chose Sebastian. It's done," I say, leaning back. But I can't ignore the knot that forms in my stomach.

She eyes me. "What were you trying to tell me earlier? It was amazing, *but…*?"

I shake my head. "It doesn't matter."

"Oh. Now you're yanking me around." She shoves me, none too lightly.

"Stop it." I slap her hand away and stand up.

"Tell me. Come on. You know I haven't gotten that far with Trevor. We're waiting until after our ceremony, and I need to be prepared."

"Wait. Back up. You decided?"

She smiles. "Yeah. Trevor asked me as soon as we came back, telling me he can't imagine life without me and all that stuff." She waves her hand like it's no big deal. "We're going to make it official soon."

I twirl and jump back on the couch, wrapping my arms around her. "I'm so happy for you! You two are so perfect for each other." I pull back. "How soon? Knowing you, it's going to be big right?"

She purses her lips but can't hide the glowing smile from bursting through. "I've already started on my dress. Wanna see?"

I shake her shoulders. "Of course!"

She opens the doors to her wardrobe and pulls out a white gown with a pink, sparkly sheen to it. She spreads out the skirts, and I suck in a breath. It's covered in light-pink, purple, and baby-blue real flowers of all shapes and sizes. Ivy lines the bodice and connects the flowers as they travel down the train. There are still various openings where she has yet to finish.

"Oh my gosh, Abby. It's gorgeous!"

She smiles. "Yeah?"

"You are going to be a princess…no, a queen. And Trevor is your Prince Charming, come to sweep you off your feet and give you your happily ever after."

She gives me a watery smile.

"I really do love him." She tucks the dress back in the cabinet and sits next to me. "I know you didn't like the whole matching thing, but your mom has the touch. I can't imagine being with anyone else. And obviously, there's something there with Sebastian." She slaps my arm as her brown eyes widen. "You totally distracted me, you fox! Please, tell me what happened."

I lean back to stare at the ceiling, tracing the ivy that crawls from her bed posts and onto the walls with my eyes. "Okay, fine. When I woke up next to him, I was surprised it wasn't…James. And I…I just felt wrong. Like, I made a mistake. Then earlier, when he kissed me, I realized the tether isn't as strong anymore. Like, maybe that was the only reason I wanted him like that."

I chew on my lip, waiting for her to chastise me. But she doesn't say anything until—

"That's interesting."

I roll my neck to look at her.

She shrugs. "Maybe it was the bond this whole time."

My mouth drops open. "You just told me I should stay with Sebastian. To stop yanking their hearts around."

"Because I thought you loved him."

"I do." That I know for sure. The bond amplifies our feelings; it doesn't make them magically appear.

She arches an eyebrow and lifts the letter. "If you had gotten this earlier, would you have still slept with him?"

I shake my head. "No. I would have fought against the bond harder."

She nods and chews on her finger. "You want to be with James?"

I think about my feelings for both men and shove my palms into my eyes. "This is a mess."

I want to be mad at William and blame him, but I can't, not after everything he's done for me.

"What's a mess?" Comes a deep, achingly familiar voice from Abby's doorway.

Abby gasps and jumps up. I'm frozen, not wanting to remove my hands from my eyes and see him. Then everything will be real, including what he told me in that letter.

I lower my hands. Abby's face is buried in James' shoulder, and he holds her with one hand, a duffle bag in the other.

But he has me captured in his hazel eyes.

Tears blur my vision, not prepared for him to be right here, flesh and bone. I haven't fully comprehended the letter, and part of me didn't believe he would actually come.

His eyes continue to hold mine and emotions flood my system. I stand, not being able to hold myself back any longer. It's really him. James is here. He's back. And if he truly still loves me—

A sob breaks through as I throw my arms around both of them. Abby adjusts so I can be in on the hug too. Sobs rack my body, and Abby steps back so James can fully wrap me into him. His earthy smell, his warmth, it's all so familiar. Like he was just out in the woods for the day.

I look up at him, and he smiles crookedly, wiping my tears with his thumb. "I was worried you didn't get my letter."

Another sob breaks through, and I can't stand to look at him. My shame and guilt radiate off me, but I also can't let him go. Not yet. He rubs my back in soothing circles, making it so much worse.

"I'm here. I know it took so much longer than expected but I had to keep my promise, even if it's a little late. You are the most important thing in my life."

I can't take it anymore and pull away from him. I shake my head. "I…I can't," I stutter, moving around him and out the door.

He grabs my hand. "You can't what?" His voice is laced with confusion, and it breaks my wounded heart.

I can't bear to look at him. He's got to see what I did all over me. I'm a shining beacon of betrayal. I try to shake him off, but he's got an iron hold.

"What's wrong?" He grabs my shoulders and forces me to face him. His eyes are so full of love that I want to collapse into a hole and let the ground bury me alive. "Is it the bond with Sebastian? Because I've been researching it, and it's normal for you to feel the way you do. And I'm okay with it. I admit it was hard to come to terms with, but my love for you outweighs all else. And I have some good ideas where we can find him."

"Please stop," I gasp.

He looks at me, concern and hurt fighting to take over his features.

"Maya? Whoa. Get your hands off her." Sebastian comes out of nowhere and rips me from James's grasp.

James opens his mouth as he takes Sebastian in and how he's holding me protectively in his arms.

His shock turns into wild rage. "I don't know how you managed to crawl out of whatever hellhole they had you in, but don't think for a second I can't put you back there." James steps toward us, and Abby grabs his arm. He tries to shake her off.

I'm frozen in Sebastian's arms, my body immobilized as it takes in the situation.

"Get off. What are you doing?" James yells at Abby.

"James, stop. Just look," Abby pleads.

He looks at us again, his dark eyes narrowing in confusion. "Maya, why aren't you trying to get away from him?"

"Because we're mates, you idiot," Sebastian growls.

Comprehension crosses his features. "After what he did?" Hurt flashes in his eyes before a mask of steel comes down.

"I didn't get your letter," I finally say.

"But...the... What's on the table?" He points inside the room. He must have seen it when he walked in.

"I only just read it *today*."

"You didn't get my letter," he says again. "So, you must have thought— Oh, Maya." His face twists in pain and his shoulders fall. "You don't have to be with this lunatic just because you're mates. But you already knew that…" He trails off, pushing his dark hair out of his face, trying to rationalize the situation.

"She chose me," Sebastian says, his voice made of iron.

I blink, and James is in Sebastian's face. Sebastian swiftly pushes me behind him.

"She didn't choose you. You forced this on her, you bastard!"

"I'm not that man anymore. She chose me. She loves *me*."

He shakes his head. "No. No. No. Maya, it's just the bond, right?"

I stare at him, and he reaches for me.

"Get out of my way," James growls, pushing Sebastian.

Sebastian grabs James's arms. I can feel the heat radiating off his back, his fire building. But he's not trying to fight James, just hold him back. "Don't do this. She doesn't want you," Sebastian hisses. "You look pathetic."

That does James in. He moves his body in a way that has Sebastian releasing him in one moment…and the next, James's fist is connecting with Sebastian's jaw.

Sebastian falls backward as James grabs me around the waist, pulling me to him.

"It's going to be okay. We're going to figure this out."

I barely hear him, because I can't look away from the fire consuming Sebastian. Flames run up his arms, and his eyes turn scorching. James pushes me behind him. I catch a glint of silver as it's pulled from his belt. Sebastian steps toward us before stiffening and closing his eyes. I watch in awe as his chest rises and falls, and the flames die out.

"Come on, Maya. Tell him," Sebastian finally says. A bruise blossoms on his tense jaw, but his voice is calm.

I look between them as a fissure cracks in my heart. Every part of me wants James. I want to be in his arms, but even now, as his hand lightly touches my arm protectively, I can't stand it. The guilt eats away at me, clawing into my deepest parts. He deserves so much better than the sick creature that I am.

I step away from him, deepening the fissure. "I…I need to think," I stutter.

Then, I turn and flee like a coward.

My tears are already soaking my shirt as I fall into my room. Climbing into my Sebastian-scented bed, I groan. I look up at the ceiling, blurred from my weeping. How many hearts am I going to break today? First William and now James…and even Sebastian with how I just ran away. I don't deserve their love. I don't deserve anyone's love.

34

Butterflies

Tap. Tap. Tap. A light knock sounds from my door.

"Go away," I call. My voice is rough. My tears have finally run dry, and my throat is like sandpaper.

"I did not just come one hundred and fifty miles for my great-granddaughter to tell me to go away."

I balk as Grandma Izalia strides through the door like she owns the place. For where once stood a frail and fragile-looking old lady, barely able to walk, now stands a strong, healthy, mighty woman with flowing black hair streaked with silver. She wears gray slacks covered in colorful flowers, with a matching orange blouse and two knives attached to a belt at her waist. She winks at me when I look from them to her.

She dances forward, and with a twitch of her fingertips, her bags float behind her like my very own Mary Poppins.

"Pick your jaw up off the floor, little lady." She smiles and tilts her head as she stands at the bottom of my bed. "I must have played that role too marvelously. Oh, but it was fun pretending to be like those little old ladies I often see in rocking chairs on their front porches…you know, like in the films."

"What?"

She gracefully sits on the edge of my bed and pats the spot next to her. I obediently scoot forward. She flicks her wrist, and a cup full of water floats toward me. I swipe it out of the air and drink it in one gulp. How'd she know I needed that? And how did she know where to even find that?

"You see, we had to make sure we could trust you and your friends first. I thought it was ridiculous, but your father is a worrier. He likes to hide me away in that house like I haven't been alive for nearly a hundred years, seventy-five of those living on the mainland. I've been a nurse, a doctor, a teacher, and many other things. I certainly know how to take care of myself." She scoffs and shakes her head.

Still drained by the intense emotions I just went through, I just stare at her, marveling.

"It feels so good to stretch my legs!" She looks at me with a sly smile. "And my abilities." She waves towards my back door, and it opens wide. A wind drifts through my room, picking up various items and setting them in their places until the breeze blows my hair off my shoulder. Something tickles my cheek, and I look down. Resting on my shoulder is that black and white striped butterfly, its wings beating slowly.

"Thank you for your service. Tell your friends," Izalia says, and the little guy flies away.

"You can control butterflies?" I gape at her.

"Not just butterflies. And I don't control them. No, I would never do such a thing. I just ask for favors, and most of them are more than willing to help. Except for bats, those pesky things. Nocturnal animals can be grumpier, you see."

I can't lift my chin off the floor. I know Terras have a way of communicating with animals, but nothing on this level. This is true magic.

"That lovely butterfly helped me keep track of you."

My eyebrows turn up.

"I'm in your corner," she says with a smile before looking around. "You guys have completely altered this place. It's lovely! So much more life than before. It reminds me of home in a way. Of course, the trees are very different, and it doesn't smell anything like the ocean, but being in the middle of nature…it's a whole different life than living amongst so many people crammed together in neighborhoods and cities." She wrinkles her nose in disgust.

"Wait, wait, wait. Back up. You've been here before?"

She looks at me, tilting her head. "My son built it for his mate. Michael's parents. Rebecca loved the forest, and Teddy had an affinity for the earth. Earth and fire. He could build anything." Her voice grows sad. "He wanted to grow old with her here and have a big family. I would have loved that for them. But it wasn't meant to be. He was called back to the earth too soon. It's been a long time since I visited."

Her voice grows distant, and I'm not sure how to respond to this wild revelation. "So, Michael has been here too?"

"Oh yes. It's his."

I shake my head. "Did my mom know that?"

She looks at me like *isn't it obvious?*

I slap my forehead. "He's the one that told her about it." And the secrets just keep unraveling. I shouldn't be surprised at this point. If I weren't so emotionally drained right now, I would be more intrigued and ask a million questions about my grandparents, but I just sigh.

"Is Michael…er…my father coming, too?"

She taps her fingers on her chin and shrugs. "He may not know I'm here, but I'm sure he'll figure it out. Yesterday, he left to track a lead about your mom, told me not to expect him back for a few days, so I decided to come see my favorite granddaughter. I've missed you."

I smile, and she clasps her hands together. "How is the boy drama going?" Her eyes light up.

My smile disappears. "Not well, actually. But does anyone else know you're here? Or did you just fly down the chimney like Mary Poppins?"

She laughs, slapping me on the leg. "Oh, girly, you are a hoot. First of all, that's Santa Claus. Second, thank you for the comparison. I love that film. And third, I was hoping you would introduce me, of course."

"As who?"

Her emerald eyes shine. "As who I am."

"My great-grandma Izalia, an original Elemental, who can control all four elements, from a distant island nobody knows about?"

The wrinkles around her eyes deepen. "Well, you don't have to tell them my whole life story. And we call ourselves Divina. You lot came up with the whole Elemental thing." She shakes her head like she's offended.

An inappropriate giggle erupts from my throat. It feels weird to laugh with everything that's going on.

"What?"

"You're just…not who I expected to walk through my door. But I needed you." I grab her hand, which doesn't feel as delicate as before. It's strong and unyielding, having done great and marvelous things. "Thank you for coming, Noni." I use the same pet name Michael used, and it feels right.

"Oh." She pouts and pulls me in for a hug. She's warm and smells like flowers.

My tears are unexpected as they fall onto her pants.

"I'm sorry," I say, sniffling and pulling back.

She pulls me against her bosom once more and rubs my back. "Shh, my child, let it all out. Noni is here."

And with that, the floodgates open until the riverbed dries up.

"When you're ready, just point me in his direction. I will finish him off for you."

I giggle and lean back, somehow feeling whole again. She's not Mom, but the feeling is similar. "No. It's me that deserves a punishment."

Noni wrinkles her dark eyebrows, but before she can respond, the door bangs open, and we both turn. Abby comes in with somebody hot on her heels. I don't see who they are, because Abby whips around.

"Get out before I turn you into a tree," Abby threatens.

"You can't do that." Sebastian's voice reaches us, and I cringe. I'm not ready to talk to him yet.

"Fine then, I'll…sic a bear on you."

"How are you going to get a bear in here?"

In profile, I see her eyes bulge. She puts two fingers in her mouth and whistles loudly.

"Okay, okay. I'm coming back in five minutes, though."

"No, you're not," she says, slamming the door in his face and locking it behind her. Finally, she turns with a smile that falters when she sees my grandmother.

"Grandma Izalia?"

"It's good to see you, Abby. I'm guessing that boy out there is why my granddaughter has been crying for the last hour?"

I look at her. It was not an hour. Well, unless she's talking about the time before she arrived as well. I sigh. She knows everything.

Abby looks at me and tilts her head. "Eh…not the *only* one."

Izalia looks mildly surprised. "Oh, it's that William boy too. Huh?"

"He certainly didn't help." Abby chuckles, and my look silences her.

"Who else?" Izalia looks from me to Abby.

"My brother." Abby just can't help herself.

Noni puts a hand to her mouth. "Oh dear. You have gotten yourself in quite the lovers' quarrel, haven't you?"

My head falls into my hands. "I don't deserve their love."

"Of course you do! You are quite the gem. Never say that." Noni grabs my chin and makes me look at her. "Never say that."

I grumble, and she releases me. "Come sit, Abby, let's figure this out."

"What if Sebastian comes back? Or *James*?" I say, starting to panic.

Noni wiggles her fingers, and the door starts to vibrate. Then, it *disappears*. Abby's mouth drops open, but at this point, I realize she could probably literally do anything. Stop time, turn me into a shoe, pull a car out of her bag. So, I'm not at all surprised that my door is simply gone. Or I'm too emotionally exhausted to care.

"Just an illusion. It's still there, but your boys won't be able to find it. You have all the time in the world to sort this out now."

"Right," I say, folding myself onto the pillow as my stomach growls.

"Or until dinner," Abby says, flopping next to me, still peering at the door nervously. "I've never seen an Aura do that before."

Noni shoots me a wink. Abby doesn't know that she can control all of the elements. Looks like she's an Aura now.

A yawn breaks through as I close my eyes. My body is exhausted from all the physical and emotional turmoil I've experienced today. Where should I even start to tell my grandmother about this complicated love life of mine? I think back to when I first met James and fell for him. Images of us under the canopy of trees become blurry behind my closed eyelids until all there is are green wisps and lovely voices.

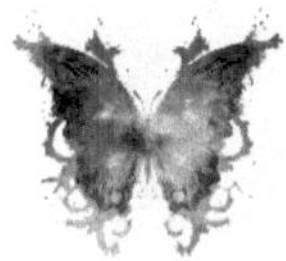

I jolt awake, having had a dreamless sleep for once. I rub the sleep from my eyes and look around for Abby and Noni. Fading sunbeams light my room a deep orange. I peer at my clock. Whoa. I slept all day. It's already nearing 5:30 in the afternoon.

"Rise and shine, my lovely," Noni says.

I spot her on my chair. She's now wearing a dress the same shade as my beige armchair, blending in seamlessly.

"I'm so sorry."

She stands, places something on my coffee table, and looks me over before sitting beside me. "You look better." She touches my cheeks. "More color. How do you feel?"

"Great, actually."

She looks at me sheepishly. "I may have done a little something to help."

"What do you mean?"

"I could feel your dreams." She shudders. "I banished them from your mind while you slept. No wonder you slept so long. How long have those nasty things been bothering you?"

"Pretty much since the Coms attacked us, Sebastian forced me to bond with him, my mom got kidnapped, and James left me."

Her eyes bug out, and she places her hand on mine. "My poor child. You have some deep trauma in there that is manifesting through your dreams.

"Is this another Divina thing?" I ask, not wanting to figure out which traumatic thing is causing these nightmares.

She shakes her head. "No. Well, a little. I used to be plagued by nightmares after I left my island. While I was a nurse, I became very interested in mental health as well. A friend taught me some dream work techniques, and I found that, if I combined them with my unique abilities, I could help even more."

"Can you teach me?" I ask, fully sitting up.

"Maybe. But first, you need to learn about your own mind." She taps my head. "While I'm here, I can continue to banish them for you. Or you can face them."

"Face them?"

"Your dreams. They're trying to tell you something."

"What are they trying to tell me?"

"Oh. That is for you to figure out."

I stand, my shoulders sagging. Like I haven't been trying to figure that out all summer. "They're probably telling me I need to make up my mind," I murmur on my way to the bathroom.

"That's a good start!"

I smile at her before closing the bathroom door and rolling my eyes behind it.

I bring Noni to dinner, ready to introduce her to people, but instead, they welcome her with open arms, call her by name, and chat like they're finishing a conversation that started ages ago.

Sitting down with our food at a table holding Juliet, Ann, and Cal, I turn to my little brother when he waves enthusiastically at her. Him too?

"What were you doing while I was out?" I ask her after taking a few bites of the salad, stifling the intense hunger from not eating all day.

"Abby showed me around," she says before digging in.

"Since you're Maya's grandma, that makes you mine, too, right?" Cal asks.

I gag a tomato out of my throat as I blink at him. I made Mom tell him that we have different biological dads, and he took it smoothly—almost too smoothly, like he didn't quite understand. We clarified that Dad was, and would always be, *our* dad, and he never brought it up again. Not until now.

"Of course!" Noni says.

Cal brightens. "I've never had a grandma before."

"Oh, you have many grandmas. You just haven't met them." He thinks that over as she turns to me. "This is delicious. I might just stay. Your father is going to have to rip me out of here kicking and screaming."

"What about Sarah?"

She purses her lips. "You do realize she wasn't actually my nurse, right? I am very much not a crippled old woman."

"Oh."

I swallow the sting. So many people have lied to me, and it's starting to get *really* old. But it's also understandable. They wanted to get to know me first before revealing her true nature. Izalia is a rarity. And didn't I want to do the exact same thing? It seems to be the world we live in now—deciding who to trust, even if they are family—*especially* if they're family. People can do all sorts of terrible things in the name of trying to protect loved ones.

"I do love Sarah, though. She did a phenomenal job. I might just hire her for real." She chuckles. "Well, that is, if I ever leave this place." She lowers her voice so only I can hear. "I didn't come very often after Teddy built it. I was a little mad he moved so far from home."

"Home?" I take another bite of my food; the tangy dressing explodes in my mouth.

"Florida."

I nod, greedily storing the bits of her backstory away for later.

"But, once they had Michael, they finally buttered me up for a visit. He was the most darling baby." She looks far off as she finishes the rest of her food.

I wonder what this place was like back then. Before I can ask, a strong presence enters the room

The tether pulls on me like it's wrapped around my heart, and he's tugging on the other end with all his strength. Sebastian sits next to me, his heat blanketing me. He kisses me on the cheek, satiating the pull, dimming it to a dull simmer.

"You're awake," he says.

I finally look at him. His face is full of love, longing, and a hint of worry in the scrunch of his eyes.

"Yeah. I just needed some sleep. Especially after…" I swallow my words, my face heating as his chest bounces in a silent chuckle.

He brushes his fingers down my arm, bringing with it flashes of our most intimate moments.

Standing up, I grab my cup of water and drink it in one motion. "Need some more water," I mumble, turning away.

That's when I feel another presence, not quite as all-consuming as Sebastian's but like a physical piece of me has walked in. Without meaning to, I meet his gaze.

James's hazel eyes widen when he takes me in. They soften as he walks towards me. I want to run to him, throw my arms around his neck, and never let him go. I take a small step, but the tether stops me cold, reminding me I'm already taken, reminding me that my actions resulted in me never being embraced by that man ever again.

I turn towards the kitchen—the only other exit in the room.

My cup clangs against the hard ground right before James calls, "Maya, wait!"

I break into a run, but James is faster. I make it inside the kitchen when he grabs me by my shoulder.

"Maya, I *know*. Abby told me everything I missed. But it doesn't matter. I still want you if you'll have me."

I shake my head. No, there's no way she would tell her brother about what I did with Sebastian. I step back, but he steps with me. He grabs my other shoulder and makes me face him.

"I'm ruined," I say, a tear slipping down my cheek.

He brushes it back. "No, you're not. So what? You love Sebastian. Of course, you do. He's your mate. But I don't care. I love you. Do you hear me? *I love you* with my whole being and everything I am. You are my every breath, Maya. I physically cannot leave you again. I won't leave you again. You could love a hundred men, but it would not change a thing. Like I've told you over and over. I'll love you *always*."

A strangled cry or gasp heaves from my chest, and I go limp in his arms. He tucks me into his chest. There is no way he knows. He would not still love me if he knew the truth.

I glance into the commons, where Sebastian struggles against something. He's trying to stand but can't, like an invisible rope ties him to his seat.

Noni catches my eye and winks, but I can't move or feel anything.

James picks me up gently in his arms and carries me into the hallway and out the door. He carries me all the way to the tree line and then through the trees, right to our bench. He sets me down on it and sits on the ground, placing my hands in his. He kisses them slowly, one by one, and then just holds them to wait.

I haven't been out here since before the Coms attacked us and my world fell apart. The leaves are starting to change color. Where they were once a vibrant green, they are now adorned by orange and yellow tints. They will continue to change until they float to the ground. Just like me, a wilted leaf. I've changed. He loves the old Maya, not this one.

Closing my eyes, I focus on the sounds of the forest, its familiar earthy smells and calmness. It's like when I'm in the water. I feel whole out here like I do when I swim. His strong hands are wrapped around my own, unmoving. Not rushing to calm my nerves like William's gentle circles. Not rushing to heat my skin like Sebastian's sensual caresses. Just waiting for me to be ready.

"James," I breathe, opening my eyes.

He's sitting back on his heels in the dirt, looking at me expectantly. It's been so long since I looked into those hazel depths, studied his high cheekbones and hard jawline, felt the stubble surrounding his lips. I feel myself waver, wanting to let him in—to tell him I love him, too, and to choose him—but the guilt crawls up, like a fungus, twining around my heart, rooting deep.

I tug on my hands, and he immediately releases them.

"I need to get back," I murmur and stand.

He stands with me. "You don't want to talk?"

I sigh. "About what?"

His eyebrows turn down in hurt and frustration. "You're not going to sever the bond then? You choose him?"

I open my mouth to tell him that I do want him, but the guilt-ridden roots deepen. "I...I don't know what to say."

I leave him there, and I don't turn back.

35

Intruder

A week has passed since James arrived, and I haven't talked to him again, despite some lingering looks on both our parts. Sebastian has taken up residence in my room, but so has my grandma. Wixx offered her a room right next to mine, and she sleeps there—I think. The rest of the time is spent in her permanent place on my couch. She's there when I wake up and when I fall asleep. She claims she just wants more time with me, which I know is true, but she's also watching Sebastian.

I blink at the light coming from the bathroom as Sebastian steps out. I yawn, and he notices before turning the light back off. I'm again enveloped in darkness, but I can see his silhouette approaching me.

"Sorry if I woke you. They want me out there earlier and earlier, it seems," he says, sitting on the edge of the bed, sliding his hand through my hair.

They've been working him hard, rebuilding Legion Headquarters. He leans down to kiss my temple like he does every morning. Usually, I either pretend I'm still asleep or Noni is already here. I glance at the couch, but it's empty. Sebastian seems to notice, too, because the kiss moves to my mouth, and his hand slides underneath my neck, arching me toward him. My spark reacts, wanting to pull him closer, but I've gotten better at ignoring it. My heart is nothing but a dull ache these days.

I pull back, and he sighs. "I know, I know. I'm sorry."

I shake my head. "We're bonded mates. I'm the one that should be sorry."

"You have nothing to be sorry about. I know you need time."

Our conversation from the day after James made his grand entrance echoes in my mind. We were standing on my back porch watching the sunset, and Sebastian started kissing me. It was romantic and perfect, but something uncomfortable stirred inside me.

"I need some time," I told him. *"With James back, all these feelings came flooding back, and I just…"*

Sebastian grabbed my hand tenderly. *"It's okay. Like, I didn't even know who you were just a couple of weeks ago."* He chuckled. *"You can have all the time you need. I'm not going anywhere."*

His eyes were full of solemn understanding, but the words were too similar to James's. They made me squirm.

Now, he's looking at me with the same expression, and he's been true to his word. Giving me space and time.

I watch him go, feeling conflicted and guilty. I roll onto my side, but my door opens back up, and Noni takes her spot on the couch, a new project in hand. She's taken up knitting. I don't know where she got the yarn—probably the basement, since she has a better idea of what's down there than us. She's made blankets, shawls, hats, and tiny clothes, which I'm guessing are for the children here. They're piling up on the end of the couch. It's such a grandmotherly thing to do.

I smile, watching her work for a bit as golden light begins drifting into the room. A slight breeze ruffles my hair just as my eyes start to feel heavy.

"What are you thinking, girly?"

I muffle an ineligible response and roll back over, closing my eyes. Maybe she'll think I've gone back to sleep.

Suddenly, I'm being nudged over, and I begrudgingly make room for her as she climbs into the bed.

"It's been a week. Anyone can see you're unhappy," she says.

"I'm not unhappy."

"You haven't left this room but to eat."

"Not true! I've…helped Abby."

Abby's ceremony is in two days, and I've tried my best to help her with preparations, but that girl has a one-track mind. She wants to do everything, and I seem to only get in the way.

She pats me on the leg. "Come on! We're going outside. You need to practice."

"I'm fine."

My back door bursts open, and a strong gust of wind blows in picking me up.

"Hey!" I squeal but continue to rise and float out of the room. I thrash and kick, but fighting against the wind and Izalia's powers is pointless. "Noni, put me down!"

"No. You need some fresh air."

Ugh. I stop fighting and fold my arms around myself in contempt, which doesn't last long as I near the railing of my balcony. My eyes widen as I levitate over it. Noni walks underneath me as she guides me to the pond. I'm a balloon, and she's holding the string. The chill morning air raises goosebumps on my bare legs.

"This is ridiculous. I'll walk, okay? Put me down."

She smiles up at me and shakes her head.

As we near the water, she still doesn't let me go. I fly over the glass surface until I'm hovering right over the heart of my pond.

I narrow my eyes at her. This has to be just for show. I'm in my pajamas, it's freezing, and the sun hasn't even fully risen. She wouldn't…

But a smirk twists her lips.

"Don't you dare."

She winks, and I gasp as she releases me. My stomach flies into my throat, my arms flailing before I splash into the water.

For a moment, the water cocoons me, as the bubbles burst all around. The shock of the cold wears off quickly, my skin numbs, and I let myself sink, blowing the air out of my lungs. My feet hit the muddy bottom. I dig my toes in, allowing that small angry part of me, mad at the fact that my grandmother just dropped me into an ice-cold pond, to flare up and then disperse. The other emotions I've been pushing down throughout the week awaken. Instead of the water calming me, my nerves buzz, as if a thousand tiny bees have found a home in my veins. I move my hands gracefully in and out, building up the energy until I feel like a high-voltage electricity wire, every part of me pulsing, needing an outlet.

The water heats around my skin, warming my body until I can feel my toes again. I twist and swirl my hands faster and faster and push off the ground just as the burning in my lungs becomes too much. My built-up power unleashes, and I blast up and out of the water. I soar into the sky like a firebird, flames burning away the water droplets as I let it lift me, higher and higher.

I laugh in delight before noticing the treetops and how high I've actually launched myself. My fire sputters out, and I fall. My laugh turns into a shrill scream as I descend much too fast. Before I strike the water's surface, my body slows, and I lightly hit the water.

When I swim back up, I spy Noni on the shore, hands on her hips, beaming.

"Thanks." I chuckle.

I swim ashore and stand before her, my navy pajama shorts and T-shirt soaked, water dripping down my legs. I point at the sky. "Did you see that?"

She laughs with a nod. "Anyone within a mile radius saw that."

"Wow. That felt good. A little scary. But amazing."

"Gotta work on the landing."

"Do you think I could do that again?"

"Definitely. And with the height you got to, I doubt I'll even need to help this time," she says with a knowing smile.

"Wait a minute, that was you?"

She pinches her fingers together, leaving a little space. "This much. It was mostly you. You have a lot of power within you and at your fingertips. I just helped you release and harness it." Her eyes sparkle. "There is so much more you can do."

"Okay, you convinced me. Can I at least put on my training clothes?" I say, peering down at my wet pajamas.

She waves her hand, and I speed off to my room. By the time I throw on a sports bra and workout shorts, the euphoria starts to wear off, and my thoughts return to Sebastian and James.

I stop before Noni, the dull ache returning as the sun ascends over the mountains, lighting up the world.

Noni places a hand on my shoulder. "My poor child. Love is an amazing thing, but it can do such awful things."

"I brought it on myself. Don't pity me, please." For the first time in weeks, I'm not thinking about the tether binding me to Sebastian nor the love shadowed by the guilt I feel when I think of James. I feel like me again. "Practice is exactly what I need."

She looks me over once before clasping her hands together. "Let's get started then."

By the end of an hour, I'm panting, sprawled out on the grass. I haven't had a real trainer since Seth. There were Ignas who took pity on me and taught me how to harness my fire, but none of them were anything like Seth. He knew my strengths and weaknesses, when I needed to be pushed, and when I needed extra time. I miss him. But Noni—she's a machine.

She stands on the edge of the pond, wielding all four elements, her dark hair flowing behind her. Earth, water, fire, and air swirl around each other. I've never seen anything like it. We've grown a small audience, and everyone is fascinated by Noni's methods. She deemed our community safe enough to reveal her true nature. I don't know if it's the smartest thing. What if the Coms find out about her? She'll be their top target. But if I were her, I'd be tired of hiding my true self all the time too.

Everyone wants to be taught by the true master, so she spends the rest of the day being pulled between different people. I spend the day making up for my moping by pulling my load in the community, helping with every meal, and assisting anyone else who lets me, except those rebuilding Legion Headquarters. I avoid that area because of Sebastian, and I'm also a chicken and bypass the gardens, where I know James might be assisting his mom. I find Cal and give him some more Lympha lessons. Mom will be proud when she sees him and the rate he's picking up everything.

I also wonder if it'll make her sad, though, that she missed the exciting first months of him figuring out his abilities.

As I return to my room, I'm physically exhausted from the day but feeling more accomplished than I have since we returned from our trip. That's the key—get my body moving so my mind doesn't have time to drag me down.

Noni sits up on the couch, a bright smile on her face. She taps the cushion next to her and pulls me into a hug when I sit. "Feels good, huh?"

"Yeah. You were right."

She shrugs. "Always am. Now. What would you like to know about me?"

I turn to look at her. "What do you mean?"

"I am ninety-five years old." She cocks her head. "Well, I think I am. Ninety-something." She waves her hand in the air like her age doesn't matter. "My days are numbered, and I've had a lifetime of experiences that can aid you."

"Tell me what your childhood was like," I say giddily, tucking my feet underneath me.

She smiles and settles into the couch. "I was an energetic young child, always seeking adventure."

Noni goes on to tell me about an island full of beauty, peace, and wonder. And how everyone had an essential part in keeping it that way. I can't get my questions out fast enough as she tells me about a city made entirely of glass and the different types of jobs people had, including protectors who controlled storms around their island. That's how they have isolated themselves for so long and why nobody knows of their existence. She tells me she misses the sunsets over the water and the galaxies covering the night sky. Her people lived in harmony with nature. It's how they survived for hundreds of years, only taking what was needed, and giving back the rest. The way she describes it makes me long to visit.

This is how the next couple of days pass. Noni training me by day and telling me stories of her island by night. Cal joins on the second night, then Abby, Juliet, and Ann on the third. By the fourth, the whole gang, plus some, are piled in my bed, hanging off my couch, or sitting on the floor to listen to her dreamlike stories.

One night, Sebastian sits at the foot of my bed with my feet in his lap as Noni talks. Cal asked her about the island's wildlife, so she's going on and on about the different reptiles, fish, monkeys, and other exotic life. I don't know if the animals she's talking about are unique to her island or if they're just different names for more commonly known animals. It doesn't matter though. I'm caught up in the magic of it all until Sebastian slides his finger across the inside of my foot.

I jump and he smirks. He does it again on the other foot, and I have to hold back from kicking him. I raise my eyebrows at him, and he shrugs. He starts rubbing my feet and I settle back onto the pillow, then catch James's eye from across the room. He's in one of my armchairs, observing me. He holds my stare, and I look away, back to Noni who is smiling wide. But I can't get back into the story. Sebastian drums his fingers on my ankle, and I peer at him.

He smiles, holding my eyes, seeming to know what I'm thinking. This is the first time I haven't minded him touching me. Maybe that's the cure. Time. In time, I'll be okay.

My head falls against the wall as a wave of exhaustion hits. One moment, I'm listening to Noni talking about colorful birds and the next I wake up from a vivid dream about dancing around a bonfire on a beach.

I look around my dark room, wondering where everyone went. Did I fall asleep? Huh. Noni is sound asleep beside me, and Sebastian's soft snores drift from the couch. I settle back onto my pillow. Noni's stories are rubbing off on me. At least it's a nice change from my usual nightmares, not like I've been having them. Noni has kept them at bay, just like she's promised.

But with her help, I've had to keep my promise of trying to understand the reasoning behind my dreams. She has walked me through some meditation, and surprisingly, instead of figuring out my newest dreams, I remembered a few snippets of the nightmares I used to have before we found Sebastian—the dreams I could never hold onto. Even though it's wild, because we're not an Aura couple, I'm pretty sure that I had somehow entered Sebastian's mind during that time, because the bits and pieces I can remember are of him being tortured. Noni thinks it's possible with my bloodline, but it doesn't make sense on his part.

I close my eyes, expecting to drift back off, but I'm wide awake. Giving up on sleep, I tiptoe to the hook in my bathroom, grabbing my swimsuit to sneak out for what used to be my usual late-night swim. With Noni training me and pushing me to my limit, I've been so wiped out that I've been sleeping all night.

After twenty minutes of swimming, my stomach twists. I try to push past the gnawing hunger, but it intensifies to the point where I have to pull myself onto shore. I glance at my watch. There are still a couple of hours until breakfast. I can wait. After a second lap, I'm absolutely starving. Grabbing the robe I hung on a tree, I head inside.

It's eerie walking through the manor at night while everyone sleeps. I round the corner to the kitchen and stop short. A light is bathing the hallway. Who else would be up this early? It's probably some Terras getting in extra early food prep for the day.

As I'm rounding the corner, I hear a familiar deep voice. I stop to listen.

"We'll need at least thirty of your best legionaries," he says.

"And you're sure we can get her and the others out?" Wixx responds.

"I certainly hope so."

"That's not good enough, Michael."

I suck in a breath. My father is here?

"What do you want me to say? You know the risks if we—"

"What are you doing here?" I ask, stepping through the door.

Wixx and he sit on a couple of bar stools at the island in the middle of the kitchen, mugs grasped in their hands.

"Maya!" Michael stands to make his way over to me. He pulls me into a hug that I don't return, too shocked to move. "I was going to come see you when you woke up, but you found me first." He smiles.

"What are you doing here?" I ask again, looking suspiciously at Wixx. "Do you know each other?"

"Wixx is an old friend," he says.

My eyes widen and I shake my head. I need to stop being so surprised by these things. It *is* his house. I'm sure everyone but me knows this.

Wixx's curly afro bobs. "A very old friend. Statistics, was it?" she says, eyeing him.

That pulls me up short.

He shakes his head. "Calculus."

"You went to school together?"

"I used to fancy the sciences but decided I liked people more on the outside than the inside." She laughs.

It's hard to imagine her being something other than a commander in the legion, but she must have had a career beforehand. I cock my head at her. Teacher? No. Military? Maybe. I know many of the other legion commanders were once in a branch of the military before the Elementals got kicked out and built the legion.

"Did you know Wixx here operated the Humanitarian Emergency Response Center in New York?" my dad says, looking at her.

"That's amazing," I say, truly awestruck by this new information about her.

Wixx beams, but then her smile falters. "It was, but sadly, we were one of the first targets. All relief centers across the country fell into chaos as everyone turned on each other. Nothing could have prepared us for that." She shakes her head, banishing the memories. "Back to your father here," she says, joining us at the kitchen opening, mug still in hand. "The legionaries on watch alerted me to an intruder." She throws him an irritated scowl. "You could have waited for the sun to rise at least."

He shrugs and she continues. "When they brought him in, I recognized him, of course, and he filled me in on how you and his grandmother were here."

"You know about Noni?" I ask.

He smirks. "There is very little of what Izalia does that I don't know."

"Come sit, Maya. We'll fill you in. Want me to get you a cup?"

My stomach rolls as I peer at the coffee sloshing in their mugs. "I was looking for food."

I make myself some toast, grab an orange, and sit down. "So, you're here to take Noni back?" I say over a mouthful of bread.

He smiles wide. "Maya, I found your mom."

I almost choke on my food. Tears spring in my eyes. "You could have started with that!"

"I've been following quite a few leads since your visit. Yesterday, I was in Seattle, and I found them. They're holding your mom and many others from your base there. As soon as I found out, I came straight here." He looks at Wixx. "To hopefully receive help getting them out."

"Of course! When do we leave?" I ask, unable to hold back my enthusiasm.

"It's not that simple, Maya," Wixx says.

"What do you mean? We know where they are. Let's go get them." I hop off the stool.

Wixx grabs my arm. "You and your friends were very lucky you got out of those places unscathed, but we're talking about the biggest Com headquarters in the United States. They won't even let you in the city that surrounds it without being tested, let alone trying to get inside the prison."

I turn towards my father. "But you have a plan, right?"

"I do. But we can only pull it off with help." He looks at Wixx again.

She shakes her head. "I need to talk with the others. There are many risks. And that's not even counting that I'll be leaving my people without protection, having a good chunk of our legion gone."

"You can't just leave them!" I say, growing a bit hysterical.

"I'll call a meeting for the morning, and then you will have your answer. That's the best I can do." She stands.

I step toward her and Michael holds his arm out in front of me with a look.

I sigh. "Okay."

I watch Wixx leave and sit back down to finish my food. Michael found my mom. I can't believe it. She's alive. A part of me had started to believe that maybe she wasn't and I would never see her again.

"We'll get her out."

I look up at my father, whose eyes are full of conviction, and smile. "Thank you."

"I'm just glad I was able to find her for you. It's the least I can do for not being in your life for the past eighteen years."

I shrug. "It wasn't your fault. Oh. And it's nineteen now."

His eyes fill with emotion. "You had a birthday?"

I nod. "September 2nd"

He smiles. "I knew it was sometime this part of the year. I'll have to get you something!"

I shake my head. "No need. Everyone spoiled me two weeks ago. I still even have some leftover cake Abby made me." I doubt it's edible now, though.

His face falls. "I'm glad you had a good birthday. I just…" His eyes glisten, and he clears his throat. He reaches out as if to grab my hand, then hesitates, laying it on the table instead. "I'm here now and have no intention of leaving."

My heart constricts. "Wait, like you're going to *stay* here?"

"I have some loose ends to tie up in Portland, but yes, that's the hope for after we get your mom." He hesitates. "If you guys will have me."

I know this place belongs to him, and he has no need to ask permission, but still…

I grab his hand and smile. "I would love that."

36

A Bunch of Girls

"You've revealed *everything*?" Michael seems more shocked than angry as I unabashedly listen from the bathroom door.

"Michael. I'm old. No, not old. *Ancient*." Noni pauses. I wish I could see her face. I imagine her pointing out every wrinkle. "I'm done hiding. And I think it's about time the Divina step down from their high rock and join civilization." She lowers her voice. "They can help."

"What are you suggesting?"

There's a sound of paper rustling, like she's handing him something.. Now, I *really* wish I could see what's going on.

"When it's time," she says.

Michael mumbles something I can't hear, and then there's a shoosh before Noni says, "We need to get down there, Michael."

I make my appearance then, covertly looking for the papers, but nothing is out of the ordinary on the table or couch.

The three of us head to the dining hall, where Wixx will make her big announcement. I contemplate asking them about their conversation, but I have a feeling they don't want me to know. Izalia has been so forthcoming lately that I have no doubt she'll reveal the information they're keeping from me when it's time.

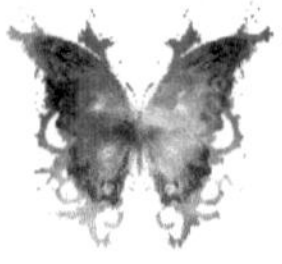

I stare down at the tofu-filled casserole on my plate, trying not to gag. It was so nice getting a chance to eat real meat and eggs on the road, and I would kill to have this be filled with those things. Everyone is in attendance for the upcoming announcement. People who aren't eating line the walls of the space. My leg bounces up and down as I push my food away from me.

Sebastian places his hand on my bouncing leg. "It doesn't matter what she says. We're still going. We'll get her out."

Everyone close to me knows what's happening after I rounded them up early this morning. I barely manage to offer him a smile as bile rises.

I take a huge swig of water and look around the crowded room. Some people are still filing in, but it should be about time. I find James easily. His eyes are on his feet, and one of his hands is gripped tightly in his mom's, like she will never let him go again. He seems to sense my stare, because he lifts his chin and meets my gaze.

My heart stutters unevenly, and Sebastian's hand suddenly weighs a thousand pounds. He offers me a half smile before whipping his head toward the front of the room as Wixx and other newly promoted commanders enter through the kitchen.

A hush falls over the room. I'm surprised to see Abby's fiancé, Trevor, among them. He must have finally gotten that promotion. Hopefully, that's a good thing. I peer at Abby across the table, who's beaming with pride. I wait for her to catch my look, but she's in her own world.

"Abby?" I whisper.

She blinks at me, and I gesture towards Trevor.

"I didn't know. It must have happened this morning," she says, holding that wide smile.

"Do you think he'll vote for the mission?"

"Oh yeah. He's got your back, girl."

A tiny bit of my anxiety lessens.

"Attention, everyone!" Wixx begins. "Thank you all for coming this morning. We have received some good news. Our commanders have been found!"

Everyone claps and whoops, but not to the point I would think at the declaration. Word must have spread already about what the meeting is for. Some are shooting others meaningful looks.

"It's all very exciting, but that means an important decision needs to be made. How to get them back."

An eerie quiet falls over the room, as if everyone is holding their breath.

"We have talked as a committee, and because of the risks and dangers of this mission, it will be a volunteer mission only. And only trained legionaries may go."

No.

"Commander Collins has volunteered to lead the mission," Wixx says as Trevor steps forward.

Abby gasps and I can feel that gasp to my very core. I can't look at her. It's one thing to go with a group of us, but to lead a mission on a volunteer basis? It could be suicide. I was willing to take that risk, but not Trevor. If something happens to him—

No.

I start to rise, but Abby grabs my hand from across the table. With tears in her eyes, she says, "It's okay, Maya."

"No, it's not. Not for me."

Her grip on my hand tightens as she yanks me back to my seat. "It's for all of them, Maya. We need to get *all* of them back. Commander Lawrence, Barlowe, Zhang, and the rest of our people."

I swallow and nod, looking back to Wixx. The commotion dies down and Wixx continues.

"If you would like to join Commander Collins, please come to the front."

This is it. Those who volunteer could make or break this mission. Michael was saying something about needing at least thirty last night before I interrupted him and Wixx. I try to find him, but he's sitting two seats over and facing away, his posture rigid.

James is the first to break from the wall. His mom whimpers as he kisses her on the cheek, whispering something in her ear. My stomach rolls into a tight ball. Sebastian squeezes my hand before riding James's heels. William appears, and the trio makes their way to the front. I can't help but wonder if they would be doing this if my mom wasn't involved, and without a doubt, I know they would. They each have a strong drive to protect, probably one of the few things they have in common.

A couple of others whoop and shoot to their feet to join, including Josh. I'd pretty much forgotten about the man we found in the caves this summer. He's kept his word on staying far away from me since I've been home. And it looks like he's made a couple of friends, as two others join him. I don't hold what he did against him anymore. If I can forgive Sebastian, I can certainly forgive Josh for trying to protect his people. But I may be alone in that sentiment.

"Oh, hell no," James says, turning on him.

"Come on. You know I'm a good soldier. You can use me, man," Josh says.

"Nope."

When Josh reaches Trevor, James stands between them, almost nose to nose.

"I want to help," Josh says calmly, not flinching at his closeness or the lethal glare in his eyes.

Trevor pushes James aside. "We can use him."

James shakes his head, and I swear I hear him murmur, "As bait, maybe."

I think I'm right by the way Trevor smirks.

A couple others join, including Rachel, the Terra girl in the legion that I once was jealous of because she and James were friends.

Wixx frowns when nobody else moves, not even the two other commanders beside Don, who's overseeing the whole thing with a bored expression. Or maybe he just can't see in general? It's clear now who voted for going and who voted for staying.

Eleven people, including Michael, is nowhere near enough. I look at the faces of the rest of the legion, and find them either stoically staring ahead or looking back and forth, to and from the group, apparent indecision on their faces.

I stand up. "I'm joining."

I walk straight to the front, despite the murmuring and Wixx's shake of her head. "I may not be a legionary, but I'm trained by the best." I nod toward Izalia, and she smiles proudly. That smile gives me enough confidence to show off. I pull the fire from within, directing it to my left palm. With my other hand, I harness water from the nearby drinking glasses. The two elements swirl together in front of me. "Try me. I'll put any y'all on your back."

There are some chuckles, but nobody protests.

I look at Wixx, dropping my hands. "I'm joining."

"Well, if she's going. I am, too! They've got my dad." A shock runs through me as a girl from the nearest table stands.

"Me too!"

Another girl stands, and then another, and another until the number of women volunteers almost equals the number of men. My grandmother, Abby, and Juliet are among them. Pride swells within me.

One of Josh's friends, the tall one with jet-black hair and sharp cheekbones, raises his voice. "No way. A bunch of girls will just slow us down."

Before I can see who moves, a gust of wind blows him into the air so hard he flips twice and lands on his butt, his long legs spread out in front of him. People snicker as Juliet slowly lowers her hands.

"We are not just a bunch of girls," she says, flipping her hair and stepping over him.

He blinks up at her as his anger dissolves into awe. I can practically see the heart eyes forming.

The way Wixx is beaming at us makes me think it wasn't her idea to exclude us. "Okay, settle down, everyone."

She turns to the other commanders, one whose voice rises above the others.

"Absolutely not," says a blond, burly man I don't recognize. He must be new to the base.

The five commanders murmur amongst themselves before the blond guy leaves the room in a rage.

Wixx faces us again. "Women may go if they wish, but I want to warn you how dangerous—"

The cheering in the room muffles the rest of her words.

In the end, we have twenty people who volunteered, and we are set to leave in three days, after the girls in our group get some minimal training—the only prerequisite to our joining.

I catch up to Michael before he leaves. "This is good, right?" I smile at him, but when he turns, his face is pained. He tries to hide it and pull up a matching smile, but he's not quick enough.

"What is it?"

"Would you hate me if I told you not to come?"

"Oh, not you too."

He places a hand on my shoulder and looks around before pulling me into a corner of the room. "I don't know if we'll be coming back."

My stomach drops. We don't have enough people. He thinks this mission will fail.

I shake my head. "No. It's enough. It has to be."

He scratches the side of his head. "I'm just being paranoid. You're right. It'll be fine." He smiles, but it doesn't reach his eyes.

He's gone before I can say anything more. I turn and scan the people who volunteered and can't help but feel an air of foreboding. Is Michael right? Will most of us not survive if we go? I look at William, Sebastian, James, Abby, Juliet, and Izalia.

Who among them will come back? Can I survive if one of them doesn't?

No. The answer is that I won't survive losing any single one of them.

37

Tortured Proximity

ichael's words push me to train harder than I ever have before. I train my fire with Sebastian after breakfast. I train my water with Wixx after lunch. I train both together with Izalia in the afternoon. And when twilight begins to descend, I swallow my conflicting feelings and go to find James. I hope not to need it, but knowledge is power. If anything happens to my abilities or I'm weakened somehow, I need to know how to use weapons. And there is no one I know better with them than James.

I walk around the lake, crossing the old imaginary border that kept me contained for so long. Three-quarters of the cube-shaped glass building rises to my left. It's so close to being finished. To my right, I recognize the spot where Sebastian and I had our first date. The tiki torches are gone, and the firepit is overgrown, but the rocks are still there as a silent reminder of our time together.

Abby told me James and Trevor were at the training area, and I'm glad for it. I'll need a buffer. The area is just a glorified field, a space big enough for the legion to control the elements and practice their combat skills. I settle onto one of the benches surrounding it, spotting Trevor's bright red hair right before finding James' dark curls. They are in hand-to-hand combat. A few others are in the space, primarily those who had volunteered. Juliet's long, flowing, white hair stands out as she spars with the dark-haired guy she made a mockery of this morning.

He smiles wide as he lands on his back and Juliet shoves a giant stick into his side. Juliet giggles as she helps him up. William is further away, helping two girls, but I catch him eyeing Juliet every now and then. I can't tell if it's the watchful eye of a friend or something more. My attention returns to James. He's dressed in a sleeveless top, his hair tied up in a bun on the back of his head but most of it is falling out. His shoulders and arms glisten in sweat as he dodges a move from Trevor, thrusts one arm out to grab the back of Trevor's neck and pushes him off balance. James then kicks a leg out, and Trevor goes down hard. Before he hits the ground, James is on top of him, a knife to his throat.

A shock runs through me, but also something else—an excited thrum—that I ignore. Trevor pats him on the hand, and James releases him.

"You got me that time." Trevor grunts as he sits up to catch his breath. "What are we at, six to seven?"

James grins. It's been so long since I've seen him smile. Every time I have caught him watching me, it's with that hard mask of his. But he doesn't know I'm here yet. I'm not currently breaking his heart. It brings me back to the trees, when it was just me and him, and he would flash those wonderful, warm smiles every chance he got. He seemed to save them up, just for me.

"If it makes you feel better about yourself," James says, offering him a hand. Trevor slaps it away.

I laugh, and James instantly turns my way. He wipes the sweat from his brow as he cocks his head. The mask doesn't return, though. If anything, mischief lights his eyes.

This is my chance. Or I can be a chicken and ask somebody else, *anybody* else.

No. I can do this.

James meets me halfway and makes a show of looking around. "Your *mate* isn't out here."

"I know."

He steps closer to me, much too close, and leans down. My breathing hitches as he lowers his lips to my ear. "Did the wolf let his little lamb out of his sight?"

I ignore the delicious shiver that runs through my body and push him away, but when my hands make contact with his chest, I hesitate.

He grabs my wrists and pulls me closer. "Come out to play?" His voice is all wrong, mocking when it used to be soothing.

"Stop."

"Why? Worried I'll break his toy?"

"Stop it!" This time, I do push him. Fire tendrils slip over my fingers as he stumbles.

He smiles a heartbreakingly beautiful smile that clouds my thoughts. "There she is."

I look at his chest. It's easier if I don't look into that stupidly gorgeous face of his. "You know, I came out here to ask for your help, but if you'd prefer I ask somebody else, fine." I turn on my heel to head to who knows where, but his hand wraps around mine.

"I'm sorry. I'll be good. What do you need help with?" His eyes are sincere, the sarcasm gone. I don't blame him though, I'd be mad too. Just like William, he can't possibly understand what's between Sebastian and me. Even *I'm* beginning to understand it less and less.

"I need you to show me how to use a gun."

His eyebrows rise. "You have one?"

I shake my head. "I don't want one either. But I thought it would be good to know…just in case."

He nods, and more wayward curls fall out of his bun and into his face. I want to reach out and push them back, but I ball my hand into a fist instead, digging my fingernails into my palm.

"Let's do it. But we'll need a little bit more privacy. Don't want to start a war again by getting a certain fire-wielder angry."

I glare at him.

"Too soon?"

He leads me into the trees, not our spot, but a more open area that looks like it was decimated by the bombings. Terras have regrown everything around the manor back to its former glory, but anything past the tree line was left untouched.

James drops the bag he ran back to the manor to get. He also changed out of his sweaty clothes, as he now wears a fitted, black V-neck. He digs three silver cans out and takes them to the center of the field. He sets them on a burnt tree husk and whistles loudly. After peering around, he walks back to me.

He sees the question in my eyes. "Just making sure there are no animals in the vicinity for you to—" He makes a slicing motion along his neck and sticks his tongue out the side of his mouth.

I cover my laugh with a cough. "I'm not killing any bunnies."

"Hopefully." He pulls a smooth, black handgun out of his backpack.

I immediately take a step back.

It's in my hands as I hold it against Sebastian's chest. A shot rings out and he's falling to the ground, the light leaving his eyes.

I blink away the image hastily, but not before James catches it.

His eyebrows turn down in worry. "We don't need to do this."

I push my shoulders back and move closer to him.

He eyes me warily before saying, "It's just an object. There is nothing to fear from the gun itself. It's whoever is wielding it. And you will wield it. You will be the one in control."

I nod, swallow, and hold out my hand. He places it into my palm and wraps my hand around the handle. It's unnaturally heavy for such a small object, cool to the touch.

"Unless you're ready to shoot, always keep your finger off the trigger like this." He moves my pointer finger so it aligns with the barrel of the gun. He taps a small switch on the other side. "This is the safety. Right now, it's on, so it can't shoot. But when you're ready, you'll flip it off and aim toward those cans."

"Safety on, shooting off. Safety off, shooting on. It's backward, got it."

He wrinkles his brow at me, but I'm too busy studying the cans across the field to comment. It can't be that different than aiming a fireball, right?

I slowly lift the gun with my hand toward the cans. "Wait, do I just press the safety or flip it like a switch?" I swing toward James, and his eyes widen. The gun disappears from my hands in a flash.

"Never point a gun at somebody unless you want to kill them. Actually, I take that back. Planning my death is probably your favorite pastime."

"Oh. Sorry." I frown and then the last part of his sentence hits me. "Wait, what?"

He slides something from the gun's base. "This is a magazine; it holds the cartridges. This one is empty." He shows me a rectangular black object with holes in it, nothing inside. "And this one is full," he says, showing me another before placing it back in the gun.

"This gun is loaded, Maya. No pointy, pointy." He makes a show of pointing it at the ground and I nod.

"Why would you think I want you dead?"

He shrugs. "I'm sure I put you through hell when you thought I abandoned you, and then you came all the way across the country for me and I treated you like crap on the bottom of my shoe." He places the gun back in my hand. This time he wraps his arms around mine, positioning my fingers exactly. He pulls up the gun so it's at eye level with the silver cans and slowly moves my pointer finger to the trigger. He takes my other hand and wraps it around the gun for added support.

His next words are a caress on the shell of my ear. "Then you didn't get my letter and thought I was the most despicable person you've ever known. I don't blame you for moving on, Maya. I just wish it wasn't with *him*."

"James, I—"

"Shhh. The safety is off. I want you to take a deep breath and pull the trigger."

I blink, distracted by his words, the gun in my hand, and the feel of his body pressed up against mine. Without thinking, I pull back the trigger, and a loud pop sounds out.

My hands jerk back. James stabilizes me, though, so I don't do something stupid like drop it. That wasn't too bad.

As soon as he moves my hands to lower the gun, his body against mine becomes my main focus, his rich, earthy scent fills my nose.

But he moves away too soon, leaving the gun in my hands. Cold air replaces his warmth. I blow out a breath. *Get it together, Maya.*

He points toward the cans with a smile. "Look, you got one first try!"

"That wasn't me! That was you. I don't think I was even looking."

His eyes widen. "Maya!"

"Sorry," I mumble, lifting the gun to try on my own.

"You need to rack it."

"Whaa?"

He takes the gun from me and pulls back on the top part until it clicks. "This strips a round from the magazine into the chamber so you can shoot. You must do it every time."

"Right." I take the gun back and aim at the cans. He was right. The far left one is gone now. I aim for the next can, but I'm not sure which eye to use, so I use both.

Even though I'm ready this time, I still jump a little at the loud noise and the gun's recoil, but I'm proud of myself for not dropping it. I squint to see if I got anything, but the cans remain intact.

"Was I close?"

"Eh. You weren't standing right. Here." He grips my hips from behind, and an electric shock goes through me. He kicks my right foot into a wider stance, almost toppling me over. He grips me tighter, and I stifle my gasp. "Keep your feet aligned with your shoulders."

When I nod, he slides his hands up my frame to my shoulders. "You need to relax. You're too stiff."

Hmm. I wonder why. Not that his hands are all over my body, and I'm trying and failing to tamp down the fire igniting in my veins. His hand moves down my right arm, skimming the tender spot where my arm bends. I bite the inside of my cheek to keep myself from leaning into him. I've never known touching an arm to be so…intimate. But I want him to do it again and again.

"Lock both your arms." His voice drops an octave, making me think I'm not the only one affected by our proximity. With his next words, I can almost feel his lips against my neck. "It's okay to close an eye to focus better."

His hand moves slowly back up my arms, touching that tender spot again as the other snakes up my neck. My hands shake.

"Tsk tsk. Don't hold it too hard, Maya. Firm and steady." His fingertips brush my face, and the tiniest gasp escapes my lips. His hard chest stiffens against my back and his thumb grazes my bottom lip.

I bite it.

His forehead drops onto my shoulder as his knees seem to buckle behind me. I don't move an inch as he struggles to right himself. He sucks in a strangled breath and brushes my left eye.

"This eye. You can close this eye." His voice is husky and tortured, and oh, how it fills me.

Confidence bursts through me, and I aim and fire, knocking the middle can clear off the tree. But I don't celebrate or even move. It's silent as James's ragged breathing begins to slow in tune with mine. And finally, achingly slow, he steps back.

I lower the gun and turn around. His eyes are full of want—no, *need*.

"I don't want you dead, James. I never thought those things. If anything, it was the complete opposite. I—I never stopped wanting you. Even when I should have." The words tear from me before I can stop them, and he closes the gap between us.

His hands are in my hair and on my neck, gripping my back. The gun disappears from my hands, but I don't dare touch him back. If I do, then I'll be lost in him forever. He cups my face tenderly, his lips just inches from mine, waiting for permission. For a moment, I think I'll give it to him. It would be so easy to succumb to these feelings ravaging my heart.

"James, I can't." It's torture to say the words.

With that, he releases me like I shocked him. He moves to pick up the gun, which is wrapped in a root. James, either consciously or unconsciously, had the little guy take it from me. He flips the safety, releases the magazine and puts them into his pack separately. He throws it over his shoulder and without looking at me, heads back into the trees.

I trail after him. "Wait, what about—"

"You're amazing, Maya. Quickest study yet!" He says it too cheerfully.

I trip over roots and brush to try to keep up with his pace. "James, there's one more thing."

He stops and I almost run into him.

"I don't know if I can, Maya." He shakes his head, the sorrow in the words striking my heart like tiny arrows.

I could ask somebody else. I *should* ask somebody else. Instead, I walk around him so he can see me. His face is masked as he stares to the right of my shoulder.

I slip the knife from my boot—his knife. "Teach me how to use this?"

He looks at the knife, his face softening a tiny bit, before searching my eyes. "You kept it."

Not wanting to speak and betray the tumultuous emotions battling inside me, I only nod.

"Have you used it?"

I shake my head. "It can't be that hard, though, right? Just point and stab?"

His lips curve up at that. "Point and stab? Doesn't look like you need my help then."

I shift on my feet, biting my bottom lip. His eyes zone in on that tiny motion, and I remember so acutely what it's like to have his lips on mine. His hand flexes and his eyes heat, before he blinks it away. He swipes that same hand through his hair.

"Okay, but we better get back to the training field. If I'm alone with you any longer, I'm going to do something we'll both regret."

He brushes past me, his fingers reaching for mine almost like he doesn't realize it. In a moment of weakness, I move my hand so he can touch me. One last touch.

But that touch is my undoing.

Blue flames erupt from the spot and travel along my skin, reacting to him and his words. I marvel at them and know beyond a shadow of a doubt that I share his same torture. If his lips are close to mine again, nothing will stop me from finishing what we started.

38

Unearthly Melodies

Quiet sobs emanate from behind Abby's door. I hesitate to knock. With her ceremony in the morning, I came to see if she needed anything before I called it a night. I don't know if she'll want to see me now. I'm sure she blames me for Trevor having to lead the mission that we're leaving for in twenty-four hours. I swallow my selfishness and push the door open.

She looks up from her ceremony dress piled in her lap with tear-stained cheeks. "We shouldn't be having a wedding right now."

"Oh, Abby." I run and throw my arms around her. "Of course we should. It is exactly what we need right now, something to celebrate."

She sniffles, and I rub her back. "I'm scared, Maya."

"Me too," I admit. "It's okay to be scared, though. I mean, who wouldn't be, right?"

She nods and wipes her nose.

"This ceremony tomorrow is why we're doing this. So we can thrive and stop living in fear. We can't let them win."

"We can't let them win," she repeats, hiccupping.

Suddenly, an alarm pierces the room. We freeze, staring at each other with widening eyes. It's part of the new security system Wixx installed, so we'd all know if there was another attack. This alarm is *not* a drill.

We thaw from our frozen state and dash into the hallway, now swarming with people. Unlike the chaos of that so-called drill months ago, people are calm because they know what to do. That's what happens when people aren't lied to and forced into a tiny, obedient box. Many shuffle down the steps and continue to the bunker, while others move outdoors, preparing for battle. Abby and I join them.

My knife is strapped to my thigh for better access, with a sheath gifted by James after our lessons. He didn't get as close to me again, unlike whatever insanity washed over me in the forest, but there were still some heated moments. The audience helped keep my emotions in check. William also joined in training me, and I'm much more confident with my knife now. He was right; it's much more than just "point and stab." I feel ready, remembering what James told me.

"Focus on your fire and water powers, but if you feel fatigued, go for the weapons. The gun for longer range targets and the knife for closer sparring."

He insisted on giving me a gun, and even though I'm a bit more comfortable with it after our training, I still don't want the thing anywhere near me. I took it not to cause a scene in the moment but stuffed it in a drawer as soon as I returned to my room.

We bust through the doors outside, and part of me wants to tell Abby to go to the bunker, but her face is determined, even in her hot-pink pajamas. I wish she would have at least thrown on a jacket. She's just too exposed like that, a bright-pink target.

The legionaries are lining up along the east perimeter. The sun has long set, and darkness sweeps over the land. Other than a soft murmuring, it's quiet as we join them and await what is coming for us. There's no whirring of engines, at least. My pulse thrums in my ears. Will this mean I won't get the chance to save my mom? That I will never see her again?

Someone grabs my hand, and I look up to find Sebastian.

"We can't be sure that they're hostile. It's a small group," he says.

I wrinkle my brow. "You saw them?"

"Just some fuzzy images on a screen. It even looked like…" He shakes his head.

"Looked like what?"

"Like there were children with them?"

My eyes widen as I push past him and through the gathering legion.

"Maya!" Sebastian calls, but I ignore him.

Men curse and grunt as I shove and elbow myself to the front. A group of people have just broken through the trees in the distance. Wixx stands on guard, leading the charge, as water swirls around her. Three other commanders, including Trevor, surround her—their elements on full display.

"Wait! Stop!"

Somebody grabs me around the waist, pulling me back. I pull the knife from my thigh, swing around, and put it to their throat.

"Let me go," I growl.

The legionary who was stupid enough to try to stop me holds his hands up, and I sprint towards Wixx.

I grab her arm. "Wixx, stop!"

The commanders turn on me, but I ignore their hostile expressions—except Trevor, who is more surprised—and lock eyes with Wixx.

"Maya. If you want to be in this, you have to follow protocol. Get back!" she snaps.

"No, they're not hostile!"

Her eyebrows turn down as she hesitates slightly. Swirling elements gather around from the legion behind us as my heart rate skyrockets. The small group is getting closer, and I can see their faces in the light of our elements.

"How do you know?" she hisses, turning back toward the group, which is being led by a redheaded couple.

"Because that's my brother."

After the rest of the legion scatters, a small group of us, consisting of my father, Izalia, Sebastian, William, James, Wixx, Abby and Trevor, welcomes the intruders.

Thomas wraps me in a warm hug, eyeing our father behind my shoulder.

Michael pats him on the back. "I didn't think you'd come."

He shrugs. "You said you needed people when you visited, and we have people." Thomas winks at me and adds. "And I couldn't let my little sister have all the fun with those Com bastards. He told me you managed to break into two of their facilities?"

I smile as my father and brother look down at me in pride. They're the same height, probably around six feet, and share many of the same traits, including the striking eyes. We both got our hair from our mothers' sides, though. However, Thomas's son has Michael and Izalia's dark hair. Genetics work in mysterious ways.

"It was nothing," I say.

Thomas laughs loudly and shakes his head, pointing at me. "You're badass. My sister is badass!" he yells louder.

"Shh! Your kids are right there," I say, looking over to where Izalia stands with Claire and their children.

"Oh, they've heard worse. And besides, they're soaking in all the grandma snuggles."

Izalia beams as she holds their baby boy on her hip and twines her hand into their daughter's hair as she talks to Claire.

"Thank you for bringing them," Michael says, voice full of emotion.

"It's been too long without family. My children deserve it, despite my feelings on the matter," he says gruffly.

"Which are?" I ask.

"Jeez, sis, already prying into my personal life?"

I shrug. "You'll get used to it." Somehow, even though I barely know him, Thomas does feel like family already.

"I still can't believe you didn't tell us," William butts in, flinging an arm over my shoulders.

I look up with a grimace, but his lips hold a small smile. It's possible he even figured it out before by the way he doesn't seem the least bit surprised.

"I know. It was a lot at the moment, and then there just wasn't a good time." I shrug, even though it's a terrible excuse.

Abby bumps me with her hip. "He'll annoy the heck out of you soon enough," she says, eyeing James.

I can feel where he is, even though I refuse to look at him. The way his body heat wrapped around me earlier is still too fresh in my mind. I can't give in to those feelings.

"Then it looks like big brothers aren't much different than little brothers. Cal is going to love you guys," I say, taking in my new family. I went from losing my mother and only having Cal to having a big family including in-laws.

Cal is with the other kids in the bunker but should be coming out soon. Then, everyone I love will be together…except my mom. I swallow. Soon, I'll see her soon. And now, we have a real chance. Thomas and his people have increased our numbers to thirty-five, and everyone is in better spirits for it. Seeing Michael smile finally calms my nerves enough to be in the moment with everyone.

The gathering eventually moves indoors, as the night's chill settles into our bones, and the littles start crying, needing a place to rest. Izalia offers up her room—not like she uses it much anyway—and soon we all find sleep.

"Was mine like this?" I ask Juliet as we finish draping the chairs in white cloth and tying them in green sashes.

"Worse, Abby was a monster. At least she's not down here ordering us about."

I giggle but quickly sober, remembering that she was not only putting together my ceremony but busting James out of jail that day. No wonder she was a monster.

"Are you playing?" I ask.

Juliet smiles and nods. "They found me a new harp."

"Good. Abby will love that."

Soon everyone is settled in their fancy seats in the gardens, awaiting the beautiful bride. Trevor stands underneath the decked-out arch, as handsome as ever, exotic flowers drifting in the wind. Juliet and I are on the other side as her bridesmaids. I'm standing as Juliet plays the harp next to me. Abby wanted it just like a Com wedding. William and Cal stand next to Trevor as his groomsmen. William is the epitome of a heartthrob in his black suit vest and white collared shirt and tie, his hair perfectly mussed. And Cal—Mom would have loved to see him all dressed up. He looks older, more like Dad, with his little bow tie.

Juliet's music flows with the birds' songs, creating an unearthly melody as the front doors of the manor open. Ann steps out, holding my niece Loreline's hand. Abby made her a last-minute flower girl, and Ann was thrilled not to have to do the "walk of embarrassment" alone. They toss white rose petals on the grass, making a walkway for—

Everyone stands as Abby steps into the doorway, Mrs. Stevens holding her hand. Tears stream down the woman's cheeks in an unending flow. Knowing her, she's probably been crying since she saw her daughter.

James is on Abby's other side, his arm hooked in hers, which is holding the bouquet I helped with—well, if helping counts as holding the ivory-colored ribbon as Abby wielded her powers to create the masterpiece.

As soon as I spot James, I can't take my eyes off him. He's stunning in a dark suit. The collar of his shirt is open as he's forgone a tie, looking like Abby tried to wrangle one on him and he ripped it off moments before stepping to the door. The thought makes me smile. His hair is combed back out of his face, except for one curl that has gotten loose, hanging over his left eye. My heart squeezes as he finds me. His hazel eyes don't leave mine as they close the distance.

The people around us fade into the background, and I can almost imagine that this is *our* ceremony day and all of this is for the two of us—that he's mine.

But I blink and it's gone. I rip my eyes from his to look at Abby. It's her day. I've already had mine.

She's radiant in her pinkish-white gown made of flowers. The train flows behind her, the flowers moving along the grass like they're alive. Ivy has grown from the bodice, wrapping around the tips of her shoulders and curling around her neck, making it look longer. Her auburn hair is in an updo, a flower crown circling her head, and a few curls framing her face. She only has eyes for Trevor.

As the trio step in front of us, James kisses her temple and moves to stand beside William and Cal. Mrs. Stevens gives Abby a tight hug before wiping her eyes and sitting down. Trevor, who looks dashing with a new haircut where the sides of his head are trimmed short and the top is styled expertly, takes her hands, a silent tear slipping down his face, which Abby wipes with the tip of her manicured finger.

"You're going to make me cry and ruin my face," she teases, but I can hear the emotion in her words as she holds back her tears.

Trevor kisses her hand. "Nothing can ruin that face, my love."

I'm bawling by the time Don completes their bonding ceremony, so happy for Abby that my heart could explode. If anyone deserves such happiness, it's her. They kiss with the heat of a thousand suns and throw their hands in the air as they face the crowd. We erupt in cheers and swarm the merry couple.

That night, after a party that puts any event this place has ever seen to shame, Cal lies in bed with me. We have the room to ourselves. Noni is with her grandchildren, and Sebastian told me during the one dance we shared that I probably wouldn't see him for the rest of the evening as they have some plans to hash out before we leave in a few hours. I would have joined, but when Cal unexpectedly asked to sleep in my room, I didn't hesitate.

"Promise me you'll come back," he says.

I shift onto my elbow to look at him. He avoids my gaze. "I came back last time, didn't I? And I *will* have Mom with me this time."

He peers up at me. "This feels different than last time."

"It is. This time, we have a lot more people to back us up."

He moves into a sitting position and plays with the buttons on his nightshirt. "Can you stay?"

His big blue eyes pierce mine. It's been a long time since I've seen that fear there. He usually tries to put on such a brave front. I pull him to me and smooth the back of his head, where his hair is sticking up at all angles. He wraps his arms tightly around me.

"I have to go get her, Cal." I pull back to look into his red-rimmed eyes. "I promise I'll come back."

He settles into the crook of my arm as I play with his hair. "Keep your little cousins company, okay? Show them around. You know all the best spots."

Cal yawns. "You mean my niece and nephew?"

I smile. I'm glad he's taken on the uncle role so exuberantly. He knows he's not technically related to them, but that has never mattered to him. Family is family, no matter if they share blood.

Cal falls asleep fairly quickly, and I know I should get up and prepare to leave in the next hour, but instead, I study him.

His face isn't as round anymore, and he's becoming lankier as he grows, barely able to fit in my lap. But right now, he looks so young, with his dark eyelashes flat against his rosy cheeks and his plump lips jutting out. An image of holding him like this as a baby floats into my mind, and an unsettling feeling wiggles into the pit of my stomach. For a moment, I consider staying. He's lost so many people already. But the moment passes quickly, and I slip out of the room.

I'll be back.

I have to.

39

Seattle

The drive to Seattle feels unusually long, probably because we have to stay off all the main roads, and nobody is in a chatty mood. I ride with my father and Noni, sitting in the back seat between Sebastian and Presley Reed, one of the girls who volunteered.

Presley used to be in a tight-knit trio of friends, the quietest among them. I know she's a Terra but that's about it. The other girls matched, bonded, and left the community months ago. Presley was matched, too, but she's not bonded, so something must have happened.

I peer at her sleeping figure slumped against the window, wondering why she volunteered. I should be sleeping, too, using this five-hour drive to rest, but I can't. Instead, I watch the taillights ahead of us. We're behind the lead truck, holding Abby and her new commander mate with James, William, and Juliet. Thomas is in another. Claire stayed back with the children.

As we approach the city lights, Sebastian's hand tightens around mine. I peer at him, but he seems calm and collected. He looks down at me with a smile. But it's a bit tight-lipped. I squeeze his hand in return.

"It's gonna be okay," he whispers.

I nod, wondering if he's trying to reassure me or himself.

My father clears his throat. "We're about ten minutes from the wall around the heart of the city. There's a pull-off up ahead where we'll stow the cars."

"And you said there is a section we'll be able to slip through, right?" I ask.

They explained the plan to us before we loaded into the vehicles, which initially had only a third of us going through the wall. But Trevor tweaked it so we would enter at different times. The first group will be scouts to ensure we find a safe way in and deal with any Coms on the way. The second group includes me to get my mother and the others out. The third group will head to the water where we will make our escape and be ready to aid us if we need it. Most of the girls are unhappily in that one. But once Trevor convinced them that lookout was just as important, they obliged. I overheard Trevor assigning Abby to the third group and was pretty relieved she didn't fight it.

Noni looks back at me with a smile. I wish I had that same positivity, to not even look a *little* worried. Maybe I would if I had all four elements in my arsenal of power. I have two, though, and that's more than anyone else can say here.

The truck stops and we pile out. Before us rises a metal gate that extends to our right and left as far as I can see, reminding me of the types that are kept around prisons. It seems as if the whole community here are prisoners, not just my mom. Who would choose to live like this?

I peer up at the stars to calm my nerves, but there are none. The glow from the city beyond the gate is too bright.

Abby bumps me with her hip, startling me out of my reverie. She rubs her hands together. "This is going to be fun."

I give her a look. This coming from the girl who froze before going into the Com headquarters in Portland. She must have been thinking the same thing because she says, "I admit, last time I was terrified. But this time—" she shrugs, "—I don't know, Trevor makes me feel more confident."

I understand that feeling—the person you love hyping you up, making you feel like you can conquer the world.

"Are you scared?" she asks.

I start to shake my head but stop myself. "A little."

Her eyes widen. "You, scared?" She holds up a hand. "Three weeks ago in Portland, San Francisco, Salt Lake—" she lifts a finger with each city, "—you were kicking butts and taking names." Abby looks around before pulling us deeper into the shadows, away from the gathering group and incoming Jeeps and trucks. "Tell me."

I'm suddenly relieved she knows me so well—knows I'm holding back. I spill everything.

"It was different before. I was putting myself at risk...but now?" I look past Abby at Noni, who's talking with Juliet; my father, who's probably explaining the plan for the tenth time to one group; Sebastian, who's in a heated conversation with the blonde commander I'm not fond of; William, chatting with Thomas and his group, who just climbed out of a truck; and James, who's leaning against the closest Jeep, watching me. A shiver runs down my spine.

"Everyone I love is here," I whisper, more to myself. Then I look at her and choke out, "What if something happens?"

She pulls me to her chest, and I swallow my tears. I cannot cry and be weak right now.

"There's nothing to worry about. Your grandma could probably pull this all off single-handedly and give the Coms life lessons in the process."

I chuckle despite myself and pull back, my eyes burning to release the emotion. I open my mouth to respond, but James appears next to us, and the words get stuck in my mouth.

"Are you okay?" He looks at me, really looks, like his eyes can sear straight through me to my core. It makes me want to really start crying.

Abby weaves her hand around my back, pulling me against her, and turns toward him. "Yup."

He ignores her, not taking his eyes off me. I hold his stare. Abby peers at me and lets me go.

"I'll just be over here," she murmurs, getting the hint.

Neither of us acknowledge her leaving. James takes a step toward me and slowly brings a hand up to my face but pauses and lets it drop. Pain flashes in his eyes before he hides it behind a mask of indifference. I grab his hand, not meaning to, but I can't stand to see him in pain. I hold it to my face.

"I won't let anyone hurt you." His warm, sweet breath swirls my hair.

"I'm not worried about me," I say.

He smiles tightly, his finger caressing my temple, sending sparks down my frame. "Of course not. You have the gun and knife?"

I debated taking the thing but ultimately decided it would be stupid not to. Thanks to Abby's excellent seamstress skills, I have both strapped to my thighs behind hidden pockets in my cargo pants for easy access. Unlike James, who looks like he's carrying around a whole weapons department on his belt, anyone who attacks me won't see it coming.

"Maya?" Sebastian calls from afar.

I drop James's hand as his mask pulls back into place. I hate that he wears a mask. I prefer the mocking over his acting like he doesn't care.

"I'm over here," I say, stepping around James.

James grabs my hand, and I turn back to him. "I won't let anything happen to your family, Maya." Of course, he was listening to my and Abby's conversation.

I look into his hazel depths. "You can't promise that." My hand slips through his grasp as I walk away and back into Sebastian's arms. But before I do, I hear his voice on the breeze.

"I promise, Maya."

Sebastian takes my hand and pulls me toward the growing group around my father and Trevor.

"All their firepower is along the water and the other side of the city. This section along a park is the least guarded. They keep the prisoners in the heart of the city, about three miles in," Michael says.

Trevor's voice rises. "Diego and Michael will bring the first group through here." He points to a section of the wall.

All I see is the dark fence with no openings. Trevor nods to Diego, the blonde commander who got upset with all the girls who volunteered. He separates himself from the group when his palms begin to glow red and flames crawl up his arms. He grabs the gate, and the chains melt, falling to the ground with a clank, leaving a hole big enough for a large person to fit through.

Impressive.

Nine others separate themselves and join Diego, including William. I reach out for him, and he kisses my temple.

"Already worrying about me?" William teases. But I don't respond. His eyebrows turn down as he grabs my hand and rubs the back of it. It does nothing to soothe my nerves. "I've done loads of missions like this. Now *you*. Don't do anything daft, okay?" He nudges me and I finally nod. He moves his eyes to Sebastian as somebody else tugs on my arm.

Before I look away, William and Sebastian close their hands along each other's forearms in a sign of kinship. A jolt of surprise goes through me. Another tug on my arm has me turning away before I can say anything.

Sebastian releases me as Michael pulls me in for a hug. Unlike the awkward side hug I got when we left his house, this is a genuine, warm, fatherly hug. I'm suddenly five years old in his arms as I imagine what it would have been like for him to have been a part of raising me. *He's here now.*

"If anything happens, run and don't look back. I love you," he whispers in my ear.

I pull back to look at him, but he has already released me, heading for the wall, William ahead of him. My stomach tightens. Why would he say that? Does he not believe this will work?

A numbness takes hold of me when Sebastian's hand finds mine again. I'm numb as Trevor talks to and directs people. I'm numb as I walk to my assigned group, and somebody imparts instructions. I'm numb as I watch my father and William cross the barrier and disappear beyond the wall without a backward glance. That oh-so-familiar and diluting numbness is back once more.

High Alert

After an hour of holding my breath, we finally receive the message on Trevor's communicator. Each leader of the three groups has one, just in case Auras can't use their air-linking abilities. Group two gets the all-clear to move forward.

Sebastian helps me up from the ground, where we waited not-so-patiently against the tall gate blocking out the moon's light. The last of the trucks have been stashed in an abandoned building nearby and we're ready to go.

We gather with ten others near the opening. We don't get any other information about the state of the first group. I want to ask, but I bite my tongue. They would tell us if something happened.

I study the faces in our group and do a double-take. James is in our group. He's near the front having a heated conversation with the commander in charge of our group, Lliam, I think. I thought—or hoped—James would stay in Abby's group, but who am I kidding? This is *James*. He doesn't know how to take a backseat in the action.

Three other girls are in our group, two of whom are not legionaries: Camille, a Lympha with short black hair and piercings in her nose that weren't there a few months ago, and Presley. I know why Camille is in this group; her father is among the commanders who were taken, but Presley? I still don't know why she came, let alone how she was put in the most dangerous group.

Then I see why. Presley takes Camille's hand and nuzzles into her side. Huh. I didn't know they were together. Relationships with the same gender were forbidden during the matching, but Wixx apparently lifted that unsaid rule. Good for them to find love in the chaos.

Out of the other seven in our group, three of the faces are familiar. There is Cody, an Igna, and Foster, an Aura I've seen train with William occasionally. Then there's Rachel. Her dark pixie cut has grown to her shoulders since she last helped Seth train me, but she is still just as intimidating as when I first met her. She has muscular arms, a confident stance, and intense eye contact with the other guys, holding her own as a woman in the legion. She talks with two tall, very muscular men with similar features, all dressed in legion black near the fence. I recognize the last two as part of Thomas's group. My brother, Thomas, is in the third group with Izalia, and I'm pleased with how that turned out.

Everyone seems calm but also focused and ready. They're used to doing stuff like this, unlike me. I'm so far out of my league here. Maybe I should have stayed back. If I get somebody killed, I don't think I'll ever forgive myself.

Trevor moves into our circle, clearing his throat. He looks at each one of us. It's the first time I don't see him as Abby's beau, or now mate. His eyes are clear and full of electricity. If he was an Igna, they would probably be lit up right now. It seems that he truly feels like he has the weight of our survival on his shoulders as he talks to us.

"…stick with the plan. Good luck." He ends the inspired speech that makes my nerves fill with something other than anxiety. We've got this.

Our group files through the dark opening, the burnt edges of the gate sticking out haphazardly. James is the first to step through. I peek over my shoulder one last time. Abby is chewing on her finger, but when she sees me, she smiles and gives me a thumbs up. Trevor joins her and gives me a nod, his face still serious. Izalia blows me a kiss that feels like butterfly wings against my cheek. She's almost lost in the darkness with her dark clothes and hair wound around her head like a halo, but I see a speck of color under jacket and smile. Thomas gives me an encouraging nod. They are all safe for now.

I turn back around and Sebastian guides us through the opening. We're the last ones to go through.

My eyes have long since adjusted to the darkness, but it feels as if we've been sucked into a black hole inside the wall. My feet step noisily onto dead leaves and sticks, and I wince. I still have my hand in Sebastian's, which I'm grateful for, since he seems to know where we're going. We walk for a while, and the silhouettes of trees form above our heads. A field opens before us, just past the trees, but we head in a different direction, around the outskirts of the field.

James is far ahead, stopping occasionally to put a hand on a tree before continuing. He's the leader of our group, I realize with a start. Is that what he was arguing with Lliam about? Two leaders butting heads? It makes sense, though. He's a born leader. He truly cares about his team and always puts their needs first, which is why he was gone for so long. If not for that part of him, he would have come with me when we found him in Texas. His love for his team made him stay and ensure they would be okay. But what about me? I wasn't okay. He knew I was going into Com territory. Why didn't he want to be there?

A part of me knows that he was trying to protect me from Talia but I can't help the selfish thoughts from taking hold. He wasn't there when I needed him most. I did have my own group at the time. But still, it's not like we had any experience. He chose his team over me in the end.

James stops up ahead where the trees end, waiting. When we catch up, he lowers his voice. "The path we have planned out should be completely clear from the first group, but keep your eyes peeled. You never know." He doesn't even look at me before trudging ahead.

Sebastian leans down. "You good?"

With James and Sebastian with me, I find that my confidence is higher, but my father's warning is still ringing in my mind. "Yeah, you?"

He touches my chin. "Always, when I'm with you."

That touch causes my spark to grow, and heat laces my body. I turn away from him, embarrassed. We're in the middle of a critical mission in enemy territory. How could my body still respond like this? My feelings for him are so entwined with the bond that I can't even tell which is which anymore.

"Come on," I whisper, marching ahead. He's at my side with one long stride, his arm brushing against mine. I try to ignore the heat and look around like James told us to.

We're next to a large sign with faded letters: *Jefferson Park Golf Course.*

I peer back at what I thought was a field. In reality, it's an overgrown golf course. It still has hints of its former beauty in how the trees perfectly encircle the entire field, and parts of the brush are in equally distanced spheres.

We come over a hill, and I see it—the Seattle skyline. The buildings rise in the distance, dotting the night sky in warm light. I can even make out the Space Needle, its pointed tip spearing into the full moon like a head on a spike. I wince at the imagery. I had wanted to go as a little girl but never got the chance. Mom came to Seattle once for work and told me how beautiful the view from the top was. I just hope that her experiences here have helped her somehow while she's been imprisoned.

On several occasions, I have to stop to keep my heart from jumping out of my chest. Every sound puts me on edge. Being in the open is nerve-wracking, but we aren't in the open for long. James keeps us against buildings and under any tree cover we can find. We stop occasionally to reach out with our senses and harness our Sages. My flames are hot and ready inside me, a stoked fire waiting for their first victim. The first sign of danger, and I'll light up like a torch. My body also keeps up a constant vigilance about how far the nearest water source is. I have to admit, Igna abilities are much more convenient.

I peek at Sebastian. He's looking around uneasily, his eyes twitching back and forth, his jaw set. I wonder what it's like for him to be going back into a city, toward a prison like the one he was kept in. I wince as the few images I remember from my dreams—or possible memories from Sebastian—flash in my mind. He's endured such unspeakable pain. At least he has his powers back now. I haven't seen him use them since that unfortunate day last week when I found James's letter. I wonder if they have grown to what they used to be or if his inability to control his anger has grown with it.

I quickly banish the thought. I've forgiven him. Forgive and forget and move on.

His eyes land on me, and even though I can tell he's nervous, he smiles at having caught me staring at him.

"Get down!" James hisses from up ahead as he dives under the canopy of a building's entrance.

We're in the middle of a city sidewalk. The streetlights aren't on, but up ahead on the road, lights from a vehicle are heading straight for us. Sebastian and I aren't near any entrance or alley, so I fall flat onto my stomach, pulling Sebastian along with me. We army crawl toward a tree and a bush between two slabs of the sidewalk. It's a skinny tree and a tiny bush that smells like dog pee. It'll hardly obscure me, let alone the both of us. But there is nowhere else to go.

The headlights grow closer, and I squeeze my eyes shut.

James appears at our sides, wrapping his arms around the both of us. I stiffen under his touch as the bush grows three times its size, enveloping us in its leaves. None of us breathe as the large truck rumbles past.

Suddenly, I'm back in the forest with James, hiding from our people as we try to sneak out of the base. It takes all of my self-control not to lean into him.

The moment is over quickly, and James releases us. Sebastian and James rise, and both hold hands out for me. I hesitate before grabbing Sebastian's hand. James's hand drops, and he turns around without a word.

"Hey, thanks, dude," Sebastian says, sounding genuine.

James looks over his shoulder and catches my eye. "It's why I'm here."

We continue on the same road but at a brisker pace than before as we urgently try to get off the streets. But with every corner we turn, hiding spots become sparser as the city grows denser. We're within a mile of our destination now, and it's eerily deserted. Whatever the first group did, they did a good job. Every time we step on a new road, I breathe a sigh of relief that their bodies aren't sprawled out on the pavement.

Grouped close, everyone is on high alert. The first group is supposed to message us their exact location so we can meet up and plan our next move. By now, group three should be on their way to the water's edge, ready to come to our aid or provide cover fire for us on our way out. Getting in is supposed to be easy, but getting out may get messy.

Once we get within a couple blocks of their headquarters, James turns around, his expression strained. "Something is wrong."

"What do you mean?" asks Presley, who has shown incredible focus and agility so far.

"Group one has been radio silent. They should have been keeping us updated on their location. Foster can't hear them, either." He catches all of our eyes. "There is nobody out here."

The words drop straight through me. He's not just talking about the Coms.

"I think we should go around and regroup with the others. It could be a trap."

My heart beats hard in my chest. William. My father. No. "No." I walk forward. "I'm going in."

James blocks me. "It's too dangerous without word."

I shake my head. "I am going in." I move past him, but he grabs my arm.

"No. We're going back."

I try to shake him off, but his grip is iron-tight.

Sebastian is on us in an instant. "Let her go," he says with a low, calm voice.

James gives him a stern look, daring him to do something, before setting his eyes on me. "You're not going in." He still doesn't let go.

Sebastian's voice grows more deadly. "I said, let her go."

James ignores him again but loosens his grip. I stay quiet, unmoving. Tension radiates off Sebastian as he fights to control his emotions. I look at him then, but there is no fire in his eyes like I expected.

"Would you like me to do something?" His voice is even but his posture is rigid.

James scoffs and turns to face him, his hand still laced above my elbow. "What are you going to do? Beat me to a pulp again?"

I suck in a breath as Sebastian's face pales.

"James," I hiss.

He looks back at me and slowly lets me go. I move away from him and put a hand on Sebastian's chest. His eyes are far away. Does he remember?

"I agree with Maya. I want to go in," Camille says, stepping up to us.

The rest of the group seems to have been silently watching our little exchange until now. Presley and Rachel join Camille with agreeing nods. James raises his eyebrows and looks to the rest of the group.

"What about you guys?" he asks, folding his arms and leaning against the dumpster we're camping out behind.

There are some murmurings, until, one by one, they join us girls.

"We've come too far to quit," one says.

"We need to get our people out," Lliam, the other commander, who seems to have stepped down after his and James's discussion, adds.

Who knows if that's what they really want or if they just don't want to be shown up by a bunch of *girls*? It's probably the latter, according to the looks they're giving each other. *Men.*

James shoves a hand through his hair and shakes his head, looking up at the dark sky like it can give him the answers he needs. "Fine." His chin dips back down. "But we're not going in blind. Foster. Your skills will come in handy. Join me up ahead, and we'll scope out the place first. Find another entrance."

I open my mouth to complain about not staying behind, even for recon, but James gives me a look. As in, *shut it before I throw you over my shoulder and drag you out.*

I roll my eyes, and I swear I see a faint smile pull on his lips before he says, "Let's find a spot for you guys to wait that won't get you shot."

After James sends a quick message to the third group, we end up in a parking garage with two cars that look like they've been sitting there for twenty years.

After James and Foster leave, one of the tall men, whom I now know as Rus, walks up to the red car and whistles. "I wonder if she still works." He tries the door handle, but it doesn't open.

"Here, let me," says Cody. He places his hand on the window and closes his eyes. His dark skin glows, and the glass melts around his hand. He shoves his hand in and unlocks the car from the inside.

He climbs in and opens the top visor. When he doesn't find anything, he dips below the steering wheel. A few sparks flash before the engine revs. He sits up with a huge smile.

"Looks like you've done that before," I mutter, and he winks at me, climbing out.

Presley says, "What if someone hears that?"

"She's right. Shut off the Camaro," Sebastian grunts.

I look at him, surprised he knows what kind of car it is. He's staring at Cody, who caresses the steering wheel like he wants to kiss it.

"Ya'll are no fun." Cody shuts off the car but continues to rub the wheel like he's about to go for a drive. "Let them come. This baby is faster than anything they've got."

"Yeah, we'll just all shove into the whole two seats," snorts the other tall guy, Ren. I believe Rus and Ren are brothers—twins by the way I keep mixing the two up.

"I'll ride on the roof!" Rus chirps.

Lliam opens the trunk. "We could probably get one or two in here."

"*You* maybe. But not me. I'm not a pretzel. I call shotgun," Rus says.

Lliam shrugs, not saying anything against the comment since he's the shortest person here—even shorter than me. As Rus is about to get into the seat next to Cody, Rachel moves him out of his way with her hip and sits down, sticking her tongue out at him.

His eyes narrow as he grabs her foot.

"I don't think you want to do that," Rachel says, a sensual slur to the words that make me think something is going on between the two of them.

Despite being deep in enemy territory, and with the possibility of, any minute, being found out and slaughtered, I smile. I peer at Sebastian, watching them with mild interest. "You don't want to claim your spot?"

He smirks. "Oh, I have my eye on something else." He grabs my hand and pulls me along. I follow him to a corner of the garage, where, sitting in the shadows, a black Harley is parked. He places his hand on one of the handlebars.

"Have you ever ridden one?"

He shrugs. "My family had dirt bikes when I was little. How different could it be?" He flashes me a genuine smile, and I can't help but smile back. "Wind in my hair, my girl on the back." He moves to face me and intertwines his arms around my waist.

"Bugs in your teeth," I tease.

He chuckles and leans his head down. "Good source of fiber," he whispers before his lips are on mine.

I sink into him and his warmth, happy to be in his arms—forgetting about everything else for a moment. I let myself enjoy him and stop thinking, burying the guilt and worry, letting the bond takeover for once. Pulling him closer, I grab the back of his neck, deepening the kiss. Fire dances on my skin, and I feel my control loosen as it lashes out for him.

When I pull back, he releases me. I force the flames back into myself, breathing hard.

He rubs my cheek with his thumb. "I love you."

I don't say it back, but I smile, and he leads me back to the others. Clarissa and Presley had the same idea as us because they are off in another corner. The boys and Rachel sit against, on, and in the car. Their jokes from earlier have dwindled into a nervous chatter. The way Rus plays with Rachel's gloved hand confirms my suspicion about their relationship. I'm happy for her to have found somebody.

A part of me feels shameful seeing all of them, knowing I roped them into doing something they didn't want to do. I stow it next to my other regrets. Guilt is me, and I am guilt. Will I ever feel light again?

Rachel catches my eye and smiles. I can't bring myself to smile back. She cocks her head and comes my way. She nudges me with her elbow, settling against the wall I'm leaning against. Sebastian keeps a relaxed arm over my shoulders.

"How are you?" she asks.

I bite the inside of my lip. "You really okay with this?"

She holds up her left wrist, wrapped in a red bandana with sparkly lettering I can't make out. "This belonged to my sister. The Coms killed her."

I wince.

"If I had the opportunity to save her life, nothing would have kept me from her. That's why I joined the legion—to save our people. And that's what we're doing."

"I'm sorry you lost your sister."

She rubs the jeweled letters on the bandana. "Her name was Robin. Pretty much the opposite of me, girly in every way that I'm not. It was just the two of us." She smiles. "She wouldn't have approved of me joining a legion full of men. She would have scolded me for a while, tried to convince me to leave, but she would have eventually given in." Her smile widens. "But only so I could give her the inside scoop on the most good-looking ones." Then, her smile disappears as she eyes the brothers. "She would have loved Ren and Rus. Twins for twins. She always dreamed we would bond to another set."

My heart breaks for her—not only a sister but a twin, her other half. I doubt there is a deeper, natural bond out there.

"But to answer your question. Yes, I'm okay with it because I'm okay risking my life for a better future. I chose this knowing

I could get killed. If it's my time…it's my time. At least I got to live."

Her words bring back a conversation from months ago with Trevor. He had told me that we choose to be killed. I couldn't make much sense of it then. But now, being here in the middle of the war. He was right. Life or death is a choice. But I would make one small change. It's more of a choice between living and surviving. We could simply survive or we can risk death and *live*. Rachel wants to live and I think I do too.

My heavy thoughts are interrupted by incoming footsteps. Everyone straightens, preparing themselves. I pull my fire so it's just underneath my skin. I wiggle my fingers, ready.

James rounds the corner and we all deflate. He scans us and his eyes flash when he sees me. "Breaks over. Let's go get our people."

After telling us that they found an open window in the back of the detention center, we follow him to a concrete building that probably has seen better times, James points toward a busted-out window…on the third floor. My mouth falls open, but I quickly close it as everyone else prepares for the jump, as if it's nothing. At least it's set behind a ledge or maybe that's a balcony?

"Why doesn't it have bars or something on it?" I ask.

James responds, "The prisoners are kept in the lower levels under the city."

I peek at Sebastian, worried this is unearthing some trauma, but his face is blank, not readable in the slightest. Underground seems like a common theme for where they keep Elementals locked up.

"There're no outside entrances to them, so this is as close as we can get."

Foster launches Lliam up and through the window like it's nothing. Our group gets thrown into the air one by one until it's my turn. I look at Foster nervously. His blond hair reminds me of my other favorite Aura, who launched me over a wall when running away from cops. How different could this be?

I eye the small opening. "What if you miss?" He raises an eyebrow at me. "Sorry, don't feel like face-planting into a concrete wall," I mumble.

"I don't miss. Ready?" he says roughly, sweat dripping down his forehead. This must be taking a lot out of him.

"Guess so."

I'm not sure how to stand as he grabs me around the hips from behind. I'm about to ask him to count to three when he hoists me into the air. I'm airborne for a moment as I rush toward the window. I swallow the scream and brace myself for impact.

My foot connects with the ledge, and I duck so I don't whack my head on the other ledge above my head, as there are two more stories above this one. Somebody grabs my wrist and pulls me in.

Everyone is scattered in a dark room filled with boxes. In the corner near the window, a weathered desk is piled with dead leaves and other undistinguishable items. The window looks like it's been busted for a long time. Ren is at the door, peering out a small window at the top.

"This place looks deserted," he says.

Sebastian appears behind me the next moment, then James and Foster last. He's breathing hard as he sits on the ground, leaning his head back against the wall. James steps toward him, and he waves him off.

"Just need a moment. You guys were a heavy lot."

I take my water from my hip and drink almost half of it. I've been saving it for just this moment. I wipe the water off my mouth, feeling ready.

"What's the plan now?" My mother could be just beneath my feet. Trepidation courses through me. We're so close.

Once Foster has recovered, we file out of the room. I hate that James is leading, but I remind myself he's probably done this hundreds of times. My fingers twitch, waiting for any sign of movement as we round corner after corner. I keep a silent recollection of all the water sources I feel.

When we reach the ground floor, my gut screams that something is terribly wrong. Why is nobody here? Where are our friends?

I push to the head of the group. "James," I whisper. He rounds on me, his eyes darting around nervously. "We need to leave. You're right. There is something wrong."

His eyes land on something over my shoulder and widen in fear. Immediately, I release my flames, whipping around.

"Too late for that," the darkness responds.

A Fighting Chance

We're surrounded.

There is no escape.

I can't tell how many Coms there are, but it's certainly more than our measly twelve. Their weapons are all pointed at us, fingers on the triggers, as they circle.

Ready to kill.

Time has stopped. Our choice between this breath and the next will determine whether we get out alive. If everyone I love will continue to have a heartbeat or if we will end up on this cold-tiled floor, soon to be forgotten. Just another casualty of war. Anyone can make this choice. Just a twitch of their fingertips and everything will implode. My mind races, remembering the exits I know of. We can run up the stairs and escape out the window we came in. We could charge the front door.

Or we can fight.

Sebastian meets my gaze from across the room where I left him along the edge of the room. There's an incremental nod of his head, and I know what to do. But can I be fast enough? Faster than the time it takes them to register we're fighting back and pull their triggers? Faster than a bullet?

I meet James's stare, uncannily similar to Sebastian's. I know he's thinking the same thing. We have to fight our way out.

I'm relieved that Trevor's group isn't here yet. Abby, Juliet, Thomas, Izalia. One of them will take care of Cal for me. My heart cracks, ripping the hole wider. I'll have to break my promise to him.

Anger flares inside of me. I barely keep the fire contained to my skin. No. I will not break it. I will live. We will all live.

And with that thought to fuel my flames, I detonate.

Directing my flames to the half on my side of the room, I hope Sebastian follows suit on his. I keep the wall of fire up, not knowing how many I take out, but if they can't see us, we'll be harder to shoot. I pull the water I located earlier and create a wall of water behind the flames. Then, I whip around to a frenzy behind me.

Singed bodies lay on the floor, revealing a direct path to the front door. Sebastian is covered in fire, throwing flaming balls around him. A vortex of my fire and water swirls around us as I spot Foster moving his hands through the air.

And James. James has his hands on the floor, deep in concentration. Camille and Presley block him from view, deflecting every bullet shot their way with a mixture of water and earth.

The Coms lower their weapons and charge for them instead. Keeping my shields up, I launch myself toward the two Com men. Their eyes aren't on me as I connect my foot to one of their faces, and he collapses into the fire. Blinding white light flashes in the other one's face, and he grabs his eyes, dropping to the ground.

Shouts come from the back of the room. I whip my head around to see the front doors wide open. Giant roots crawl through them and drag away Coms, kicking and screaming. I risk a glance at James, standing again, kicking the blinded man out of his way.

He grabs my hand. "Let's go!" he shouts, running before I can respond, but not for the entrance.

As we race down a hallway, I look behind me for Sebastian. A Com jumps out, and I slash with my knife on instinct, not remembering when I even pulled it out. The man grabs his chest and keels over. Behind him is a scene of flames, wind, red-tinted water, dirt, and falling bodies as the stench of burnt flesh and blood saturates the air. I don't see Sebastian.

"Wait. We can't just leave them," I say, pulling James to stop.

"We're not. We're getting your mom." His eyes are wide and full of adrenaline.

I look back again. Should I stay and fight or use this opportunity to save my mom and the others? That is why we're here.

He sees me struggling with the decision, so he decides for me and tugs me down the hall. I let him.

"They'll be okay. Sebastian can wipe out the lot of them if he desires. And the third group is almost here. My communicator broke during the attack." He lifts it to show a bullet in the middle of the screen. My eyes about fall out of my head.

He shrugs. "Guess it's my lucky day. Juliet reached out. Did you not hear from her?"

I shake my head in a daze. James could have died. Death is just one bullet away… I try to focus back on what he just said. Juliet reached out through an air link. I haven't heard from her or William. Why haven't I heard from them? Too many emotions run through me as he pulls me through a door, and we descend the stairs. Fear for everyone who's out there fighting. Agony, knowing the rest of my friends are on their way to this bloodbath. Confusion at what James just said about Sebastian being able to take out everyone? And surprisingly, a little jealousy that Juliet linked with James instead of me. Maybe she's mad at me about William?

Oh, William. *You better be okay, or I'm going to find you just so I can kick your butt for telling me not to worry*, I shout with my mind, frustrated I can't open an air link with him.

Down, down, down the stairs we go, deeper underground. The air becomes stale, and nausea rolls in my stomach.

"I don't understand," I say, referencing his comment about Sebastian.

He gives me a quick look and continues to descend, pulling me along. "Think Juliet still likes me?"

I shake my head at him, making jokes at a time like this. Besides, their courtship was like a day long. "No, not Juliet. About Sebastian. What do you mean, he can wipe out everyone if he desires?"

"You didn't know?"

"Know what?" My voice rises, echoing off the concrete walls. We skid to a halt in front of a large steel door blocking our way. James tries to open it without luck.

"I got this," I say, pushing him aside. I try to remember the way those boys did it when they melted the gate and the glass. Placing my palm around the doorknob, I push all my energy and fire into my palms.

"I've been watching Sebastian train for the last week," James says, "and he's powerful. More powerful than he was last time. More powerful than any Igna I've ever seen."

The steel melts like putty around my fingers until a fist-sized hole forms. I stick my hand in it and pull. James helps me, and it screeches loudly as it opens.

James continues. "I think they did something to him in those labs. Something that—"

James doesn't finish his sentence because the door fully opens, and there is a man with a large gun aimed right at us.

James tackles me to the ground behind the wall as the gun fires. I cover my ears at the deafening blasts. The shooting stops and James leaps for the opening. I shriek as I clumsily crawl toward the door and fling myself through. James has one arm wrapped around the man's neck and the other interlocking it and pulling back. Both their faces are beet red, but the light in the man's eyes slowly dims until they close.

Finally, he slumps over. James releases him and stands, wiping back the hair clinging to his sweat-soaked face and neck and breathing hard.

My eyes widen. "Did you just—"

He shakes his head. "Just passed out." James expertly removes the weapons from the man, shoving one through his belt and pulling out the cartridges of the rest and tossing them down the hall. "Come on," he says, palming the last gun.

I follow him, nudging the guy with my foot as we pass. He doesn't move. I grip my knife and debate pulling out the gun, but my powers are still amped up, ready.

Then I hear them. The moaning and the crying. This prison is very similar to the one Sebastian was in—dim lights, cement walls, and the terrible smell of rotting flesh and urine. I pull the hem of my jacket over my nose and breeze past him.

"Mom! Mom!" I race down the hall, looking briefly in each cell behind large metal bars. I get to the very end and gasp. Around the corner, the prison seems to go on without end in each direction.

James comes up behind me. "Take the right. I'll take the left," he says.

I don't hesitate. I rush down the aisle, screaming my mom's name. My voice grows hoarse halfway down, and I bend over to catch my breath.

"Girl," comes a soft voice.

I stiffen to the sound. Many voices have called out to me, but this one is different, calmer. Two cells down, a young man, probably around my age, has his hands wrapped around the bars, his face pressing against them. "Girl, who are you looking for?" He has a strong East Coast accent.

I step toward him but keep my distance. "Who are you?"

"My name is Greg. I was working here undercover, and they found me out, so I might know her."

I hesitate. He will probably want me to let him out for more information…if he's even telling the truth. But what choice do I have? It'll take me the rest of the night to get through all the cells, and I don't have that long. We could be out of time already. What if I never see the sun again?

I push the thought away, deciding to take the chance. "Her name is Evelynn Mayfield. She's a geneticist commander. The Coms took her from a community in Oregon."

His eyes flicker. "A geneticist?"

I nod.

"She wouldn't be down here. They would want to use her. They'd keep her locked in the labs. I'm sure of it."

"And where are those?"

He hesitates. "Let me out, and I'll show you."

My shoulders slacken. I knew it.

"You can trust me. Come on. Would I be in here if I was on their side?"

He has a point, and I don't have the time. "Fine. But I'm an Igna. Do anything funny, and I'll torch you."

"Deal. I'll help you find your mom, and you don't burn me alive." He smiles in a way that reminds me of William—boyish and charming.

That does me in. I take the lock, and it melts underneath my touch. The door swings open.

His eyes widen as he steps out, and his smile grows. I look at him warily, but he just says, "Let's get your mom."

"Wait. Do you know about any other commanders that came in with her? There were three of them. An Aura…Lawrence, an Igna…Barlowe, and Zhang. He's a Terra."

He rubs his chin. "Lawrence? That name sounds familiar, but no. A lot of people come in here. I'm sorry."

I nod. "Did you see a large group of us come down here recently? Like an hour ago?"

He shakes his head again.

I raise an eyebrow at him and make a show of looking around. "Maybe somebody else here has more information."

He rolls his eyes. "Usually, prisoners don't come straight down here. There is a holding place they are taken to first, a couple blocks from here. Tests are run, revealing abilities and all that. They could be there."

I smile. "That's better."

We run back to where I came from as prisoners shout at us to let them out. Maybe I should. Aren't these my people? "Are there good or bad people down here?"

He cocks his head. "Both." He stops before a cell and whispers, "Penny, are you in there?"

A thin girl with large blue eyes walks to the bars. Greg lets out a whimper when he sees her and tries to embrace her through the bars.

He turns to me. "Please, can you let her out too? She's one of the good ones, I promise." He doesn't take his eyes off her, and she holds his gaze like he's the air she needs to breathe.

Their evident love weakens me, so I place my hand on the lock, heating it until it falls to the ground. He pulls her into her arms, and they kiss passionately. I avert my eyes. At least I helped one person.

He has to practically carry her, because she keeps tripping over her feet. Poor girl. She looks like a walking corpse. But not to him. He looks at her like she's the most beautiful person he's ever laid eyes on.

The prisoners' shouting intensifies but I can't take my chances letting anyone else out. The wrongness of it is almost too unbearable, and I'm about to break when we make it back to the fork I left James at.

"James!" I yell down the hall.

For a moment, there's nothing, but then I hear a faint "Coming."

After a minute of me awkwardly standing next to the madly in love couple, James appears with three people behind him. Looks like somebody got to him too. But then I see who it is.

"B—Barlowe. Zhang," I stutter.

Barlowe pulls me into a hug, and I stiffen. He has never hugged me. He leans back with tears in his eyes and looks me over. "Thank you," he says in a deep scratchy voice. For the first time since I met the Igna Commander, I begin to like him.

The third person, whom I have never met, blinks past his shoulder. She is an older woman with jet-black hair.

"This is their friend," James says, glancing at the couple beside me with a conspiratorial look.

I shrug, and he smiles faintly. His smile morphs into something else as he looks at me like…like I'm his girl. I look away quickly.

"I'm assuming none of you have your abilities?" James asks.

They shake their heads.

"But we can still fight. Don't worry about us," Barlowe says, nudging Zhang, who nods in agreement, even though his almond-shaped eyes are distant. They are both much skinnier than the last time I saw them. Zhang's cheekbones protrude from his face, and Barlowe…he's no longer huge, just regular-sized now. I wonder how Zhang feels about James letting him out of jail when he once put him in one.

The voices from the people begging to let them out are at an all-time high as we run back. I feel myself shrink. *We can't save everyone,* I tell myself, but it does nothing. We could.

I turn toward James and open my mouth, but he frowns and shakes his head, already knowing my thoughts. I seem to read his too. How would we get them out of the city? They won't all fit in the boats. We were warned it would be hard not to take everyone. Just our people. Well, unless—I don't let myself finish the thought. Everyone *will* live.

"We could at least give them a fighting chance," I murmur.

He wavers. "We don't have the time. It would take forever to let them all out."

"Just the ones we pass then," I say.

Barlowe speaks up. "I want to save everyone too. I wouldn't wish the conditions they keep us in on any living thing. But it's not a good idea. Most of these guys don't care whose side you're on, and the others have lost all their humanity."

I grimace. "But you're okay."

His amber eyes hold mine. "I'll never be okay."

I think of Sebastian and how well he acclimated after coming out. But also, how he never talks about his time in prison. I shudder at the silent horrors he's burying.

We find a couple other familiar faces, one being Camille's dad who had immediately asked about her the moment we released him. But it's not enough. There are so many others. By the time we get to the other side of the steel door, I want to throw up—the smell, the wailing, the guilt. I run to a corner, and my stomach empties itself. Tears are running down my face by the time I'm done.

James moves to hold my hair and rub my back. I wipe my mouth with my sleeve and lean against him. I let him comfort me for a moment before pushing my shoulders back.

James leads us up the stairs. The couple murmurs into each other's necks while everyone else is silent.

I peek at the woman who had come out with James. "What's your name?"

"Marley," she says. Her voice is husky, and she doesn't say anything else.

We reach ground level again, and James holds up a finger. "Give me a second."

There are no sounds of the battle we left, and I don't know how that makes me feel. He disappears around the corner as I hold my breath. The smell of burnt flesh is more potent than before. My stomach twists.

Someone pops their head back through, but it's not James's dark locks but a blond head of hair instead.

"William!" I jump on him as he embraces me. I nuzzle into his sweat and grime-coated neck, not caring. He's alive.

"Barlowe, Zhang, good to see you chaps in one piece," he says over my shoulder.

I pull back and place my hands on his face. He has a long gash across his cheek.

"I'm fine. It looks worse than it is. Let's go, everyone is waiting."

"I thought your group got taken," I say.

"We did," he says grimly.

I stare at him in disbelief and can't bring myself to ask if we lost anyone, so I follow him.

And that's when I see the bodies throughout the lobby. So many bodies. It almost doesn't look real, more like blackened props in a movie scene. The scent stings my nose, and I bury my face into William's shoulder. He pulls me quickly along the morbid path through them, like a bulldozer had come through previously.

I squeeze my eyes shut and don't open them back up until I feel the breeze on my face. Then I'm in somebody else arms— make that two.

Juliet and Abby squeal as they pull me to them.

"What happened?" I say, finally looking around. Our people are scattered throughout a courtyard, with green and orange trees arranged around a pond in the middle and brightly colored leaves floating on top.

"We got here just as Sebastian imploded. It was awesome," Abby says.

"He what?" I shriek, looking back at the building, the doors that have been ripped off their hinges, expecting to see bits and pieces of him everywhere.

Juliet shoves Abby. "He didn't implode," she says, giving her a dirty look. "But he pretty much snapped his fingers, and all the Coms became encased in fire. It was like a cartoon. We weren't even needed."

Another person grabs my shoulder, and I find Thomas. "Glad you're okay, sis. They're right. Your mate has insane powers."

"Well, where is he then?"

Thomas points to a grove of trees on a patch of grass near the outer edge of the pond. "He's with Izalia."

I rush to the trees and catch James's eye. He's talking with Trevor. He watches me for a moment before turning back to him. I reach the grass and fall to my knees next to Sebastian. He's sitting up against the tree with his eyes closed, ash and grime coating every inch of him. I can't tell where he is hurt. Noni is on his other side, hovering her hands over his body.

"Is he okay?"

Sebastian's eyes flutter open at the sound of my voice, and he smiles. I pull his hand into my lap.

"He'll be fine. He just used an excessive amount of his power. He's completely drained."

I squeeze his hand. "I heard you're pretty powerful."

His shoulder lifts slightly, but he keeps his eyes closed. "At least something good came out of that hell hole."

Before I can ask him what he means, Noni says, "This should help." Fire and light erupt from her hands. I jump, releasing his hand as they slide over his body like molten lava. My eyes widen in worry, but his face remains calm, with no sign of pain. Once his whole body wraps in light and fire, the light pulses and then dims. The flames flicker, licking over his skin until they pull back and absorb into Noni.

He sits up, blinking, his dark skin returning to normal. "Wow. What was that?" he asks.

Noni shoots us a smile. "Just a little trick I learned from the Divina."

He goes to stand, but she pushes his shoulder down. "You might feel better, but you still need to wait for your energy stores to return. Take it easy."

Now that Sebastian is doing better, I call Trevor over to tell him what we learned. But it looks like James beat me to it.

"Since nobody is attacking us at the moment, I have to assume everyone is inside, holed up somewhere. They still have our people," Trevor says.

"Wait. What are you talking about?" I look around, realizing for the first time that I don't see anyone from the first group besides William. I stand. "Where is Michael?"

Trevor shoves his hands in his pockets, eyeing the other buildings around us. "The first group got taken."

"But William…" I look for him. I did see him, right? I spot him talking with Juliet and Abby across the courtyard. I take a deep breath, trying to calm the sudden panic.

"William is the only one that escaped. Or, more likely, they let him go so we would fall right into their trap."

I wave at William, and he jogs over. "You're the only one that escaped? What happened?"

He blanches, fiddling with the knife on his belt. "It all happened so fast. One moment, we had just cleared the street a block from here, and the next, they had us surrounded. We must have missed one."

"Are they okay?"

"Me and Kyle got away but…Kyle didn't make it. He points to the slash on his face. The bullet grazed me." He kicks the ground with the toe of his boot. "But not him."

"That's from a *bullet*?" I almost scream. "You could have died, William!" I want to throttle him for being so reckless. "Why did you do that?"

He shrugs. "There was an opening, and I took it."

I wrap my arms around him and choke out a sob. I can't do this. I can't lose him. I can't lose anyone. He pulls me into him and rests his chin on my head. "I'm okay, love."

"The science building," Trevor says.

I pull away and wipe my eyes. "What?" I ask, turning toward Trevor. He's looking at Noni, who must have asked a question I didn't hear.

"William told us that's where they have our people."

"And that's where my mom is," I say, remembering what that boy I pulled out of the prison told me. I square my shoulders. There is no time to cry and be scared. We have to save our people. "Well, then, what are we waiting for? Let's go."

"You know it will be a trap, right?" William says. "They know that I know."

"And? Wasn't *this* a trap? We kicked butt," I say. Trevor's face pinches. How stupid of me to assume. "We lost somebody," I say slowly.

Trevor nods.

"Who?" I look around, trying to figure out who's missing. Then I see her. Camille is sitting on the ground next to somebody lying too still. Her dad has a hand on her shoulder. Oh no. Not Presley. Camille's torso hides the face as she caresses the head in her lap.

My heart lurches as I walk toward them, and then I notice another person on her other side. It's Ren. His shoulders are shaking as he leans over the body, and Presley sits perfectly fine next to him, staring off, unblinking. If she's there, then who—

As I get closer, I notice the red bandana wrapped around the wrist lying lifeless on the grass, the jewels on it winking in the sun.

I sway on my feet as my throat closes. *I am so sorry, Rachel.* This wouldn't have happened if I hadn't made them continue the search. This is my fault.

Sebastian is there suddenly, wrapping his arms around my waist. "I'm so sorry Angel."

I shake my head. "I—I shouldn't have pushed you guys to continue."

He turns me to face him. "This is not your fault."

"Yes, it is." My voice breaks.

"We made the decision as a unit. This falls strictly on the Coms. They killed her. They take us. They imprison us. They hurt us. But we can hurt them back." His voice is hard, unwavering.

They killed her. I can't believe she's gone. I turn around to see Camille standing up, placing Rachel's hands over her abdomen as if she was resting peacefully, before falling into her dad's embrace. Rachel wanted to save our people. She would want us to continue the mission. For Robin. For Rachel. For Seth, my trainer gone too soon. For all those that the Coms have taken from us. And what about those prisoners? Are we much better if we leave them? Doom them to death?

"We can't just leave them. There were so many of them, Sebastian. The prisoners. Stuck down there. Helpless," I say.

His face twists. Only he knows the true horror of being trapped in an underground prison.

I overhear Trevor say, "They know the punch we can pack now. They'll be ready for us."

Trevor and James stand to my right, the latter casting uneasy glances at me as he tries to pay attention to Trevor. He seems to give up as he comes my way.

"I have an idea, but it's crazy. Greg, tell them what you just told me," James says.

The boy I saved looks incredibly uncomfortable as he shuffles toward us, the thin girl attached to his side. "My dad grew up here, and he once told me that there was a great fire. The new city was built on top of an older, burnt-down Seattle. That there is a whole city with passageways and tunnels down there." He looks at James.

My eyebrows turn down. "And?"

James's eyes flash. "And that's how we get in to save our people. To save your mom. And you're right. We shouldn't leave all those prisoners down there." He looks back at Trevor with a wicked gleam in his eye.

Trevor pinches the bridge of his freckled nose before sighing. "Lead the way down to the prison."

42

The Sunken City

James was right. This is crazy.

I watch as prisoners get released one by one, some of them whooping in the air, others crying uncontrollably, and a couple shooting dirty looks my way, like I'm the one that put them in there. It wasn't hard to convince each one before releasing them that they had to join us for their freedom. The guard James and I had encountered was gone, making the pit grow in my stomach. But there is no way he knows of our new plans, just that James and I were down here.

Terras work together to block the entrance to the door we came through, collapsing all walls so none of the prisoners can escape through the back. This leaves us with only one way out.

Fighting.

Queasiness writhes in my gut, and panic claws at my throat being down here again, knowing we could be trapped indefinitely.

"You sure you know the route?" I ask James.

"As sure as one can be who pieced together this underground hellscape with old plans." He smirks.

I want to hit him.

"Yeah, yeah. The labs aren't that far. It'll be fine," he says.

I guess they used to do tours down here, and Greg knew where to find the old flyers and maps. Supposedly, these tunnels should go right under the science building, even though *Public Library* had been stamped onto the same building. The maps are old, from before the war started. Who knows what has crawled down here since or what has fallen into more ruin. For all we know, the ceiling could cave in on us at any moment.

I step closer to Sebastian as one of the prisoners eyes me from over James's shoulder. The man's eyes flicker to Sebastian before turning around with a smug expression. It seems they don't forgive me for leaving them all down here earlier. *I came back for you*! I want to shout at him.

Trevor and James lead our group of escapees, with a few up ahead to ensure we don't fall into a sinkhole or something. I walk closely behind them, and Sebastian is directly behind me, so I don't have to keep checking my back.

With orbs of white light guiding our way, we move through deeper and darker tunnels. Dust motes fly in the air as our feet pick up dirt that hasn't been touched in years. Water drips from somewhere far off. I feel the call of it in my bones. A damp, unpleasant smell fills my nostrils, but it's at least better than the putrid smell of the cell block.

The rocky walls morph into windows, doors, and decaying signs as we enter the first signs of a city—just like Greg had described—a burnt, decaying city directly under the new one. I step over a massive cement block, and we shimmy along in single file to prevent falling into a crater-sized hole.

Purple hues dance across our heads, and I peer up. A skylight filled with rectangular violet glass pieces shines down on us, allowing in light from one of the streetlights above. I breathe in, feeling a tiny bit better. We're not that far from fresh air. Exhaustion creeps into my limbs as we walk, the effects of this all-night mission finally catching up with me. I fish out the guarana leaves Abby gave me and shove them in my mouth, swallowing the bitter taste. Supposedly, it's the correct amount for my weight, so I won't crash like last time.

William, Juliet, and the other Auras in our group carefully move rubble out of our way. I wince, looking up warily, waiting for it to fall on top of us and bury us down here forever. A charred barbershop sign hangs on a wall, and a bit of red is still visible on a busted-out light.

"This place is a time capsule," Abby murmurs to my left as we pass four dirt-filled glass bottles on a window ledge. "Greg, what was the history of this place again?"

Abby stops to look around for him. Voices murmur behind us before Greg pushes his way through.

"What?" he asks, looking between us.

We continue walking again as Abby gestures to our surroundings. "Why is this still here?"

He scratches his ear as more people turn to face him. "If I remember correctly, it was the fire from 1889. It destroyed like thirty city blocks. They elevated it, but rebuilt some shops underneath the new street level, businesses operating at both levels."

Curious, I pull my jacket sleeve over my palm and wipe away some dirt on the window to look inside. I snap my finger, and a flame casts a bit of light inside. A red circular couch sits inside, draped with pieces of what look like clothes.

"In the early 1900s, the bubonic plague hit, and it was all shut down for fear of the rats."

A bar is against one wall, with turned-over bar stools and glasses on its ledge. In the corner, a rusty 100-year-old cash register sits next to a sign that reads *Tony's Speakeasy*.

"Then, like thirty or forty years ago, it was excavated and preserved. I did a tour once when I was little, but, of course, historical stuff like this got ignored when the war started." Greg's voice drifts forward as people pass us, but I'm stuck on the scene before me.

Sebastian's breath is on my neck. "What do you see?"

"A window to the past."

I step back as a shiver runs down my spine. This place is straight from the 1800s. I wonder what it was like to be an Elemental back then, enjoying this club with whoever you liked, not worried they'd slit your throat.

Something scurries across my feet, and I hold in a yelp. Abby shrieks in front of me a second later.

"Please tell me that's not what I think it is," she says.

Nobody responds until James says, "You're in their home, Abigail."

She snorts and moves closer to Trevor.

"You don't like rats?" he asks her with a tilt of his head.

"Rats? Just because I'm a Terra doesn't mean I love every foul creature out there. Did you not just hear Greg? They gave everyone the plague. No, I have no love for rodents, Trevor."

He chuckles as we come to a fork in the tunnel. James pulls out his map. His eyebrows turn down as he studies it, his face cast in shadows.

"Maybe you should ask the rat," I mutter.

It's meant as a joke, but Noni steps from behind me. "That is brilliant. Give me a moment."

My eyes widen as she stoops down. When she stands back up, a big ugly rat is cupped in her hands.

Abby backs away, and I try not to gag. I know they don't have the bubonic plague now, but there's no telling what other diseases it could be carrying. Noni tenderly pats it on the head with one finger and nods before putting it back down.

"Left!" she calls out.

James's mouth gapes, but he quickly recovers, and he and Trevor turn left. I'm surprised none of the Terras thought of it first. How they communicate with animals must be different from what Noni does.

We don't walk far before she tells us to stop.

The shuffling of our group and the muffled conversations quiet down. She moves us aside and steps toward the wall. A light orb brightens where she's standing, showing us an iron ladder fastened there. It was deep in the shadows, and we surely would have missed it.

"The labs are above our heads," she says.

Trevor and James talk among themselves. Trevor doesn't need anyone's advice on leading his mission, but he obviously thinks highly of James. I would guess it's either because of James's experience or because he's now his brother-in-law. Maybe both.

Trevor turns and raises his voice so even the ones at the back can hear. "We'll go up in groups of fifteen."

I don't know how many are with us now that we have the prisoners, but there have to be at least sixty. Our odds are much better than they were.

"Spread out and be quick. I want to hit them before they know what's happening. If things take a turn, get out." He grips the first rung on the ladder and takes a deep breath. "I'll go up first."

Abby stiffens next to me but doesn't say anything. He's about to hoist himself up when she grabs him. He turns, and she pulls his face to hers, taking him in a heated kiss. When they pull apart, he looks at her full of love and adoration. My heart aches. If anything were to happen to him, it would ruin her.

She places her hand on his cheek before he pulls up and climbs. We all watch in silence. He pushes against the ceiling, but nothing happens. He shoves harder, his arms shaking as he grunts, but it still doesn't budge.

"I'm sure they blocked it off. Here, allow me. I should be able to unseal it," James says.

Trevor climbs down, and Abby grabs onto him happily. But now James is the one who will open it and be the first to stick his head through. For all we know, we could be entering the very center of the facility. I have a sudden desire to throw myself on him like Abby did Trevor. Knowing I can't, I hug my arms around myself and bite the inside of my cheek, silently pleading that he won't be able to open it. *Somebody else, anybody else.*

He places his palms on the ceiling, and wood planks crack and shift. They fall away, hitting the floor with a crash. I wince. *Can they hear us?*

Behind the planks, a square concrete slab with a metal handle in the center appears. James grabs the handle and pushes. A scraping sound claws at my ears as a crack forms on one side of it.

"Some help here?" he grunts.

Trevor climbs the ladder, and James makes room for him so they're both balancing on one rung. William and Foster situate themselves underneath, palms up to assist with their aura powers. One big push and it bangs open.

I wince again. They definitely would have heard that.

James is through the hole first, and Trevor follows closely behind. I hold my breath, straining my ears for any sound.

"Come on up," Trevor's whisper travels down.

Others follow suit, climbing the ladder until it's Sebastian's and my turn. He goes first. The rusted iron rungs are surprisingly warm underneath my freezing hands.

Sebastian offers me his hand as I climb into a dimly lit room. The light from underneath the door shines onto storage boxes lining the walls, cleaner than the last storage room we entered—if you can even call it that. This is more of a closet. There isn't nearly enough room for fifteen. I barely squeeze in amongst the dozen others as the rest of our group waits below, ready.

The only sounds come from our breathing and shuffling of bodies to make more room. The space is quickly heating up, vastly different from the cold climate underground. Sweat beads on the nape of my neck as a couple more bodies squeeze in.

There's a shift in the atmosphere when Trevor clears his throat. We all look at him, alert and ready, as he grabs the doorknob. My heart pounds in my ears, and I grasp onto my flame and feel for the closest water sources.

The door swings open, bathing us in yellow, fluorescent light. Trevor stumbles back as if he wasn't the one to open it. My eyes adjust, trying to make out the silhouette in the doorway. Before us is none other than the familiar strawberry-blonde hair and widening blue eyes of my mother.

43

Bloodshed and Magic

She doesn't move. None of us do.

I know I should be freaking out, but my first thought is that she looks okay. Her face isn't hollow, and she doesn't have the same emptiness in her eyes the other prisoners do, that even Sebastian did for a while. The next thing I notice is that she's in blue nurse's scrubs, not the gray drab of the prisoners. She's holding a small box of medical supplies that promptly hits the floor and jostles me out of my shock.

Fear grows on her face, and she takes a step back. I don't blame her. She's now looking into the eyes of quite a lot of escaped prisoners.

I shove my way through the few people in front of me before she takes off. My movement rouses everyone into the present again.

James, who is almost directly in front of her, steps forward. "Evelynn."

She blinks at him, recognition wiping away a little bit of the horror on her face. Then she searches the other faces in the room until she finally lands on mine.

I break free from the group when she finds me, throwing myself on her and burying my nose into her familiar scent. Before I can fully come to terms with her being flesh and bone beneath me, she pushes me off her and back into the closet.

Pain slashes through me, gutting me to the core. I've been looking for her for months. Why would she shove me away? Her daughter?

She looks around quickly before scrunching up her nose and pushing her way in. Kicking the box she dropped into the room, she closes the door behind her. She taps the wall, and light floods the room. Her eyes grow once more, taking us all in.

"Why are you here?" she hisses. Another stab to my insides. Not the greeting I thought I would get from my mother, who I haven't seen in almost five months, and who I'm now breaking out of prison.

"Mom, it's me," I stutter.

"Yes, Maya. What in the world are you doing here? And you freed *all* of them?" Her voice shakes.

I don't know what to say. Doesn't she *want* to be saved? *We're doing this for you.*

Rage boils within me. "We're saving you!" I want to throttle her. I just found her, and I want to throttle her already.

Her head falls against the door as she places her hands on her face like we're some huge inconvenience and not risking our lives to save her butt.

"Michael told me his group was the only one, and he certainly didn't tell me you were here." She turns to James. "And you." Then she points to Abby. "And you!" She hasn't seen Sebastian yet. He must still be at the back of the group where I left him. "You cannot be here. Go back the way you came."

"Mom. we're not going anywhere without you and our people." I can't believe that I have to argue this with her.

"Maya, you don't understand. You just need to go." Her voice takes on a desperate note.

"Commander Mayfield," Trevor interrupts. "Maya is right. It is our mission to retrieve you and the others. Do you know where they're keeping Michael and his group?"

She pulls a hand down her face. "Yes. But you won't get past him."

"Who?" Trevor and I ask at the same time.

She hesitates. "Their leader."

"We'll take our chances," Trevor says, holding back a smile.

She looks at him grimly as a wave of foreboding washes through me. "He's not just a Com. He was…made. He's very powerful with unusual abilities."

My eyes widen. Could it be the man that Michael told me about? The Com they gave abilities to and then became power-hungry?

I grab my mom's hand. "I don't know why you're walking around free, and from that box of supplies on the ground, helping."

She grimaces at the box she dropped, which contains rolls of bandages, gloves, and other small items scattered on the floor at her feet.

"I don't care," I continue. "We all do things to stay alive. But we are here. We are ready to fight. There are more down below. We can do this with your help. Mom, help us save you. Help us save everyone."

Her eyes glisten and she wraps her arms around me. I thaw a little, having missed the warm comfort of her hugs. "You have grown." She sniffles and pulls back. Her lower lip wobbles. My mother is not a crier. "I'm so proud of you. But I can't let you walk into your death."

She steps back and presses a button on a gray device on her waist. "You have five minutes before they are here. Go!"

My stomach drops. "Mom. What did you do?"

James lurches for the device and shatters it on the ground.

She shakes her head sadly. "It's already done."

For a beat, James stares at her, hurt and anger evident on his face, and she stares back, sorrow and a silent pleading sketched into every deepening line. Everyone waits to see what he'll decide. Not Trevor, not me, but him. James. It doesn't matter what group of people he's with. People look up to him to lead—to decide our fate. He's a natural-born leader. It must have been hard for him to push down those impulses when he was pretending to be a regular legionary all those months ago.

I blink, and he's throwing the door open and pulling two guns from his belt in one swift motion, launching himself down the hall. Trevor is on his heels. Even though it's the worst time to have such thoughts, all I think is how good he looks in that all-black uniform, hugging his muscular figure, with a gun in each hand, leading the charge, ready for a fight.

The thought dissipates quickly as my mom and I are shoved from the door, and everyone runs out, following suit. The prisoners hold a hodgepodge of weapons we found on our journey underground, from crowbars and bats to pieces of wood. It's quite a frightening scene. But they have a hindrance, unable to use their powers. Hopefully, we can come out on the winning side between their brute force and our abilities.

"No!" Mom screams.

I look at her, coldly. "You promised to put Cal and me first, remember?"

Her face doesn't register my words as she just stares, horror-stricken, at the flood of legionaries and prisoners leaving the storage room. Her frame begins to quake.

"It was the last thing you said to me!" I grab her shoulders and force her to look at me. "You said we could go anywhere. Us. Not just me and Cal. Our family. I'm not leaving you." She's staring at me, but I can't tell if she's absorbing my words. "We're fighting, whether you like it or not. This is the last chance you get. Tell me something to help us. Anything!"

She covers her face and cries. I let her go, not comprehending. This is *not* my mother. My mother would never just give up like this. What happened to her?

Somebody places their hand on my shoulder. "Come on, we need to go."

I look at Sebastian. There's understanding in his eyes as he looks down at my mom. She's now crumpled to the floor in a fit of sobs, not even registering the fact that Sebastian is alive and here with me. He looks deep into my eyes, communicating something. And then I understand. I crouch low and lift my mother's face to meet my eyes.

"We're bringing you home today, Mom. You don't have to be afraid anymore."

That causes her to burst into more sobs. Sebastian bends down and picks her up. People are climbing from the opening in the floor and rushing into the hall. Sebastian cradles my mom like she's a child as we join them. Her eyes are closed. She's still weeping, but her lips are moving, mumbling something incoherent.

Sirens wail through the building, and thunderous footsteps join the noise into a chaotic symphony. We follow the flow of people. Some branch off toward rooms and other hallways. Sebastian won't be able to fight with my mom in his arms. She'll come to her senses and help, right?

I look at her again, and she has her eyes locked on mine, but it doesn't look like she's seeing me. Worry grips me but I push it down. She'll be fine.

We come to a large opening with a high glass ceiling, covered in hundreds of diamond-shaped windows that flow all the way to the floor. Early morning light streams in, piercing the elements swirling between large pillars and throughout the extensive space as legionaries fight. The prisoners are in hand-to-hand combat. Bodies are dropping, and I can't tell who is on whose side. Sebastian nudges me, and we trail around the room's rim.

My eyes widen when I spot Noni, a spot of color among the waves of black and green. Her black hair falls out of her braid as she takes out six Coms with a wave of her hand. And I was worried about her. She's the most powerful one here. She expertly swings her arms and blasts a ring around her with fire, water, and air weaving together. She then raises her palms, and the glass ceiling shatters above our heads.

Everyone gasps and throws their hands up as a million glass shards are about to rain down upon us. I press myself against the wall, away from the vicious onslaught, but at the last moment, the shards freeze midair and turn into flaming glass arrows, piercing every Com in the room. One man falls at my feet, convulsing and choking on his blood before his body slumps.

I recoil from his body and look up at Noni in awe as she wipes sweat from her forehead and catches my eye with a wink.

Everyone else scans the bodies in disbelief. There's a beat of silence before shouting and cheers erupt. They then run down the halls leading further into the building, hopefully towards where they're keeping our people.

My mother seems to awaken from her dreamlike state. She swats at Sebastian's arms, and he releases her. She stands up, her eyes scanning the room.

"Only one person could have done that." She looks toward Noni. "A Divina. I don't believe it." A glimmer of hope flashes in her eyes.

Noni comes our way, her colorful, floral top dancing around her. "Hello. You must be Maya's mother. How wonderful it is to meet you finally!" she says, like we're not in a war zone but getting together for breakfast on any Tuesday morning.

My mom doesn't respond, just stares at her with disbelieving eyes.

Noni smiles, the wrinkles on her face becoming more distinct. "I'm your daughter's great-grandmother." She lowers her voice. "But between you and me, let's leave that 'great' off."

"My daughter's what?"

She smiles and thrusts her hand out. My mom takes it carefully. "I'm Michael's grandmother. I'm guessing he didn't tell you of his heritage?"

"He had a few unique properties from studying his blood samples. But I never would have guessed…" She shakes her head. "The Divina all died off hundreds of years ago. I've heard rumors about a possible civilization living in a remote place somewhere. But that's like believing in Atlantis. Never in a million years… If you're here, then…"

I've never seen my mom so short of words, but hearing her talk like this, like herself…hope blossoms within me.

"You're correct. We don't leave our island," Noni says.

My mom's eyes widen as she mouths "island," like she's just made a rare genetic discovery—in a way, she has.

"But I did. Many years ago." Noni flashes me a look, and the beautiful story of love, loss, and sacrifice about how she came to be on the mainland, which she only told me a few nights ago, fills my mind.

My mom's eyes widen. "Could I have a few samples? I just need—"

Shouting echoes from one of the halls, silencing my mother.

"We shall be going! Could you tell us how to get out of this place by chance?" Noni asks, looking at my mom expectantly.

My mom points down the middle hallway. I roll my eyes. Oh, so she'll act like a human being for *her*. I should have guessed Noni would be the one to snap her out of it. She has a way with people.

She's magic.

"Wonderful!" Noni starts for the hall and yells over her shoulder, "Come along!"

My mom looks at me and then back at her, eyes still wide. I take her hand and exhale as she follows. Sebastian stays close to her side, just in case.

Noni doesn't lead us down the middle hallway, though. We turn down the one with all the shouting and gunfire. As we round the corner, it's a similar scene to what was in that great room, but on a smaller scale. People spill out the doors into an outside common area. Tables and chairs are scattered, being used as weapons or shields. The once beautiful shrubbery and flowers are trodden down, splattered with things I don't want to look too closely at.

I feel him before I see him. James still has that gravitational force around him, like when I first met him. I always know where he is in a room. I continue to scan the area for my friends and spot Trevor and Abby next, back-to-back, fighting. Using both of their abilities, water and earth, in a way I have never seen before, so seamlessly, almost like they can wield each other's.

Then it hits me. They *can* harness each other's in a way. As a bonded pair, their powers strengthen and flow as one. I have yet to try it with Sebastian.

A man jumps in front of us with two knives, wielding them expertly, slashing them through the air. He throws one directly at Sebastian's chest.

I throw my hands up, but before my fire or water unleashes, somebody else's water encases the deathly blow in midair, and it falls to the ground.

I look next to me at my mom. She takes the water-encased knife and throws it back at the guy. I look away just before it slices through his throat. Mom stuns me even more by running head-first into the chaos, her water taking out Com after Com.

"She's back," Sebastian mumbles, throwing his flames outward.

The heat hits me, electrifying and accelerating the pulse thrumming through my veins. His power clashes with mine, and I welcome it, joining our abilities together. And just like I saw with Trevor and Abby, I easily synchronize with him, feeling my power increase tenfold, like there is a never-ending source.

We use our combined powers to make a path through the fighting, singeing anyone that comes close. Sebastian covers me as I open the closest door. The room is empty. We move to the next one and the next. We keep pushing until we've searched every room on this wing.

When I spot my mom across the decimated common area, we head for her without speaking. It's as if he's also connected to my every thought, not just my power.

"Mom! Where are they?"

She looks at me, breaking her concentration, and somebody swings toward her back. Sebastian blasts the guy away.

"They're on the second level," she says, "probably right above us."

We wasted so much time searching this level. I feel dumb for not asking her sooner. I nod, and we head for the stairs. My mom is on our heels, protecting our backs.

As I peer around from this new vantage point, I can tell we're winning. The Coms are starting to notice, too, as most of them are making a run for it. I meet James's eyes and nod toward the stairs. He'll tell Trevor and Abby. But where are Juliet and William? Noni and Thomas?

We finish our ascent up the stairs and come to a deserted hall.

"It's just down here." Mom points past a wall of windows that overlooks the outside commons toward white double doors. "But I need to tell you something first," she says.

Ugh. I do not have time for her to try to talk me out of this again. I brush past her, heading for the doors. Pounding footsteps come from the stairs, and I whip around as Abby, Trevor, and James make an appearance, out of breath and covered in blood, but they're here.

Between the six of us, we've got to be able to take out the poor schmuck guarding our people, since I'm pretty sure we've already taken out most of them.

I'm almost to the doors when they open, and a familiar bald man glides out, hands in his pockets and a strange expression on his too-thin face.

Like a cartoon character, I screech to a halt, and Sebastian runs into me, grabbing my arm to keep me from falling face-first onto the tile.

"Kirt! I'm so glad you're okay. Now you can help us, too," I say.

Commander Kirt Lawrence still has that odd expression—a smirk, but more lethal-looking, and his eyes are different. I step toward him, but my mom grabs my hand and yanks me away.

I look back to shake her off, but that same terrified, balancing on psychotic expression she had when I first found her takes over her face once more.

"It's what I was trying to tell you," she murmurs. I can barely make out the words. "The one in charge…it's him."

44

Twisted Shadows

"What are you talking about? It's just Kirt," I say, scrutinizing both of them.

It's the same man who came over for BBQs with his family when I was little, the same man that I've seen give Cal a bottle and do his little girl's hair, the same man that took over the legion and protected us while in the manor. The same man I've grown to love and respect as our leader, no matter how much I might have rebelled against him because he's Kirt. Just Kirt.

His smile grows. "How many times have I told you to call me Commander Lawrence." His voice chills me to the bone, icing straight over my flickering spark. Did they change him somehow? Like the Rogues, Michael and Thomas's people talked about?

I step back, and he takes note of it, cocking his head like a predator and nothing like the man I thought I knew.

"I've always thought of you like a daughter. I don't wish to hurt you."

"Why…why would you hurt me?" I stutter.

He doesn't have that dead look in his eyes they talked about. They are gray and full of malice. No, he has not been changed. I know the answer in my gut, but I need him to say it. It can't be true until he says it.

He smiles sadly. "I've hurt a lot of people. Starting with my own family, unfortunately." He looks at me pointedly. "That was an unfortunate accident, though. A casualty of war like so many others." He shakes his head like he's talking about accidentally running over a squirrel, not murdering his entire family.

I try to swallow, but my throat is too dry, as if I haven't had water in a week.

"People who get in my way. People who think they know better." He shrugs.

I take another step back. James comes to my other side, and he and Sebastian flank me. I feel stronger with them there and push back my shoulders. "You're the Com that was made into one of us."

He rolls his eyes. "Into one of you," he scoffs and then says, louder, "Like I would want to be one of you!" He raises his arms, and shadows grow and stretch up the walls, swarming the hallway as his wind whips my hair across my face and electricity dances on his skin.

"I am so much better than any one of you. Than all of you combined, really." He laughs. Slowly, the shadows disperse, and the wind calms. "Because I like you, Maya. And because your mother has helped me so much these past few months." He looks at her, and I follow his stare.

A few feet away, she stands as still as a statue. She's so pale, truly frightened by this man…no *monster*.

"Point and stab," James murmurs under his breath.

I'm not sure I even heard him. But it reminds me of the extra weapons I have on my person. I feel the tiniest bit better; Kirt's only weapon is himself.

"I'll give you and your friends a choice. It is so nice to see you, Sebastian, by the way." He winks at him. "Getting her to bond with you took some…effort. But you managed to do it. Good for you."

It makes me want to puke, him praising Sebastian, only knowing him as his worst self. Like forcing the bond on me is something to be proud of. The nausea that has been plaguing me more often than not returns again. I swallow it down.

His gray eyes move to James. "And still pining after her. *Tsk. Tsk.* She is a bonded woman now. I should punish you." He lifts a hand.

"What's your deal?" I yell, stepping toward him, in front of James, my hand hovering over my hidden gun.

James and Sebastian step with me. Kirt smirks at them but lowers his hand.

"Right."

At that moment, William and Juliet glide into the room.

"What'd we miss? Oh! You found Commander Lawrence, great!" William says.

He and Juliet are in the same state as the rest of us, breathless and covered in grime. It's so nice to see them okay, but at the same time, I'm absolutely heartbroken. All my friends are here. How are we all going to get away from this monster unscathed?

Kirt frowns. "You sure have a lot of friends, Maya."

Abby grabs William's hand, shushing him as I turn back to Kirt. I don't respond.

He raises a caterpillar eyebrow and continues. "My deal. Stay with me and help the cause, and I promise that your *friends* will be safe. I've been wanting to study that DNA of yours for quite some time."

I think of how my mom reacted to Noni and am so grateful she isn't with us. He would want her too.

"So, this *cause*. Wiping out the Elemental race, I'm guessing? You want me to help with that and be one of your experiments."

"However, you want to look at it." He interlaces his fingers behind his back to wait for my answer.

It's my mom who answers. "You can't have my daughter, Kirt." Mom walks ahead of me to stand in our path. "You said you would leave her alone. I've already promised to help you."

With a twitch of his fingertips, she flies across the room, slamming into the wall with a sickening crunch.

"I don't need you anymore," he says, bored.

I scream and run towards her crumpled heap. A force stops me and slides me close to Kirt against my will, turning me toward him.

"What is your answer?" He places a finger on my cheek.

My chest burns, and I blast my flames outward.

He winces and pulls his hand back, sucking his finger. "Ouch."

He thinks that hurt, wait until—I rip my knife out from my sheath and aim for his chest, just like James taught me. Kirt makes a surprised sound as I pull the knife out of him, not sure where I hit.

Warm liquid drips over my hand. Without looking at him, I turn and run, free from whatever invisible binds he had me in. I think of Santa Rosa, when Juliet, Abby, and I combined our powers when we were captured, and an idea forms.

"Santa Rosa! Now!" I scream at Juliet and Abby. I pray they remember.

They look between themselves then back at me, a moment of hesitation, before tree branches crash through the far window and vines slither past. Sebastian grabs my hand, his fire sliding up my arm.

I turn to see Kirt grimacing, one hand pressed into his side. Dang, I missed. Vines wrap around his legs and arms, forcing his hand away from his wound. James catches on and more roots slither in, and together, they wind around him quickly.

He bears his teeth as a manic laugh bubbles out of his throat.

I gather water and take aim. Sebastian squeezes my hand, and I feel an influx of power rise like a tidal wave. More water travels from Trevor across the hall, and we have him encased in no time.

He frowns at us, like this is just a minor inconvenience, bubbles forming around his lips.

Juliet is next. The water ices over. William joins her as they turn him into a human popsicle.

Trevor runs for the double doors Kirt came through and throws them open. I glimpse the first group of people who had come ahead of us, all lying on metal beds, before I go to my mom, my knife clattering next to her. I kneel beside a small pool of blood forming underneath her head and push my shaking fingers into her neck.

A few too-long seconds pass of nothing, until a faint pulse thrums against my fingertips. Sebastian is at my side, placing his hands against her head. I grab his wrist.

"Wait, we shouldn't move her. It could make the injuries worse."

"We don't have a choice. We have to get her out of here before…" His eyes flick to Kirt, and I nod. Who knows how long we can keep him trapped in there?

He slowly rolls Mom to her back. There is a large gash on her forehead, blood filling her hair, turning it a dark shade of red. He lifts her as I hover my palms over the gash, sending water into it and hope it's healing her. The blood flow decreases as I take my hands off. She hangs limply in Sebastian's arms.

William and Juliet layer more frozen water on Kirt's icy cage, but we don't have much time.

Unease fills me as shadows from the corner of the hallway shift. I run into the room behind Sebastian as Abby and Trevor finish unhooking the last person. The machines beep angrily at them. Our people are still out of it, I throw water onto the lot of them, and they all sputter awake. Michael looks around wildly before his eyes land on me and then my mom in Sebastian's arms. His face crumples.

"The window!" James yells as branches from a tree smash into the window and hook inside the lab. "Climb down the tree, now!"

Our people rise, but they're wobbly on their feet. We help them, and I grab my father's hand. He still hasn't taken his eyes off my mom.

"She's alive," I tell him.

"I didn't know Lawrence would be here, or I never would have come." His face is ashen, and his green eyes flick to the hall toward Kirt and then back to my mother.

"Well, I'm glad you didn't know then."

After helping Michael over the ledge, I grab someone, then someone else. Sebastian jumps from the window, flames burning brightly underneath him to slow his descent. He lands softly, my mom still in his arms. I'll have to get him to teach me that trick.

"William, Juliet, come on!" I look back at my two friends, who have their hands out, keeping Kirt in the solid block of ice. They are so focused that they don't see the shadows stretching closer to their feet.

I bound towards them. "Look out!"

William pushes Juliet into the lab's safety as the shadows wrap around his ankles and tug his legs from under him. He lands hard on his side with a grunt.

I grab Juliet's shoulders to keep her from falling and rush past her. I shoot flames at the shadows, but they do nothing. Then water. Still nothing. The shadows drag him down the hall, away from the still-frozen Kirt, and I chase after him.

William kicks and claws at his ankles, but there is nothing to touch. A spiral of wind flings his hair upward, but his power does nothing to fight the shadows. They are taking him to the stairs. What would hurt a shadow?

"William, try your light!"

Now that I think about it, Kirt has never cast light orbs. Lots of wind, but never light. Didn't Michael say that his powers were similar to ours but twisted?

William shoots a blinding white light out of his hands. The shadows wither away. He slows just as he's about to be launched down the metal stairs. I reach for him and help him up.

Once he's safe, I keel over, panting hard. We stare into each other's eyes not believing what just happened—attacked by *shadows*? Who ever heard of such a thing?

But then William's gray eyes widen as he focuses on the something behind my shoulder. I turn as Kirt flicks a piece of ice off his shoulders.

"Looks like I have my answer," he says casually, dusting ice shards off his dark clothes. He doesn't even wince when his hand brushes where I stabbed him. He must have healed himself while encased in ice.

We launch for the stairs, taking two at a time, shadows nipping at our heels. William shoots his light behind us, but where he pierces one, another takes its place.

The downstairs is deserted, disarray left in the battle's wake. Our people are gathered in the outdoor commons area, heading out of the section that will take them out of this building of horrors. We head down the opposite hall, leading Kirt away from the others, into the same hall from which we first came.

As we slide into the great room, we stop short. Standing in the middle of the vast space is Kirt, waiting. The shadows surround us in full force. William and I are thrown into the air. I reach for him, but the shadows tighten around my neck, cutting off my air supply, and keeping me from even looking William's way. I can only stare at a smiling Kirt as he squeezes the life out of me.

The edges of my vision darken, but then the force lifts.

I inhale and look at William. His face is turning an awful shade of purple.

"Let him go!" I wheeze out. I kick my legs, but I'm stuck. My hand hovers over where my gun hides, but for all I know, he can stop a bullet with those shadows. I have to distract him.

"Be my experiment, and I will."

"Fine! Just let him go!" I say immediately.

I hear William intake air and watch the color return to his face. Out of the corner of my eye, I spy storm clouds gathering above our heads.

"How do I know you mean it?" he asks.

"Take my blood right now. I don't care!" I say, flinging my arms towards him as an offering.

He releases me, and I collapse onto the hard, tiled floor. I stand, noticing William is still hovering above my head. "Let him go too."

He shakes his head. "Nuh-uh. Not until I get your blood."

I thrust my arms out toward him, palms up. "Go ahead."

"Judith!" he calls, and a woman with short blonde hair, wearing scrubs, comes running in. "Get me a needle and a vial, please."

She nods and disappears. Where the heck was she hiding?

I stare him down to wait. And keep one ear to the sky, listening to William's storm clouds swirling above us, growing angrier by the minute.

Judith returns quickly, her heels clicking against the bloodied tile. Kirt tapped his foot thirteen times. I bet if he got to twenty, she'd be dead. Sweat beads on her forehead as she looks from me to him. I suddenly feel bad for her. How did she even come to be here. Is she a Com or an Elemental indebted to him? If he could hoodwink my mother, he could do it to anyone. On the outside, we're all the same—Elementals and Coms. This war is stupid. And it's all his fault for the divide between us.

I keep my eyes trained on Kirt as Judith pulls out a long silver needle in my periphery. His eyes move from me to the needle. In one motion, I rip the gun from my leg strap, tap the safety off, and shoot.

45

The Beast Inside

I wait for Kirt to drop, but nothing happens. Then, with widening eyes, I realize my mistake. I didn't rack it. I go to grab the top part of the gun, but it's ripped from my hands. Kirt narrows his eyes on me before they flick to William. My heart drops.

"No!"

A choking sound emanates from above me, and I look up in horror. I twist my hands and throw a fireball at Kirt. He steps to the side, and without even looking at me, shadows wrap around my body, freezing me in place.

"No! Stop!" My eyes fill with tears as Kirt slowly, lazily, looks toward me.

All the while, William chokes and thrashes above me.

"Now, Judith," Kirt says.

She pushes a needle into a vein at the crook of my arm, and I barely feel it as my blood empties into a clear vial. Her hands shake, the only sign of her not wanting to be involved.

"Please, stop! Don't kill him! I'm sorry, I'm sorry!" I cry. The tears flow harder, and I can barely see him or William, but I can hear him. My heart deteriorates listening to his suffocation, but it means he's still alive. He's still fighting. How long can somebody go without air?

"You're a monster! A monster!" I scream, fighting against the bonds.

He doesn't show an ounce of mercy, but his eyes shift down the hall.

No. Please don't come after me. *He'll kill you too!* I shout in my mind to whoever is behind me.

Judith pulls the needle out of me, and my blood drips onto the linoleum. Then I realize that small sound is the only thing I hear. Nothing is coming from the boy I love above my head.

"No!" I scream, my flames bursting out from within me directionless. The pain is too much to bear.

"What are you?" Kirt's voice reaches me, and I realize the shadows have slackened.

I turn my head to find Noni standing beside me, a golden glow around her body like a literal angel—a savior. But I can't bring myself to feel anything other than utter despair.

Kirt is blown off his feet, and William topples to the ground next to me. Once I'm free from the shadowy bindings, I throw myself on him and gather his body in my arms.

I tap his grime-coated face. "William! Please wake up! Please!"

He doesn't move. His chest doesn't rise.

I do the only thing I can think of and lower my mouth to his. I blow life inside of him once, twice, three times—

I lean back, but he's so achingly still. I shake him. "William! Please come back to me! I am so sorry." I sob and beat on his chest before blowing air into him again.

His eyes fling open.

"William!" I cry, wrapping my arms around him tightly as he does the same. "I thought you were dead!"

"I thought I was too. Did…did you snog me?"

I shake my head as my tears soak his vest. "It was CPR, you fool! Never do that again!"

He pulls back and wipes the tears from my face. "Sorry, love."

Together, we stand, him shakily as he leans heavily on me. We face the monster, hand in hand. William strokes circles on the outside of my hand. I believe he's come to find it just as soothing as I do. I squeeze him back, still not believing that he's okay. I take a deep breath and notice again the swirling clouds above us.

"Some bad weather is blowing in, huh?" I ask, sniffling.

The side of his mouth quirks up slightly, but he doesn't take his eyes off of Kirt, who's now standing, looking pissed.

His shadows gather around Noni as she walks towards him. I gasp and step toward her, but she glows brighter, and the shadows dance away. They can't touch her. She's the light that casts out the darkness. She glances back at us.

"Go. Your friends are waiting."

We back up to the hallway entrance, which will lead us out, but we hover along the room's edge. I can't just leave her here alone with that monster.

"You can go," I whisper, pushing William away.

He pulls me with him, an iron grip on my hand. "I'm not leaving your side. Anyway, I'm the backup." He looks up at the sky, which is swirling and growing, turning shades of purple and black. My hair stands on end, feeling the electric current growing.

"If you have any sense, you'll get out of here, old woman," Kirt growls.

She sweeps him off his feet with a flick of her wrist, and he curses.

"You asked for it," he grunts, standing once more.

Before he can do anything, she unleashes a massive fireball. No, not a fireball. It's an animal running on four legs toward Kirt.

His eyes widen, shooting electricity out of his hands. It skewers the animal in half just as it's about to engulf him, sending tiny little flames dancing around his body instead. But he's so distracted by the fire that he doesn't see the wave of water directly behind the animal. It smashes into him, swirling around his body, raising him into the air. His face twists in rage as he thrashes inside.

"Enough!" he yells as the water bursts, some droplets landing on my skin across the room.

Shadows encase his body, raising him high above Noni's head. Lightning sizzles on his skin. He spreads his arms out wide. Noni throws light bursts toward him, ripping holes into his shadows, but there are too many of them.

He looks down at her, his lips spreading into a dangerous smile as he clenches his fists.

With an avalanche of snaps and pops around us, the outside of the wall separates from the beams behind it. William and I dive to the side before the falling debris can crush us. The metal beams rip from their structures with a deafening crack and head straight for Noni.

Water, wind, and fire wrap around them, barely stopping the assortment of beams from hitting her. But as she focuses on that,

Kirt unleashes shadows and electricity from his body, using the same tactic to distract her as she did him. She doesn't see them coming.

"Noni, watch out!" I scream, standing up, readying to throw all I have at Kirt.

She twists to face him just as lightning strikes the ground before her. It is not Kirt's lightning, though; this one is from the swirling purple clouds above our heads.

It blocks most of Kirt's impact as his lightning meets it in a vociferous strike. I cover my ears against the deafening noise vibrating my skull as she and Kirt hit the ground.

I hold my breath when Noni doesn't move. A woman her age probably would break every bone in her body with a fall like that.

I run for her, jumping over bodies and debris. William calls for me, but I don't slow. I'm almost to her when the hair on my arms stands on end. I dive out of the way as electricity strikes where I stand. I look up at the monster.

He's back on his feet now, grinning. "I don't miss, you know," he says.

"Bastard."

I step for her, but he wiggles his pointer finger at me. "Nuh-uh. I think I'll keep her. Slice her up bit by bit and study what makes her tick."

I scowl at him. Rage boils up, and I shoot my fire at him. I don't wait to see if it hits its mark. I clear the beam between Noni and me.

Crouching down, I exhale with relief as her emerald eyes open.

"That one hurt. I'm no spring chicken anymore," she grunts, pulling herself up on her elbows.

The room darkens as power grows around us. The metal beams swing back into the air.

"Is anything broken?" My heart beats loudly in my ears as I glance behind me at the massive tornado of shadows, lightning, and metal. But it's not the only thing swirling.

"No, I don't think so. Would you be a dear and help an old woman up?"

I take her fragile hand. How can something so tiny and breakable house such strength and power? I keep one eye on the metal beams swinging dangerously closer to us as I help her up with ease. She's as light as a feather. How has Kirt not blown her away?

We barely reach the hall's entrance when the wind is upon us. It pulls me back, my feet sliding against the linoleum. I catch myself on the wall, digging my fingers into the jagged edges, and look back as a vast, thunderous tornado touches down between us and Kirt.

My jaw drops. This tornado makes Kirts look tiny and pathetic. William stands dangerously close to the whirlwind as he controls the beast. Kirt is nowhere to be seen, lost somewhere in the chaos. Hopefully, he will get skewered with one of his own metal beams.

"William!" I scream, but I'm not the only one to say it. Somebody grabs my hand, pulling me from the wall and into his arms.

"William! Get out of there!" Sebastian yells again. There's no response. "Damn it. He can't hear us." He looks down at me, taking a quick scan of my body. "Are you okay? Looks like we missed an epic fight."

I nod, taking quick stock of my body. The only pain comes from where the nurse stabbed me with her needle. "We?"

"We," James says, taking Noni's arm to steady her as she leans against the wall.

She pats his hand with a smile and straightens.

He shakes his head in awe at what's going on around us. "Who knew William had that beast inside him?"

"I did," Sebastian says, letting me go. His jaw sets as he prepares to throw himself into the cyclone.

I grab his arm. "You'll die out there."

William is just a vague silhouette at this point, standing in the eye of the storm.

"Don't do anything rash. I'm working on it," Noni says. She grits her teeth, her eyes closed in concentration. She wobbles on her feet, and all three of us reach out to grab her. "There!" Her eyes open. They are two glowing emerald orbs.

Something barrels down the hallway and blurs past us. I gasp as a huge mountain lion leaps into the tornado. I expect it to fly into the air and out of sight, but it lowers its body to the ground so its belly almost brushes the surface and stalks its target—William. My heart pounds.

"No!" After all this, William is just going to get eaten by a giant cat?

I'm about ready to throw myself out there, but Sebastian grabs my arms. "Wait," he says.

My eyes widen at him. He points toward the cat.

It inches closer to William and stops just near his feet. It doesn't attack but nudges him with its nose. William looks down, and the center of the tornado fades a bit as he jumps back.

I swear I hear a scream through the deafening roar of the wind. Imagining his thoughts on seeing a mountain lion tapping on his leg has my lips pulling up.

Enough of the tornado dampens that Kirt's shape comes into view too. His hands are in the air, shadows swirling around him, yards away from William, as if he's collecting them from the earth's four corners. Even a tornado doesn't have a chance against something that isn't physical.

The big cat grabs the bottom of William's pants and starts dragging him toward us. My lips quirk up even more at the sight. William fumbles to keep his pants up with one hand, and the other still faces the tornado, keeping it strong and swirling. I know he must be cursing at the animal.

The mountain lion with William in his mouth reaches us and finally drops him.

"Bloody hell," William says, but he doesn't turn toward us as he focuses his energy on the tornado.

I smack him on the arm. "William! Are you insane?"

He shakes his head, still focusing.

"Come on we need to get out of here. Bring it with us!"

He looks at me like I'm the crazy one. I don't give him the chance to argue. I grab the back of his shirt, glancing at Sebastian for help. He stoops low to grab William around the waist, probably planning to throw him over his shoulder, when his eyes suddenly widen.

It all happens too fast. One moment, Sebastian is next to William and me, and the next he's gone. I lunge forward as arms wrap around William and me, and we fall backward on top of each other. The end of the hall caves in around us.

James pushes me forward to avoid getting hit, but now he's in the path of the crumbling walls. I scream as I'm pulled backward by an unknown force. The same force pulls James, and we're all sliding down the hall, inches away from being smashed by chunks of ceiling. I scramble to my feet, and we make a run for it.

Something slashes into my arm as I throw myself into the open air. The four of us tumble down a steep slope. The breath wooshes from me as a large male body lands on my chest. He jumps off me quickly and air fills my lungs once more.

We pant and cough as James helps me up. I look around for Noni, whom William is holding up. She's slouched on her knees, breathing hard but okay. William's face is caked in sweat and grime, and one hand is still raised in the air.

I whip around. Behind us the tornado is tearing its way through the building, following us. I gape.

"I didn't mean it literally! Stop it, William."

He shakes his head, his eyes bloodshot. "I can't. My energy is spent. I—I can't control it now." His arm falls to his side limply.

"Maya, we need to run." James is at my ear, pushing me away from the cyclone coming for us.

"But Sebastian." I grab my chest, feeling for the tether. "He was right there. What happened?" My hair whips around my face as I stare at the incoming behemoth. Sebastian is in there.

James grabs my hand and yanks me away. We're all running again down the street between the line of buildings. I can see the water ahead, far down the road. I ignore the ache in my muscles and my legs screaming at me for rest. I ignore the tether pulling me in the opposite direction and the tears stinging my eyes. The sky is gray and angry above our heads. The wind howls behind us, and trees tear from their roots. Buildings crumble on both sides of the street. I duck my head just as a stop sign flies past.

At the end of the street, we stop short. In the intersection ahead of us, just two blocks from the pier that holds a towering Ferris Wheel, more fighting has broken out.

Can we not get a single break?

Juliet's white hair is the first thing I see, swishing elegantly through the air, battling two Coms simultaneously. Wait, no—not Coms. They have powers, water by the looks of it. Rogues? She kicks out and swings back, blasting away one's water so it engulfs him instead of her, before turning the others into ice, incapacitating them. Even in battle, she's beautiful and graceful.

I grab William who looks like he's about to pass out.

"William! It's Juliet!" I point, and he sees her. I don't have to say anything else.

She stiffens and looks our way. She gives him a brief nod as they make their mental connection. After finishing off a Com with a flick of her wrist, she closes her eyes in concentration.

James pulls me toward the fighting as I watch Juliet raise her hands. A couple of other Auras do the same—the strength of many. I peer over my shoulder, but the raging tornado is still heading our way like it's angry we created it and wants retribution. People are now noticing the incoming beast. They scatter like ants. Our people head for the water. The Coms run in the opposite direction. A couple of them stay and continue to fight, even though they're outnumbered twenty to one. What would compel them to keep fighting?

The boats are ready and waiting in the port, beyond the pier, keeping their distance, just in case. But our escape route is set, and the plan is in motion, except for one detail—Sebastian isn't here.

We reach Juliet, still deep in concentration as a man with short dark hair stalks her.

James raises his gun. "If you have any sense, you will join your friends."

The guy doesn't seem to hear him—or doesn't care. He flings his arms forward, a crack forming in the earth. James closes it before it reaches Juliet and pulls the trigger. The man crashes to the ground.

James places a foot on his chest. "Just stop!"

He thrashes from underneath the boot. James is trying not to kill him. I step closer.

The man flails, his eyes bloodshot and lifeless like something else is pulling the strings on him.

"He's a Rogue," comes a voice.

I look up to find Thomas staring down at the man on the ground. I sigh inwardly, grateful that he's in one piece.

James winces as the man claws at his foot. He shoots him in that arm. The man doesn't even flinch, just keeps writhing towards James.

"I've never seen one," James says. "Is there anything we can do?"

Thomas shakes his head. "His soul is gone." Thomas brings up a hand as flames gather in his palm.

"No, I'll do it. He won't feel a thing," James says. "Maya, you may want to—"

He doesn't have to finish. I squeeze my eyes shut. It doesn't matter that I've already seen so much death. If I have the choice, I'd prefer to have fewer reasons for more nightmares.

The shot rings out and the thrashing and grunting from the man stops.

Somebody pulls me into a hug.

"I'm so glad you're okay," Michael tells me. He pushes back to take me in, emotion lighting his eyes before they land on the man James just shot. He frowns.

"Would you have been able to help him?" I ask.

"Maybe. Each case is different. How long it's been since they've been altered. How strong they are. How much of the person is still in there."

I nod as James brushes past me. Michael's words ring in my ear. *There are many things worse than death.* This is worse than death—turning into a Rogue, being forced to hurt and kill people as your own body becomes a prison. Dread curdles in my stomach.

I step away, shake off the feeling, and scan the dispersing crowd for familiar faces, hoping to see others I love. I'm surprised that quite a few prisoners stayed to fight, but many have disappeared, as expected. I spot Trevor's flaming-red hair and expect to see Abby not too far away, but I can't find her auburn bob in the crowd.

"Where is Lawrence?" Michael asks.

"He and Sebastian are in there somewhere," I choke out, referencing the cyclone and the rubble that used to be the science building.

But when I look back, the cyclone isn't coming for us any longer. It's veering to the right and growing impossibly stronger and faster as it chases the Coms into the city. More importantly, there is a perfect path back to Sebastian.

"I'm so sorry, Maya." He says it like Sebastian is already passed saving. "But we need to get out of here. Now." He turns toward Thomas and Noni.

The tether is still there, strung tight toward the decimation. I'm not leaving him with that monster.

"Still a badass, I see," Thomas says.

I flash him a tired smile. He has just let go of Noni, who was leaning heavily against him. Michael picks her up in his arms and starts for the water. My heart goes out to her. It's the first time she's looked her age since her brilliant act in Portland.

"Wait. Where's Mom?"

Michael points with his nose to the nearest boat, which our group is heading to. "She's safe with the rest of the injured. Your friend Abby too."

Abby is injured? No. I swallow and push the worry down for now. She's safe and so is Mom. Knowing they're okay calms my nerves just enough for me to make my next decision.

"I'll meet you at the boat, okay?"

Noni eyes me over Michael's shoulder, and I silently plead for her to let me go. I have to save him.

She shakes her head sadly before tilting her head and whistling at James, who is holding up a very exhausted William. They both pause to look at us.

I gauge my chances, turn on my heel, and run. I take a whole two steps before James pulls me to his chest. I thrash against him, but his arms are like steel.

"I have to go back."

"That's suicide." His voice is hard, unyielding.

"He has him! Kirt has Sebastian. I know it!" I sob.

He pulls me into his chest, and the floodgates open as I pound on him weakly.

James whispers, "Go ahead. I've got her," over my head as I sob into his chest.

"But… No…I have to…" I choke, looking up at him through my muddled vision.

His eyes are sorrowful as he places a hand on my cheek. "Would Sebastian want you to go back for him?"

No way. He'd tell me to get as far away as possible. I stare into his hazel eyes, pleading for a way. They soften, and his head falls against mine. "I'll go get him."

"You said it's suicide!" I screech, pulling away from him.

"He's your mate. I don't want to see what his death will do to you."

"Oh, and you think both of you dying is the answer?"

He looks away from me, but I force his chin back to face me. "No. You will not die today, Avery James Stevens." A fire burns in my chest at the thought.

He sighs as he looks from me to the city. Sebastian is strong, stronger than most because of what he has endured—if we can just get to him without being noticed. But there is no way I can ask James or anyone else to come with me to find Sebastian.

And then there's Kirt. He won't let me just leave if I go back. He did get my blood; maybe that was enough.

A pit forms in my stomach. I know better. Nothing will ever be enough for that man. He will continue to take and destroy as long as he lives. If I don't get to Sebastian now, I may never see him again.

The fire swirls and grows within me as I glance beyond James toward the boats and our people—my *family*.

They'll try to wait for me, but they won't, they can't risk their lives for one person. They'll have to leave. I wouldn't want them to stay. But then, even if I do find Sebastian, how will we escape?

My body fights against itself as I look between the city and the bay that's calling me home. The tornado, having run out of things to destroy or to fuel it, finally makes its way back into the clouds in the city's center. Juliet and the other Auras bring up the rear, right behind Thomas and William, their energy reserves depleted. They drift farther away as they pass the last buildings. James's chin-length hair whips around his face as he watches me, awaiting my answer.

I feel the exhaustion creep its way into my muscles as they start to protest me even standing. The sun rises higher in the sky, baking my skin. It would be so easy to give up.

Straightening my shoulders, I wipe the tears from my cheeks. "I'm going." I turn and head up the hill.

James joins me but doesn't stop me. Instead, he launches into what he does best. Leading.

"We killed most of them. It's just Kirt. I'll go in first, and you wait for my word. With just the two of us, there is a chance we can get in and out undetected. But that depends on whether Kirt has anything other than what he's shown us up his sleeve. I've gathered that his powers are a flip of ours: Shadows, electricity, and metal. I wonder if there's anything else."

James continues to think aloud, formulating a plan on the spot. But with every step, dread curls around my stomach. With this decision, I could lose both of them, but I can't physically leave Sebastian. I have no choice. He's my mate, and we are one. I must save him. And James will not let me go on my own. It's completely selfish of me, but I'm glad he's coming. I can't do this without him.

A reflection of light catches my attention from the road ahead. I stiffen. In between the decimated buildings, far up the road, is the unmistakable form of Kirt Lawrence. His bald head always glistened in the sunlight. He has a huge gun pressed against his shoulder, directed at us.

Time slows as I grab onto James. To push him out of the way or pull him close for one last embrace, I'm not sure. Before I can, a missile whistles over our heads, and an explosion rocks the earth behind us, straight into the heart of our people.

I capture James's hazel eyes in mine moments before my body is violently ripped away.

Ethereal Light

Blue sky stretches above me. The storm-ridden clouds from earlier have turned into a twisting black wall of smoke, disrupting the beauty.

I would think I'm dead if it wasn't for the burning in my lungs. Panic prickles through me like a thousand needles as I try to get my lungs to work. Then, the pain blossoms from my back and radiates into my legs.

I open my mouth to scream, but I can't. My lungs won't work. I envision William in front of me, telling me to breathe with him. Finally, oxygen rushes in, and I roll achingly slowly to my knees, coughing as the smoke burns my lungs. I scan the unrecognizable sight before me.

There is a small crater where our group had just been walking, half the pier is collapsed into the water, including the towering Ferris wheel.

Bodies lay everywhere.

Some are frightening still. Some are moving, but barely. And others, who were on the outside of the blast zone, are slowly rising to their feet like me. But I wasn't nearly as close. If I'm aching at this distance, I can't imagine what they're going through. Part of me is glad the smoke distorts their faces. I can live in delusion for a little bit longer before my heart is undoubtedly ripped from me.

I get to my feet with effort and trip towards my people—my friends, my family. They were all down there. I choke on the smoke, and my eyes water, but I don't stop. I stumble into somebody. It's the thin girl from the cell. I assumed she would have already been on the boat. Did she come back to help those who were injured?

She's looking down in horror. At her feet lays the boy from the cell who had helped us, Greg. If it weren't for him, we wouldn't have been able to get anyone out. His eyes are wide and frozen. Gone.

I look back at the girl, who is shaking uncontrollably now, and wrap my arm around her. I nudge her away, but she won't move. She's surprisingly strong as she pushes me off her and collapses to the ground. I step toward her, but there are so many others I need to find.

I let her be, and I look for a familiar face. Emptiness swallows me as I stare at those on the ground. So much death. Some are people I had just started to get to know. Wide, lifeless, gray eyes and blonde hair have me sucking in a breath and choking again, though I quickly realize it's not William, but Foster. I lean down and close his eyelids before continuing.

Most of the bodies are charred beyond recognition. I cover my nose with my jacket to block the ungodly stench and swipe at my right eye, which won't stop watering. I recognize another whose face is only half charred—Cody, the smiling Igna boy, who pretended to drive the Camaro in the parking garage. He's not smiling anymore. My stomach rolls and then heaves.

As I empty the contents of my stomach onto the scorched earth, I feel the pull behind me. Sebastian? I turn, and James wraps me in his arms.

"Maya." James caresses the back of my head, holding me tight.

I breathe him in, so utterly grateful, then lean back. His face is bloody and black with soot. "Have you found anyone?"

His eyes darken. "I saw—"

He doesn't get the chance to finish because something behind me has him stiffening. Rage morphs his features. I know by the bleak feeling in my gut who it is before I turn.

Stepping out of the smoke is Kirt, a shadow army flanking him, a menacing smile forming on his lips. Lightning sizzles on his palms, dancing on his fingertips.

"Should have taken my deal, kid," he says before hurling lightning straight for us.

A wall of earth shoots out of the ground, taking the force of the impact. James grabs me and runs for the water. Layers of rock launch from the ground behind us, protecting us from the onslaught of Kirt's lightning.

But we don't get far before shadows wrap around our feet, and I smack face-first into the hard ground. James groans next to me. The shadows climb my body like ice-cold vines, and I writhe to get free, but they're too strong.

Light. I need light. A memory surges to the surface of blue light coating me while kissing James, of it dancing on my skin at even the thought of being close to him. I know that unique power is in there.

I focus on the spark in my chest, trying to harness that part of me when I'm with James, but only orange fire licks my skin, doing nothing to the shadows.

Kirt stalks toward us, only a couple of feet away now. There is no more time to think.

"James, kiss me!"

His struggling stops next to me, his eyes widening. He doesn't voice his confusion, though, just leans in and brushes his lips against mine.

Warmth fills me, making my very bones vibrate. I feel it—the light. Joy, happiness, and pleasure swirl inside. I grasp it, holding on tight, as I deepen the kiss. His lips open, and his tongue teases mine. Fire explodes from within the deepest part of me.

I break the kiss in a gasp. Blue light and flames shimmer brightly on my skin, causing the shadows to skitter away. With my hands freed, I pull James towards me and swallow him in my light.

Kirt steps over us. "How sweet. One final moment before you die." He eyes me. "*Tsk. Tsk.* You're a bonded woman. Don't you know what this will do to your mate?"

"I'm right here, and it hasn't done a damn thing." Sebastian launches himself at Kirt, fire wrapping around his entire body.

Kirt yells as the flames encase him as well. Lightning and shadows strike out, but Sebastian holds tight, even as his eyes begin to roll to the back of his head, and he shakes violently. His fire doesn't let up as it swirls and engulfs them both. Kirt screams and writhes against Sebastian's iron hold.

They fall to the ground together and Sebastian's eyes flutter closed. My hand flies to my chest.

That link to him, the tether that binds us, the strong sense of him and the need to be with him…dampens.

I scream, shuffling to my feet, and do the only thing I can think of. I grab a hold of the water from behind us and tidal wave it towards them. It hits all four of us, extinguishing the fire and separating them. I crawl to Sebastian and grab his face, shaking him. He doesn't move.

"Please wake up. I love you, Sebastian. I love you! Please don't die."

I place my head on his chest. It's silent. Nothing. The tether withers, an ache growing in the center of my chest. My back arches, and I fall onto him. I stroke his cheek, trying to hold onto that last wisp between us.

"Please," I whisper, my tears dampening his already wet shirt.

James falls to his knees at our side. His hands are on my shoulders, trying to pull me off, but I refuse to let go.

"Trust me," he says.

I lock eyes with him and nod, trusting him fully. Sliding off Sebastian and into the muddy grass, my hands hang limply in my lap. James places his hands over Sebastian's heart and pushes down, pressing repeatedly, before lowering his mouth to his. He blows in and sits back up, continuing the compressions. Again, he blows into his body.

Sebastian's chest rises and it gives me hope, but it just becomes lifeless again when James goes back to the compressions.

It'll work. It has to. It did for William.

A voice at the back of my head tells me that William had just needed oxygen, but Sebastian got electrocuted over and over again. It's not the same.

Another hand touches my shoulder, and I flinch. Noni stares down at me. Her face and clothes are caked in soot but otherwise seems unharmed. I'm so happy she's okay, but I can't voice it. I feel broken, like I'll never be whole again.

Noni lowers herself down and places a hand over James's. "Let me."

James nods and sits back on his heels, breathing hard. Noni places her hand over Sebastian's heart. She thumps once, and a jolt goes through him, zapping his entire body. She waits. Then she does it again—this time, a jolt along with light. She waits. He doesn't move.

She grunts and grabs my hand. "I need your help."

I just look at her. She places my hand on his chest.

"I need you to focus on your powers and his. You're still connected to him. Use everything. Push it all inside of him, okay?"

I nod weakly and close my eyes. I focus on that flame inside of me. It's so tiny. I've used so much of it already. I let my love bloom outward. The love for my family. My love for Sebastian. My love for my friends. And even my love for James. I know it'll always be there, no matter who I choose or how often my heart breaks. I let it push my flame outward and into my palm. I focus on my water powers and all the skills I learned growing up, pulling its essence into my palm.

Then I search for that part of me that is linked to him. There! The tiniest sliver of the bond, barely hanging on. A light breeze could break it in half.

I grab hold and pull. An echo of his powers on the other end pulls weakly back. I grab onto it with all of my dwindling strength. My spark ignites and burns, blooming brighter and hotter until everything inside of me and who I am incinerates and I am left with one purpose, one thing keeping me tethered to this world— him.

"Okay!" I yell through gritted teeth.

Noni sucks in a breath and pushes my hand into Sebastian's chest so hard I swear I hear bones crack. A jolt reverberates through him and into me. I fall into Noni, and she holds me upright.

All my power is sucked away.

Gone.

I don't feel a single trace of my flame. She helps me sit up as my eyes roam over his body, looking for any sign of life. His lips are blue, and he's still so pale.

It didn't work.

I'm so sorry I failed you, Sebastian. You proved to me that you could change, but I couldn't.

I still love James. Even now, the tiniest part of me is grateful that it's not James lying on the grass, lifeless. Without the strength of the tether, I feel that love and need for James so immensely that it could swallow me whole if I let it.

Guilt crashes over me, too strong to contain, pushing bile up my throat. I fling myself back and puke in the grass again. Nothing comes up though. I dry heave a few times before Noni grabs me. Tears stream down my face.

"It's all my fault, Noni," I cry.

She grabs me, her face bright, as she looks down at him. "Look."

I look. Sebastian's chest rises, and his face fills with color. His eyes flutter open. I didn't think I would see those ocean eyes again. I fling myself on top of him, and he slowly brings his hand around my waist as I sob into his neck. At the contact, tendrils of power seep back into me and my spark flickers once more.

"Did I die?" He groans.

"You sure did. And your mate brought you back to life," Noni says.

His eyes flicker to mine.

I lower my mouth to his. His body stills and I pull away. Nobody else would have noticed the hesitation, but I did. He didn't want to kiss me—a first.

Slowly, I help him into a sitting position.

"What about…him?" Sebastian asks, looking around.

I hadn't even thought about Kirt. I look over at his body, charred on the ground. "Looks like you did your job well."

"Good."

He rises to his feet, taking me with him. He pulls me against him. I study his face, but it's a mask as he scans the field around us. He limps down toward the water, his arm tight around my waist.

When we reach the rocks, I grab his face to look at mine. "Are you really okay?"

He nods. "Thank you."

"You're the one that saved my life," I remind him. He sacrificed himself for me *and* James. My heart swells.

He frowns. "And then you saved mine."

I laugh breathlessly. "What, you didn't want me to save you?"

I thought that would pull a smile out of him, but his frown deepens. "No, I did not." He looks at me seriously.

"Sebastian. You don't mean that."

His eyes flick away and back to mine.

Unease fills me. "What happened earlier? Before you…died, back at the building. Did he take you?"

A deep line forms between his dark eyebrows. "One of his shadow limbs grabbed me as we turned to leave." A muscle ticks in his jaw, and he turns away. "Nothing worse than what I've already experienced," he murmurs.

I can tell he doesn't want to talk about it, but why would he say he didn't want me to save him? It makes no sense. Something must have happened. I think of the moment before he came—when I kissed James.

I gently place my palm against his cheek. It's unusually cool. "Is it me?"

He covers my hand with his but still doesn't look at me.

He shakes his head and sighs. "I felt that I finally made up for what I did to you, but then you went and saved me. We're out of balance again."

"Sebastian. We're mates. That's what we do. You don't owe me anything."

Something flickers in his eyes before he looks back at me. "If you say so."

I shake my head at him, then I look up the hill at everyone making their way down to us—those that are left. It's hard to look too long at the charred bodies covering the landscape. But I need to know who made it. Abby and my mom were safe on the boat, but what about Michael, Thomas, Trevor, William, and Juliet? My stomach clenches when I don't see them.

I let Sebastian guide me to the dinghy that will take us to the boat—or more like yacht.

I count three decks, each in a flurry of motion, as we step on board. There are so many injured people lying on the dock, and from the moaning, more are inside that I can't see. Those who are mostly unscathed are healing others who are worse off.

Even though I want to walk through the boat and find my loved ones, I know this is more dire. With my fire and water powers, I can help twice as many. I get to work, starting with a woman about my age in a gray prison uniform at my feet. I kneel next to her as Sebastian goes to another.

"Do you happen to be an Igna or Lympha?"

Her blood-coated face blinks up at me, and her cracked lips form the word "Lympha."

I nod, grabbing some water from the sea and swirling it around her. It's more difficult to wield with my power still drained, but I make do with tiny amounts of water at a time. She winces as the salt meets her wounds but then relaxes as the healing begins. She stands with me once I'm done.

"Thank you." She smiles. "I'm Lilly."

I nod. "Maya." I look around for another to help.

Lilly uses more water to clean the grime off the rest of her body. "I'm sorry about your guys' commander. What a shame."

I stiffen and turn. "Who?"

"The red-haired fella?"

My breath leaves me, and I rush for the stairs. After searching the second and third decks, I head for the quarters below decks. There are three boats, though. Abby may not even be on this one.

The next level is even more cramped with bodies, but I spot a bob of auburn hair immediately, sitting on a lower bunk bed. She looks at me as I near. Her face is red and puffy, tears sliding down her cheeks.

"It's gone," Abby gasps. "The connection is just gone! Maya, it hurts. It *hurts*!"

I hold my arms out for her, and she collapses into my arms.

"My mate! He's gone!" she wails.

We sink to the ground together. Her grief shatters what's left of my strength, and all the thoughts and fears I've been trying to push down rise to the surface like a buoy. What if they are all gone? Wasn't Trevor near my father? Thomas and William were there somewhere too. I'm hopeful for Juliet, who was near the back, but she could have easily been—

My tears mix with Abby's for I don't know how long. Finally, a hand on my shoulder raises me. I settle Abby back on the bed and follow Noni up the stairs without a word. The other two boats—one which holds my mom—are ahead of us in the bay as we distance ourselves from the city. Sebastian is at the railing, looking down at the water, the muscles in his arms flexing and relaxing as if preparing for another onslaught.

"I wanted to say goodbye, my dear," Noni says.

"What?" I look around between the two land masses in the bay. We're almost to the open ocean. Where does she think she's going?

"Your father and Thomas are still alive, and so are your friends. William scared us for a bit, having thrown himself over your friend Juliet during the explosion, but he'll recover."

I throw my arms around her. "Thank you for telling me, Noni. I was so worried."

She pats my back and holds my gaze in hers. "You'll need them for what's to come."

My eyebrows scrunch together.

She looks me over with a watery smile and grabs a wisp of my hair. "My lovely girl."

I'm about to ask her what in the world she's talking about when shouts come from the back of the boat.

I slowly turn and can't believe my eyes. It's straight out of a horror movie. The scorched corpse of the man is walking toward us…a literal zombie come back to life.

I watch in dread as electricity cracks his skin and it falls away, leaving a scarred, freakish-looking monster underneath. It's as if that is what was there this entire time, and we just overlooked it. The monster he truly is.

"How?" I choke.

We're still too close to shore to be safe from him. I grapple for the last of my energy reserves and focus on my Sage—the water hitting the boat, the sea salt breeze curling around my hair. I pull the wave toward us, propelling us faster, but I stare in shock. His shadows are already on their way, reaching the end of the crumbling pier, gliding over the half-submerged Ferris wheel, and floating over the water.

Noni touches my wrist, drawing my attention. Her expression hasn't changed from her earlier rambling.

"I'm ready," she says softly.

I shake my head at her. "Noni, he's back!"

"It's okay. I'm ready," she says again, smiling as she stares beyond me. Not at the monster, but beyond him, beyond the land surrounding us, toward the sea, as if she can see her old home from here—her island.

"Ready for what?" I cry. I pull the waves in more, but all my energy is spent from saving Sebastian. The waves fall flat. The shadows are almost to our boat.

She turns to me, and a magnificent smile graces her face, making me forget everything else. A tear rolls down her cheek, not of sorrow but of insurmountable joy. "To see him again."

I'm about to ask who when it clicks. The story she told me about her love, who sacrificed himself. She'd only shared the intimate details of her heart with me a few days prior. Suddenly, I know exactly what she's planning.

She brushes a kiss on my temple, squeezing something into my palm. "This is for you. I love you, my darling girl."

"Izalia," I gasp. But before I can take another step to hold her back, she vanishes into wind and sunlight.

I trip over my feet to get to the railing, to jump into the water, create a tsunami, launch a fireball, do *something*. She can't do this on her own. But I don't see her in the water.

Somebody grabs my hand. I twist to find Michael. I didn't know he was on this boat.

"She's going to get herself killed!" I wail.

"It's her last wish. To sacrifice herself for those she loves. Just like Theo." His face is calm. He's accepted it.

I know that. Deep inside I know that. But she's a part of my family. A part that I just got back. I can't lose her so soon. I go to grab the railing but metal digs into my palm.

Opening my hand, a beautiful golden ring with a sparkling sun in the center winks at me. Izalia's ring. The only piece of jewelry I ever saw her wear. I swallow hard, still not wanting to believe it.

Her form appears far ahead, directly in front of the vile monster of a man. I lean against the cold railing, the ocean water spraying onto my hands. I slip the ring on so I don't accidently drop it. I hate that it fits perfectly. She should be still wearing it.

A warm hand covers my own and, without looking, I know it's Sebastian, his heat seeping into my body.

We drift further and further away, my energy fading fast as I lean into Sebastian. I don't want to watch but can't peel my eyes away, barely making out the two shapes on the shore, when a powerful, bright-white light illuminates the length of the coastline—more brilliant and ethereal than the sun. I shield my watering eyes, but still, I don't look away. The sight burns into my memory forever.

When the light dims, there is nothing on the shore.

Nothing at all.

My body feels detached as the ocean waves rock us. So many thoughts swirl in my mind, but I don't have the strength to grasp one and give it much time in my head. My tears are long gone.

Sebastian slumps against me as he sleeps, our backs against the railing I have yet to leave. I keep his hand in mine, tracing the veins and then the sun on my finger. Some people sleep, while others watch the coastline, waiting for something to happen.

I don't blame them.

Part of me is waiting for Kirt to jump from the water and kill us all. But he's gone. She killed him.

She's gone.

I can barely think of it before another lump settles in my throat. I have my mother back. Michael told me her injuries would heal. He didn't mention the injuries *inside* of her, though. In whatever condition she's in, at least she's back. Cal will be happy that I kept my promise.

There's a flutter at the edge of my vision—a beautiful white and black butterfly coasting in the wind. I sit up, watching it. What is it doing way out here? It's not like we're that far from land, we've just barely made it out of the bay. But there is nothing for it in these waters.

It descends until it lands on the railing next to my face, its wings flapping up and down like an eye winking.

"Good thing you found us," I murmur, raising my hand toward it.

It immediately flutters to my fingers. When it touches me, an electric charge goes through me and the butterflies' wings look like they are made of flames. I blink and the wings return to normal between one flap and the next.

It's *her*. I look around, expecting to see Izalia sitting somewhere on the boat, engaged in one of her many stories, but her beautiful floral skirts are nowhere to be seen. I *feel* her, though—an overwhelming feeling of joy, contentment, and love. She's happy. Wherever she is, she's back with her love. I smile as I raise my fingers and the butterfly flies away.

"Goodbye, Izalia."

47

Tiny Spark

Two weeks have passed since the battle in Seattle. Not like anything has changed. Killing their leader and destroying a major city just angered the Coms, fueled their hatred against us. What Kirt Lawrence started cannot be stopped. We can't stay at the manor. Preparations to leave are already in motion as we brace for retribution.

Two weeks since William was injured. His body was severely burned from the explosion. Auras were able to quicken the healing process, but parts of him were too badly damaged to heal properly. The doctor worries about his eyes the most. Despite the scarring and hazy vision, my little sunshine-attention-seeker has never been happier. While bedbound to allow his skin to heal more naturally, Juliet flutters around, caring for his every need and changing his bandages. He thinks it's because Juliet feels terrible since he got hurt while protecting her. I'm trying to not-so-subtly hint that she's hopelessly in love with him. When Juliet isn't there, I stay with him, finally getting to repay all those months he comforted me at my worst. I don't think he knows how to struggle, though. Just this morning, he was joking about *his smoking-hot body*.

Two weeks since Noni's passing. We had a beautiful funeral for her at the manor. Hundreds of butterflies were present, and I swear there was a sea salt breeze that blew in. Her presence was strong, as if her arms wrapped around me while we tossed flowers into the lake and shared stories about her. She had only been with these people for a short time, but everyone had something to say about her. Her impact will be one for a lifetime.

Two weeks since Sebastian has been himself. He's distant. But it's not like I've been much better. There is a rift between us that we're dancing around. He hasn't mentioned anything about the kiss between James and me, but I know he saw it. I've been waiting for him to ask so I could explain, but I don't want to be the one that brings it up.

He also hasn't said anything more about what happened when Kirt took him. So here we are. Barely talking. Sleeping in the same bed, but barely touching, despite the pull.

I fold my arms as a cool breeze tickles my neck, whispering that fall has descended. The flowers on the hibiscus rose we planted in my grandmother's honor dance amongst the branches. It's one of the few flowers that bloom in early autumn, and its vibrant tropical colors remind me of her. This is where I come to talk to her now. There's usually a butterfly or two in the vicinity.

One sits on a branch not too far away now. Noni's body may not be here, but her presence is.

I study its yellow wings as Sebastian walks up behind me. I feel him quite acutely, the tether stronger than ever. Having it gone for that short moment when Sebastian died and realizing how powerful my love for James was underneath, the tether seems more like a chokehold these days—a lie.

"Can we talk?" His voice is soft, careful.

I nod without looking at him and follow his shadow to a bench near the yellow butterfly. I count each flap of the butterflies' wings, gaining strength to tell him the truth.

At twenty-four flaps, I finally look at him. His expression is pained. I swallow my words.

"We need to talk about it."

There are so many things that "it" can be. I wait as Sebastian leans against the bench, his face contemplative. He cut his hair short again, his face clean shaven, now looking more similar to the man I first met but also so far from him.

He turns to me, his chin set. "Maya, do you love me?"

"Yes," I say automatically.

"Do you still love James?"

I don't answer right away, but I told myself I would be truthful. "Yes."

He nods, not acting the least bit surprised. "I saw the way you lit up when you kissed him. Just like the time I found him in your room." He winces. "You've never had that reaction to me."

He's right. I haven't. Wait, how does he know that?

"I didn't tell you about that," I say slowly.

"Huh?"

"About when you found me with James. William couldn't have told you about that incident. He wasn't there."

Sebastian's face goes blank as he scratches his chin. "You must have."

I shake my head. "No, I remember every single thing I told you about my relationship with James, and I never mentioned that horrible morning."

Sebastian looks away from me, but I grab his chin. He's hot to the touch, more so than usual. "Are your memories coming back?"

He looks at me for another moment before his face slackens. He nods.

I gasp. "Well…that's…good, I guess."

He raises an eyebrow. "Is it?"

I think that over. I never actually planned for this. How it would make me feel for him to remember doing all those awful things. "When?"

He rubs his chin and looks at me guiltily.

"How long, Sebastian?"

He lets out a long exhale. "Ever since those guys roughed me up the day we got here."

My eyes widen and I stand, needing to distance myself from him. "That was more than a month ago. Has it just been a few things here and there?"

He bites his lip.

"Everything?" I whisper, taking another step back.

He nods slowly.

Betrayal stabs me in my stomach. "You have known everything this whole time?"

He doesn't say anything.

"What the hell, Sebastian? That's not any better than the old you."

Hurt flashes across his face, but I don't let up.

"You pretended to be somebody you weren't back then, and you're just playing me for a fool all over again. I believed you had changed. I do love you. I slept with you and sealed the bond, if that isn't proof enough!" My voice turns shrill, and I have to fight to gain control of the flames that want to burst from my body.

He stands, grabbing my shoulders. "I have changed!"

I shake my head and back away from him. And for the first time since I kissed him in Michael's house, I'm afraid of him.

He must see it in my eyes because he raises his hands and backs away. "Let me explain."

Heat gathers behind my eyes. "I want to sever the bond," I say before he can.

"What?" His mouth drops open, his arms falling to his sides. "You won't even let me explain? Our first hiccup and you want to sever our bond? Just like that."

I can't tell him the truth—that I don't want to be with him, that I love James and always will.

"This isn't just about me, this is about *him*," he spits, as if he read my mind. Rage boils in his eyes as those flames dance across his pupils. I flinch and his face softens. "You think I would hurt you?"

I step away from him and recoil when my back hits a tree, Izalia's tree. An image of him pummeling James, blood flying everywhere, fills my mind and I flinch again.

He shakes his head. "You'll never be able to truly forgive me. We fight, or I get mad over something inconsequential, and you're immediately scared of me." He places his hands over his face and takes a deep breath before letting them fall to his sides again. "A part of you may be able to forgive me, but the trauma I caused…it will always be there, just waiting for me to slip. It doesn't matter what I do." The realization hits him and his lips part.

A part of me wants to comfort him and tell him that I do love him, but he's right. I can't even listen to his side of the story. I jump straight to the worst conclusion, and I can't control how my body reacts to him in his moments of anger.

"Okay, I'll do it. Let's sever the bond. Tonight. So, you can finally be free of me." He turns and walks away. In a flash, he's swallowed by his flames and is gone.

I can breathe once more. This is what I wanted. It's what I was going to ask for anyway.

But instead of feeling immense relief, I crumple into the grass, sobs escaping my throat.

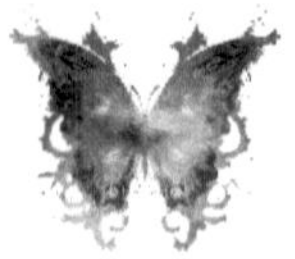

The curtain of night descends as I wait for Sebastian and Don, the High Aura, near the water wheel. I told no one. Not even James. It felt wrong to go straight to him. I do love Sebastian, despite everything. I love him. And that love isn't going to just go away. I'll need time before I can be with James. And I'm not doing this just to be with him, anyway.

I'm doing this for me, for my future, so I can make a true choice instead of it being thrust upon me time and time again. And Sebastian was right. I can't control the way my body reacts to him. He's proved multiple times that he's changed. He even *died* for me. But my body will never forget.

I take a deep breath as his shape forms in the darkness. I don't look up as he wavers a few feet away. I could slice the tension between us with the blade strapped to my thigh.

Before one of us has to speak to the other, Don appears from behind him. "You two are sure about this? There is no knowing how it will affect you. It's not often that a bonded pair wants it broken, especially after it's sealed."

I avoid Don's gaze, not wanting to see the judgment there. A nervous energy vibrates my bones and swirls in my gut. "You have done this before, right?" I ask.

"Once," Don grunts.

"And how did it turn out for them?"

"I don't think you want to know."

My eyes flash, and I can't help but look at Sebastian. His face is as hard as stone as he stares at him. "We're sure."

"Okay, then," he says, rubbing his hands together. "You don't happen to have the same knife that the ceremony was performed with, do you?"

Sebastian's face twists in pain, but he still doesn't look at me. He does remember everything.

"I do." I lean down and slide James's knife out.

"It's not necessary, but it does help make the process a little easier, since that is the knife that connected you two. Sebastian, take the knife. You were the one to make the final incision, correct?"

Sebastian clears his throat, barely able to get an audible yes out as I hand him the knife. It's as if we are living it all over again.

"Take each other's hands," Don instructs.

Sebastian still doesn't look at me as he steps closer and places his hands, palms up, in front of me. I place my hands in his, the heat immediately traveling up my arms and warming my chest. I swallow hard.

"As the earth has given, let her taketh away. Water that gives us life. Earth that gives us refuge. Air that gives us breath. And fire that gives us warmth. Let the link that binds these two mates together be severed forever."

Colors swirl around us just as they did during the ceremony. I watch the blue, green, white, and red wisps in the air, swirling faster and faster.

At last, I look at Sebastian. He's watching me with tear-filled eyes. My heart squeezes.

"I'm so sorry I forced this on you, Maya. I haven't apologized since getting my memories back. I was out of my mind, I admit. Strung up with jealousy and rage. I hope that this can help heal those wounds that I caused. I should have told you when my memories came back and should have offered to break it then. How could I continue to push this onto you? I'm a selfish bastard, and I will never forgive myself."

He takes the knife in his palm and slits across the raised line on his palm, turning it into an X. Crimson blood pools and drips off his palm.

"Be happy, Maya." He hands it to me.

I place the tip against my palm and look up at him. His blue eyes are bright with sorrow and regret.

"Thank you." I drag the blade across the scar.

I scream.

It feels as if I stabbed myself directly in the heart. Sebastian yells in pain, too, and we both fall to our knees. He places his bloody palm over my hand and looks at me, his pupils blown wide, his body convulsing as he pants. My body twists as I fall onto my side in the dirt.

I grit my teeth. The tether is embedded deep inside of me. It twists and turns, trying to free itself. I grab my chest, as if I can yank it out myself and make this misery end.

Before, when Sebastian had died for a moment, it was as if the tether just quietly disappeared, a dull ache replacing it. But *this*. We're cutting into our very souls, digging it out with our fingers.

Sebastian leans over me, placing his hands around my face. Even though I know his own bond is twisting in pain, he says. "Focus on me."

My heart pounds.

"Remember our first kiss?"

My thoughts go to the dark hallway and how William had wanted to kill him.

"When I threw us in the lake," he says, his eyes scanning mine, willing me to remember.

"You…thought I was burning…alive…tried to put…me out."

He smiles, but it comes across as a grimace. "I was so freaked out and so happy—" he stops to pant and grit his teeth before continuing, "—at the same time. I had been wanting to kiss you for so long."

The story distracts me. The pain is still there, but my mind isn't focused on it as much.

"You didn't think twice about hurling yourself in the water." I yelp as another wave of pain comes. "I thought you would have just launched *me* in."

Sweat pools above his brow. "I'm happy to get wet for you."

A weird snort comes out of my mouth, and I realize I'm trying to laugh through the pain. Flames dance on my skin, the pain seeking an outlet.

His body twists off me as fire shoots out of him, up to the sky. The flames curl around the moon.

My soul slides through a paper shredder. My back arches as the tether finally pulls free, and I slam back into the ground.

The relief is immediate, but a hollow hole replaces it. The pieces of my soul intertwine around it, rough and jagged.

I breathe hard as I look at Sebastian. His eyes are closed. I sit up and grab his hand. They fly open.

"I don't feel you anymore," he says.

I look at our hands. There is no heat. The pull is gone. I release him as he pushes himself to a sitting position. Every square inch of my body is caked in sweat. I stand, and a wave of dizziness washes over me. I teeter, and Sebastian steadies me.

"How do you feel?"

I search for my flame and blow out a breath when I find it, strong and steady inside. "Okay. You?"

He flicks his wrist and fire forms in his palm. He shrugs. "I guess we'll see."

"Don left us," I say, looking around.

Sebastian scoffs. "I wouldn't want to see that either."

He's got to be here somewhere, in case we had died or something. I let out a shaky breath, not believing we just went through that. My body feels completely depleted.

"I need a swim."

"I think I'm going to leave," he says, looking toward the trees.

"Leave?"

He rubs the back of his neck. Then his face twists in disgust, and he wipes his palm on his pants. "You probably don't want me hovering around as your constant reminder."

I shake my head. "You don't have to go."

"It'll be good for me. And it's been a bit since I've seen my family."

"Okay." I hover awkwardly before throwing my arms around him. "Thank you." I breathe in his spicy aroma one last time.

"You were never meant to be mine," he whispers in my ear before walking off.

I watch him go until fire envelops him and he disappears for good. I rub my chest, still feeling a slight ache where the bond was ripped from me.

A midnight swim will do me good, help calm me so I can sort through these conflicting feelings. I slip off my shoes and am balancing on a rock when sharp, stabbing pains pull at my stomach.

"Oh!"

I step off the rock and bend over, pressing my hand to my lower abdomen. This is nothing compared to the pain I just went through, but still. *Now* is the time my body decides to give me cramps? It's like a sick joke, the universe telling me I haven't suffered enough.

I lie back in the grass and look at the stars. I feel lighter, freer, a bit hollow, a bit sad, but okay. I'm going to be okay.

For the first time in my life, I get to choose what happens next. I'm no longer forced to stay somewhere just because other people tell me it's where I belong. I'm no longer forced to choose between two matches. I'm no longer forced to be bonded with Sebastian. I don't even have to choose to be with James. I can choose me.

I'm finally free.

Somebody's big head blocks the stars from view. I twist to see my mother peering down at me. She's in her pajamas, her hair pulled back into a tight ponytail.

"Hey."

She hasn't been herself since we returned. I'm not even surprised to see her wandering around this late at night in her PJ's.

It's nice to have her back, though. Cal has been stuck to her hip since their reunion. She tilts her head and narrows her eyes at me.

I sit up and wince, grabbing my stomach. Her eyebrows pull down.

"Just cramps," I say, waving off her worry.

She crouches next to me, placing a hand on my belly.

"What are you doing?" I ask, stiffening.

My mom shushes me and closes her eyes in concentration. When they open again, a wide smile stretches on her face.

"What is it?"

She shakes her head in wonderment and offers me a hand. I stand up and vertigo hits me again. She steadies me.

"Don't worry it's normal," Mom says. Her smile is starting to diminish, but her eyes are full of a light that I haven't seen in too long. I keep waiting for her to fall back into psychosis. Some days are better than others, but she's trying. I look at her quizzically.

"What are you talking about?" I ask.

"The dizziness, the cramping. I'm guessing you also get nauseous? Really hungry? Have you had any vivid dreams?"

I stare at her uncomprehending.

She laughs. "Where's Sebastian?"

"Sebastian? Mom! Please tell me what you're talking about."

"Well, I can't be sure without doing some tests, but…" She grabs my hand suddenly and places it on my stomach. "What do you feel?"

Maybe I was wrong. She's definitely falling back into psychosis. Nonetheless, I do what she instructs. My stomach is flat underneath my hand. The ache of the cramp is settling. I feel a bit hungry, I guess. I'm about to tell her that, when I do feel something abnormal—a tiny little foreign spark in a place I wouldn't expect. Could it be a side effect from breaking the bond? Unease washes over me.

"What is tha—"

"You're pregnant, honey."

I frown, shaking my head. No, I'm having cramps. I stop myself. When was my last period? I turn away from her and count on my fingers. It's been six weeks. My eyes widen.

"You can feel it. All Lymphas can, since the fetus resides in amniotic fluid—*water*."

"No."

She tugs me back around, but I don't see her. I can't see anything beyond a haziness that fills my vision.

"What's wrong? Is it Sebastian? You don't think Sebastian will be happy?"

Sebastian. Sebastian is the father.

A spot near the trees where he disappeared comes into focus. "Sebastian is gone. We broke the bond." My words come out dull, lifeless.

She gasps, and I turn away to look over the dark water, the moon rippling on its surface, my hand still over my stomach. It's not like I never planned on becoming a mother. I was fully planning on it just months ago when I was matched to Sebastian and William. But *now*? Like *this*? I've just let the father of my baby go. I'm finally free from other people making choices for me.

"Mom? Are you sure it's not something else? I did just break the bond. Maybe there are effects of that going on with me?"

"I mean…yeah. It's possible," she says hesitantly.

I nod. She definitely believes I'm pregnant. But it's not like my choice is gone if I am, right? If I don't want…

An orange butterfly that looks like curling flames lands on my shoulder, tickling my cheek, and my mind fills with images. Images of two futures. One path brings a peace that resonates deep in my soul. The tiny spark gives a jolt, warming and spreading toward the gaping hole where the bond with Sebastian used to be, smoothing the hard, jagged edges.

A new bond. A new connection. A new choice.

My hand curls around my flat stomach as I promise the tiny spark something.

I choose you.

EPILOGUE

Sebastian

The fire burns away, and I'm left standing outside the cave that holds the legion's Jeeps. Her sweet, fruity scent is still all over me. It's like a knee to the groin. It sucks being selfless.

It physically hurts not to feel that cord binding me to her any longer, to know she's no longer mine.

I melt a hole in the rock and step into the cave. Hopefully, they won't be too mad at me; it's an easy fix for the Terras.

I pass the Jeeps, hoping she's still here.

"Yes!"

The sleek black motorcycle sits in the corner, untouched from the day I convinced Commander Zhang to let me save it during a training exercise in a nearby town. I slide a hand down the engine and instantly hear my mom's voice.

Those machines should not be on the road. One wrong move, and you're roadkill. And I'm not coming to scrape your body off the road, Seby.

My poor mother. She had to have known she'd lose the fight with motorcycles and dirt bikes with all boys.

I swing my leg over the seat and turn the ignition. I'll have to swipe a helmet in town—for my mom's sake. I should have at least grabbed some supplies. All I have are the clothes on my back and the memories of Maya's skin against mine. I'll never feel that again.

An ache builds in my core, but I drown it out with a rev of the engine and launch into the night.

The trees fly by, and I barely have to pay attention to when to swerve. My reaction time and so many other things have been nearly perfect since I regained my abilities. I'm a lot stronger and capable than I was. I think that's why I have been able to control my anger now when it used to take every ounce of willpower just to dampen it. It's too bad I didn't have this back when I first met Maya. Then, none of this would have happened.

I push those hard memories away. I shouldn't have told her. *No.* I'm glad I told her. It's better to be honest and screwed than— Nope. It just sucks.

I slow the motorcycle a bit, knowing I can't push this baby as fast as it can go yet. But once I'm on the open road, it's all over.

That ache in my core continues to grow, and even the adrenaline rush the bike is bringing isn't dulling it. I grab my chest and rub circles, like that can do anything. I love her so damn much.

I slam my fist onto my leg, but that pain doesn't help either. The ache grows and expands, running down my extremities and up my neck. I shake my head, but it travels, muddling my brain and resurfacing memories I've tried to bury. Needles going into my arms, legs, and chest, nasty fluids being forced down my throat, unbearable pain over and over and over again as the Coms shatter me, then piece me back together just to do it again.

Then, the last time, with Commander Lawrence—no—Kirt—evil maniac Kirt. He strapped me down with those shadows and shoved stuff down my throat. That nurse put something in my arm.

The crazy look he gave me when they finished, like I was his new plaything. Boy, was he wrong. I wasted his ass. But he had said something to me before he died, whispered it in my ear as he writhed in agony—wanted to mess with my head one final time.

I shake my head. Nope, not going there.

I swing my bike around another tree, almost to the road. The ache, muddling my senses and making me feel like I'm not quite here, finally dampens but is replaced by something else. Electric, icy-hot tendrils shoot through me, and I cringe.

I jerk the handlebars, almost hitting a tree, and the bike wobbles beneath me. What the…?

It happens again, but this time, I'm ready. I mash my teeth together and focus on the rushing scenery ahead. The tendrils climb through me, taking control of my limbs, making me feel like I'm made of Jell-O. My arms and legs are too heavy all of a sudden. The tendrils claw their way to my brain, hooking in and pulling up terrifying evil thoughts.

I blink, but all I see is red. I try to stop the motorcycle, but my body won't listen. My hand revs the bike, and I shoot off like a comet. Panic claws at me, trying to get my hands and feet to obey, but they won't. My mind cages me, pushing me down, down, down as a monster rises inside.

"They all deserve to die," he thinks.

He skids onto the main road as a manic laugh bubbles inside him—me—us. The wind is blessedly deafening as the motorcycle reaches its top speed, but it's not enough. He wants more. More speed. More power. More of *her*.

"No! You can't have her!" I yell from my cage, rattling the bars, desperately reaching for my limbs.

"Not yet. I have something to do first," he replies.

He grabs Kirt's last words to me, playing them in our mind, strengthening his resolve.

"Once you're released from her, you will burn them all to the ground, my boy."

Author's Note

Thank you for reading! I hope I didn't put you through too much emotional turmoil. I wrote this book along with a prequel that tells Izalia's story. This will be the next book releasing and I encourage you to read it before the final installment in The Spark Series coming in 2026. If you don't want to miss any announcements and updates on these books, make sure to follow me on Instagram @samchristopherwrites and join my email list through the QR code below.

Every review helps me reach more readers. If you feel so obliged, please leave a review on Amazon, Goodreads, B&N, or social media.

About the Author

Samantha Christopher is a mother to three boys and lives in the Pacific Northwest. When she's not wrangling her wild children or two dogs, you can usually find her hiding in her bedroom with a bag of Sour Patch Kids and a good book or typing away at her next story. If you want to follow Sam, you can find her on Instagram and TikTok @samchristopherwrites or visit her website for all things reading, writing, and the joys/chaos of motherhood by following the QR code on the previous page.

Acknowledgments

What a wild ride this last year has been! Thank you for taking a chance on a new author and loving The Spark Within so much that you read this second book. I couldn't keep writing without all of your support. The community of readers and writers I've met through social media has been huge in bringing these books to the world. I couldn't do it without my street team's continued support, encouragement, and sharing all the things—love you guys so much!

All glory to God. I must thank my heavenly father for putting me on this path and bringing me such wonderful readers.

Alan, my husband, soulmate, and best friend, I couldn't write any of these books without you! Thank you for kicking me out of the house so I can write undisturbed. Thank you for being my backboard for bouncing ideas off of and listening to my constant ramblings about these characters that are always in my head. I love you more than words can say.

My three chaotic, fun-loving boys. I write for you. I write so you know that you can do anything you put your mind to. Dreams require work, dedication, and a bit of craziness. I love you three with my whole heart and I can't wait for the day you can read these books.

To all my friends: Alyssa, Kristen, Becca, Liz, Karly, and so many of you who are always asking about my writing and books and just love my characters as much as I do. You are the first to volunteer to read and I'm so grateful for your support and love!

My early readers, Becca, Erin, Liz, Jessie, Brinna, and Alyssa, your feedback was extremely helpful. Thank you! And a huge thanks to my editor, Shannon Cave. This book would not be as polished without you.

Maria Spada, my poor cover designer that has to put up with my constant emails for changes, tweaks, and random ideas. Thank you! You are exceptional at bringing what is in my mind to life.

I'm grateful for my parents—all of you, Mom, Dad, Nick, Vikki, Keith, and Carol. Thank you for your support, encouragement, and for telling random strangers and friends about my book. You guys are the best!

These books are my babies; just like it takes a village to raise a child, it takes a village to bring a book about! I'm so grateful for all the people I've met on this journey who have helped me in one way or another. From sharing a post I made on social media, to buying the book, or just asking about my writing. It all helps keep me moving forward on this overwhelming yet rewarding publishing roller coaster.